PRAISE FOR MEG CABOT

"In a world that feels increasingly dreary by the day, we can count on her delightful narratives to distract and entertain."

—*Time*

"Through her books and heroines, Cabot offered escapism and empowerment right when I needed it most."

—CNN

"Meg Cabot is a fabulous author."

—*USA Today*

"Meg Cabot is best known for her books for younger readers, but her adult fiction is a total delight."

—PopSugar

"There is a school of thought that says reading should be entertaining, and this is exactly what Meg Cabot produces for us: fun."

—*Publishers Weekly*

ALSO BY MEG CABOT

Little Bridge Island series
The Princess Diaries series
The Mediator series
The Boy series
Heather Wells series
Insatiable series
Ransom My Heart (with Mia Thermopolis)
Queen of Babble series
She Went All the Way
The 1-800-Where-R-You series
All-American Girl series
Nicola and the Viscount
Victoria and the Rogue
Jinx
Pants on Fire
How to Be Popular
Avalon High series
Airhead series
Abandon series
Allie Finkle's Rules for Girls series
From the Notebooks of a Middle School Princess series

Enchanted to Meet You

A Witches of West Harbor Novel

MEG CABOT

AVON

HarperCollins books may be purchased for educational, business, or sales promotional use. For information, please email the Special Markets Department at SPsales@harpercollins.com.

FIRST EDITION

Library of Congress Cataloging-in-Publication Data has been applied for.

ISBN 978-0-06-326837-1 (paperback)
ISBN 978-0-06-332019-2 (library hardcover)

23 24 25 26 27 LBC 7 6 5 4 3

For Benjamin, who is magic

Content Warning

Some unethical use of magic. Sexual references and scenes. Mild stalking and magical violence. Mentions of the execution of persons accused of witchcraft four hundred years ago. Magic spells (of Northern European origin).

Disclaimer

The author cannot and does not guarantee any specific results from the use of spells in this book. Never use magic in the place of competent professional help.

Enchanted
to Meet
You

Jessica

To honor the Mother Goddess, the giver of life and creator of all things, celebrate her bounty in the Fall, when her fruits are most plentiful.

Goody Fletcher,
Book of Useful Household Tips

"Your mother is magic."

That's what my father told me one day when I was nine, and had been sent to my room for being disrespectful.

I don't remember now exactly what I'd said. Nine is the age when trouble can start for so many girls—but it's not necessarily our fault. We're best friends with someone one minute, then by recess we've been replaced. Usually we have no idea why. Meanwhile, our baby teeth are being pushed out of our head by our adult teeth, yet we're still young enough to believe in unicorns. It's a dizzying, disquieting time.

But 9 is also one of the most powerful numbers in the world of witchcraft. It represents selflessness, humanitarianism, compassion, and generosity—all the qualities a good witch aspires to possess.

Of course I didn't know any of this when I was nine. All I knew then was that I was miserable, and I was taking it out on the person who meant more to me than anyone else in the world—my mother.

"What do you mean, Mom is magic?" I'd asked my father suspiciously.

"I mean that if you're respectful and do what your mother says," my geeky bookkeeper father explained, sitting so awkwardly on the edge of my pink canopy bed, "she can make life really easy for you. But if you treat her badly, like you did today—well, things aren't going to go so great."

It's the rare nine-year-old who would realize that her dad was only trying to express his own feelings for his wife—a woman he was so deeply in love with, he did, in some ways, think she was magical. My dad, who knew that I loved fairy tales and princesses, was simply trying to explain to me in words he thought I'd understand that if I stopped taking my growing pains out on my poor mother, life would improve.

He could have no way of knowing that I'd take him literally—that in my nine-year-old brain, hyped up on Narnia and Disney, all I heard was that my mother was magic, which made her a witch . . . and that made me a witch, too.

Our family, I deduced, must be descended from a long line of witches—powerful ones, probably, who could read minds, cast curses, and fly. Soon, because of my magic mother, I'd be learning to fly, too.

Of course nothing was further from the truth. My mother's people were hardworking Italian immigrants who'd arrived in the United States at the turn of the twentieth century—same as my father's, only his family had come from Minsk. The closest any of them ever got to anything remotely witchy was when my parents moved from New York City to the small town of West Harbor, Connecticut, to open an antique shop. West Harbor was only a

hundred and fifty miles south of Salem, Massachusetts—though
my family never traveled there.

By the time I was old enough to figure out that my father
hadn't meant his words literally, it was too late: I'd read everything I could about "the Craft" in the library and on the Internet
(which, in those days of dial-up, was quite an accomplishment for
a kid), and was well on my way to full-blown *Sabrina the Teenage
Witch*-hood, though I never did learn to fly.

But by then I didn't care. Although I know some people—
especially those belonging to the World Council of Witches—
would disagree, you don't have to be descended from a witch
to practice magic. Anyone can effect change by using the energy
within and around them. It's all about their will and awareness . . .
and intentions, of course.

And since that day in my bedroom, my intentions have been
nothing but pure. I've never wanted anything except to be the
best good witch that I can be.

So the summer before my senior year of high school, when
Mom brought home an ancient—but amazing—book from an estate sale, I begged her to let me keep it, rather than sell it in
her shop. So old the binding had come loose and the edges of its
handwritten pages were close to crumbling, the book smelled of
vanilla and lavender and secrets. As I carefully turned the pages
and spotted words like "lover," "waxing," and "threefold," my
heart began to pound.

Mom and I were getting along much better by then because
I'd realized my father had been right: my mother *was* magic . . .
just not the kind of magic I thought he'd meant. My mother was
magic like all mothers are magic: she loved me unconditionally.

And I loved her right back . . . enough not to worry her by
telling her the truth.

"Of course you can have it, sweetie," she'd said, kissing me airily on the top of my head. "Though why you want it, I can't imagine. It's just an old Puritan recipe book. Are you going to start making pottage stew for us now?"

"Maybe, Mom," I'd said, carefully turning the pages of Goody Fletcher's *Book of Useful Household Tips*. "Maybe I will."

Jessica

Captivate thy love by preparing a pottage stew, and then consuming it before him.

Goody Fletcher,
Book of Useful Household Tips

Today is the day. It has to be. Dina said she overheard Rosalie Hopkins last night at Dairy Queen say she's going to ask Billy Walker to the Homecoming dance.

If that happens, Billy will say yes, and I'll never have a chance with him. I can't compete with Rosalie. Her dad owns the biggest luxury car dealership in the tristate area (as she never misses an opportunity to remind everyone). Plus she gives blow jobs on the first date.

Not that I'm judging her for it. I'm not, at *all*.

It's just that since I spent last semester doing study abroad in Europe, I found out a few things—and I don't mean how much better the bread is in France. I mean how intimate relations are actually *supposed* to work.

So now when I go down on someone, I expect to be gone down upon in return.

I strongly suspect, however, that Billy Walker has no idea how to orally pleasure a woman.

This isn't his fault, of course. Sexual education in this country is a disgrace.

But that's okay. I don't actually mind that I might have to spend many hours teaching Billy—slowly and carefully—how to properly satisfy a woman.

Which reminds me: another reason it has to be today is that tonight is the full moon. According to Goody Fletcher's book, love spells are the most powerful when conducted under a moon that's growing fuller (so that "his love for thee will grow apace").

So I've only got about twelve hours to get this done, or I'll have to wait a whole month, by which time Rosalie will definitely have already gotten her lips all over Billy.

Fortunately we had all the ingredients—or the most important ones, anyway, according to the book—in the fridge. So last night, while Mom and Dad were at Ethan's soccer game, I visualized my own attractiveness and lovability while chopping them up and cooking them together.

The only problem is that the ink Goody Fletcher used is so faded (and, to be honest, her cursive so spidery and hard to decipher in places), I couldn't always read the words.

I'm pretty sure this doesn't matter, however, since magic isn't about your tools, but your intentions. Which is good since I have only the best intentions toward Billy and, according to Goody Fletcher, I'm supposed to "rub garlic round a wooden bowl, then eat the pottage from it" in front of the person I'm hoping to attract.

But I'm not about to stand in front of Billy Walker in the cafeteria and eat pottage stew out of a wooden bowl rubbed in garlic. As Dina rightfully pointed out, in all the years we've gone to school together, Billy and I have never eaten at the same lunch table. He's always sat with the jocks, and I've always sat with Dina and the rest of the emos and goths. It's going to look weird enough when I casually stroll over to his table, eating stew out of a wooden bowl from home instead of pizza off a paper plate from the hot food line.

Also, I have Chem class with him right after lunch. I want to entice him, not disgust him with my garlic breath.

So it's a no-garlic pottage stew out of Tupperware for me.

I really hope my intentions prove strong and pure enough for this spell to work. I don't know how much longer I can go on being Billy's lab partner and nothing more, when all these years I've loved him. And he and Rosalie would be so wrong for each other, it's actually gross.

Jessica

> Keep out unwelcome guests (from evil spirits to garden
> slugs) by sprinkling a little salt across thy threshold.
>
> Goody Fletcher,
> *Book of Useful Household Tips*

I should have known. I should have put it together right away,
what with all the signs the universe was practically hurling at me:
Floods. Fire. The return of neon.

But as usual, I was clueless. So clueless that when the tall guy
dressed all in black wandered in off the sidewalk during my annual "Fall into Fall Apparel" sale, I didn't think twice.

Why would I? I mean, yes, the sign outside my shop has the
words *Enchantments: A Women's Clothing Boutique* carved into it in
broad hand calligraphy (then painted in gold leaf for maximum
impact).

But I get male customers all the time. So I didn't even catch
on when, instead of glancing around at all the extremely tasteful
(if I do say so myself) racks of dresses, blouses, leggings, jackets,
scarves, and jewelry, this guy simply stood there in the doorway
and stared.

At *me*.

We get all kinds during leaf peeping season, so this didn't strike me as odd. It was kind of flattering, in fact, because this guy was sexy looking, and apparently alone. There wasn't a ring on his wedding finger, either. *Nice*, I thought.

"Well, Mrs. Dunleavy," I said, turning to the mayor's wife—and my best customer. We were standing in front of the full-length mirror beside the dressing room doors. I wasn't trying to hurry her, but sexy single guys don't walk into my shop and stare at me every day. "How do you feel in this one?"

Margo Dunleavy, as always, sighed uncertainly at her reflection. "I just don't know, Jess. Do you think it's a little . . ." She lowered her voice so that the hot guy in the doorway, clearly eavesdropping on us in a low-key kind of way, wouldn't overhear. ". . . *risqué*?"

"Absolutely not." I straightened the hem of the close-fitting—and slightly revealing—burgundy silk gown. "It's the West Harbor Tricentennial Ball. When will there ever be another occasion like this? Not for three hundred more years."

I tried to ignore the fact that my reflection in the mirror wasn't nearly as flattering at the moment as that of the mayor's wife. For one thing, I wasn't wearing a practically bespoke evening gown. And for another, I'd been working hard since early morning getting things ready for the blow-out sale, so my dark curls were secured to the top of my head with a plastic claw clip, my cheeks were pink and damp with sweat, and I was wearing a jumpsuit—in *neon yellow*.

That's because jumpsuits for women my size—five foot nine and two hundred pounds—sell out in minutes in all the good colors. I have to save all the best colors (black, obviously) for my customers.

At least I'd remembered to tie one of the cute silk scarves from our new floral print line around my neck. But still, I looked like what I felt: a sleep-deprived, slightly cranky, full-figured thirtysomething witch in a neon yellow jumpsuit.

But maybe those were all the things Hot Doorway Guy looked for in a girl? It had been so long since anyone at all had been interested in me, I'd take a guy who liked neon, so long as he was gainfully employed and chewed with his mouth closed.

"And this dress fits you like a glove," I pointed out to Mrs. Dunleavy. "It's like it was *made* for you."

Because, although the mayor's wife didn't know it, the dress *had* been made for her—well, tailored, anyway. Because as soon as it arrived, I'd set it aside, knowing it would be perfect for her—with a few little adjustments of my own.

"Oh." The older woman fingered the delicate cloth longingly as she gazed at her reflection. "I have to say, I do love it. And the price is just right, as always. But Rosalie Hopkins and some of those other women from the Yacht Club—"

My voice was sharper than I intended it to be. "What about them?"

"Well, I just wouldn't want them to think I was"—her voice dipped even lower—"*putting on airs.*"

"Who cares what anyone else thinks?" The mere allusion to Rosalie Hopkins—not to mention the Yacht Club—was enough to cause me to momentarily forget my fatigue, as well as Hot Doorway Guy. Margo Dunleavy was one of the sweetest women in West Harbor, but, like so many caretakers, she always put others before herself. The upcoming ball was the perfect time for her to shine, if only she'd let me do my job and make it happen. "If you feel good in it, that's all that counts."

"Well." Mrs. Dunleavy chewed worriedly at her lower lip. "I suppose that's true. Rosalie says she's going into the city to buy her gown." Margo's gaze met mine in the mirror. "Which I told her is a mistake!" she added quickly. "Support local businesses. You know that's always been one of our campaign slogans."

"Thank you for that. I wonder if this will help." I draped a navy crepe de chine shawl around Mrs. Dunleavy's bare shoulders. Dotted with crystals that shimmered when they caught the light, the shawl brought out the silver in the older woman's hair, as well as the sparkle in her dark eyes. "Now what do you think?"

Margo Dunleavy caught her breath and, right there in the mirror, a transformation seemed to take place. Suddenly, she was standing taller, her shoulders thrown back, her cheeks aglow with a color that hadn't been there before . . .

. . . and I knew I'd worked the magic I'd been hoping for.

"Oh, Jess!" she cried. "I love it!"

"Do you?" I beamed. This was the part I loved best about my job—what made all the late nights and hard work worth it. "I'm so glad. And again, not that it matters what anyone thinks but you, but I'm sure Mrs. Mayor will love it, too."

"Oh, I think you're right. I'll take it. I'll take them both, the dress and the . . . the . . . whatever this blue thing is."

"Great. We'll wrap them up for you." I was grinning—until my gaze returned to the doorway of my shop, and I caught sight of my afternoon visitor once again. He was still looking my way—but unlike me, definitely not smiling.

And that's when, for the first time, I noticed that Hot Doorway Guy had a bright silver amulet hanging from a black leather cord around his neck—an amulet I recognized immediately once he stepped out of the doorway and some of the bright afternoon sunlight spilled in from behind him.

No. That was my first thought. Just *no*.

What did the World Council of Witches want with me? Their

bylaws made it very clear that I didn't qualify for membership—
not that I cared to join their ultra-exclusionary club.

And choosing clothes for women that made them feel sexy
and confident couldn't *possibly* count as a violation of using magic
without—

"Jessica Gold?" Doorway Guy said, in such a deep voice that
nearly every customer in the shop spun around curiously to look
at him, and then—the ones who knew me, at least—at me.

And though the expression on his face was carefully neutral,
my heart started banging in my chest.

Run, I thought. *Run.*

But where? Earlier that morning I'd propped open the shop's
front door to welcome in not only the crisp autumn breeze,
but the many out-of-towners who'd come from the city to look
at the leaves, which had recently peaked in color, setting the
forested hillsides around Connecticut's Gold Coast ablaze in brilliant swathes of red, gold, and orange.

But now as tourists strolled down the Post Road past Enchantments' open front door and peeked inside, all they could
see was this guy's broad-shouldered back as he stared at me, refusing to budge until I spoke with him—and blocking my only
path of escape.

Great. So not only was I being held hostage by a member of
the WCW, I was losing potential sales, as well.

It's really no wonder witches have such a bad reputation.

Fine. I wasn't going to run. Even if I had somewhere to go,
that would be undignified.

"Uh, Becca," I said to my trusty sales assistant. "Could you
ring up Mrs. Dunleavy's purchases after she's changed? I have to
meet with this, er, gentleman here for a few moments."

Gentleman. Yeah, right.

"Of course." Becca's dark eyes were wide with curiosity and

concern as she watched the tall stranger follow me into my small, cluttered office in the back of the shop—curiosity because she'd never seen this man before, and concern because . . . well, my office was a well-known disaster area, and I'd never allowed any-one in there before—anyone except Enchantments employees and Pye, my cat and our official shop mascot.

"Sorry," I muttered as I lifted a pile of unpriced bralettes in order to make room for him on the office's only visitor's chair.

Since there was no place to put the lacy bralettes, however, due to the piles of other merchandise, not to mention the bags of candy I'd bought (and already begun snacking on) to give out during the Post Road's Halloween Trick-or-Treating, I could only set them on the desk in front of me . . .

Which meant that I was now going to have to have a meeting with a member of an association that billed itself as "the world's largest professional organization meant to advance the common interests of witches" over a pile of ladies undergarments.

But then I reminded myself that I didn't care. There was nothing for me to be embarrassed about or ashamed of. Women needed stylish, comfortable bras, and there wasn't anything about his organization that advanced *my* interests.

"Look, Mr., er," I began.

"It's Derrick," Hot Doorway Guy said. "Derrick Winters."

That threw me. Whoever heard of a WCW member named *Derrick*? Most of them were proud that they could trace their "magick" lineage back to Colonial times, or even earlier. They all had names like Elizabeth Carrington or John Ayres or, in the case of West Harbor's local rep, Rosalie Hopkins.

Hot Doorway Guy didn't even look like a member of the World Council of Witches, except for the amulet. He looked . . . well, more like someone who *hunted* witches: tall, dressed all in black, lanky as a cowboy, but wearing biker boots—a rarity in this affluent part of Connecticut—with long blond hair tied back into a low messy knot at the nape of his neck, several days' growth of whiskers, and angular features. His slate-gray eyes seemed to be judging all my sins at once: the disorganized office, open bags of Halloween candy, the yawning window behind me (for Pye to leap in and out of as he conducted his patrols between my house and the shop), and of course, the jumpsuit.

Still, the amulet didn't lie. It was a slim crescent moon attached to a full moon, a design worn by all members of the WCW (which I'd never be), representing Gaia, the Greek goddess of creation.

I decided my best defense was to take the offense.

"Well, look, *Derrick*," I said. "I don't know what they've told you about me. And I don't know what you thought you saw out there, either. But I can assure you, it wasn't magic."

He raised both golden blond eyebrows. "What wasn't?"

"What you saw. First of all, I would never, *ever* cast a spell on someone without their consent. At least, not anymore. Spells cast as a juvenile shouldn't count, in my opinion."

The eyebrows went up even more, but before he had a chance to say anything, I barreled on.

"I ordered that dress with Margo Dunleavy in mind, and the shawl, too." I rubbed my knuckles, remembering how I'd been up sewing on the crystals until well after midnight, knowing Mrs. Dunleavy would be coming in today. My joints were still a little sore. "She's the mayor's wife. This town is having a ball to celebrate its Tricentennial—"

"Yes, I noticed. The banners hanging from every single streetlamp were hard to miss."

But he didn't say it in an admiring way. He deadpanned it, the corners of his mouth turned up into a smirk.

I thought I knew what he was thinking—or what a rational

person would be thinking, anyway. I forgot for a moment that WCW members aren't rational.

"Yeah," I said. "I know. And, for the record, I, too, am against celebrating the three hundredth anniversary of the theft of land from its indigenous people."

When his eyebrows only furrowed at this, I went on, quickly, "But the town council decided that if we threw a Tricentennial Festival the weekend of Halloween, complete with a ball in the village square, people would show up, and we'd make a lot of money. And it turns out they were right—tickets for the ball are two hundred dollars a pop, and they're selling fast. Mrs. Dunleavy out there is the one who proposed that the sales go to West Harbor schools' arts and music departments instead of beautifying the beach near the Yacht Club." I tried to keep the self-satisfaction out of my voice over this turn of events, since Rosalie Hopkins was the one who'd made the Yacht Club beach proposal. "But that's how Margo Dunleavy is—she goes out of her way to do kind things for people. She doesn't even have kids! That's why I thought it would be nice if she had something really spectacular to wear to the ball. But I *don't* cast glamours on my customers. *Ever.* So you can go back and tell the Council they're wasting their time. I haven't broken their rules."

Satisfied I'd put him in his place, I leaned back in my chair and thought about rewarding myself with a miniature Snickers bar, but decided it wouldn't be dignified.

"Well," Derrick replied, slowly. "That's all good to know. But that's not why I'm here."

"Really?" I was shocked. From what I'd read on the various spellworking message boards I belonged to, the WCW was always sticking its nose where it wasn't needed, much less wanted. "Why are you here, then?" Suddenly realization hit, and I slammed both my hands down on either side of the pile of bras and pushed myself up to my feet. "Wait a minute. You can't be telling me I'm on the Council's shit list for something I did more than a decade ago, when I was only a teenager?"

"Ms. Gold," Derrick said, his eyebrows raised again. "I think you ought to sit down."

"It's Jessica. Or Jess. And no, I won't sit down. Just because you uptight wand-clutchers can trace your magic lineage back to your ancestors on the *Mayflower*, you think you're so superior to the rest of us. Well, let me tell you something that no one else has probably ever had the guts to: Hereditary witchcraft? That isn't a thing. There's no genetic marker for magic. *Everyone* has psychic ability. Some people are simply more in touch with it than others, and that's because they've *worked* at it. They've honed and practiced their craft. That's all there is to it. Having a relative who was hanged for witchcraft in the sixteen hundreds doesn't make you any more of a—"

"Ms. Gold." The leather of his motorcycle jacket creaking, Derrick reached across my desk and laid a hand upon my shoulder. "I said, *sit down*, please."

Instantly, a fizzy sort of . . . lightness came over me. That's the only way I could describe it. It started where his hand touched my shoulder, then traveled down my arm to the tips of my fingers until it enveloped my entire body, robbing me of the tiredness I'd felt all day. Not only my tiredness, but the soreness I'd been feeling in my knuckles from sewing half the night, and my feet from being on them all day, hand selling dresses for the ball.

Instead, a delicious warmth descended upon me, as if I'd been wrapped in a blanket made of the golden autumn sunlight outside. Even when he drew away his hand—which he did almost immediately—the light, warm feeling stayed with me, and the pain didn't return. I felt . . . well, *good*.

"What," I asked incredulously, sinking down into my chair, "was *that*?"

"I don't know what you mean." He was all business. "Ms. Gold—Jessica—I'm here to deliver a message to you, and it's not about your illicit glamour-casting or whatever else you seem to think."

"I said I—"

"Don't cast glamours. I know. I heard you. Again, that's not why I'm here."

"Okay." I felt an endorphin rush as strong as if I'd just eaten a bag of chocolate bars, only without the bloating and regret. "But seriously. You *have* to give me that spell."

"I don't know what you're talking about. What I do need is for you to listen to me. I'm here because you've been chosen."

"Chosen?" I shook my head, still enjoying the effervescent fizz in my veins. "Chosen for what?"

"Not what," he said. "Who. Jessica Gold, you're the Chosen One."

Jessica

For lasting love, carve thine initials into an apple, then thy lover's initials on the other side. Slice the apple in two. Feed thy lover the slice with thine initials, and thyself the other.

Goody Fletcher,
Book of Useful Household Tips

The spell worked.

Last night I heard the strangest noise as I was lying in bed, wondering why Billy had shown no sign at all during Chem of having been affected by the sight of me eating pottage stew in front of him in the caf.

At first I couldn't figure out what the noise was. It sounded kind of like when Dina and I go out cruising with Mark in his Mustang along the country roads outside of East Harbor, and gravel flies up and hits his fenders.

Only I was in my bedroom. On the second floor of my house.

Then I heard it again. And again.

I realized it was coming from my bedroom window, and it *was* gravel: someone was throwing bits of gravel at my window from the street.

Of course I figured it was Mark and Dina. It's the kind of thing they would do, sneak out on a school night and throw rocks at my window to get me to come join them on another one of their lunatic adventures.

But when I went to my window to look down into the yard, it wasn't Mark or Dina standing there in the light of the full moon.

It was Billy Walker.

I didn't know what to do, especially when he saw me looking down at him and started waving his arms and whisper-yelling, "Jess! Jess, it's me, Billy!" Loud enough for the entire neighborhood to hear.

Naturally I had no choice but to open my window and whisper-yell back down to him, "Oh my God, Billy, would you please shut up? Do you want to wake up my parents?"

"Shit," he said, ducking and looking around like my dad was going to come out of the house swinging an axe or something. "I'm sorry. I just—I really need to talk to you."

Don't get me wrong. I was delighted to see him. He looked so cute, standing down there in his red-and-gold letter jacket, with his dark hair all messed up like he'd just rolled out of bed or had been working out or something.

But I'd already wiped off all my makeup and washed my face and put on my goofiest flannel pajamas and done my wet hair up in braids so it would be nice and wavy in the morning instead of riotously curly. I didn't exactly want to go bouncing down there and have a big heart-to-heart with the boy of my dreams in my current state of what the French call *dishabille*.

But it didn't look as if I had much choice.

"Can it wait until morning?" I whispered down at him.

"No," he said. "There's something really important I need to ask you."

Oh my God, I realized in that moment. *The spell worked. He's going to ask me to Homecoming. Me, and not Rosalie Hopkins.*

Who cares if he sees me without makeup on and my hair done up in braids? That's not going to change his mind. Not now.

Goody Fletcher's spell had worked.

"I'll be right down," I said, and closed my window against the chilly night air, jammed my feet into a pair of UGGs, and flew silently past my parents' and little brother's bedrooms, down the stairs, into the kitchen, to the mudroom where I threw my winter coat on over my pajamas and, unlocking the back door, crept outside . . .

. . . directly into Billy Walker's strong, warm embrace. Because he was standing right there, waiting for me.

"How did you know where I live?" I asked.

"I came here for your birthday party when we were six. You showed us all your room, don't you remember?"

"Oh, yeah," I said, and I did dimly remember it, though it was hard to remember anything at that moment because suddenly Billy's lips were on my cheeks, my hair, my lips, kissing me as if he could never kiss me enough, which was exactly what I'd always dreamed of, though I'd never dreamed of it happening here, in my backyard, in the middle of the night with me in my winter coat and pajamas and Billy's skin feeling so hot against mine, like he was running some kind of fever. And that wasn't all of his I felt against me, either.

"Are you"—I managed to gasp, coming up for air after a particularly intense kiss, with tongue—"all right, Billy?"

"Yeah," he murmured, sliding his lips down my neck. His big football player fingers were fumbling at the buttons of my flannel pajama top. "Are you? Is this . . . is this all right?"

"Yes. More than all right. It's just a bit . . . sudden."

"I know. But you've been so nice to me all year, helping me in Chem the way you have. I'd have flunked by now if it weren't for you, and Coach would've kicked me off the team for sure. It's so sweet of you, and . . . well, I've wanted to kiss you like this for so long, Jess. I just never worked up the courage until tonight. I can't believe you like me back. You do, don't you?"

"I do." Understatement of the year.

"Oh, man. That is so great. *You're* so great. . . ."

This was very gratifying to hear—almost as gratifying as his cold, strong fingers felt a second later around my boobs when he finally got my top open and, with a strangled cry, buried his face against my throat.

But it still wasn't exactly what I'd been hoping for.

"Didn't you say you had something you wanted to ask me?" I said as I very delicately pushed his head lower.

"Oh, yeah." He mumbled something that I couldn't understand because his mouth was full of my boobs.

"Billy." It was one of the hardest things I've ever had to do, because the sensation of his hot tongue on my nipple had set off a veritable geyser of lust in my pants.

But I needed to hear the words, so I tugged his head away by his hair. He stared up at me, his eyes as drenched in desire as my pajama bottoms.

"Wha'?" he asked, stupidly.

"Homecoming," I said. "Who are you taking to Homecoming?"

"Oh. You, if you'd go with me, Jess. You."

I let go of his hair, and his mouth went right back to my chest, before sliding lower. Then lower. "You," he murmured again, like an incantation. "You, you, you, you."

Jessica

Samhain is when the wise goodwife finishes her preparations for winter. Animals should be fattened up enough for culling. Fruits, herbs, and harvest vegetables should be preserved for the cold winter days ahead.

Goody Fletcher,
Book of Useful Household Tips

I started to laugh—until I realized Derrick Winters wasn't joking.

"Wait," I said. "The Chosen One? _Me?_"

Apparently he was serious, since he produced a pile of paper from the inside pocket of his leather jacket and unfolded it.

"This was copied from a witch's grimoire found plastered into the wall of a house in upstate New York," he said. "It's thought to have been hidden there nearly four hundred years ago."

"Wait." I couldn't believe this was happening. "This isn't an _ancient prophecy_, is it?"

He eyed me sternly over the top of the papers. "Ms. Gold, I can assure you that though you may find it amusing, what's happening here in your town is deadly serious."

"What's happening in my town?"

He stared at me like I'd just asked if the sky was blue. "A

ENCHANTED TO MEET YOU

rift. A shift in the cosmic balance. Are you honestly telling me you haven't noticed? Nothing unusual at all lately around West Harbor?"

"Well, no, not really." When he continued to give me the hairy eyeball, I said, "I mean, I've been a bit busy getting ready for this sale." When the disbelieving look turned into bewilderment, I explained, "My Fall into Fall sale? I have it every year. It's when we slash our prices to get rid of all of our summer stock to make room for our winter inventory—"

Now the look turned to one of impatience. "Ms. Gold. Are you serious? You've noticed *nothing* strange around this village at all lately? Sinkholes? Missing pets? Unusual weather patterns? Anything unusual at all?"

"Well, if you put it that way . . ."

You couldn't be a witch—even a nonhereditary witch like me—and not have some inkling when things weren't quite right. Dina had been complaining for months that West Harbor real estate sales were down, while sales in neighboring Greenwich and Fairfield remained as brisk as ever. The shop next door to Enchantments had had a *Vacant: For Lease* sign in its papered-over display window for months, and I'd even noticed a slight decline in the usually vigorous market for my wide-leg loungers.

All of those things could be explained by a local—*very* local— economic slump.

But the wolf Mark swore he'd seen along the jogging trail while he'd been out for his daily run the other day? There hadn't been a wolf spotted in Connecticut since the seventeen hundreds, when colonists, fearing for their livestock, hunted them into extinction.

Yet the more we tried to convince Mark that he'd only imagined the one he'd seen—or that it had been someone's husky escaped from its leash or backyard—the more he stuck to his story.

Now I was wondering if he might actually have been right.

And then there was the water.

"I mean, sure, there've been a few odd things here and there," I replied, carefully. The pleasant glowy feeling his touch had wrapped me in had all but disappeared, and I was beginning to feel something else instead . . . a slight chill. It wasn't coming from the open window behind me, either. "Some flooding in town. Every time there's a king tide or it rains more than a fraction of an inch, the Post Road floods, especially in the cafeteria over by the high school. That never used to happen. And there've been some odd animal sightings. But that kind of thing is going on all over the world, isn't it? Climate change, or something—?"

"No." Derrick's silver gaze was steady. "It's because of the rift right here in West Harbor. And it's going to keep getting worse every day until the Chosen One puts a stop to it."

"And by the Chosen One, you mean me? All because it says so in some book someone found buried in a wall? Oh, *come on*." I guffawed, but the air around me did seem to be getting chillier. "You know this is basically the beginning of every supernatural horror film ever made, right? You can't actually believe it."

"I do believe it," he said quietly. "Because I've seen it happen before, dozens of times. I'm sure you've heard of it happening before, too. Towns just like this one that were wiped off the map like they never existed—"

"You mean by fire or flood? Those were natural disasters."

"Were they?" His eyes glowed. "Or was it because of an old wrong, a crime committed long ago that was never righted, so that the forces of evil were allowed to fester beneath the town until finally they created a rift they were able to slip through and destroy the area completely?"

"Oh." I blinked. "I hadn't thought of that."

Except that I had. A crime committed long ago that was never righted? I had personal knowledge of such a crime . . . several such crimes, actually. I'd contributed to them. I'd always wondered when—or if—anything would ever come of them.

I guess I had my answer.

"But what if that evil could have been stopped?" he went on, those silver eyes gleaming excitedly. "That's why I'm here. I'm hoping to keep such a rift from happening to West Harbor—but I can only do it with your help."

"Okay," I said. No way was I going to mention having personal knowledge of any crime that might possibly have contributed to the evil festering beneath my town. I was going to keep it cool. As cool as a witch in a neon jumpsuit could keep things. "In that case, yeah, I think maybe I should hear about this ancient prophecy of yours. Just to be on the safe side."

Looking pleased, Derrick lifted his stack of papers and began to read aloud from the first page. "'Every thirteenth generation, a child is born. Into this child, the light will be implanted—'"

Implanted?

"'—by one trained to wield it. That child will become the bringer of light. Through her, compassion and empathy will be reborn. Through her, harmony in nature will once again be restored. Through her, evil will be extinguished—'"

"Sorry to interrupt." My heart, which had already been drumming at the possibility of my having contributed in some way to the formulation of this supernatural fault line, was beginning to slam inside my chest. "But was this fact-checked by anyone? Because it seems a bit—"

"There's more." Derrick pointed to his paper.

"I'm sure. But—"

"Just let me get to the end. 'Without her, hope dies. And without hope, humanity dies itself. And because there will always be those who prefer evil,'" Derrick continued reading, "'she must be protected by the one who is chosen. When the Bringer of Light is joined by the Chosen One, her power will increase tenfold. Because it is only with light that evil can be destroyed, and it is only with light that life can flourish.'"

I realized my hand had crept toward the amethyst stone I always wore on a silver chain at my throat—or had worn, at least, since the trouble with Billy. Amethyst had protective properties, and the stone had always worked.

Up until now.

"There," he said. "That's it. This is your copy to keep." He laid the folded pages on top of the pile of lacy bralettes between us. "You can ask your questions now if you still have any."

"Um," I said, the cheesiest of the supernatural horror movies I'd watched obsessively as a teen now replaying on a loop in my mind. "Listen. I'm sorry. But if the Council sent you here to implant the light into me so that you can protect it, I'm going to have to give that a hard pass."

He stared. "Pardon?"

"Not that I don't think you're attractive, because I do." Like, *majorly* attractive—except for the part where he worked for the WCW. "I like the witch hunter vibe you have going on there with the hair and the leather jacket and the boots and everything. And I *love* that thing you do with your fingers—you're going to have to show me how you do that. But the whole reason I'm on continuous birth control is so no implantation-type situation can ever take place. And before you say anything about how I'm missing out on the joys of motherhood, I don't consider myself child*less* as much as child-*free*. I love kids, but I tried the relationship thing, and it *really* didn't work out, so I'm done with all of that. I'm happy to be a single, prosperous, child-free business witch with my own home and a cat. So while I'm sorry about this rift thing,

I have to decline your invitation. Do you want your parking validated? Because I can do that."

The corners of Derrick's mouth twitched. I wouldn't have said he was smiling, though. That seemed beyond his emotional range. "I'm not here to implant anything in you, Jessica."

"Oh." I had to admit that, despite having meant every word I'd just said, I felt a little disappointed. Derrick Winters may have been with the WCW, but he was hot. Living in a village as small as West Harbor, the dating prospects were appallingly slim, especially when you were looking for someone who was supportive of entrepreneurial businesswomen and uninterested in any kind of long-term relationship. If I'd *had* to have sex with him—in order to save my town—it would not have been the worst thing imaginable. "Then I don't get it."

"*You* are the Chosen One." He tapped the parchment paper. "The One selected to implant—and protect—the light."

I shook my head. "And how am I supposed to do that, exactly?"

He reached for the papers he'd laid on the pile of bras and unfolded them again. On the second page was what looked like a bio that included a full color photo—a school photo, from the looks of it, and not a very good one—of a shyly smiling brown-skinned girl, a teenager in glasses and braces.

"Esther Dodge," he said, and tapped the photo. "Through forensic genealogy, we believe she's the Bringer of Light."

"*She's* supposed to save West Harbor from the rift?" I gaped. "She's just a kid!"

"She's sixteen. But even so, if she's the witch we seek, her powers—coupled with yours—are all that can save this town."

I studied the photo skeptically. "Really? What type of witch is she?"

When he looked blank, I prompted, "Storm witch, cottage

witch, hedge witch, sun witch?" There were almost as many kinds of witches as there were spells. Each of them drew their power from different types of energy, but they were all legitimate practitioners of the Craft—in my opinion. As a member of the WCW, he might disagree.

"Right," he said quickly. "Right. Well, the truth is, I don't know if she's even aware of her powers. That's where you, as the Chosen One, come in. Only you can determine if Esther truly is the Bringer of Light, by awakening that light within her yourself."

Awakening sounded a lot better than implanting, but it was still pretty vague. "How do I do that?"

"In my experience," he said, "if you're truly the Chosen One, it will come naturally. According to my sources, her family isn't magically inclined, so you'll probably be the first witch she's ever met."

Great. No pressure. All of this sounded horrible. "But why me? Why am I the Chosen One? Why not you, since you obviously know so much about it?"

He scowled, though at the calendar on my wall, not at me. "I don't have the necessary skills. You do."

"Necessary skills? But I don't know anything about—" Then I realized what he meant by necessary skills. "Is it because I'm a woman and she's a sixteen-year-old high school girl, and you're . . ." My gaze strayed from his eyes to his whiskers and leather jacket. ". . . you?"

"I don't know what to tell you," he said, flatly refusing to acknowledge what I was saying. "Our research says the Chosen One is you."

"Uh-huh." Typical Council member, never taking accountability for anything. "Your *research*. Tell me this, then. Since when has the WCW been using forensic genealogy to test members of

the public—minors, I might add—for proof of supernatural ancestry? Besides the fact that it's stupid, is that even legal?"

Now his scowl was definitely directed at me. "Ms. Gold, you
do realize that every moment we spend here, arguing over this, is
another moment the forces of evil are able to gather strength,
don't you?"

"Oh, the *forces of evil*." I widened my eyes at him mockingly,
but truthfully, his words gave me another chill—enough so that I
reached for a mini chocolate bar. Suddenly, I needed the comfort
of a quick hit of sugar.

I hated the World Council of Witches, but I loved my town—
obviously, since I'd moved back to it after college, and was sitting
here listening to a WCW member explain to me how I could save
it from ruin when every instinct in my body was telling me to
run—run far away from him.

But a stronger impulse was compelling me to stay. Stay and
right the wrong I was pretty sure I was at least partially responsible for committing.

"How exactly am I supposed to protect this girl—sorry, the
Bringer of Light—who I don't even know from the *forces of evil*?"
I asked. "This is West Harbor. People here hardly bother keeping
their doors locked at night. I don't even own pepper spray."

"Well, I suggest you start keeping your doors locked at night.
This village is very quaint, but it's only forty-five miles from New
York City." One corner of his mouth was turned up, which for
him I guess counted as a smile. "And I'm fairly certain the powers
of evil are resistant to pepper spray."

"Is that supposed to make me feel better about any of this?"
The chocolate wasn't helping. "What does the Council think it's
doing, anyway, putting all the responsibility of saving the universe
on me and a teenaged girl?"

"Not the universe. West Harbor."

"Right. Sorry." I stared down at the photo. It wasn't every day that a hot guy walked into my shop and told me that the fate of the universe—well, okay, my small town—rested on my shoulders. Maybe that's why it took me so long to realize the girl's maroon sweater vest and yellow striped tie looked familiar. "Hold on. Does she go to school *here*—West Harbor High?"

"I'm told that she does."

"That's where I went to school. Is that why I'm the Chosen One? Because I'll have some kind of rapport with her?"

"It's possible," he said. Then he added, carefully, "That and the book."

I raised my gaze to blink at him. "What book?"

"Don't you have some sort of ancient book of spells . . . ?"

Comprehension dawned. "Goody Fletcher's book? Oh my God, who told you about that? Was it Rosalie Hopkins?" It had to be. God, I couldn't believe this. Rosalie had been itching to get her hands on that book since high school.

His gaze, which had always been sharp, became razor-edged. "So you and Rosalie Hopkins are friends?"

I opened my mouth to blurt out the truth—that Rosalie Hopkins and I were mortal enemies, and that if the rift was my fault, she was at least as responsible for it as I was.

But that didn't seem the wisest thing to say in front of someone who'd been sent to help repair it.

"We went to school together," I settled for saying instead.

Was it my imagination, or did he seem relieved? Some tension went out from beneath the padded shoulders of that motorcycle jacket, anyway. "That's probably how the Council found out about the book, then. And also probably why I was asked to give you this."

And then, to my utter horror, he tossed a silver amulet—an

exact replica of the double moons he was wearing—onto the pile of lacy bralettes between us.

"*What?*" I stared down at the talisman in complete shock. "Are you kidding me? I'm not wearing *that*."

He shrugged again. "Suit yourself. It's for your own protection, but whether or not you wear it makes no difference to me."

I glanced from the amulet to his face, flabbergasted. "But I thought those were only for people like you."

"Me?"

"Members of the World Council of Witches."

Like all members of the WCW, he was a supremely good-looking and confident—one might even say *over*confident—person. But suddenly, he seemed uncertain, shaking his head and stammering. "I . . . I . . . I'm not a member of the WCW."

"You're not?"

"No. What would make you think that?"

I pointed wordlessly at the amulet around his neck.

He fingered it in surprise, seeming to have forgotten he was wearing it. "Oh, right. You do know that this is the symbol of Gaia?"

"Yes. But it's also the symbol of the World Council of Witches."

"But they don't own the trademark on the symbol for the ancestral Mother Goddess of all life, do they?" The bitter sarcasm in his voice was oddly soothing. "No, they don't, despite what they might think. So I suggest you put it on. It's not pepper spray, but it's better than nothing."

Reluctantly, I lifted the amulet he'd tossed at me. The metal felt cold and hard against my fingers. Rosalie wore one exactly like it, usually tucked away on a silver chain beneath her inevitable cashmere sweater set, where she thought no one would notice it.

I did, though. I'd noticed it long ago . . . and also noticed that Rosalie's mother and grandmother wore similar ones.

It took me years to realize exactly what the pendant represented—and that I was never going to get one like it.

Until today, apparently.

Derrick was pointing to the open window above my head. "Aren't you worried about break-ins?"

"No. It can't open any farther than that, it's been stuck that way for years. But it's fine, my cat uses it to get in and out. If you don't work for the Council, how did you get all this stuff, like the forensic genealogical report on Esther, and copies of the prophecy about her, and everything?"

"Other entities exist in the world besides the World Council of Witches," he said. The sarcasm was back. "Entities that care as much as you do about saving this town from evil."

"Right, right." That called for another chocolate bar. "And precisely how long do we have before that happens? Did your bosses at this mystery entity give you a deadline?"

"Yes, actually," he said, with a brisk nod. "Halloween."

I choked a little on some peanuts and caramel. "I'm sorry—did you just say *Halloween*?"

"Yes. You know that Halloween is when the veil between this world and the spirit world is at its thinnest. That's when we'll have the best chance of defeating this evil." He must have noticed my expression, since he asked, "Sorry, is that inconvenient for you?"

"Yes, actually. Halloween is next week. How am I supposed to save West Harbor from being rifted, or whatever it is, in *a week*?"

"I don't know." He was edging toward the door. "But I'd think you could start by contacting Esther and—"

"Please don't say the word *implant* again."

That caused both corners of his mouth to turn up—a hard-won victory for me. "I was going to say, see if you think she truly is as gifted with magic as we've heard."

"Right. And how will I let you know if I do?" I'd already scanned the papers he'd left me, and seen that they had no phone numbers or email addresses or anything listed on them that could be considered remotely useful information. This was one thing I'd always hated about the witching world. The magic was wonderful, but witches themselves could be so flaky—except of course for Rosalie Hopkins, who was a stickler for the rules, and loved nothing better than coming after those of us who didn't follow them to the letter—except herself of course. She defied them flagrantly. "Or are you just going to dump all the responsibility for this girl and the continued existence of West Harbor into my lap and then leave town?"

"I would never do that," he said, as if he were not standing by the door, looking ready to do exactly that. "I'll be around, enjoying the quaint ambience of this picturesque little seaside village during its Tricentennial celebration. You'll be able to find me when you need me. In the meantime—how do they put it on the Council? Oh, right." And then he smiled—an actual smile, showing a set of white, even teeth. "Blessed be."

Then he was gone, leaving me with only a pile of paper, a pendant, a task I didn't have the slightest idea how to accomplish, and the sinking feeling that West Harbor's "rift"—which apparently only I could heal—might somehow have been caused by me in the first place.

Jessica

To rid thyself of unwanted pests place a turnip near thy breasts.

Goody Fletcher,
Book of Useful Household Tips

Today at lunch, Billy came and sat next to me. Because of course he did. Dina and Mark and everyone else were cool about it . . .

. . . until Billy got up to get us more soda—Coke for him, Diet Coke for me. That's when Mark burst out with, "I can't believe this, Jess. He's sitting with us *again*? When is this going to end?"

"Mark!" Dina cried.

"What?" Mark looked mad. "It's true. That guy's a dope. Worse, he's a dope I have to sit with at lunch every day because Jess put the hex on him with her witchy magic."

I glared at Dina reproachfully. "You told him?"

Dina gave an apologetic shrug. "I had to tell him. He kept asking why a jock like Billy was sitting here with us emos. He pretty much knew already anyway after the thing with the stew a few weeks ago. You did look kind of weird walking around the caf and eating it, instead of sitting down like a normal person."

"You girls." Mark looked at Dina and me and shook his head, his long black hair swaying against his leather-jacketed shoulders. "Goddamned witches. Is that how you got me, Dee? You cast a spell on me, too?"

Dina grinned and reached out to pinch one of Mark's cheeks. "I didn't have to cast a spell on you, honey. You've been in love with me since the moment you saw me."

"Lucky for you that's true." The adoration that was always in his eyes when Mark spoke to or about Dina softened them, and suddenly, the two of them were kissing. I sighed and looked at the dome-shaped skylight above our heads.

Being a witch is hard, no matter how pure your intentions might be. And being a solitary witch might be harder than anything— AP Chem included. Obviously I had let my best friend, Dina, in on my secret, way back in middle school.

Fortunately Dina took to magic like a duck takes to water, and the two of us had formed our own little mini-coven. It's nice to have someone to try out spells with, even if most of them didn't seem to work—or at least not the way we meant them to.

But I can't say Dina's boyfriend, Mark, is always one hundred percent supportive of our mystical endeavors.

"But *you*," he said to me, his gaze hardening, when the two of them resurfaced from sucking face. "Billy Walker? *Really?*"

I smiled and ate some more of my peach yogurt. "Don't you worry about Billy. I'm taking good care of him. Reeeeaaaal good care of him."

Dina burst out laughing while Mark gagged. "I'm gonna puke," he said. "And what's worse is, you don't even know what you're doing."

"Oh, I know *exactly* what I'm doing," I said, licking my spoon and thinking about the night before. Billy had shown up—as he had every night since I'd cast the spell—and sprayed my window with pebbles. Then the two of us had snuck out into his truck, where I'd undressed him . . . and allowed him to undress me. I'd stepped up my nightwear since I'd realized romantic moonlit rendezvous were his thing. Instead of my flannel pj's, I'd started wearing the lacy camisoles I'd bought at Victoria's Secret in the vain hope that someone might see me in them.

Turned out those hopes weren't so vain, after all. My inner thighs still tingled from his whisker burn. Billy had proved a very quick—and eager—student of my personal brand of sexual education.

"No, you don't have any idea what you're doing," Mark said. "Because if you did, you'd know just how much of a dope that guy is."

"Oh, give it up, Mark." Dina rolled her eyes. "Just because Billy likes football—"

"It's got nothing to do with football," Mark said. "Sal's a football player, and there's nothing dopey about him." Dina's older brother, Sal, had graduated two years before us and gone off to Syracuse on a football scholarship. "I'm talking about Billy, and the shit he says when you girls aren't around."

"Oh, you mean *guy talk*?" Dina aped her boyfriend. "I can't wait. Come on, tell us. What kind of shit does Billy say?"

Mark shook his head, suddenly reluctant to speak—which for Mark was unusual, so it had to be bad. Mark's father had passed when he was young, leaving Mama Giovanni's, the family restaurant, to be run by Mark, his mother, and his three sisters. Mark was intensely protective of both the restaurant and all of the women in his life, and that included his girlfriend—and her best friend. Still, he ordinarily wasn't shy about sharing juicy gossip.

"Come on, Mark." I had a hard time imagining Billy saying

anything so awful that Mark wouldn't repeat it. "What did he say? You can tell me. I won't get mad."

"Well." Mark glanced over my shoulder to make sure Billy was still out of earshot, then leaned forward, the sleeve of his leather jacket squeaking against the smooth laminate of the cafeteria table. "Okay. If you must know, he won't stop talking about how much he loves you."

Dina's brow furrowed. "Is that all? What's wrong with that? I think that's sweet!"

"No, I mean—he won't stop talking about it. It's *all* he talks about. Billy used to talk about how he couldn't wait to graduate and go to Notre Dame on that football scholarship he got. But now all he talks about is how he can't wait to graduate and move to Manhattan and live in a loft with you, and run Jess's errands while she's in class at FIT."

I froze with a spoonful of yogurt halfway to my mouth. Dina and I exchanged nervous glances. "*What?*"

"Yeah. I thought that might get your attention." Mark opened the Tupperware containing the lunch his mother had made him. Mama Giovanni's lunches were legendary. But for once I was more interested in what Mark had to say than in what he was eating. "Billy doesn't want to go to Notre Dame anymore because that'll mean being away from his precious Jess. He's going to skip college altogether and go straight to work at some union job if he can get it, so he can start saving up to buy you a great big fat diamond engagement ring, because he's so in love with you, he wants to mar—"

"No." I set down my yogurt, feeling suddenly ill. "Please. Stop."

"Hey." Mark shrugged. "I don't make the news. I only deliver it."

"But moving to Manhattan and finding a cheap loft to live in is what *we're* supposed to be doing together after graduation," Dina reminded me.

"Yes." I felt numb. "I told Billy that. But he must think now that he and I are together . . ."

Dina looked heavenward and sighed. "Oh, *Jess*."

"See?" Mark shook his head. "This is what I was trying to tell you nutjob witches. It's great you wanted a date to Homecoming, Jess, but you went a little too far. Now the slob's in love with you. *More* than just in love with you: he wants to marry you and fill you with baby Billies."

"Oh, God." I dropped my head down onto the tabletop. "What have I done?"

Dina patted my shoulder. "Don't worry," she said. "We'll figure something out. Maybe there's a spell in Goody Fletcher's book that will undo it."

"And by the way," Mark went on, polishing off his cannelloni, "there is no way you two are going to find a cheap loft in Manhattan. Those only exist in those dumb rom-coms that you love to watch. And I would know because my uncle Richie is a contractor on Staten Island."

"Here, Jess." Billy had come back. He slid a frozen Snickers bar as well as a can of Diet Coke in front of me. "I got you this as well as the soda. I know how much you love chocolate."

I felt a wave of nausea sweep over me. It wasn't the frozen Snickers, though. It was Billy, and what I'd done to him. This wasn't what I'd intended. This wasn't what I'd intended at all.

Oh, God. What had I done? And how was I going to fix it?

Dina was right: the book. There had to be a spell in Goody Fletcher's book that would undo this mess. There just had to be!

Jessica

Boil together equal parts fountain water and pure honey.
Add a little nutmeg and dressed ginger, along with the
rind of half an orange or lemon (if one can be found).
Let stand till lukewarm, then add three parts rum.
All who drink in good cheer will be friends for life.

Goody Fletcher,
Book of Useful Household Tips

"Wait," Dina said over hot toddies that night on her brother's
front porch. "This guy wants you to *what*?"

"Implant the light into this girl," I said. "And then guide and
protect her. Because she's the Bringer of Light."

"What does any of that even mean?"

"How should I know?" I took a sip of my drink. "But the fate
of West Harbor depends on it."

"Well, screw that." Dina—still as petite as she was in high
school, but now brunette with blond highlights—sat cross-
legged on the porch swing beside me. "Why doesn't this Derrick
just do it himself?"

"I told you, he can't. Only I can do it, because I'm the Chosen
One."

"Yeah, about that. How do you even know any of this is legit? There isn't a single guy on here who matches his description named Derrick Winters." Dina waved her phone at me. "Not on any social media platform that I can find."

"Not everyone is on social media, Dina. Especially witches."

"Yeah, but this guy isn't on Classmates.com or LinkedIn or *anything*. Did he not go to school? Has he never had a job?"

"Apparently this *is* his job," I said. "Driving around, telling women their towns are in mortal peril, and that they're the Chosen One."

"*I'm* the Chosen One!" Dina's seven-year-old nephew, Toby, out in the front yard, declared as he swung his light saber in the direction of his older brother, Daniel. "Stand down, villain!"

"You're not the Chosen One," Daniel scoffed, his own glowing plastic saber cutting a swathe of brilliant red light across the darkened lawn. "*I* am. Prepare to meet your doom."

"Neither of you have been chosen for anything except bed," their mother, Yasmin, declared as she came out onto the porch carrying a thermos containing more hot toddy, since our mugs had been running low. "Head on inside now. Your father's waiting for you upstairs to help you brush your teeth and put on your pajamas."

"Aw, Mom!" Both boys put up considerable resistance, but were eventually wrangled inside, leaving us in blissful quiet—for the moment, anyway.

"So let me get this straight." Dina's sister-in-law settled onto one of the cushioned wicker couches and pulled a faux fur blanket over her lap, since the autumn air had become more chilled than brisk once the sun went down. "You're saying a wizard walked into your shop today and said the world was going to end if you didn't find this little high school girl and implant the light into her? And you believe him?"

"Uh," I said. Dina and I exchanged glances. Dina and Yasmin got along well—well enough that they'd taken over Dina's dad's old real estate law office together, right across the street from Enchantments, and adorably renamed it DiAngelo & DiAngelo, Sisters In Law.

But that didn't mean book-smart but tenderhearted Armenian American Yasmin was a believer. She tolerated what she called our "little hobby," but only because she seemed to view it as a harmless vestige from our school days together—like cheerleading, except that school spirit had been the one kind of spirit that had never held any interest for Dina and me.

"First of all, a male practitioner of witchcraft is a witch," I said. "Not a wizard or a warlock. The word *witch* is gender neutral."

"All right," Yasmin said. "No need to get defensive."

"And he didn't say the world was going to end," I went on. "Only West Harbor."

"Well, that's a relief." Yasmin's tone was mildly sarcastic. "But what does this male witch expect you to do? Just walk up to this girl and say, 'Hi, hello, I'm the Chosen One, come with me if you want to live'?"

"It *is* hard to believe," Dina said. "I'm not saying the stuff he said about the rift isn't true. Obviously we've seen the flooding with our own eyes—and Mark's wolf, if it even *is* a wolf, which I still doubt. Mark knows Italian food and cars, not wild dogs. But how does this guy know about our rift, especially if he isn't affiliated with the WCW?"

I shrugged. "How would I know?"

"So why do you even trust him?"

"I . . ." I held my mug in both hands, letting the hot beverage inside thaw my chilled fingers as I remembered the look on Derrick's face, so urgent and serious, as he'd spoken to me that afternoon in my office. But more than that, I remembered the shock of electric warmth that had gone through me when he'd touched my shoulder—and the oddly reassuring comfort of his sarcastic words: *Other entities exist in the world besides the World Council of Witches. Entities that care as much as you do about saving this town from evil.*

"I don't know," I said, finally. "I just do."

"Great." Dina pushed her foot against the porch railing, making the porch swing we were sitting on sway. "So you just have a *feeling* this guy is legit. A feeling that has nothing to do with those great big shoulders of his that Becca keeps talking about."

I frowned at her. "Give me a little credit." But Becca wasn't wrong about the shoulders.

"Are you sure he didn't put a spell on you?" Yasmin asked worriedly. "Or a hex, or whatever it is you witches do?"

"He didn't put a spell on me." I put out a foot to still the porch swing. The delicious dinner we'd had—takeout from Mama Giovanni's—wasn't settling too well in my stomach. I told myself it was because of the swaying of the swing, but I worried it was due to the memory of Derrick Winters and his impressive . . . message of impending doom. "Clearly the guy knows what he's doing. Why else would I be picked out of all the witches of West Harbor to be the Chosen One?"

Dina nearly spat out her drink. "Oh, right! Sorry. I forgot. Your spells always work out great."

I laughed, but Yasmin looked confused.

"Wait." She looked from her sister-in-law to me. "I thought there was that whole thing in high school with—"

"Honestly I *am* a little astonished they picked me and not you,"

I said to Dina, to change the subject from Billy. "Your bakes are legendary. I don't know why you went to law school instead of culinary school."

"One chef in the family is enough." Dina meant Mark, with whom she'd moved in after returning to West Harbor post–law school. Mama Giovanni was *not* happy that they'd yet to tie the knot.

"I just want to know what long-ago injustice was committed here in this town that never got rectified, and created this so-called rift." Yasmin was looking thoughtful. "West Harbor's crime rate is really low. The only thing I can think of that might remotely qualify is the Valentine's blizzard of 2006. Do you remember that one?"

Dina and I exchanged uneasy glances, neither of us certain how to reply, but Yasmin, not noticing, continued. "Sal was telling me about it. West Harbor was the hardest hit area in the state. It came on so suddenly, everyone was completely unprepared, and the power went out, and some people got trapped in their cars on the interstate? But I wouldn't consider that a *crime*. It was just *weather*. It wasn't anyone's *fault*. It was . . ."

Her words trailed off as she finally caught a look at our faces. Then she slapped a hand over her mouth, her eyes wide as she whispered, "Wait. *Was* it someone's fault? Was it . . . was it witches? Can witches *do* that?"

"Some witches can," Dina said. "A storm witch, especially. But Jess and I aren't storm witches. We're cottage witches. We can both do amazing money spells, but we had nothing to do with that blizzard." Her dark-eyed gaze narrowed, sending me a clear warning: *Do not talk about this with my sister-in-law.*

No worries. The last thing I wanted to do was dredge up the memory of the blizzard I—however accidentally—had a hand in causing.

"But that's terrible," Yasmin cried. "Does this Witch-Council-whatever-it-is punish witches who do that? Generate giant storms that hurt people?"

"Sure." I took a big gulp of my drink, hoping the alcohol would help. It didn't. "It punishes nonmembers, like us, who they don't consider true witches."

Now Dina was rolling her eyes at me. "If the witch has a good enough reason—"

"*No*," I said firmly, cutting Dina off. "That's the whole reason the World Council of Witches was formed, back in the eighties. Too many people were running around doing horrible things to other people in the name of witchcraft. Something had to be done to separate them from *real* witches, so this guy—Bartholomew Brewster, who's descended from a man accused of witchcraft in Salem—founded the WCW. It started out as a tiny group."

"But over the decades the group's gotten bigger and bigger." Dina took over my explanation, probably because she was worried I was going to start popping off about what really happened that Valentine's Day. "Especially as people have found out through DNA ancestry research that they're related to someone who was once accused of practicing witchcraft. And now Bad Old Bart calls himself the Grand Sorcerer."

"Wait." Yasmin blinked at us. "So a *guy* started it?"

"Yes," Dina said. "Of course a guy started it. In ancient times, it was usually women who practiced the art of healing. Every society had goddesses to whom they prayed for health, who helped supply the herbs they needed to cure what ailed them, and midwives and priestesses to apply them. It was men who began accusing these women of being witches, and the medicine they used magic, because they were fearful of losing their power and status in society. So they had them killed. Because men are and always have been jealous of women's power, especially our innate psychic power, and always attempt to co-opt it whenever—"

Now I rolled my eyes. "Dina. Come on. Not all men."

She scoffed. "Oh, really? Fine. With the exception of Mark and Sal and maybe like four other guys I—"

This was the point at which Dina's brother, Sal, opened the porch door and stepped outside, a bottle of beer in his hand. "Well, the kids are down, finally. I had to read them two chapters of a book about a half dog, half man who solves crimes. What are we talking about out here?"

"Oh, not much." Yasmin slid over on the wicker couch to make room for her husband. He was as large as Dina was petite. Strangers found it hard to believe the two were related. "I was just getting a history lesson about the World Council of Witches."

Sal looked puzzled. "The World Council of—?"

"A man came to visit Jess in her shop today," Dina interrupted her brother, loudly, "and said she was the Chosen One, and that if she didn't implant the light of magic into a girl, West Harbor is going to be destroyed by Halloween."

"Oh." Sal sucked on his beer. "That's a new one. What girl?"

I pulled out the papers Derrick had given to me. He hadn't told me that I had to keep my mission a secret, after all. And if there was anyone in town I thought might know Esther, it was Sal.

"Oh, sure," he said, after giving the photo a quick glance. "I know her."

Bingo. I feigned surprise. "You *do*?"

"Sure," he said. "Esther Dodge. Smart kid. Quiet." After a devastating knee injury that had ended his fledgling pro football career, Sal had surprised everyone by returning to college, getting his masters and PhD, then becoming principal of West Harbor High. He now ruled over our former school like a firm but gentle giant. "She's a witch?"

"Only potentially."

"Wait. We know the Dodges!" Dina plucked the page with Esther's photo on it from her brother's hand. "They own West Harbor Brewport! Yaz, we helped them with that property line dispute, remember?"

"Oh my God." Yasmin's dark eyes went wide. "That's right. The Dodges are so fun—they still give us free nachos at Tuesday Night Trivia. Is Esther as fun as her parents?"

"No." Sal stretched, then wrapped one of his comparatively massive arms around his wife, who snuggled up to him for warmth. "Esther's shy. I've hardly ever seen her talk to any of the other kids in school. She doesn't do any extracurriculars. And at lunch she sits under the Emo Dome by herself."

"Oh!" Dina clutched her heart, looking stricken. "The poor thing!"

"What's an Emo Dome?" Yasmin asked.

"It's the part of the cafeteria that's under a large circular skylight," Sal explained. "It's supposed to give the kids some natural light during the long winter months, but instead all it does is flood every time it rains."

"But why is it called—?"

"Oh, right. Because the goth and drama and band kids traditionally sit there."

"Jesus, dude." Dina glared at her brother. "How have you still not put a stop to that?"

Sal shook his head, looking confused. "To what, the flooding? Do you think I haven't tried? No one can figure out where the water is coming from. The roofers say it isn't coming from the sky-light, and the plumbers say it isn't coming from underneath—"

"No! To the kids calling it the Emo Dome. It's pejorative. And this is the twenty-first century. Why are kids still segregating themselves into these dumb groups, anyway? The goths and the emos and the band kids and the jocks. Why can't they all sit together?"

"Uh, gee, Dina, I'm sorry if the high school where I work is actually reflective of what is happening in society today. People tend to want to hang out with people they like. Why don't you and Jess start hanging out with Rosalie Hopkins? Why do you have to be so pejorative?"

"That's not even how that word is supposed to be—"

"Would you two knock it off?" I rolled my eyes. This was one of the problems with being friends with a brother and sister. The squabbling didn't end. "May I remind you that we've just been told our town is in mortal peril? Who cares about the Emo Dome? Sal, can you write me a pass or something so I can go over to the school and have lunch with Esther on Monday? I don't want to get in trouble for trespassing on school property as a nonparent, or whatever."

"Oh, that's so sweet." Yasmin stroked her husband's arm. "Sal, write her a pass. Then Esther won't have to sit alone under the Emo Dome at lunch anymore."

"No, I can't write her a pass," Sal said. "That would break about ten state and probably federal laws. Especially for Jess to come onto school property and proselytize about witchcraft—"

"It's not proselytizing when it's to save the town," Dina snapped.

"I highly doubt the school board will see it that way," her brother snapped back.

I realized as I listened to my best friend bicker with her brother that I'd made a mistake: I probably should have kept my mouth shut about Derrick's visit to my shop.

Except that West Harbor was a small town, and Becca couldn't stop blabbing to everyone she knew about the tall, handsome stranger in biker boots I'd spent such a long time talking to in my office. They'd have heard about Derrick eventually.

But I could have told them what I'd told Becca: that he'd been an eccentric billionaire, looking to buy property in town, including Enchantments, as an investment, and that I'd sent him on his way.

"Listen," I said, putting my mug down on the porch railing with a thump. "If this whole prophecy thing that Derrick told me about really is as dangerous as he says, maybe I should have left all of you out of it."

Dina stared at me with her mouth hanging open. "Left us out? Are you serious? Of *course* you had to tell us!"

"Yeah," Sal said. "I need the advance notice to get gas for the generator for when the End of Days comes."

Yasmin gave him a sour look. "Of course you had to tell us, Jess. How could you even *think* otherwise?" She turned her big brown eyes toward her husband. "There must be some way you can get Jessica a pass to talk to Esther during school hours without upsetting the school board."

"Why can't Jess talk to the kid outside of school hours?" Sal asked. "Then none of it will be my problem."

"Yes, but then there's a chance Esther's parents will find out." Yasmin blinked. "And you know how people can be about witchcraft."

"Actually Esther's parents would probably be pretty open-minded about it." Dina looked thoughtful. "Remember last year at the Brewport's Halloween costume contest? Virginia Dodge dressed like Ursula, the witch from Disney's *The Little Mermaid*. Of course you can't guarantee that anyone who loves Disney movies enough to dress like the witch from one of them is going to be open to the idea of their kid actually *being* a witch, but—"

Sal looked upset. "Isn't Ursula an *evil* witch in that movie? The boys were just watching it. That witch was definitely evil."

"It depends on your point of view," Dina said. "Ursula made a business agreement with the Little Mermaid—her voice in exchange for a pair of legs—and then the Little Mermaid tried to renege on the contract. Personally I don't blame Ursula for being pissed."

"The mermaid was underage," Yasmin disagreed. "You know perfectly well that contracts signed by teenagers can't be enforced and are therefore voidable."

"Whatever," Dina said. "The fact remains that witches are notoriously misrepresented on film. Look at almost every female villain in every princess film ever—"

"Oh, for God's sake." Sal started to get up. "If the world's really going to end, I'm going inside to play as much *Call of Duty* as I can."

"Wait!" Yasmin turned to her husband. "What about that mentor program? The one that helps pair local business owners with high-achieving students, and guarantees them college scholarship money? You were telling me just the other day that you need volunteers, so I'm sure there must be room for Jess—"

Sal winced. "That program is so that students can learn about the advantages of a business education," he said, "not *witchcraft*."

"I'll tell Esther all about the challenges of being a female entrepreneur," I promised. "And witch."

"The Brewport is one of the most successful businesses in

town," Dina pointed out. "Why would Esther's parents sign her up for a mentor?"

"Hello," Yasmin said, rubbing her thumb and fingers together and waving them in Dina's face. "Free scholarship money. Doesn't matter how well you're doing financially, every parent wants more. Of course they're gonna sign her up. I'm going to sign the boys up when they're old enough."

Sal dropped his head into his hands. "This is *not* happening."

"It's okay, Sal," I said. "I'm the Chosen One. I'll be a good mentor to Esther. I won't let anything weird happen to her or your school."

"Oh, sure," Sal said through his fingers. "You mean like with Billy?"

In the stunned silence that followed, I could hear Sal's neighbors' television next door, and farther off, the soft sigh of the sea. No one spoke—no one even seemed to breathe—until Dina said, finally, "That was harsh, Sal. Way harsh. You *know* that wasn't Jessica's fault."

"Yeah, come on, Sal." Yasmin looked mortified on her husband's behalf. "Billy is completely over Jessica. He's married now, with kids. Dina and I saw him the other day at Stew Leonard's. He seems really happy."

"See?" I smiled, though I wasn't sure it was convincing. "I'm not saying Billy didn't go through a hard time—who didn't, as a teenager? But he's happy now. Everybody's happy. Now let's make sure they stay that way. Write me a pass so I can meet with Esther."

Sal lifted his head, but he didn't look thrilled. "Fine. Whatever. You witches are going to do what you want anyway. You always have, and you always will."

"Yay!" Yasmin flung her arms around her husband's neck and kissed him, while Dina and I exchanged looks of relief. It was a small victory, but it's important to celebrate the small victories.

"Oh, shit," Dina said a second later, after glancing at her phone. "I gotta go. Mark's working late at the restaurant, and one of us has to go home and let the dogs out. Jess, did you walk over? Do you want a lift home? Or would you rather walk?"

"Ride, please." I only lived a couple blocks away, but my feet were aching from having been on them all day. The Fall into Fall sale had been a success, but it had taken a physical toll. I couldn't help thinking about the warm, restorative blanket in which Derrick's touch had wrapped me earlier, and how it had made all my pain disappear. Was it only his fingers that possessed this magical healing power?

Oh my God, what was the matter with me?

"What's up?" Dina demanded, as we got into her car. "You're so quiet. You're not pissed at Sal for that dumb thing he said about Billy, are you?"

"What?" Startled, I reached for my seat belt. "Oh, no. No. Sorry. I was thinking about something else."

"About Billy? I thought you'd let that go. It wasn't your fault. And he's completely over you. Yasmin and I really did see him with the kids at Stew Leonard's the other day. He honestly does seem happy now. Ish."

That *ish* caused my heart to twist with guilt. I hugged myself, even though it wasn't all that cold out. "I wasn't thinking about him, I swear."

"Okay, good." Dina switched on the engine. "Because I want to hear more about this guy from the store this morning. Did he really have silver eyes? Because that's what Becca is going around telling everyone."

"I wouldn't say they were *silver*, exactly. . . ."

Except that, as we pulled away from her brother's house, I

could have sworn I saw Derrick's silver eyes flash at me from behind the wheel of a Fiat 500 parked just down the road.

But that was impossible. Because that would mean Derrick
Winters had been sitting in an absurdly small car watching me
drink hot toddies all night.

And that was too stupid to possibly be true.

Derrick

Calling oneself a Witch, possessing the ability to cast spells, and/or performing magick, does not make one a True Witch. Only proof of descent from a known Witch makes one a True Witch.

Rule Number One of the Nine Rules
World Council of Witches

For a moment Derrick was convinced Jessica had spotted him, even though he'd chosen his hiding place with care, then cast not one but two protection spells around his vehicle to keep her from noticing him. She didn't strike him as a woman who would take kindly to being followed, even if he was only doing it to protect her.

But she certainly wasn't making it easy, sitting on her friend's front porch and discussing the situation loudly enough for all the world to hear, while under the influence of alcohol, no less.

Everyone who knew him well knew that Derrick liked a glass of whisky or two now and then—but never when there was work to be done.

And there was plenty of work to be done right now—not that anyone in this pretentious little village seemed to realize it.

Derrick had never been anywhere with so many one-way streets, signs directing people to the "sea"—which turned out actually to be the Long Island Sound, and so virtually without waves—and organic coffee shops designed to look like English cottages.

Maybe that's why everyone in West Harbor was so pretentious: they were all overcaffeinated.

Everyone except Jessica Gold, that is. She was nothing like Derrick had been expecting. He'd done his homework: she had an active and lively social media presence, as one might expect for someone who owned a clothing boutique.

But the videos of Jessica vamping around in her shop's latest fashions hadn't prepared him for the reality of meeting her in person: the riot of black curls that framed her heart-shaped face, the pink of that bow-shaped mouth, or, most distractingly of all, the liquid depth of those large brown eyes, and her big, happy laugh.

Why hadn't anyone warned him? That the woman upon whom the success of this mission depended had a laugh that made his knees feel unsteady, a face the perfect shape for cupping in his hands, and a taste for miniature chocolate bars?

None of this was sitting well with him. None of this was right. None of this—

The car he was tailing pulled into the driveway of a cheerful yellow cottage a mere block from the public beach. Jessica got out of the passenger side.

"Good night!" she called to her loud friend. "Thanks for the ride!"

The friend said something indistinguishable, then drove away. Jessica climbed the steps to the front porch of her cottage. Unlike the yards of her neighbors, hers didn't have a single jack-o'-lantern, scarecrow, sheet hung to look like a ghost, or fake gravestone. The front of her shop downtown had been tastefully decorated with artificial gold leaves to celebrate both the season and its owner's last name, but there was no sign that Halloween was approaching outside her home.

At least until she reached the front door, when a black cat leaped from the tidily stacked woodpile and met her, arching its back in joyful greeting.

"Pye," he heard Jess say in an affectionate tone as she reached into her bag for her keys—she did, indeed, lock her own front door, despite what the rest of the residents of West Harbor might do—and the cat rubbed itself against her legs. "Good boy. Did you have a nice day? What did you get up to? Are you ready for dinner?"

He saw the cat's mouth open and close in reply—a pink flash, a meow too high-pitched for him to hear from where he sat. And then both Jessica and her cat disappeared through the front door into the warm, brightly lit house. A second later, the porch light flicked off, and Derrick was left alone in the darkness of her road, watching the shadows for a threat only he—

His cell phone rang. He glanced at the number on the screen, rolled his eyes, then answered it. "What?"

"And a good evening to you, too," the caller said, sounding amused. "Why so surly?"

"Because I'm in West Harbor, Connecticut." Derrick felt a wave of anger for having gotten himself into this position in the first place. May the Goddess forgive him. "Am I supposed to be happy about it?"

"Oh, I don't know. I can think of a few reasons why you might be. But I'm glad you followed my advice."

"Advice?" he grunted. "Pretty sure it was an order."

"It was *advice*. In any case, how is it?"

"Not exactly how you'd said it would be."

"Really?" The caller sounded mildly curious. "How so?"

Because Jessica Gold is warm. And beautiful. And funny. And trusts him, even though she shouldn't.

But of course he couldn't say any of that.

"Well, first of all, because you said it was so damned urgent I get here right away," he said, "I flew here instead of riding, so I had to rent a car when I arrived. But because it's something called 'leaf peeping season,' all the decent-sized options were taken."

The caller laughed. "Aw! Poor you."

"Yeah, well, I'm glad you find it funny, because I don't. All the hotel rooms are booked, too. So unless a place opens up soon, I'm going to be sleeping in this car—"

The caller's voice sharpened. "You aren't supposed to be sleeping at all. You're supposed to be protecting her."

"And I will," Derrick said. "But it's a little hard when you won't let me tell her the truth."

"Just stick to the plan." The caller's voice softened. "If you stick to the plan, everything should work out fine."

Derrick didn't express his doubts about that. The plan had been made before he'd known that Jessica Gold had skin that looked as soft as silk, and eyes that sparked like fireworks when she laughed. And how much he liked the sound of that laughter.

"How does she seem?" the caller surprised him by asking.

When Derrick replied, he kept his tone carefully neutral. "Good. A little confused, and possibly a bit frightened, but willing to take on the assign—"

"Not the Gold woman," the caller said. "The other one."

"Oh." Of course. Derrick cleared his throat as he watched a blue light flicker in one of the rooms in Jessica's cottage. She'd turned on the television. He wondered what she was watching, then found that he didn't care. Whatever it was, he wished he was inside, watching it with her, preferably on a wide, soft bed. But a couch would be fine, too. "I haven't seen her yet."

"Will she be ready in time, do you think?" The caller's voice was unsteady.

"I don't know." Derrick surprised himself with the honesty of his answer. He watched the blue light in Jessica's house dance and wave. "She'll have to be, won't she?"

"Yes," said the voice on the other end of the line, sounding sadder than he'd ever heard it. "We have no other choice."

Jessica

Always remember: what thou give to thy neighbor will be returned to thee threefold.

Goody Fletcher,
Book of Useful Household Tips

"I know what you did," Rosalie said.

"I don't know what you mean."

I wasn't lying, either. A lot had happened since that terrible day I'd found out Billy intended to give up his college scholarship to follow me to New York.

I'd headed straight home from school and consulted Goody Fletcher's book on how to reverse a love spell.

I'd spent the next few weeks carrying the tip of a turnip root around in my bra. I'd cleaned my entire house from top to bottom (to the surprised delight of my parents) to encourage the "removal" of negative energy, as well as lit a candle and left it to burn overnight (in a plate where it was unlikely to catch any curtains on fire), wishing Billy's ardor for me to melt away like the candle wax. I even wrote his name on a slip of paper and stuck it in the freezer (since we didn't have an icehouse), all while patiently explaining to Billy over and over that, while I still wanted to be friends, I was no longer interested in a romantic relationship. He needed to go to Notre Dame in the fall like he'd planned, and live his best life.

None of it worked. Billy still stubbornly showed up almost every night to throw pebbles at my window and, when I pretended to be asleep, sobbed and called my name until I finally gave up and came downstairs to meet him. The last thing I needed was him waking up my parents, not to mention the neighbors.

I had dark circles and bags under my eyes from lack of sleep. My grades had taken a massive nosedive, and I'd put on a ton of extra weight from all the Snickers bars I was comfort eating.

My parents were planning a huge eighteenth birthday party for me at Mama Giovanni's on Saturday night (not my *actual* birthday, which fell on Valentine's Day, the following Tuesday), and I was afraid to invite anyone except my closest friends, since I knew if Billy found out about it he was going to show up and ruin it.

Obviously Rosalie had seen the existential angst on my face, sensed something was up, and followed me into the girls' room to do battle.

"You know *exactly* what I mean." She was so angry she'd forgotten to snap the gum she habitually chewed. "I know you used a love spell on Billy Walker, because there's no way he, of all people, would ever fall for a hot mess like you."

"First of all," I said, snagging a paper towel to dry my hands from the dispenser. I hoped she couldn't see that my fingers were shaking. "The name-calling is unnecessary. And second of all, this is Connecticut. Where would I even get a love spell?"

"Cut the bullshit, Jessica." Rosalie's lip gloss, like everything else about her, looked perfect. She was right: there was no way, except through the use of witchcraft, that a big slob like me should have gotten Billy Walker over her. It defied the natural order of things. "I know when someone is screwing around with magic. My eleventh great-grandmother was accused of witchcraft, right here in Connecticut. She would have been hanged for it, too, if she hadn't been rich enough to bribe the judge to banish her instead."

I couldn't believe what I was hearing. "Wow. So does that mean you're a witch, too?"

"What do you think?" Rosalie sent me a withering look.

Okay. So Rosalie Hopkins—cheerleader, president of the senior class, and shoo-in for prom queen—was a witch.

But maybe . . . just maybe . . . this was the answer to my prayers.

"Okay, then, I'll level with you." I tossed my wadded-up paper towel into the trash can behind her. Unlike my mom, who ran an antiques store downtown, I threw away things I didn't need as quickly as possible. "My mom bought this book at an estate sale. It was in amongst a bunch of other old books. It turned out to be a book of spells. There's a love spell or two in it, and I did use one on Billy, but now—"

Rosalie's mouth had dropped open, revealing her pink tongue and even pinker gum. "*You* have a grimoire?"

"I guess? I don't know what that is."

Rosalie looked toward the fluorescent lights overhead, seeming to fight for patience. "I can't believe *you* of all people have a grimoire when you don't even know what one is. You'd better give it to me."

"What?" Rosalie had always been entitled and rude—she'd been at my sixth birthday party, too, along with Billy, and demanded that I give her my new Barbie Ballerina—but this seemed a little much, even for her. "No."

"You've got to, Jess. For your own good. You clearly don't know what you're doing. You know Billy gave up his scholarship to Notre Dame, right?"

I nodded, swallowing painfully. "I don't understand it. I've done every binding and banishing spell in the book. I don't get why none of them are working."

"There are *binding spells* in there? Look, you *need* to give me that book. Let me buy it off you. How much do you want for it?" She reached into her bulky, overloaded patent leather Marc Jacobs tote for her wallet. "I only have about two hundred on me, but I can go to the cash machine after school and get more."

"Rosalie." I couldn't believe this was happening. It was only third period. I wasn't even fully awake yet. Maybe I was still dreaming. "The book's not for sale."

"Don't be dumb, Jess. I know your parents don't have the kind of money mine do. Let me take Billy off your hands by doing the love spell myself, so he'll fall for me and leave you alone. This is a win-win situation for both of us."

I stared at her. She sounded exactly like her dad—Ken Hopkins of Hopkins Luxury Motors—on the commercials that played endlessly between segments on the local news. I was operating on zero sleep, but suddenly, I did almost feel as if I'd found the solution to my problems.

Or had I?

"I don't know if that's the best idea, Rosalie," I said. "Look how that spell turned out." I gestured to my reflection. I hadn't even bothered unbraiding my hair that morning, let alone putting on makeup. I looked like a human-sized Raggedy Ann doll. "I'm not happy. Billy's not happy—"

"Yeah, that's what I'm saying. Of course the spell didn't work right for *you*," Rosalie sneered. "You're not descended from an actual witch. I am. Magic is in my *blood*."

I was confused. "So?"

"So," she said, with exaggerated patience. "Haven't you heard of the nine rules?" When I stared blankly, she went on, "Of the World Council of Witches? Established in 1983? Okay, well, let me enlighten you, then: rule number one is that only someone descended from a witch can perform actual magic that works."

Suddenly all of my tiredness faded. I not only no longer felt tempted to take Rosalie up on her offer, I felt the hair on the back of my neck rise. I'd never heard of the World Council of Witches or the nine rules up until that very moment. Was I surprised to learn that there was some secret witch society that Rosalie Hopkins belonged to but I'd never known existed? No.

Was I pissed about it? Yes.

"That is the stupidest thing I ever heard," I said. "And it isn't true. Who made up that dumb rule?"

Rosalie, looking bored, tossed her smooth, shining hair. "I don't know, Jessica. I don't *make* the rules. But I do know that amateurs shouldn't be going around playing with forces they don't understand. Look what happened when you did. So hand over the book to someone who knows what she's doing, and isn't some *cottage* witch."

I blinked at her. "What's a cottage witch?"

"*You.* Someone who just messes around with herbs and things in her house and *ruins lives*."

She said it like she didn't know that women around the world had been using herbs and other plants to heal and nourish themselves and others for thousands of years.

It was weird she didn't know that. Hadn't she researched the history of witchcraft?

Then it hit me: of course she hadn't. She was descended from witches. When the first rule is that the only True Witch is one who is descended from a witch, why bother learning anything else?

That wasn't the only problem with Rosalie's rules. The other problem (at least for her)?

They didn't apply to me.

"Magic is for everyone," I said stubbornly. "Even so-called cottage witches."

"Oh, yeah? Then why did your little spell go so disastrously wrong?"

"I don't know." I began moving toward the exit. "But I don't think giving the book to you is such a good idea. I think I should probably hang on to it, and keep it safe. I mean, if a simple *cottage witch* like me could cast a spell from it as powerful as the one that made Billy fall in love with me, maybe it should just be destroyed."

Rosalie's face fell. "Wait. No, don't do *that*. That's not—"

I had no intention of destroying Goody Fletcher's book. But Rosalie didn't need to know that.

"And I think we should leave Billy alone, too."

Rosalie, her expression stunned, stepped in front of me, blocking my path. "What do you mean, leave Billy alone?"

"I mean neither of us should do any more spells on him. Maybe he'll work things out for himself if we'd just let him be."

"*Work things out for himself?*" Rosalie looked shocked. She'd stopped chewing her gum again. "Why would I want him to *work things out for himself?* Billy and I were meant to be together. Do you know who his father is?"

Billy's father was Will Walker of Walker Hardware. There were seven locations in the tristate area. Everyone I knew owned a snow shovel they'd bought at Walker's.

A Walker and Hopkins union would form one of the wealthiest

family dynasties in West Harbor history—possibly all of Connecticut.

"Billy and I would be together by now if you hadn't come along with your stupid cottage magic and ruined things," Rosalie went on. "But fortunately, I know how to fix it. Just give me the book, I'll do the spell and take him off your hands, and in a week, it will be like none of this ever happened, and everything will go back to normal."

I thought about it. I had to admit, the idea was tempting. To be able to sleep through the night again? To have good grades again? To see Billy laughing and being the sweet guy he'd been before any of this had happened?

Yeah, I thought about it. But only for a second.

"No," I said, and shook my head.

"What do you mean, *no*?"

"I mean no. What about Billy?"

"What *about* him?"

"Shouldn't he have a say in this? If this whole thing has taught me anything, it's that human beings have the right to their own autonomy, and should be free to love who they want without the interference of magic."

Rosalie snorted. She actually snorted. "Oh, please. Boys like Billy *need* witches like me to tell them what to do, so they don't make dumb decisions that will screw up the rest of their lives like he's doing right now. So just hand over the book, and I'll clean up the massive mess you made, and everything will be all right."

But still I hesitated. Alarms were sounding in my head—and in my gut. Something was telling me that giving the book to Rosalie Hopkins would be a massive mistake.

"I can't, Rosalie," I said. "I'm sorry. The book says that what you give your neighbor comes back to you, times three. If you do a spell and your intentions aren't—"

"Oh, no." Rosalie's pretty face twisted into a mask of rage. "Don't you *dare* give me that Rule of Three crap. You know as well as I do that rules like that don't apply to witches like me!"

I knew no such thing. All I knew was that the bell had long since rung. At the sound of it, a first year I hadn't even realized was in the restroom with us had burst from one of the stalls and, after giving Rosalie and me a wild-eyed glance, flew out the door, not even pausing to wash her hands. That's how much she didn't want to engender Rosalie's wrath.

I should have followed her, because now all of that wrath was focused on me.

"You want to worry about my *intentions?*" Rosalie was breathing hard as she stared at me. "Then worry about what I *intend* to do to you if you don't give me that book *today*."

I don't know what I expected her to do to me. Hex me, maybe? Put a curse on me? But certainly not what she did, which was glance toward the restroom's ceiling tiles and, a second later, raise her arm and cause them to unleash a torrent of rain down on me.

Of course it wasn't really raining indoors. What Rosalie had done was set off the fire sprinklers.

But as far as I could tell, she hadn't done it by lighting anything on fire. She'd done it with her mind, and by muttering a short incantation, none of the words of which I managed to catch. I was too busy ducking to avoid the deluge of water, and reevaluating my position on giving her Goody Fletcher's book.

"Rosalie," I cried from beneath the bank of sinks, where I'd gone to crouch to avoid getting soaked (it wasn't helping). "We're both witches. We should be working together, not against one another."

Rosalie, who was standing in the alcove by the doorway where the sprinklers didn't reach, and so hadn't gotten a drop of water on her, looked down at me pitilessly. "Nice try. But only one of us is a *real* witch. And even worse for you? I'm a storm witch. And I'm going to keep making it storm until you give *me* the book."

"All right." I couldn't believe the words were coming out of my mouth. But I was freezing cold, soaking wet, and scrunched beneath a bank of bathroom sinks. What else was I going to say? "You can have the book. Just make the water stop!"

As suddenly as the cascade of water had started, it stopped, and Rosalie was all sweetness and light again. "There," she said, smiling. "That wasn't so hard, was it?"

I rose cautiously from beneath the sinks. The floor and stalls were soaked. So was I. "Where did you learn to do that?" I asked in wonder.

"From my grandmother," Rosalie said, patting her perfectly straight hair. "Now, when can you drop off the book? I need it soon. I want Billy to take me out for Valentine's Day."

Of course she did.

"About that . . . I can't give you the whole book—but I can give you the spell I used on Billy," I added quickly, when I saw the rage rush back into her pretty face.

"What?"

"You don't have to pay me for it. You can have it for free. And then you can use it on Billy, and he'll be yours." It went against everything I thought was right, but it was the only way I could think of to get Rosalie—and Billy—out of my life, and also not get drowned in my own school. "That's what you want, isn't it?"

But before Rosalie could reply, the door to the girls' room opened and Dr. Fields, our guidance counselor, poked her head in, looking around in surprise. "What on earth is all the commotion going on in here? Why is it so . . . wet?"

"I don't know, Dr. Fields." Rosalie's cold blue eyes were like twin icicles. "I just walked in. I thought I smelled smoke, though."

Dr. Fields frowned. "Jessica Gold, were you smoking in the girls' room?"

"What? No!"

"Well, that's the only reason the sprinklers would have gone off. Come with me to my office, please."

"Your office?" I couldn't believe this was happening. Up until a few months ago, I'd been a good girl. I'd never done anything wrong in my life. And now look what was happening to me. "Yes, Dr. Fields."

I could feel Rosalie's icicle-blue gaze stabbing holes in my back as I left.

But I didn't care anymore what happened between her and Billy. I'd keep my word and get her that spell. What she did with it was her problem.

Jessica

Into a carafe, mix chocolate and snow with salt. Stir together for some time. When mixed, eat with spoons. Lasting friendship soon will follow.

Goody Fletcher,
Book of Useful Household Tips

By noon on Monday, I was sitting in the same high school guidance counselor's office I'd sat in more than a decade earlier.

At least the new guidance counselor (whose title was now apparently "student success coach") was thanking *me* for showing up, instead of me thanking her for taking the time out of her busy day to help keep me from getting drowned by Rosalie Hopkins.

"You don't have any idea how hard it's been to get volunteers for this new mentoring program," Dr. Garcia was gushing. "We've been trying to get the word out, but people simply don't seem to be responding."

"Well." I couldn't help staring at the poster hanging behind her head. With all the technological advancements in the past decade and a half, could they not have come up with some new motivational posters for counseling offices? This one was of a daffodil sprouting from the earth, and urged me to *Bloom where you're planted*. It was almost identical to the poster Dr. Fields had had up in her office! Ugh.

Except wasn't this exactly what I had done, by returning to my hometown after college and buying a home and business here? Could it be that the inspirational messages on the posters in the guidance office at my high school *had actually worked*?

"Everyone is so busy these days, I guess," I said, dragging my gaze from the poster. "Especially with the tricentennial coming up."

"You're right." Dr. Garcia shook her head, then brightened. "But anyway, I think you and Esther are going to be a great match. I'm so glad Dr. DiAngelo thought of pairing up the two of you!"

"Me, too."

Ha! Like any of this had been Sal's idea. In fact, when he'd seen me enter the administrative offices, he'd hurried away in the opposite direction—not running, exactly, but moving as quickly as a man his size could without breaking into a sprint.

But the paperwork for my mentorship with Esther had been approved and was waiting at the front desk, so I couldn't be mad at him.

"Now, don't be discouraged if Esther seems a little on the shy side," Dr. Garcia warned me. "She's not exactly an extrovert, like you, Jessica. But I think once you break the ice, you'll find that she's a deeply intelligent, intellectually curious girl. Not exactly a joiner, but very willing to learn, if you can just get her to open up."

"Great." I clutched my bag—the largest tote I owned—into which I'd stuffed my secret weapon: a plastic container full of the sweet baked goods that Dina had spent Sunday afternoon whipping up for the occasion.

It was devious. It was underhanded.

But it was exactly what any good cottage witch would do . . . and what I needed if I was going to save West Harbor . . .

. . . and get rid of Derrick Winters and his distracting silver eyes.

"Now, I'm not sure exactly what period Esther has next." Dr. Garcia turned toward her desktop.

"Lunch, I think?" I feigned ignorance. "It's noon, so . . ."

The student success coach seemed surprised when her computer monitor confirmed the news. "Oh, yes. Well, look at that. You're right! Esther has lunch now. Although I don't know how you're going to find her—"

"Oh," I said, rising confidently from my chair. "I'll manage. I used to go here, after all."

Dr. Garcia smiled. "That's right! Well, don't forget to wear your—"

I waved the security badge that hung from a lanyard around my neck as I backed out of her office. "Got it."

"Oh." The phone on Dr. Garcia's desk began to ring. She glanced at it distractedly. "Oh, dear. The senior parents this year—they're so demanding."

I waved as she picked up her phone, and mouthed, pointing at her cardigan, which I'd ordered just for her, *It looks good!*

Thank you! she mouthed back.

Then I shouldered my tote bag and set off.

One thing I'd forgotten in the years since I'd graduated from high school was just how *young* teenagers were. Had I really ever been this small, this fresh-faced, this awkward, and this *anxious*? Since I couldn't bring myself to look at my diaries from when I was in high school, that probably answered the question. That and the way my palms got clammy just reaching to pull open the door of the cafeteria.

The kids who came into my shop to try on my clothes were often giggly and occasionally even shrill in their excitement when I helped them find the perfect gift or accessory.

But the wall of sound that hit me as I entered the cafeteria of West Harbor High was a thousand times louder than that because it was joined by the clank of silverware hitting plastic meal trays, the thunder and squeak of rubber-soled athletic shoes against tile flooring, as well as the cacophony of teenaged voices, all trying to be heard over the sound of the video games they were playing on their cell phones. That, plus the sight of the hokey Halloween decorations on the walls and the overwhelming smell of industrial strength cleaner and burnt pizza brought me right back to the mid-2000s.

Thank God I'd had Dina and Mark and, yes, even Goody Fletcher's book to help me through my teenaged years. Otherwise, I might have ended up like the small, forlorn figure I immediately spotted sitting all by herself beneath the Emo Dome.

Esther.

I'd have known her anywhere, and not just because Derrick had given me her photo and she was the only African American girl in glasses under the Dome. But also because she was wearing a black zippered sweatshirt over her school sweater vest, black Converse high-tops beneath her uniform khakis, and was intently reading an actual book with what looked like a homemade black knitted book cover over it. The jury was still out over whether she was a witch, but she certainly had the look down.

"Esther?"

With all the anarchy around us, the girl hadn't noticed me approach. She glanced up from her book at the sound of her name, her dark eyes wide. "Yes?"

"Hi. I'm Jessica Gold." I slid onto the bench across from her.

The tables in the cafeteria must have gotten a lot smaller than they used to be, because it seemed like a tighter fit than the last time I'd eaten there. "Your new mentor. From Reach for the Sky— locals helping locals reach their goals? I own Enchantments, the clothing boutique over on the Post Road."

The girl continued to stare at me unsmilingly. All around us, chaos reigned. Down the table, a group of boys were screaming in excitement as one of them won a game he was playing on his cell phone. The number of four-letter words the boys used to celebrate this victory was astonishing even to me, and I enjoyed a good swear word.

Esther seemed oblivious to the din. "Right," she said finally, and gave one of the protective braids into which she'd twisted her long, dark hair a flick, so it settled behind her shoulder with the others. "Dr. Garcia said you'd be coming by."

"Yes!" I gave her my biggest smile. She was prettier in person than she'd been in her picture, with strikingly large eyes and a pouty mouth. She was so slim, a good breeze off the Sound might have blown her away—probably, I noted, because she wasn't eating properly.

"Did you not get lunch?" I asked, realizing there was nothing in front of her—no tray, no sandwich container, not even a bag of chips, only a refillable metal water bottle. "Aren't you hungry? You weren't waiting to eat until I got here, were you?"

She gave me a tiny, polite smile. "No. I normally don't eat lunch."

"Oh, you have to eat lunch! It's the second most important meal of the day, after breakfast."

"Is it?" Her eyebrows were raised skeptically.

"It absolutely is." I tried not to allow myself to be distracted by the fact that the gamers down the table were now sitting on the actual tabletop, and thumping their feet excitedly against the bench I was sitting on every time they scored. "Your brain can't retain everything it's learning in school if you're not eating enough. Did you know you burn more carbs thinking than you do working out?"

"You do?"

"Well, okay, maybe not while working out, but definitely while doing math and stuff as opposed to vegging out in front of the TV." I turned to my tote bag and began rifling through it. "Here, I brought you some brownies, homemade by my friend Dina. She's an amazing baker—"

As a fellow cottage witch, Dina was also as aware as I was that cocoa, butter, and sugar promoted feelings of peace and harmony, both of which came in handy when trying to make friends with a possible teen witch.

For the first time Esther actually looked interested in something I was saying. She leaned forward so that she could see into my tote. "Are they vegan brownies, by any chance?" she asked. "Because I'm vegan."

I winced. "No. Sorry."

"Well, I guess it wouldn't hurt to try one." Esther shrugged her slim shoulders as I pried the lid off the container, and the scent of fudgy brownie filled the air.

"Here you go. Help yourself."

"Thanks." Esther selected one of the smaller brownies and bit into it delicately. A second or two later, her face transformed, going from merely pretty to outright beautiful as she smiled—a genuine smile this time, not one of politeness. "Wow. This is really good."

Was this it? Was this the light? Had I implanted it merely with my presence and Dina's good baking?

But no, it didn't appear so. Butter, cocoa, and sugar were merely making her happy.

"Thanks. So, uh . . . your parents own the West Harbor Brewport?"

She nodded, concentrating on the flavors in her mouth. "Yes."

"That's a great place. I go there a lot. I belong to a team that competes on Tuesday Night Trivia."

Her smile turned polite again. "Oh?" The median age of attendees of the Brewport's trivia night was around thirty-five, so I could see how this information was not exactly impressive. "My mom and dad want me to start hostessing there. They want me to 'come out of my shell' as they call it." She made air quotes with her fingers. "And also learn how to manage my money and develop a strong work ethic—which I think I already have, but whatever."

"Oh, really?" I pointed at the book in front of her. "You look like a hard worker to me. Doing homework at lunch?"

"Oh, this isn't homework," was Esther's surprising reply. She'd finished her first brownie and was now digging into the plastic container for a second, larger piece, her veganism apparently forgotten for the moment. "It's a book I'm reading for fun. Did you know that the first citizen of America ever to be tried and hanged for witchcraft was a woman in Hartford, Connecticut? And it happened in 1647! That's almost fifty years before the Salem witch trials."

I stared at her. "I did know that." Hadn't Sal—and Dr. Garcia—said this girl was shy? She didn't seem shy to me. Also, had she said *witchcraft*? She was reading a book on witchcraft for *fun*? Had the light been implanted when I wasn't looking? "Are they teaching that in U.S. History now? Because they sure didn't when I was in school here."

Esther snorted. "Oh, please. I only know because I saw something about it in the Tricentennial Celebration stuff. A ton of women were accused of witchcraft right here in West Harbor. Or rather, the settlement that would go on to become West Harbor in the seventeen hundreds."

"Oh." Of course. Rosalie was head of the Tricentennial Celebration Committee. She would have made sure that information about her witchy great-great-grandmother got out. "I see."

"I thought it was so interesting, I went and asked the librarian here at the school library if there were books about it, and she found this for me." She peeled back the book's cover so I could see the title: *A History of Witch Trials in Western Europe and the U.S., 1500–1700.*

"And how are you liking it?" I asked, ridiculously nervous about her reply.

Esther took a swig from her water bottle and shrugged again. "I don't know. Obviously, it's pretty upsetting. So many of the people who were accused of witchcraft in those days were women who'd inherited wealth or property from their husbands. When they didn't want to remarry or sell their property to certain men, bang! They were found guilty of fraternizing with the devil, hanged, and that property suddenly went to their neighbors. Pretty convenient, don't you think?"

I nodded and broke off a piece of one of the brownies in the container, then shoved it into my mouth to keep myself from saying the wrong thing in reply.

"And some of the other accused," Esther went on, having gotten a good head of steam going, "were just people other villagers had it out for. Midwives who'd had a baby die on them through no fault of their own, or poor women who spoke ill of the rich men in charge. The whole thing is simple misogyny. One woman got accused because her neighbor saw her dancing under a tree after a couple of glasses of wine. Can you *imagine*?"

Thinking of Rosalie, who would definitely complain if she saw her neighbor dancing tipsily under a tree, I said only, "I could, actually."

"And here's what gets me: people—especially women—are still being accused of witchcraft today, all around the world. We need to set an example that persecuting women for their beliefs is wrong. Massachusetts has officially exonerated everyone who was executed for witchcraft in Salem. That needs to be done everywhere."

Oh my God. This was it. This had to be it. The light had been implanted—by *education*. All I'd had to do was show up with brownies and listen.

"Maybe that's something you could help with," I suggested.

"What do you mean? Like go into politics?"

"Well, no, not that, exactly."

I was really floundering here. There had to be some way I could find out if Esther was the Bringer of Light before the bell rang, and she had to return to class. Why hadn't Derrick given me more information about just what, exactly, I needed to do in order to determine whether or not this girl was right for the job of saving West Harbor?

"What about writing?" I punted, since I couldn't bring myself to say the words *Do you believe in magic?* to her. "Journalism? Is that something you'd want to study in college or . . . ?"

"Journalism?" Esther made a face. "No. What I really love is science. I'm thinking about majoring in psychology. There's a mental health crisis in this country. The demand for psychologists is off the charts—as you can probably tell." She sent a menacing look in the direction of the boys. "Brayden over there is a prime example of a kid in need of dialectical behavior therapy."

That was not at all what I was expecting to hear from a sixteen-year-old. Granted, I don't normally hang around sixteen-year-olds—except to pass them items they wanted to try on through the dressing room curtains at my shop.

Still, I was pretty sure this was exactly the kind of thing the Bringer of Light would say. And even if this kid wasn't the savior of West Harbor, I was surprised to find that I liked her enough that I actually wanted to be her mentor—her academic mentor, not her witch mentor. Although both would be fine with me.

"That sounds amazing," I said. Then I added, "You know, working in fashion retail can be a little like being a therapist in some ways. People need a lot of positive reinforcement and reassurance while trying on new clothes."

Esther smiled at me, going in for a third brownie. "My best friend Gabriella loves your store. She's always in there buying stuff—like those lounge pants you sell, the tie-front ones in the different prints? You're wearing a pair now."

"Oh, the bamboo loungers." I nodded, feeling even more buoyed. I was glad Esther had a best friend. And of course I loved it when anyone said something positive about the shop. I hoped Becca was having an okay time running it without me. But it was a Monday morning after a weekend sale, when things were usually slow, so she'd probably be fine. "Yes, they're very popular. So soft and flowy and romantic."

"Yeah," Esther said. "Well, Gabby's a Pisces, so she loves anything flowy and romantic."

I paused as I reached for another brownie. "You like astrology?"

"I love it," Esther said. "Of course astrology is a pseudoscience, but I find that a person's star sign can often be surprisingly accurate about many of their character traits."

I was already trying to figure out how I was going to report this to Derrick. He didn't exactly strike me as someone who put a whole lot of faith in star signs.

"Well," I said. "I don't know if you can definitively—"

"Like you." Esther was polishing off her fourth brownie. And they were pretty big brownies, too. "Aquarius, right?"

I stared at her. "How did you—?"

"It's pretty obvious. You've got the flowy romantic thing going on with how you dress, too, just like Gabs. But you're reserved—until you get to know someone. Then you're warm and friendly. So you have to be Aquarius on the cusp of Pisces. A Valentine's Day baby, maybe?" At the sight of my stunned expression, she nodded. "Yeah, that makes sense, because you definitely seem like the creative type—and a romantic, even though you've been a bit disappointed by love, haven't you?"

I stared harder. I might even have been goggling at her. "H-how—?"

"It hasn't made you bitter, though," she added hastily, mistaking my wonder for disapproval. "You believe in love. You just think it's better to be alone than with the wrong person. Which is so totally Aquarian, and I so totally get. No point in wasting time on bad company. Oh, and you're a witch, right? But a good witch—at least, you try to be." She shoveled the largest bit of brownie yet into her mouth.

I gaped at her. "How—how did you—?"

She took her time chewing and swallowing. "Well, the witch part was easy." She pointed at the pendant I'd forgotten I was wearing around my neck.

"Y-you," I stammered, fingering it. "You've heard of Gaia?"

"Sure. Hasn't everybody? She's like, Mother Nature, right?"

"Um . . . yes. But the rest of it . . . How . . . ?"

Then, as the table we were sitting on shook because Brayden won the game he'd been playing, and was stomping around on top of it in triumph, Esther banged her water bottle down and shouted, "Brayden! What have I told you about putting your feet on the table? Get. Down!"

On the word *down*, the cafeteria table where we were sitting gave a mighty wobble—only this time it wasn't because anyone was stomping on it. It was as if a massive hand reached down, grasped the end of the table where the boys were sitting, lifted it a few inches in the air, and shook it.

Only there was no one at the other end of the table lifting it to shake it.

And when the shaking stopped as abruptly as it started, an ashen-faced Brayden climbed meekly down from the tabletop and mumbled his apologies to Esther.

"Sorry," he said, bowing his head almost as if to a queen. "My bad, bro."

Esther rolled her eyes tolerantly. "I'm not your bro."

"I mean Esther," he said.

Esther glanced back at me and grimaced apologetically. "Brayden can't help it. He's an Aries with ADHD."

I gazed in awe at the teenaged girl sitting across from me as she dug into the last brownie.

"H-how did you do that?" I demanded breathlessly. I hadn't seen a display of magic that powerful since—well, since Rosalie.

"I don't know." She gave another shrug and sipped from her water bottle. "It's just a thing I've always been able to do. Gabby says I've got the 'gift.' I don't know if that's true, but whatever it is, I figure it will come in handy when I go to college. Keep the frat boys in their place!" She laughed.

It was fortunate that the bell rang just then, because I was too shocked to say anything more. I had, I knew, found West Harbor's Bringer of Light.

"Well, I better get to class," Esther said, scooping up her book, water bottle, and enormous black backpack. She looked at me curiously, probably because I was just sitting there in stunned silence. "But this was nice. We should do it again sometime."

"Yes." I roused myself. "We should. Tomorrow?"

Her eyes widened. "That seems a bit soon, but I guess if it fits your schedule—"

"It does!"

"Oh. Well, I do want to go to NYU to have the urban experience, but my parents say that place is stupid expensive. So I could really use that scholarship money."

"Great." I quickly pulled my cell phone—and something else—from my bag. "Let's exchange numbers, and then we can figure out a time to meet again."

"Oh." She could not have looked less enthused. "Okay. Sure."

It happened so quickly, she didn't notice. As she was typing, I slipped the amethyst stone from my necklace into a side pocket of her backpack.

After everything that had happened with Billy, I'd sworn to myself never again to use magic on someone without their permission.

But this was different. This was to protect someone.

Did I feel bad that I was lying to a child? No. If Derrick was right, and catastrophe was coming to West Harbor, it would be worth it.

Besides, we lie to children all the time about things like Santa Claus and the Tooth Fairy. Then when they get older we tell them other lies, like that there's no such thing as magic. What I was doing seemed mild in comparison, especially considering the magic I'd just witnessed Esther use with my own eyes.

After Esther thanked me politely for my time and the brownies and headed back to class, I noticed the boys follow her, murmuring amongst themselves in what I felt was a semi-worshipful manner. Surprisingly, Brayden in particular looked smitten.

My God. Esther hadn't been sitting alone because she had no friends. She'd been sitting alone because she wanted some time to herself. Esther was a teenaged witch queen.

I packed up Dina's now-empty brownie container and then, looking down at my phone, texted Derrick.

Hi, it's Jess. Met with Esther. Pretty sure she's our Bringer of Light. When/where do you want to meet to talk about it/plan next steps? Let me know.

I put my phone away, shouldered my bag, and headed toward the closest exit, which fortunately led straight out to the lot where my car was parked, since I could see through the skylight overhead that it looked like rain—which was odd because the sky had been a bright, cloudless blue when I'd walked into the school.

Then, just as I was about to reach the exit, my gaze fell on a folding table set up near the soda machines, with a sign hanging from it that screamed:

SIGN UP HERE FOR THE CHANCE
TO BE A WEST HARBOR HARVEST PRINCESS!
Get college scholarship $$$
for helping your hometown celebrate its
Tricentennial!

I'd never heard of a Harvest Princess before. But I was so shocked at the regressive antifeminist sound of it that it took me a few seconds to notice the slim woman in the pale pink sweater set and tweed slacks standing behind the table, staring at me, hatred in her ice-cold blue eyes:

Of course. Who else? Rosalie Hopkins.

Even worse, beside her stood a tall, broad-shouldered man in a crewneck sweater and khakis, looking everywhere but at my face: Billy Walker.

Derrick

Any spells cast by a Witch must be to seek harmony
with—not harm—humans and the earth.

Rule Number Two of the Nine Rules
World Council of Witches

Derrick gulped down the remainder of the coffee in his compostable cup from Wake Up West Harbor. He had to admit it
wasn't the worst coffee he'd ever had. It was actually pretty good.

He also felt much more awake, which was a relief after the
miserable night he'd spent in the cramped seat of his rental car
outside Jess's cottage. At least now he was better able to focus
his gaze on the front doors of West Harbor High, through which
he'd watched her disappear an hour earlier.

For such a relatively small town, West Harbor seemed to have
a decent high school. This one boasted an eleven-hundred-seat
auditorium, a newly resodded football field, and a four-bay auto
shop garage with two lifts.

He only knew this last part because he could see the lifts from
where he was parked, since the bay doors had been open to let in
the sea breeze. Some of the kids had even come out of the shop to
vape and enjoy the warm midday sun on their faces.

At least until that sun suddenly disappeared behind a dark bank of clouds. The wind picked up, too, right around the time he received a text from Jessica saying that she thought the girl was the Bringer of Light. The wind sent autumn leaves streaming past his car, and caused the kids to duck hastily inside. The American and Connecticut state flags, which had been hanging limply from a pole just outside the school's front doors, swelled and snapped in the gale, and thunder rumbled—not in the distance, but seemingly directly above him.

Derrick decided to recheck the weather app he could have sworn had told him only a few hours earlier that the day would be clear. Yes. It *still* said conditions in West Harbor were sunny, with zero percent chance of precipitation. What was going on? He was used to the changeable weather conditions of the plains out west. No one had warned him it could be like this on the East Coast, as well. Was this because they were near the sea? Or were more insidious forces already at work?

Then he heard a bang. He swiveled in his seat—as much as he could in the confined space—to make sure the kids in the auto shop were all right, but it turned out the sound hadn't come from there. It came from a side door in the opposite direction.

Through that side door burst Jessica, a panicked look on her face. She ran across the courtyard toward the parking lot as if she was being chased, though as far as Derrick could see, there was no one behind her.

Then there was a blinding flash of lightning—so bright that it illuminated the entire schoolyard—and thunder boomed again, this time sounding as if it was directly over the school.

And the first hailstone hit.

Derrick had been in hailstorms before. They happened frequently out west—though not as often as snowstorms.

He'd rarely seen hailstones this big, however. The first one landed with a thud on the hood of his rental car. He stared at it in confusion, thinking that maybe some kids were playing baseball out over on the field he'd seen behind the school, and someone had just hit a really long homer.

That's how big this hailstone was. Baseball-sized.

Then, when he saw the dent in his hood and realized what was actually falling out of the dark gray clouds overhead, he glanced at Jessica. She had frozen in the middle of the courtyard, halfway between the door she'd just burst through and the parking lot. He could practically hear the wheels of her mind spinning as she tried to decide which was faster—a dash back into the school, or to her own car?

"The school. Get back inside," he growled, switching on the ignition to his own vehicle as hailstones continued to smash all around it—and some on top of it, judging by the thumps he was hearing on the roof.

But for some reason, Jessica decided it was safer to make a run for her car. She began sprinting across the school courtyard as hail crashed down around her like rocks hurled from some unseen catapult.

"What are you doing, Jessica?" Derrick smashed his foot down on the gas pedal. For such a small car, the Fiat had a surprising amount of pickup. "What the hell are you doing?"

She'd clearly made the wrong choice. She only got as far as the sidewalk when the largest of the hailstones began to fall, smashing to the ground all around her as if targeted directly at her. Fortunately there seemed to be something hard in the tote bag she'd lifted over her head. It was acting as a protective shield against the projectiles, saving her from concussion.

But it couldn't protect the rest of her body, which was taking a beating . . . at least until Derrick steered the car up over the curb and onto the sidewalk, slammed on the brakes, then leaned over to throw open the passenger side door.

"Get in!"

Jessica hurled herself into the little car, slamming the passenger door closed behind her. He wasn't sure she even knew who was behind the wheel.

"Drive," was all she said, panting hard as the hail pelted the tiny vehicle. "Get out of here. Drive, drive!"

Derrick didn't ask questions—then. He jammed on the gas, sending them skidding across the hail-slick sidewalk and bumping down the curb back onto the circular driveway. Then he headed straight for the school's exit. All the time, thunder crashed above, and hail pelted the car.

"Are you all right?" he asked, sending her what worried glances he could spare from the road as he tried to maneuver through the storm. "Are you hurt?"

"I'm fine." She wasn't moving like someone with significant injuries. She'd lowered the tote bag to the floor of the car and slipped on her seat belt. Pushing her damp dark curls from her face, she looked over at him in confusion. "What are you doing here?"

"'Thank you for saving my life, Derrick,'" he said as he drove, sarcastically. He had no idea where he was going. Every street in this town looked the same to him, each dotted with picturesque Colonial-style houses and shops, except where the land met the sea. There it was dotted with touristy lobster shacks or docks.

But it didn't really matter, because right now everywhere he looked, all he saw was hail. They were driving at a crawl while the wipers worked frantically to clear the stones away so he could see. A spidery crack had begun to form across the windshield where a larger stone had pelted a hole into it. He'd have quite a story to tell the rental car people.

"Oh, you're welcome, Jessica," he continued in the same sarcastic tone. "It was my pleasure. So glad I could be there to rescue you when the rift beneath your town tore open and unleashed meteorological death upon you. Does this kind of thing happen often around here? Because weirdly, they didn't mention it on Tripadvisor."

She grimaced as she prodded tenderly at one knee. "This one wasn't the rift. It was Rosalie Hopkins."

"*What?*" He slammed on the brakes—not because he was shocked at what she'd said, but because the car in front of them had stopped.

She nodded. "I didn't see her at first, but it turned out she was there the whole time I was talking to Esther."

"Did she see you?" He dreaded the phone call he knew he was going to have to make, explaining all of this, even though none of it was his fault. "Talking to the kid?"

"No. Calm down. She was at a table around the corner, trying to get girls to sign up to be this year's Harvest Princess, whatever that is. Why?" Jessica continued to massage her knee. "What would be the big deal if she saw me talking to Esther? Rosalie's a member of the World Council of Witches. Do they not know about the rift and prophecy?"

He'd been sworn to secrecy. But how could he not tell her? It had been easy to shrug and say he'd stay silent when he hadn't met her.

But now that he had, keeping the truth to himself felt like a betrayal.

"They do, but they have their own theories about it," he settled for saying. "We were hoping to confirm our opinion on Esther before sharing it with the rest of the witching world. Would you care to tell me why Rosalie Hopkins would want to unleash a hailstorm upon you?"

Jessica shrugged and pulled her cell phone from her bag, then began swiftly texting someone. "Rosalie and I didn't get along so well in high school, that's all. And sometimes when she sees me now, she's reminded of it and gets . . . upset."

"That wasn't upset, Jessica. That was homicidal. She was trying to kill you."

She continued to text. "Don't be dramatic."

"I know West Harbor is sitting on the brink of disaster, but has your entire town lost its collective mind, as well?" The assault from the sky had gone from massive hailstones to rain. It was pouring. But at least the clouds had lightened, and now he could see that the reason the car in front of them had stopped was because the traffic lights at the intersection were out, making it into a four-way stop. Every car was patiently waiting their turn. Rosalie's assault had caused a citywide power outage. "That woman just tried to murder you in front of my eyes and you're saying I'm being *dramatic*?"

She turned her brown eyes toward him. They were so big and so many fathoms deep, he felt as if he could dive into them. "What do you want me to say? That Rosalie Hopkins is a storm witch who can control the weather, and that she occasionally uses that power to intentionally hurt people? Yes. But because she's a board member of the World Council of Witches, she's never gotten caught, or even remotely reprimanded for doing so? Also, by the way, yes."

"Wait." He couldn't believe what he was hearing. "Are you telling me that Rosalie has *done this before*?"

She snorted. "Oh, this is nothing. Do you remember the Valentine's Day Blizzard of 2006?"

"Why would I remember the Valentine's Day Blizzard of 2006?"

"Because that's the year we got thirty inches of snow in one weekend."

"Jessica, I'm from Montana. We get thirty inches of snow every weekend."

"Oh. Well, that much snow is pretty rare here in Connecticut. It's only happened here one time in my memory, and that's because Rosalie was mad at me over a love spell."

"A love spell?" He narrowed his eyes at her. She hadn't struck him as the type to dabble in love spells. "Why was she mad at you over a love spell?"

"Because I gave it to her, and it didn't work."

"How is that your fault?"

A car horn sounded, long and loud, from behind them. The electricity to the traffic light had come on again, and he'd failed to notice because he'd been looking into Jess's eyes.

"It's a long story," she said. "You've got the green light. If you make a left here, we'll be at my house. I'm sorry, but I need to check if my cat is okay." She waved the cell phone she was holding. "I already heard from my assistant manager Becca that Enchantments is fine. It didn't even rain downtown. The entire storm was focused on this side of West Harbor. But Pye isn't at the shop, so I'm a little worried—"

He turned left.

"Isn't Rosalie a little old to still be upset about a crush she had in high school?" he asked, as they pulled onto her street.

"I know, right?" Jessica rolled her eyes. "But it's slightly more complicated than that. Are you living in this car?"

Startled, he looked away from the hail-capped piles of leaves around her street and glanced instead at her. "What? Why would you ask that?"

"Because." She pulled a pile of compostable coffee cups from

Wake Up West Harbor from the compartment on the inside panel of the passenger door. "There are so many of these in here. And your bag is in the back seat. And this book." His copy of *Plutarch's Lives*. "And that smell—"

Alarmed, he asked, "What smell?"

"I don't know," she said, sniffing delicately. "It's so familiar. I think it's . . . cannoli? Have you been eating cannoli in here?"

"No." It wasn't his fault Wake Up West Harbor also had such a fine selection of pastries in addition to such good coffee. "Cheese Danish."

"Oh, yes. Those Danish at Wake Up West Harbor are hard to resist. Wait, stop. This is my house."

She pointed at her cottage, so he didn't have to pretend he didn't know which one it was. The storm did not appear to have done any harm to the cheerful yellow exterior or the already weathered shingled roof. Even the bright marigolds on either side of the steps leading to her front porch looked unbattered by either wind or hail.

"It looks okay." Jessica heaved a sigh of relief. "Thank God, because I'm positive my car is destroyed. Do you want to come inside for a minute? I just need to check to see if Pye is all right. He has a cat door in the back. I hope he had the sense to use it."

Did he want to come inside? He hadn't been inside a home—a real home, not a hotel room or some European villa or the bunkhouse at his father's ranch, which hardly qualified as a home—for as long as he could remember. He couldn't agree fast enough, though he tried to seem casual about it.

"I guess I could come in," he said. "Do you have any coffee?"

"Of course. I suppose coffee's the least that I owe you for getting me out of there," she said, as she unbuckled her seat belt and opened the door to exit the tiny car. "Though I wouldn't have been there in the first place if it weren't for you."

"Sorry. But it's your town I'm trying to——" He bit off the rest of what he was going to say when he saw her step out of the car, then wince in pain and clutch at the knee she'd been rubbing. In a split second, he was at her side, offering a supportive arm. "What is it?" he asked. "Are you hurt?"

"It's nothing." It wasn't nothing. She was grimacing. "I think I twisted my knee a little when I dove into the car, is all."

"Let me look at it," he said.

She laughed and rolled her eyes, though it was clear from the way she was limping as they made their way up the marigold-lined path to her front porch that she was in pain. "I told you, it's fine. You're not going to look at my twinged knee."

A second later, however, she stumbled, and let out a little cry of pain.

"That's it." Derrick leaned over and scooped her up, sweeping her into his arms and carrying her up the steps to her front door.

"What are you doing?" Her voice rose. Fortunately none of her neighbors appeared to be home, or if they were, they were used to hearing her yell, since none of them seemed disturbed by it. "Put me down!"

"I understand your embarrassment," he said in the same calm voice he used to speak to agitated animals on the ranch, "but you shouldn't be walking on it. This is a medical emergency, and you're only making it worse. Could you unlock your door? I have my hands full at the moment."

"It's not a medical emergency," she said, but she did in fact reach into her bag to pull out her keys, then insert them into the front door's lock. "I'm perfectly capable of walking."

"It's better to stay off it until it's been medically assessed."

"You're going to throw your back out."

He grunted. "Not likely." If she'd only seen what his father had forced him to lift regularly back at the ranch.

The inside of her house looked exactly the way he'd expected it to. Small and cheerfully decorated, with all the original white wainscoting and moldings, it was a classic 1920s seaside cottage—though the "sea" was only a tidal estuary a block away, and a chimney had been added during some long-ago effort to winterize the place. Floor-to-ceiling bookcases built on either side of the fireplace were crammed with books of every size and length, from tomes on witchcraft, alchemy, herbology, Italian cooking, sewing, fashion history, and the occult, to celebrity memoirs and even murder in the British countryside.

She'd furnished the living room in beachy pale blues and white, so that the black cat curled in a comfortable ball on her sofa stood out in sharp contrast to all the pastels in the room. It raised its head when Derrick deposited its owner on the sofa cushion beside it, and let out a sleepy *Meow?*

"There," Derrick said. "The cat is fine." And so was its owner.

Jessica pushed back some of the dark curls that had fallen into her face and smiled down at the cat beside her, which was stretching luxuriously in place and letting out an enormous yawn. "Yes. I guess he is. Thank you." To the cat, she said, scratching it beneath the chin, "Hello, Pye. You're a very good boy. Thank you for staying home like a gentleman and not getting killed by hail." The cat looked pleased by this praise, and stretched some more. To Derrick, Jessica said, "But listen, you can't go around grabbing women like that without their permission."

"I didn't grab you." He felt a little wounded that she wasn't more impressed with his chivalry. "I carried you because you were hurt. I already explained, it was a medical emergency—"

"Was it, though? Or are you so enamored of my body that you couldn't wait to get your hands on it?"

She was joking. But he understood now that she used humor

as a defense mechanism when she was uncomfortable, so he responded in kind, hoping it would set her at ease.

"Yes." He sat down on the couch beside her—only slightly disturbing the cat, who gave him a suspicious glance, then resettled a few inches away—and gently lifted the leg she'd injured, placing her foot on the driftwood coffee table in front of them. "This whole thing, including the storm, was all part of an elaborate plan I concocted so that I could ravage you."

"Ha!" Her dark eyes danced. She was suppressing a smile, too, so he knew his attempt at humor had worked. "I knew you were lying when you said you weren't here to implant the light in me."

He nodded and reached for the wide hem of her trouser leg. "Now that you got that out of your system, let me look at that knee."

"No!" The smile vanished, and she leaned forward to swat at his hand. "My knee is fine. There's no need for you to—"

But it was too late. He'd peeled back the flowy material of her pant leg and seen what had been causing her pain: a red welt, already purpling around the sides.

"Jessica," he said, his eyes snapping wide with concern. "Did one of those hailstones—?"

"It's fine." She tried to cover the welt by tugging down the hem of her pants. "I'll just put some ice on it later."

"It's *not* fine. Jessica, let me help you."

Before she could stop him, he laid his fingertips gently across the warm, tender skin of her knee.

Jessica

Plant marigold seeds in a sunny spot in the spring, and by fall thou wilst have golden blooms that will ward off pests and promote riches.

Goody Fletcher,
Book of Useful Household Tips

I can't say exactly what happened when Derrick laid his hands over my knee, but I can describe how it felt: like the sun coming out on a bitterly cold winter's day, warming my skin and making me feel as if I'd suddenly stepped onto a white sand beach.

And just as if I'd suddenly stepped onto a white sand beach, the pain disappeared, leaving in its place only a sweet, summery sensation.

It was incredible . . . especially since I had no idea how he was doing it. And I've been around. I went to college in New York City. I've been on buying trips to Los Angeles. I even went back to France a couple of times after my semester abroad. The French might be known for their cooking, but do you know what else they're really good at? That's right: sex.

But with all my experience, I'd never met a guy who was as good with his hands as Derrick.

"How are you doing that?" I finally asked as he bent over my knee, one long strand of his sandy blond hair falling over to tickle my skin.

He wasn't aware of it, however, because his eyes were closed.

"Could you be quiet, please?" he asked. "I'm concentrating."

"Sorry," I said. "But I'm really curious. You said it wasn't a spell. Is it Reiki? Because I understand that the World Council of Witches forbids their members from practicing hands-on alternative medicine, due to the liability issues."

"Yes, well, I'm not a member of the WCW, remember?" I noticed that he hadn't shaved recently. He'd already had a few days' growth of whiskers when I first met him. Now he had what basically amounted to a short beard. Coupled with the long hair, he had a little Robin Hood thing going on. This was a problem for me, since I kind of had a thing for Robin Hood, especially the fox in the Disney version. "That's a ridiculous rule."

"I agree," I said, averting my gaze from his foxiness. "But why do you think so?"

"Because all witches are healers."

"Uh, all witches are *not* healers. May I remind you of what Rosalie just tried to do to us back there?"

"All witches have the *capacity* to be healers," he said, opening his eyes. This close, I was able to see that they weren't actually silver, but pale blue with amber flecks in them. Oh, God. "I saw you make the mayor's wife feel better about herself when you dressed her in the clothes you chose for her. The ability to manipulate the energy around us into a force that heals, spiritually or physically, is one that every witch possesses. You have it. I have it. Probably Rosalie Hopkins has it. But how she chooses to use it, according to you, is to harm instead of heal. Perhaps that's why that love spell you gave her didn't work."

I bit my lower lip—not because I disagreed with anything he was saying, but because he was sitting so close, and he was so . . . well, hot. I mean *literally* hot. He'd lifted his hands from my knee, but I still felt the heat from his fingers there. The redness from the wound Rosalie's hailstone had inflicted still lingered, but so did the glorious feeling of his touch. I'd given away my protective amethyst, and not five minutes later, I'd been hurt in a hailstorm caused by my mortal enemy. . . .

But now my wounds were being healed by a gentle-fingered witch with silver eyes and a foxy beard. Maybe my amethyst's protective properties hadn't left me entirely yet.

"A love spell draws on positive energy," Derrick was saying, "because it represents something new and hopeful. But if the witch casting it is more used to drawing from negativity—well, you can see how a spell like that might go astray."

"Yeah." I released my lip and then leaned forward to lower my pant leg. I wasn't exactly naked in front of him, but it was starting to feel that way. Any second now he was going to notice my naked thirst for him. "I get what you're saying. And I completely agree with you . . . in theory. But like I said, the thing between me and Rosalie is a little more complicated than that."

I didn't want to remember the panic I'd seen on Billy's face in the cafeteria a little while ago as he'd tried to look everywhere but at me. I hadn't exactly been happy about running into him, either—not to mention Rosalie, or their creepy solicitation for "Harvest Princess" volunteers—but at least I'd summoned up a smile and a bright "Hello" for them both as I'd tried to hurry past.

Unfortunately a waspish "What are *you* doing here?" from Rosalie stopped me before I got to the door.

"Meeting with my new mentee." I'd known better than to mention the real reason I was there, especially in front of Billy, who—as far as I could tell—still wasn't aware of the existence of witches in West Harbor. "You know, the program the school has that matches up kids with local business owners?"

My ruse didn't work, however. Rosalie's eyes narrowed suspiciously. "I didn't know they were taking mentors for that already."

"Oh, yes," I'd said, and reached into the plastic jack-o'-lantern they had sitting on the table, with free fun-sized candy bars for the kids. I wasn't a kid, but I was a chocoholic, and even after all the brownies I'd consumed, I always had room for more. Plus the sky outside was getting darker. Surely this was simply a fluke, and not any of Rosalie's doing. But I grabbed nervously for the chocolate anyway. "It's a great program. Sal recommended it. You remember Sal, don't you, Dina's brother?"

"Obviously I remember Sal." Rosalie stared at me expressionlessly. "We had to go through him to set up this table."

"Ha, ha, right." I looked down at the candy bar I'd pulled from the jack-o'-lantern and realized, sadly, that it was a Milky Way. "Okay, well, great seeing you both. I better go before—"

That's when it happened. Billy's fingers had closed over my hand—the one holding the Milky Way—preventing me from leaving, and causing Rosalie's cheeks to flush angrily.

"Here you go," he'd said.

And, like a magic trick—though there was nothing preternatural about it—Billy slid the miniature Milky Way out of my hand, and dropped a miniature Snickers bar into it. Instead of looking everywhere except at me, his eyes were suddenly gazing hard into mine, seeming to plead *Remember?*

Though he had to have known perfectly well that, after all these years, he was never going to get what he thought he wanted from me, despite remembering my favorite chocolate bar.

That's when the first crash of thunder rattled the school. Billy instantly released me . . . and I'd careened for the exit, knowing I was doomed.

And Rosalie had let me have it, all right.

Now, safe in my own living room, I wondered if I should mention any of what had happened back in the cafeteria to Derrick. But he'd only asked whether Rosalie knew about Esther. Surely there was no reason I needed to embarrass myself any further by telling him the mortifying truth about Billy.

Except . . .

Except what if what had happened after—the blizzard, and all those poor people who nearly froze to death on the interstate— was what was causing the rift?

I didn't want to think about that.

"Anyway," I said, swinging my foot off the coffee table. I was feeling better—but also like it might be a good idea to put some distance between myself and Derrick Winters. "Can I get you that coffee? Or lunch? I don't know about you, but ever since I found out about the rift, I've been starving all the time. I have some leftovers from Mama Giovanni's—my friend's family owns it. His mother makes a great Sunday night gravy." When he only looked confused, I prodded, "You know, gravy—spaghetti sauce with meatballs and sausage? It'll just take me a few minutes to warm it up. It's always better the next day for some reason. I guess the flavors have more of a chance to meld."

When he continued to hesitate, I said, a little impatiently, "Of course I could just give you my report on the Bringer of Light over coffee and cold cheese Danish from Wake Up West Harbor. Do you have more in your car?"

He shook his head, smiling a bit. "No. Sorry, your offer is very generous. I was just thrown by the gravy reference. Where I come from, gravy only comes on mashed potatoes."

"Oh." I eyed him as he reached out to tickle Pye under the chin—and the cat *let* him. Not only let him, but rolled onto his back and showed him his belly, purring. "Yeah, I could see that."

This was nuts. As a shop cat, Pye tended to be friendly with strangers, but not *that* friendly. It had taken months after I'd adopted Pye from the shelter for him to trust me enough to show me his belly. Did Derrick's fingers have the same magical effect on cats that they did on women?

But Derrick didn't even seem to notice my cat's reaction to his touch. Instead, he climbed to his feet, pulled off his leather jacket, and walked across the room to hang it on the fish-tail coat hooks by my front door, straightening the sleeves so it hung evenly with the umbrellas and rain jackets also hanging there.

So he liked cats, and was a little perfectionistic.

This was bad. I liked men who were kind to cats and also kept things tidy.

It didn't hurt that his butt looked so nice in his black jeans, too.

". . . but you really don't have to cook for me," I realized he was saying when I was able to drag my attention away from his jeans.

"I've never been to Montana," I said, walking briskly into my kitchen. Eyes forward. "But around here, gravy is considered spaghetti sauce, and heating up leftovers isn't considered cooking."

I pulled open the door to the refrigerator as both man and cat sat and watched me, the man on a stool at the pass-through between my dining room and kitchen, and the cat on the floor beside him, since Pye was apparently now Derrick's friend for life. "Do you really want coffee, or have you had enough?"

"Is there such a thing as enough?"

"Point taken." I switched on the machine and slipped a pale blue mug beneath the spigot. It was amazing how easy it was for me to move now that he'd done that thing, whatever it was, to my knee. Was he single? And interested in female business witches? Because if we survived the coming apocalypse, he was definitely someone who'd be useful to have around, considering how often I wore out my joints on tailoring projects (and found myself the target of supernatural attacks by my former high school nemesis). "So, my verdict as the Chosen One is, Esther is the Bringer of Light."

He raised his eyebrows. "What makes you think that?"

"Hmmm, let me see." I began spooning food I'd pulled from the fridge into microwaveable bowls. "She moved an entire cafeteria table in front of me using only her mind."

He looked startled. "She's telekinetic?"

"That's what I'm assuming. Or she knows a spell that allows her to move objects with her mind whenever she needs to. But I've never seen a spell like that."

"It's high magic," he murmured. "Such spells exist in scrolls and manuscripts from ancient times, but I'm not sure how she'd have been able to get her hands on one."

"Right. But she's definitely interested in the Craft. She was reading a book on the history of the persecution of witches." I slid his cup of coffee in front of him. "Let me guess. You take it black."

"I do." He sipped, and looked moderately impressed. "This is good, thanks. Did she say why she was reading that?"

"Because Rosalie got her interested in the subject. One of Rosalie's ancestors was accused of being a witch. She's using that fact in some of her Tricentennial publicity—enough so that she's got Esther outraged that so little of what happened here back then is taught in school today, especially when it was caused by so many issues that still exist: ignorance, greed, poverty, misogyny—"

"'The imbalance between rich and poor is the oldest and most fatal ailment of all republics.'"

When I only looked at him blankly, he said, "Plutarch."

"Oh, right. Your book from the car."

Derrick nodded. "And don't forget that the Puritans also loved a good conspiracy theory. Any chance they got to blame a bad harvest or a baby dying on their neighbor having made a pact with the devil, they went for it."

"Oh, yes, of course. That's probably why Esther can't understand Salem getting all the attention for their witches when we had our own witch hysteria here forty years earlier."

"More people were executed for witchcraft there than in Connecticut, though," he said.

"Well, Massachusetts *is* the Puritan state." The microwave pinged. I transferred the contents of the bowls onto two white plates, grabbed some silverware from a drawer and a container of freshly grated Parmesan from the fridge, then brought it all over to the counter at the pass-through, pulling up a stool so I could sit across from him. "And on that happy note—*buon appetito*."

He looked down at the mess of spaghetti and garlic bread on his plate a little apprehensively, as if he wasn't sure what to do with it. But when he saw me jab a fork into my long pasta noodles, twirl them into a bite-sized portion, then pop them into my mouth, he did the same—then got a pleased look on his face.

"Hey," he said. "This is really good."

"Um, yeah." I took a swig from the ice water I'd poured myself. "What did you think I was going to do, poison you?"

He frowned as he bit into his garlic bread. If there was such a thing as a self-defensive bite, that's what he took. "No. Well, maybe. It's just that I've been here in West Harbor a few days now, and the food I've had so far has been . . . disappointing."

I laid down my fork and stared at him. "Derrick, I could have told you good places to eat around here if you'd stuck around and asked, instead of peacing out with that 'blessed be' crap. There are dozens of good places. Mama Giovanni's is only one of them. There's also the Country Gourmet—"

"I'm not in West Harbor to eat," he interrupted, although the rapidness with which the food on his plate was disappearing disproved his claim. "I'm here to save it. And you. Tell me more about Esther."

"Okay, fine. She's smart. She wants to be a psychologist."

"Good." He nodded as he sopped up what was left of his sauce with his remaining garlic bread. It was hard for me not to stare at his forearms now that he'd taken his jacket off. They were impressively shapely. "That's a positive sign. It shows she has empathy."

"That's what I thought. She was sitting alone, but only so she could read. She has friends, as well as what I'd call a lot of Big Sister Energy. She was able to get a classmate who was climbing on a table to do exactly as she said and get down—though partly only because she shook him down."

Derrick stared at me. "That's why she shook the cafeteria table? To get the boy down from it?"

"Yes. Why?"

"The Bringer of Light shouldn't be using her powers for violence—unless of course she's battling the forces of evil."

"Trust me," I said. "This kid might not have been evil, but he was super annoying."

He grinned a little. "Anything else?"

"Well, there was one other thing. . . ."

He glanced up from the meatball he was about to bite into, suddenly apprehensive. "What?"

"She read—with complete accuracy—my astrological chart, without my having told her my birthday."

Slowly, Derrick laid down his fork.

"I know," I said quickly. "The WCW doesn't hold astrology in the highest regard." The Council didn't just disregard it. I knew from online posts by disgruntled former members that they called it—along with tarot card reading, numerology, and palm reading—"the least disciplined of the divinations." But this was mainly because of social media influencers using it online for clout. That wasn't nearly as offensive—to me, anyway—as politicians misappropriating the term *witch hunt*. "But you said yourself that each witch channels the energy of the universe around her differently—or something like that. Just because Esther does it through astrology doesn't mean she isn't the one we're looking for. She even knew I was a witch. Of course, that was because you're making me wear this dumb Gaia amulet—"

His gaze on me sharpened. "That 'dumb Gaia amulet' is for your protection."

"Yeah, well, fat lot of good it's done for me so far."

He folded his arms across his chest, causing his biceps to swell. "You're not dead, are you?"

"Wow. Impressed with yourself much?" I pushed away from the counter and busied myself with clearing our lunch plates, mainly so I'd be distracted from his arms. "For your information, I could have handled that thing with Rosalie back there without your help. I've been handling her for *years* without you and your magic fingers."

"Have you, though?" He was unimpressed. "A witch with powers like that could be using them to do so much good in the world—making it rain in drought-stricken areas, or the sun come out in areas afflicted by storms. But instead she chooses to use them for petty grievances."

"How is that *my* problem?" I demanded. "I thought that's what 'entities' like yours—whatever it is—and the Council are for: keeping witches like Rosalie, who abuse their magic, in line."

He frowned. "Have you reported her?"

"No. Why should I bother? If the Council doesn't want me or witches like me, why should I help them?"

"You'd be helping the world, actually, not the Council," he said. "But I understand."

"Do you?" I glared at him. "For someone who isn't a Council member, you certainly seem to be on their side."

His frown turned into a shadow of a smile, and for once, that silver-eyed gaze seemed to soften. "I'm only on one person's side, Jessica—yours."

This reply—and the smile—was so disarming that for a second, I could only blink at him in surprise . . . until he broke the unexpectedly intimate moment by adding, quickly, "And West Harbor's. And Esther's. I'm on her side, as well. So when are you meeting her again?"

"I don't know." I had to turn away from him because I'd found the sudden softness of his gaze unsettling. I made a big deal out of putting the dishes in the dishwasher. Pye, who'd apparently been waiting for Derrick to pet him again, finally realized that wasn't going to happen anytime soon, and took the opportunity to exit through the cat flap in the back door. "It was awkward. The bell was ringing. We exchanged numbers, though."

He shoved himself away from the counter, the feet of his stool squeaking noisily against my wood floor. "If Esther is the One, we need to get started on her training right away in order for her to be ready by the Hunter's Moon."

"The what?" I turned from the sink to face him as he came into the kitchen. His gaze remained unnervingly bright.

"The Hunter's Moon. It's the full moon that appears after the harvest, when the fields have been reaped and hunters can see their prey at night. This year's Hunter's Moon happens to fall on the same night as the Tricentennial Ball, which happens to be the night before Halloween, which is when the veil—"

"Between this world and the spirit world is at its thinnest, I know, I remember." God, this guy and his prophecies. "But if the Hunter's Moon is when there's going to be some apocalyptic battle with the forces of evil in West Harbor, I don't see how Esther's telekinesis and ability to read their exact astrological chart is going to help."

"That . . . is . . . why . . . we . . . have . . . to . . . train . . . her." A muscle was leaping around in Derrick's jaw, like he was trying hard not to say something he'd regret. "Do you have any more coffee?"

"Uh, I think you've had more than enough coffee." The muscle in his jaw wasn't the only thing jumping. Some veins in his neck were also throbbing. "In fact, if you ask me, what you need instead of more caffeine is a nap. Why don't you go back to your hotel and take a little siesta? Then I can go to my shop and check on how Becca is doing. We can meet up again later and see if there's anything left of my car to salvage, and decide what to do next about Esther's training."

But instead of agreeing with my very sensible plan, he looked even more stressed, his brows lowering as he looked away. "I don't nap."

"What do you mean, you don't nap? Everybody naps. Napping is so good for you. It increases alertness and improves memory—"

"I can't go back to my hotel room, all right?" He finally raised his gaze, and when he did, I saw that his eyes looked blue and amber again. "I couldn't get a hotel room. Everything is booked solid because of all the leaf peepers and this stupid Tricentennial."

"Wait, so I was right?" I wasn't sure I believed what I was hearing. "You really *have* been living in your car?"

"No, not living in it." He was defensive, but adorably so, like Pye when he tried to leap onto the kitchen counter, but missed. "I found a twenty-four-hour fitness center. I've been showering and keeping some of my things in a locker there."

"Oh my God, Derrick, why didn't you say anything? I have a spare bedroom. You can stay here."

Now, instead of defensive, he looked uncomfortable. "That wouldn't be right."

"Why? Does it violate some HR code at the WCW? Who cares? You said you didn't even work there."

"I don't," he said. His hands had strayed toward the pockets on his jeans. He'd shoved his fingers into them like some schoolboy who'd been caught doing something naughty, when literally all we were doing was discussing what I assumed were going to be some completely platonic sleeping arrangements—much as I might wish the situation to be otherwise. Seeing his discomfort over this was truly the highlight of my day so far. "I'm supposed to be protecting you. And Esther, if she's the Bringer of Light," he added hastily.

"Well, won't it be more convenient for you to protect me from inside my house than outside it?" I brightened, a thought occurring to me. "You could even come to Trivia with me tomorrow night!"

His brows lowered in confusion. "To what?"

"Tuesday Night Trivia, over at West Harbor Brewport. Esther's parents own it. I'm on a team with my friends, and we meet there every Tuesday night—"

A loud knock sounded on the door. Derrick froze, his expression wary, as if the forces of evil might actually have already arrived on my porch. "Relax," I said. "It's probably UPS. They always come this time of—"

"Jess?" called the unmistakable voice of my ex-boyfriend Billy. "Jessica, are you there?"

Jessica

To enhance any celebration, mix saltpeter with ice. Drop
a vial of watered wine into the concoction, and soon
thou wilst have the most delectable snow thou hast ever
tasted.

Goody Fletcher,
Book of Useful Household Tips

It started out as a gentle flurry . . . just enough so that Mom had
to put on the windshield wipers as we were driving home from
Stew Leonard's.

Then the snow got heavier. And heavier. Soon it was coming
down so hard and fast that my little brother, Ethan, asked, "Is this
a blizzard?"

"No, it can't be," Dad said. "They didn't say anything about a
blizzard in the forecast."

Then the local news came on. It was official: it was a blizzard.
Airports were shut down. The highways closed to all but emergency vehicles. Even the trains that normally shuttled millions of
commuters in and out of New York City came to a halt.

Here's the thing: it never occurred to me that there was anything paranormal about it. I wouldn't even have known otherwise if Rosalie hadn't called that night on my parents' landline to ask, "How are you liking my little birthday present?"

I was confused. "My birthday's not till Tuesday."

"Yeah," she said, "but weren't you having a party at Mama Giovanni's tonight?"

"Um, I was. But we moved it to my house because of the snow." I had to stick a finger in my free ear to hear her because Mark and Dina and some of my other friends had come over. It was silly, but we were playing *Dance Dance Revolution: Mario Mix* in the living room on Ethan's Nintendo. So it was loud near the landline. "Mark's mom is here making dinner for us. Why? What's your present?"

"God, you're dumb." Rosalie's voice rose to a frenzied pitch. "Do you have any idea how dumb you are? *I'm* the one making this storm happen. It was me. I did it to ruin your party and get back at you for what you did to Billy."

"What did I do to Billy?" I was genuinely bewildered—and a little concerned. "I gave you the love spell. I thought you were going to use it on him in time to get him to take you out for Valentine's Day. Didn't it work for you?"

"No, it didn't work for me." Rosalie sounded as if she were crying. "It didn't work for you, either."

"Yes, it did, Rosalie. If it didn't work for you, you must have done something wrong. Love spells work best under a full moon. Wait until the next full moon, then try it again. And did you leave out the garlic? I left out the garlic, and I think that's what made all the—"

"The spell didn't work because Billy *was already in love with you*, you idiot!" Rosalie spat into the phone. "He just told me. He told me that we could never be together because he's been in love

with you since the beginning of the school year, when you were
so nice to him in Chem class, helping him to not flunk it and get
kicked off the stupid football team. And he likes that you're so
tall. He says he likes not having to lean down so far to kiss you."
She let out a bitter laugh. "Can you believe it? He *actually* loves
you. *Really* loves you. He always has. The only reason he's been
leaving you alone lately is because you asked him to, and he loves
you so much, he wants to make you happy. He even got his scholarship back—because you told him to!"

I stood there in complete astonishment, holding the phone
to my ear as Mark yelled, "Switching to hard mode!" and Dina
shrieked with laughter. Billy Walker was in love with me? *Really*
in love with me, and not magically in love with me?

Everything made so much sense now: why he'd refused to go
away after I'd told him I wasn't interested . . . and why the banishing spells hadn't worked.

There's no magic greater than love—real love. No power on
earth is stronger.

"You can't use a love spell on someone who's already in love
with someone else," Rosalie went on, angrily. "No matter how
pure your intentions. And you especially can't use a love spell on
someone who's already in love with you. You ate that disgusting
stew in front of Billy for nothing . . . and so did I."

"Rosalie." I was stunned. "I—I don't know what to say. I'm so
sorry."

"You don't even know the meaning of the word *sorry*." Rosalie sniffed. "Not yet. But I plan on making you sorry. First with
this storm, and then by reporting you to the World Council of
Witches for causing the suffering of others through the use of
magic. You know that's forbidden, right? That should earn you
a lifetime ban from the WCW right there. Not that you'd ever
qualify as a member anyway."

"What?" I wandered up the stairs as far as the phone cord would stretch in order to get away from the cacophony of noise below me. That didn't help me escape the rumble of thundersnow above, however. "What are you talking about, Rosalie? None of this was my fault. I didn't know Billy was in love with me. And you just said my spell didn't work! I know Billy's hurt right now, but I didn't cause that hurt by using magic. You, however, are very definitely hurting people with this storm. I just heard on the news that thousands of people are stranded at the airports and train stations and on the sides of the road—"

"If anyone's hurt, it's your fault," Rosalie snapped. "Remember this day, Jessica Gold. Remember it well. Because whatever happens, *it's all your fault.*"

Then the phone went dead in my ear. A second later, the lights went out, and *Dance Dance Revolution* died, to the groans of all my friends.

The power was gone. And with it any sympathy I might once have had for Rosalie Hopkins.

Derrick

A true Witch does not seek power through the suffering
of others.

Rule Number Three of the Nine Rules
World Council of Witches

All the color drained from Jessica's face. It was as if the voice
from behind her front door was coming from the undead.

"Who is it?" Derrick reached out to grasp her by the arm and
draw her close so he could whisper in her ear. "Who's Billy?"

"An ex."

"Is he possessed?"

"*What?*" Jessica, for all her charms, seemed to have no idea
that evil existed, despite the number of times he'd assured her it
did, and was speaking at a normal volume which anyone standing
outside the door could hear.

"Has he ever shown symptoms of demonic possession?" Derrick hissed in her ear. "Aversion to sacred things and places? Sudden ability to speak dead languages? Any festering wounds?"

"No!" She pulled her arm from his grasp and looked up at
him as if he were the one who was demonic. "Of course not! Do
demons actually exist?"

"Yes, of course demons exist! What do you think I've been trying to tell you? Angry spirits—also known as demons, or ghosts, or whatever you want to call them—are born when someone has died an unjust or particularly violent death. Your town is under attack by them, and by Thursday's full moon, with Halloween the next day, they'll be at full strength. They could manifest themselves in any number of ways—"

"Well, they haven't manifested in my ex-boyfriend."

"How do you know that?"

"Because I just saw him." She swallowed, then looked slightly guilty. "He was there today, at the high school, with Rosalie."

Derrick was so alarmed, he reached out to grab her by the arms again, this time with both hands. "Why didn't you tell me before? This is *exactly* what I was saying to you the other day about unusual activity in town. How often does he normally come over here?"

"Never, okay? But he used to come over here all the time back in high school, when we went out." Perhaps noticing his confused expression, she explained, "This is my parents' house. I bought it from them when they decided to move out to Santa Fe to be closer to my grandparents. I didn't take advantage of them, though. I paid full market price—"

He couldn't believe she was talking about her finances at a time like this. "Do I look like an accountant to you?"

"Oh my God! *Really?*" She twisted, trying to free herself from his grasp. "Look, trust me, Billy Walker is *not* in league with the forces of evil."

"Maybe not the Billy you used to know. But now—"

Another thump struck the door. This time the man's voice behind it sounded whiny and impatient. "Jessica, I know you're in there. There's a car in your driveway, and I can hear you talking."

"Oh, God." Jessica's dark eyes, as she looked up at Derrick, were wide with anxiety. "I have to let him in."

"You don't, actually," he said, forcing himself to remain calm. "Evil spirits cannot enter a home unless invited."

"You don't understand." She'd wiggled free, and was already on her way to the door before he could stop her. "It's *Billy*. He's not evil. *I'm* the one who treated *him* horribly."

"*What?*" Derrick wondered if they were in Connecticut or cloud-cuckoo-land. "I thought you said the love spell didn't work."

"It didn't. But it was because he was already in love with me."

Before this had a chance to sink in, she'd already thrown open the door. He wasn't sure who he'd been expecting to see, but it certainly wasn't the tall guy standing there in khaki pants, a sweater Derrick was certain his mom had picked out for him, and the worst fake tan he'd ever seen.

"Billy," Jessica cried. "What a surprise! Come on in."

"Hi, Jess." Billy wiped his feet awkwardly on Jessica's black cat welcome mat. If they lived through this encounter, Derrick was going to have to have a word with her, and not just about what she'd confessed just before opening the door. If you invited in every guy who called himself Billy (even though he was past thirty and didn't live in the South), and wore navy blue sweaters with tiny red lobsters embroidered all over them, you were bound to let in something diabolical.

"I stopped by Enchantments first," Billy explained, "but Becca said you weren't there, so I took a chance that you'd be—"

Then Billy's gaze fell on Derrick, who'd taken up a defensive position near the fireplace, where there was an antique stand holding a set of wrought-iron pokers that Derrick thought might come in handy should things take a turn.

"Oh," Billy said, backing up so quickly, he almost hit his head on the doorframe. He was tall—taller than Derrick, and that was saying a lot. From his height and the way he carried himself, Derrick guessed he'd probably played football once upon a time. "I didn't know you had company. I didn't mean to interrupt. Maybe I should—"

"No, no." Jessica's smile was as fake as Billy's skin tone. "You weren't interrupting. Billy, this is—"

"Winters." Derrick decided to use a different line of defense than the fireplace pokers. He crossed Jessica's living room with his right hand outstretched. "Derrick Winters. I'm Jessica's boyfriend."

Billy looked a little stunned at the word *boyfriend*, but otherwise handled the news like a champ.

"Eric, is it?" Billy said, with his bright All-American Boy smile. Literally bright: his teeth were capped and almost blindingly white. He shook Derrick's hand calmly, not trying to crush his fingers with his own even though he could have, since he had a ball player's enormous paw. "I don't think I've seen you around town before."

"It's Derrick, and no, you wouldn't have." Derrick returned to his position against the mantel. "I'm Jessica's dirty little secret."

Jessica let out a bark of nervous laughter and hurried to Derrick's side. He had to hand it to her: she was managing the curveball he'd thrown with admirable aplomb. There was only the faintest pink in her cheeks.

"There's no secret!" she cried. To his surprise, she snaked an arm around his waist. "Our relationship is just . . . new. And you haven't seen Derrick around before because he doesn't live here."

"Oh, really?" Billy's eyes were as shiny as his teeth. "Where are you from?"

"Montana," Derrick said at the same time that Jessica said, "The city."

Billy looked from one to the other in confusion. "I don't understand."

"Derrick's from Montana," Jessica said quickly, "but he lives in the city now. That's where we met, actually, at the Metropolitan Museum of Art, where we'd both gone to—"

"See the new Colombian art exhibit," Derrick said, at the same time that Jessica said, "Check out the fashion collection."

Jessica elbowed Derrick, but he only slipped his own arm around her. He liked the feel of her body against his. They seemed to fit together perfectly, like matching salt and pepper shakers. Now that he was certain from Billy's demeanor that he wasn't demonically possessed, only deeply stupid, he felt more at ease. He said, "To be honest, I think we were both just trying to get out of the heat. But instead, we found a different kind of heat." He looked down at Jessica, whose cheeks were turning an even more interesting shade of pink, and grinned. "Didn't we, honey?"

That's when he leaned over and kissed her.

Jessica

To rid a home of demons, sweep it counterclockwise with a new broom.

Goody Fletcher,
Book of Useful Household Tips

I wasn't expecting the kiss.

But I felt it. Oh, how I felt it.

If I'd thought the touch of his fingers on my shoulder or knee was amazing, that was nothing compared to the touch of his lips on mine. Suddenly every cell in my body sprang awake, like I'd been struck by lightning—but in a good way. Was there such a thing as gentle lightning?

Because that's what his kiss felt like. Lightning filled with golden autumn leaves and softly falling rain. He smelled of it, of the rain and the leaves—as absurd as I knew that sounded. He smelled of the mist that had hung over the grass when I'd left my house that morning, as clean and as fresh as newly picked apples.

And his lips on mine, rather than demanding anything, were a promise: a promise of more kisses to come. That promise was echoed in the hard outline of his body, pressed against mine. For a moment, I forgot everything else except those lips and that body—like that there was a supernatural cataclysm threatening my town, that my ex-boyfriend was standing a few feet away, and that Derrick had just accused that same ex-boyfriend of possibly being a demon, then told him we were dating.

Then he lifted his face from mine, and I saw that he looked as shocked as I did—though I didn't know what he had to be so surprised about, since the whole thing had been his idea to begin with. It wasn't until I heard a deep voice say, "Well, uh," that I was able to drag my gaze from his gleaming eyes and see Billy still standing by my front door, shuffling his feet.

"I'm happy for you, Jess," Billy said, and he actually did look happy. "It's great—really great—that you've found someone. Rosie and I were just asking each other, when is Jessica ever gonna settle down?"

Great. Forget demons. *This* was my apocalyptic nightmare.

I dropped my arm from around Derrick's waist and took a step away from him, since I could still feel energy radiating from his body to mine. I couldn't tell from his expressionless profile if he could feel it, too, but I didn't need it scrambling my senses anymore. "Oh?"

"Yeah." Billy shoved his hands in the pockets of his Dockers and rocked back on his heels, still smiling. "It's nice to see you taking life seriously for a change. You know Rosalie says that a woman's fertility begins to decline dramatically after age—"

"Okay, then," I interrupted briskly. "What was it, exactly, that brought you by, Billy?"

"Oh." He quit smiling, apparently remembering that the reason for his visit wasn't only to remind me that I hadn't had kids yet. "Right. Your car. I saw it in the parking lot just now outside the school. You're still driving that blue Mini Cooper, right?"

Bluebell! "Yes." It physically pained me to think what kind of damage Rosalie might have inflicted on my beloved vintage Mini. "Why? How bad is it?"

He winced, pulling his phone from one of his pockets. "Bad, Jess. Really bad. Much worse than that Fiat out there in the driveway."

Derrick muttered, seemingly to no one in particular, "It's a rental."

I felt a pang. Poor Bluebell. She and I had been through a lot together, including alternate side of the street parking rules in New York City during the years I'd lived there. "Won't insurance cover the damage?"

"Sure, if you carry comprehensive." Billy scrolled through some photos on his phone, then turned the screen toward me. "But I think it might be a total loss."

I stared down in horror at the photo. Bluebell was barely recognizable. Was this another one of Derrick's signs of impending doom for West Harbor? Or only another example of Rosalie's ongoing vendetta against me? How could she have been so cruel? It was one thing to have gone after me, but my poor innocent car?

"But I wanted to let you know that I'm taking care of it," Billy said quickly, apparently seeing the heartache on my face. "I'm having your car towed over to Hopkins Motors, and I'm putting our best guys on it. If they can't fix it, no one can."

I could barely look at the photos, they were so awful. I handed his phone back to him. "Thanks, Billy."

"And while your car is in the shop," he went on, shoving his cell back into his pocket, "you can borrow any other vehicle on the lot, free of charge. And if it turns out we can't repair it, I'll get you the best deal possible on a new one. Friends and family discount. Whatever you need."

"That's so nice of you, Billy." I didn't want a new car. I wanted Bluebell. "Thanks."

"Hopkins Motors?" Derrick, slouching back against the fireplace mantel, straightened.

"Yeah." Billy beamed at him. "My father-in-law owns it."

"Your father-in-law." Derrick's silver gaze laser-focused onto me. "You're married to Rosalie Hopkins."

Billy beamed. "That's right. Do you know her?"

"Only by reputation." Derrick's gaze on me narrowed. "Weird that no one mentioned to me that the two of you were married."

By "no one," I knew that Derrick meant me, and that I was going to have some explaining to do.

But how could I explain something that, even today, still caused me so much grief?

Jessica

Journal Entry from 2008

To attract good health and sweeten thy dreams, place a sprig of thyme beneath thy pillow.

Goody Fletcher,
Book of Useful Household Tips

It turned out Mark's uncle Richie had been right: there weren't any lofts left in Manhattan for college girls to rent cheap and fix up.

But there were plenty of unair-conditioned walk-ups in Washington Heights.

That's how I found myself dragging my heavy art portfolio up and down the five flights of stairs to the one-bedroom apartment Dina and I were sharing.

Not that I was complaining. My life in New York City was everything I'd dreamed it would be, and more. I didn't even mind cramming myself and my giant portfolio onto the subway every morning for my hour-long commute downtown to school. I was living in the most exciting place in the world. What could be better?

As I undid the many locks to our place and opened the door that day, I saw that the mail had already arrived. Dina usually got home before I did, grabbed the mail and brought it upstairs, then changed and left for her volunteer job at the neighborhood animal shelter. No dogs were allowed in our building, and Dina, a dog lover, couldn't stand being without one. I could hear the shower in our single bathroom running, so I knew she was already home from her puppy-loving.

The mail that day consisted of the usual pile of bills, junk, and multiple magazines to which I subscribed for inspiration (*Vogue*, *Allure*, *Harper's Bazaar*, all of which always seemed to arrive on the same day), along with one mysteriously large cream-colored envelope addressed to me "and guest." It had a West Harbor, Connecticut, return address. The sender was Mr. and Mrs. Kenneth Hopkins, Rosalie's parents.

"Oh my God," I called to Dina, who'd just that moment turned off the water. "Did you see what I got in the mail?"

"No. What?" I heard the hooks on the shower curtain rattle as Dina threw it back and stepped from the tub.

"A wedding invitation." I found a butter knife and opened the thick, expensive envelope. "Rosalie Hopkins is getting married."

"Oh, yeah." Dina appeared in the hallway wearing only two fluffy white towels, one wrapped around her body, the other around her hair. "I forgot to tell you. My mom said she saw Rosalie and her mom at the Westfield Mall in Trumbull last week, and she could have sworn they'd been looking at baby stuff in GapKids."

"Jesus!" I jumped, both at Dina's words and the cascade of fake gold rose petals that fell from the envelope when I pulled out the invitation. A confetti bomb. So Rosalie. "How could you not have mentioned that until now?"

"They could have been shopping for a relative." Dina shook her head as she stared at the mess on the floor. "But now it's looking like maybe not. What dumbass did Rosalie Hopkins get to knock her up and then agree to marry her?"

I looked at the invitation, which was exactly what I would have expected from Rosalie: extremely proper and stuffy.

Mr. and Mrs. Kenneth Hopkins
request the honor of your presence
at the marriage of their daughter
Rosalie Anne

to

William Robert Walker
Saturday, the twentieth of December
at six o'clock
First Protestant Church
West Harbor, Connecticut
Reception to follow
West Harbor Yacht Club
RSVP
Black Tie

I looked at Dina in astonishment. "Oh my God," I said, suddenly barely able to breathe. "Billy."

"No." Dina snatched the invitation from me. "No way."

But it was true.

I had to go sit down on the futon (which served as both my bed and our living room couch) because I felt a little lightheaded.

"How could he have been so stupid?" Dina raged, still staring down at the invitation.

"It's Billy," I murmured. "You know how dumb he is. He never stood a chance once Rosalie decided he was the one she wanted."

"Yeah, but he could have worn a condom. What's he going to do now?" she asked. "Drop out of Notre Dame and be Rosalie's full-time arm candy slash baby daddy?"

"I guess so." I put my head between my knees, not so much because I was still feeling light-headed, but to avoid having to see evidence of Rosalie's latest offense—the invitation in Dina's hands, the fake rose-petal confetti on our floor. Instead, I studied the insoles of my boots.

"Still, you have to admit," Dina said, "he'll make a good dad."

I didn't look up. I didn't say anything, either. What was there to say?

Then Dina's bare feet, with her dark purple pedicure, appeared in my line of vision, and I felt her sit down on the futon beside me.

"Hey," she said, patting my shoulder. "Come on. You know I'm right. He *will* make a good dad. And you know what? I bet he'll be happy, too. The only thing Billy's ever wanted is to love someone. Like, *really* love someone."

I looked up then, and gave an unsteady little laugh. "To a nearly suffocating degree."

"Exactly. I think all those spells you did for him, wishing him success, worked. *This* is what success means to Billy."

"Being a teen dad?"

"Yes. I'm serious. And you know what else? There's a reason you got an invitation and I didn't. Rosalie doesn't expect you to come to her wedding—"

I sat up so fast, I gave myself a head rush. "I would never!"

"Of course not. But she wants to rub it in your face that she got Billy and you didn't."

"*Why?* She knows I broke up with him. Why would she think I care? It's so weird."

"Oh, come on, Jess. You *do* care a little. Why else did you do all those spells? You want Billy to be happy, don't you?"

"Yes, of course I do. That's why I was so glad when he finally went off to school. I thought he might have a chance at getting away from her at last—and from me, and from West Harbor. But now Rosalie's figured out the *one way* to drag him back, and keep him there with her forever." I looked down at the invitation dangling from Dina's hand, and something clicked. "Do you think Rosalie sent me that invitation herself?"

Dina followed my gaze. "As opposed to having her mother do it? Or one of her dad's many personal assistants? I guess so. She probably took great satisfaction in it, too, licking the envelope herself and everything. Why?"

"Because there's a spell in Goody Fletcher's book that I can modify to send happiness to someone remotely." I plucked the invitation from Dina's hand. "All I need is something the person has touched."

Dina made a face. "Why would you want to send happiness to *Rosalie*? She's done nothing but try to make your life miserable. And now Billy's—if you consider having a baby with Rosalie Hopkins a misery, which I definitely do."

"I don't care about Rosalie's happiness. I care about Billy's. Rosalie's marrying Billy. And if Rosalie is happy, Billy will be happy, too. Want to help me?"

"Sure." Dina shrugged. "Why not?"

So that's how we found ourselves, a little while later, sitting cross-legged on the floor with Rosalie and Billy's wedding invitation between us. I'd circled it with gently flaming tea lights and sprigs of purifying thyme, and opened the windows of our corner apartment to let in the cool evening breeze—and of course the traffic noise from the avenue, below.

"Oh, Gaia," I said, "mother of us all, we ask you to protect this couple, and send them all the love, blessings, good health, and good fortune that you can."

Dina, whose eyes had been closed, now opened them and looked at me critically. "Sorry to interrupt, but do you really think it's appropriate to ask Gaia to send good fortune to the kids of two of the richest families in West Harbor?"

I considered this. "You're right. Let me try that again." We closed our eyes and concentrated.

"Oh, Gaia, mother of us all," I said, "please protect this couple, and send them all the love, blessings, good health, and good fortune that you can spare *from those who need it more.*"

A gust of wind blew in so suddenly from the open windows, it caused our long white curtains (repurposed bedsheets) to swell and then loudly snap. Dina and I shrieked, not only because of the sound, but because the wind blew out the flames on all of the tea candles I'd arranged around the wedding invitation, and we were plunged into semidarkness. The only light to see by was the yellowish glow of the streetlamp outside. In it, I could see the blue smoke from the candlewicks drifting across the living room.

"Holy shit," Dina said, her eyes wide. "Do you think that was a sign?"

"I don't know." I watched as the wind died, and the curtains fell back into their normal positions. The gold rose-petal confetti from the wedding invitation and the thyme had both been blown across the room and now lay tossed together in a pile. "I guess the real question is, if it was a sign . . . was it a good one, or a bad one?"

Jessica

To banish bad luck, place an egg, still in its shell, in thy bathing water under a waning moon. Dispose of the egg far from home, or better yet near the home of thine enemy.

Goody Fletcher,
Book of Useful Household Tips

"A lot of people don't realize we're married," Billy was saying, "'cause Rosalie kept her maiden name."

Derrick's gaze on Billy narrowed. "I see."

"Well, it's understandable," Billy went on. "The Hopkinses are kind of big deals around here. But so are the Walkers. Did you pass any signs on your way here from the city for Walker Hardware?"

Derrick shook his head. "Not that I recall."

"You must have. Walker Hardware is my family's company. That's why our kids are Walker-Hopkins. We tried Hopkins-Walker, but Rosie thought it sounded like some kind of zombie. A Hopkins-Walker, you know?" Billy chuckled to himself. "Hey, we just got their new school photos. Do you want to see them, Jess?"

"Absolutely." I couldn't meet Derrick's gaze. I knew he was

right. I should have mentioned that Billy and Rosalie were married, like I should have mentioned that I'd seen Billy at the high school. But so many strange things had been going on, how was I supposed to know which ones actually mattered? "How are Elizabeth and Billy Junior doing?"

"Oh, they're great." Billy had whipped out his phone again. "Billy's big game against East Harbor Middle School is coming up this weekend. We're all going to cheer him on. And Lizzie's loving being a freshman over at the high school. Did you know she's going to be a Harvest Princess?"

"No, I didn't. What exactly is a Harvest Princess?"

"Oh, it's a little something that Rosie dreamed up to get local girls more interested in the Tricentennial. The ones who get picked will serve as promotional spokeswomen for the town during the celebration. You know, they'll walk around the square, handing out pamphlets and stuff. Here, check out the kids."

"Aw." I looked down at the photos of mini Rosalie and Billy, posing for the camera in their school uniforms, and didn't have to fake my smile. I was genuinely happy for Billy. He'd gotten what he'd wanted most in life. For that, I was grateful to Rosalie. She'd given Billy what I never could—or, more accurately, never wanted to—give him. "They look great, Bill."

"Thanks. They're amazing."

Billy gazed at the photos a few seconds more—long enough for me to glance in Derrick's direction, and see him narrow his eyes at me. I could tell exactly what he was thinking: *Why didn't you tell me?*

But there was nothing I could do about it now, so I shrugged and looked away.

"Anyway, thanks for the offer," I said, "but now is not the best time for me to go vehicle shopping." The thought of wandering around Hopkins Motors and possibly seeing Rosalie again made me feel queasy. "I have to get back to my store."

"I can drop you off there, Jess," Billy said, eagerly. "That's no problem."

"That's generous, Billy." Derrick's eyes were as bright and as shiny as twin diamonds. "But I'm going in that direction, anyway. I'll take her."

Billy looked concerned. "Hey, bro, no offense, but your car isn't looking that great, either. I don't know if I'd risk driving that thing. Your windshield is—"

"It will be fine," Derrick said in a tone that caused Billy to quickly change the subject.

"You know, Jess," he said, looking around the living room, "I really like what you've done with the place since your parents moved out."

"Um. Thanks."

What was happening? I'd told a seemingly down-and-out Derrick he could stay with me—merely because he'd been living in his rental car and there was a supernatural menace threatening my town which he'd sworn he could help us fight—and now he was appointing himself my chauffeur?

And what about that kiss?

Because it was one thing to be pretend-dating a handsome stranger you were mildly attracted to.

But it was quite another to be pretend-dating someone whose kiss made you feel as if you were being caressed all over by gentle waves of rain-scented lightning, and whose lips you now wanted to feel over the rest of your body.

Was this part of the curse—or whatever it was—on West Harbor? Would it go away as soon as the Bringer of Light and I broke it? Would Derrick?

Probably. Which was fine, because the last thing I needed right now was a romantic relationship.

"Well, we'd better go, then, Derrick, since I'm running late as it is," I said, and lifted the tote I'd brought with me to the school and started toward the mudroom, where I intended to swap it out for something that did not contain crumbs from the now dented brownie container. "It was great seeing you, Billy."

"Oh." Billy looked crestfallen. "I'll walk out with you."

I managed a smile. "Great. Let me just go get my other bag."

Unfortunately, I'd hardly been in the mudroom for a minute before I found myself with company.

"Why didn't you tell me Rosalie Hopkins married your ex-lover?" Derrick kept his voice low enough that Billy, out in the living room, wouldn't be able to overhear him.

"Why didn't you tell me that you were going to tell Billy that we're dating?" I whispered back. "And he's not my ex-lover."

He raised his eyebrows in surprise. "You two never slept together?"

"Of course we did. Not that it's any of your business." I bent to transfer my wallet, cell phone, and lipstick case from my tote bag into the slouchy crossover bag I intended to take with me to the shop. Derrick was close enough that I could feel the heat radiating off his body—and smell the fresh clean scent of the bodywash from the gym. Dammit. Why did he have to smell good, too? "But it sounds weird to call someone you went out with in high school your lover. Would you call your high school girlfriend your *lover?*"

He looked taken aback. "No. Because I didn't have a high school girlfriend."

"You didn't?" I paused, surprised, in the middle of my bag swap. "Why not?" Then I gasped. Suddenly, everything made sense. "Oh my God. That other entity you work for—it's the Catholic Church, isn't it? You're a vampire hunter. That's why you didn't have a girlfriend in high school. You were too busy slaying those demons you know so much about."

He glared at me. "No, actually. I was homeschooled."

"Homeschooled?" This answered Dina's question of why she couldn't find him on Classmates.com. "Oh. So I'm right. Your dad took you on demon hunting missions?"

"Again, no. I grew up on a farm." He shrugged as if this was the most matter-of-fact, normal thing in the world. "My dad did need my help—but with the animals, not demons."

"Oh." He hadn't said this with his normal cockiness, however. I got the sense that "helping with the animals" had been no walk in the park—nor had living with his father. He didn't seem to have appreciated my vampire hunter crack, either. Had it hit a little too close to home? "Okay. Well, I didn't mention Rosalie being married to my ex-boyfriend because it didn't seem important . . . the same way it didn't seem important to you to mention to me that you were going to pose in front of my ex as my fake boyfriend, then kiss me, even though I told you, barely an hour ago, that you can't go around grabbing women like that without their permission."

He frowned, seeming to give the matter serious thought. "Right. You did. And once again, I apologize. But I only did it to protect you. At the time, I really did think Billy might be possessed by a demon."

"That is the single most ridiculous thing I ever heard."

"Did you notice his *teeth*? And his *skin*? That can't possibly be natural. Is it a glamour?" He glanced back to the living room. "It looks so real."

I stared at him. "That's called a fake tan and veneers, Derrick. Rosalie is into that kind of stuff. And Billy's into Rosalie, which is why he goes along with it. But even Billy has his limits. Like, Billy would never consent to having a glamour spell cast over him. I doubt he even knows what a glamour is, or that Rosalie is a witch."

Now Derrick stared at me. "She's a council member of the WCW. How could he not know?"

"Because Rosalie doesn't want him to know. And *he* doesn't want to know. How do *you* not know about veneers and fake tans and asking women's permission before touching them?" I shook my head. "Are you sure you're not a vampire hunter? Or is it that you just didn't have cable or Internet on the farm?"

"Yes," he said, offended again. "Of course we did. What we didn't have were any women."

I stared at him, certain he was joking.

But when he only stared back at me, I realized no punch line was on its way.

"Wait. No *women*? Where was your mother?"

"She left."

He said it simply, without any emotion. Still, I didn't need extrasensory perception to tell that this was a sensitive subject. I could see that muscle leaping around in his jaw again. *Stay away*, it seemed to scream. *Stay away from this topic.*

Yikes. Message received.

"Okay," I said, shaking my head some more while shouldering my bag. "Well, I can see that we're going to need to watch a lot of reality television to get you up-to-date on your pop culture references. Are you really driving me to my shop? Because I don't need an escort or bodyguard or whatever it is you think you are."

"If anything, I would think that what's gone on this afternoon between him"—he jerked his thumb in Billy's direction—"and his wife has more than amply proven that you do."

"Right." I took a deep breath. "I'll let you win this one. Tell me something, though. Have you always been able to do that thing with your fingers?"

"What thing with my fingers?"

"You know, that thing you did a little while ago to my knee. And then when we kissed—"

His gaze was as bright as a new moon over the Sound on a cloudless winter night. And it was focused on my lips, which was more than a little distracting—especially since I couldn't seem to look away from his lips, either. "When we kissed, what?"

"When we kissed. . . ." It was impossible to remember what I was going to say when those lips, so full and expressive, were in view, and so tantalizingly close to mine.

"Jess?" Billy startled me by calling from the living room. "Sorry, but I have to head out now. Rosie just called. She needs me to pick up some almond milk on my way home."

I tore my gaze from Derrick Winters's mouth. "Be right there, Billy!"

Then I hurried from the mudroom, silently cursing myself. If this was what it was like to be the Chosen One, I'd be more than happy to be unchosen.

Derrick

A true Witch does not worship evil, or any entity known as "Satan" or "The Devil."

Rule Number Four of the Nine Rules
World Council of Witches

Derrick sat in the chair to which he'd been relegated in the front corner of Jessica's shop—the "Friends and Family Chair," her giggly coworker Becca called it, since apparently it was where the friends and family of the shop's clientele sat and waited while the shoppers were trying on clothes.

There was a matching armchair across from Derrick's, and in it sat a small older woman tending to a toddler in a baby carriage while a younger woman—presumably her daughter, the toddler's mother—shopped. The older woman had made several attempts at small talk with Derrick, beginning with a sympathetic, "Waiting on your wife?"

Derrick had only grunted "No, ma'am" in reply. He'd learned it was better to shut down conversations with members of the public as quickly as possible, before they got too personal. Like Jessica asking about his childhood. He didn't need her knowing about that.

Not that she was a mere member of the public. As a fellow witch and the Chosen One, she was obviously significantly more than that.

But the less she knew about who he really was, the better for both of them.

"Girlfriend?" Grandma asked next, cheerfully undeterred by his curtness.

Derrick couldn't believe this. He'd staked out a fine position for himself here in this really rather comfortably soft leather armchair, with Jessica's friendly cat, Pye, sleeping in his lap, and the book he was currently reading—or could pretend to read, since he was supposed to be keeping an eye out for unusual phenomena and the demonically possessed. Here he could keep Jessica—busily slashing the prices of merchandise that hadn't been purchased during the weekend sale—in his sights.

But this grandmotherly woman kept trying to distract him. Even the kid in the stroller kept gurgling at him, happily waving a toy rabbit with a bell in its ear. The bell jingled every time the kid bounced it in his direction.

Derrick didn't have a lot of experience with kids, but he didn't dislike them. He simply wasn't there to play with a kid, chit-chat with grandmothers, or entertain the stares of the women of West Harbor. He was there to keep the Chosen One safe.

Why was everyone in this town so intent on keeping him from doing so?

"Yes, ma'am," Derrick said, to satisfy Grandma and hopefully keep her quiet. "I'm waiting for my girlfriend."

"Oh, how nice." Grandma took the toy rabbit from her grand-child's fingers and bounced it in the air, causing the bell to ring even more loudly and the toddler to shriek with delight. "Isn't this a lovely shop? My daughters buy all their clothes here. So does my daughter-in-law. Well, she's not my daughter-in-law yet, because she and my son still aren't married. Living together for years and still no plans for a wedding. I don't understand what's taking them so long. Maybe you can explain it, you look about my son's age. What's so wrong with marriage, I ask you?"

Derrick glanced at Jessica, but she was now helping the woman's daughter with a gown she wanted to try on. There'd be no rescue from that direction.

"Nothing's wrong with it," Derrick said, lowering his book. "Maybe your son is simply waiting until he's found the right person."

"But he has! Dina and Mark have been together since high school. They're in their thirties. They own a home and three beagles together. Surely they have to know by now that they're right for each other."

"Well, then what does it matter if they get married?" Derrick asked. "Maybe they don't feel they have to legitimize their relationship in the eyes of others with a big expensive party and a slip of paper."

The older woman looked horrified. "It's *tradition*."

"Aren't traditions made to be broken?"

"You sound exactly like my son. Which of the young ladies here is your girlfriend?"

Derrick was confident he was never going to see this woman again, so he pointed. "Her."

The old woman's gaze followed his finger. Then her eyes widened. "*Her?*"

"Yes," Derrick said.

"You're dating *Jessica Gold?*"

Derrick hesitated. Wait. Why did this woman look so delighted? Did she know Jessica? It was a small town. The likelihood was that she did. Had he screwed up? Oh, well, what did it matter? Like it or not, he'd be gone in a few days, either because he'd failed in his mission or because he'd succeeded, and was on to his next one.

"Yes," he said. "Jessica Gold is my girlfriend."

It felt good to say it. Strangely, invigoratingly good.

"Well," the grandmother said, beaming. "I'm so happy to hear that. It's been a while since Jessica had a nice fellow. And where did you two—?"

Mercifully, Derrick's phone rang. When he looked down at the screen and saw who was calling, he said, "Pardon me, ma'am, but I have to take this."

"Oh, please." The old woman's eyes twinkled as she reached for her own phone. "Go ahead. Don't mind me."

Derrick did mind her, however. The enemy was everywhere and could look like anyone, including this kindly grandmother—or a former high school football player who now sold cars for his father-in-law. You could never be too careful.

Derrick excused himself, laid down his book, lifted a protesting Pye from his lap, and stepped outside the shop to take his call, making sure to catch Jessica's eye on his way out so she'd know where he was. She nodded as he lifted his phone to his ear— and even though he was halfway out the door, he didn't miss the amused glance she exchanged with twentysomething Becca, the bubbly brunette who'd been sneaking surreptitious glances at him ever since he'd set foot in the place.

Did no one in West Harbor take anything seriously?

"Hello," he said into the phone when he was safely on the sidewalk outside the shop. He could still see Jessica inside through the enormous plate glass display windows, adjusting the hem of a gown the young mother was trying on. "Did you get my message?"

"Of course I got it." The person on the other end of the phone sounded grim. "Why do you think I'm calling? Are you honestly telling me that Rosalie Hopkins—"

"Exactly what I wrote to you." He didn't want to say it out loud. The foot traffic on West Harbor's main thoroughfare wasn't as bad as it had been over the weekend, but it was still surprisingly brisk for a Monday. Derrick had to stick close to Enchantments' doorway to keep out of the way—and to keep his end of the conversation from being overheard.

"We always suspected. But that kind of power—and that kind of blatant disregard for life . . ." The caller seemed perplexed. "We haven't seen anything like that since—"

"That's why I wrote. Between that and the Bringer of Light's exceptional gifts—if they're true—I have a feeling we might need to accelerate things a bit."

The caller's voice sharpened. "Accelerate them how?"

"Well, to start with, maybe by telling Jessica Gold the truth."

He didn't want to say it. He knew the kind of reaction he was going to get.

But he had to say something, because Jessica deserved the truth. If the woman was going to put her life on the line—and that was clearly what she was doing, thanks to Rosalie—she needed to know who she was really working for.

But the caller, as he'd predicted, disagreed. Strongly.

"No! Absolutely not! Do you want to get her killed?"

"She was very nearly killed earlier today," he said tersely into the phone, while turning to look through the display window. Jessica was now having an animated conversation with the toddler's mother while making subtle changes to the gown she'd tried on. Before Derrick's eyes, the woman bloomed, becoming pretty as a rose. But not as pretty as her stylist. "If I hadn't been there—"

"Then stay there. Continue doing what you're doing. Don't let her out of your sight."

Derrick fought for patience. "Please explain to me how I'm supposed to do that. This isn't the Middle Ages. Did you know that following a woman everywhere she goes can be considered harassment?"

The caller scoffed. "How is it harassment when you're saving her life?"

"When she doesn't know that's what you're doing because she doesn't realize the enormity of the threat against her." Derrick reached up to squeeze the bridge of his nose. His eyes hurt. Was it all the caffeine, the lack of sleep, or the absurd amount of stress he was under? Probably all three. "Look, I was thinking: What if we changed things up and simply eliminated the threat against her?"

The response was immediate—and exactly what he'd expect. "No! You know how I feel about bloodshed."

"I'm not talking about bloodshed." Probably. "A simple binding spell would keep the woman from doing any more harm. And it would be what she deserves—she's a menace."

"You know what the penalties are for casting a binding spell on a Council member?"

"Lucky for me I'm not a Council member, then, isn't it?" he quipped.

"Very funny. But you know it's too risky. You're right that she's a menace—but she's a menace with powerful magic that we might need on our side when the time comes . . . if we can turn her, that is."

Derrick raised his eyebrows. "You aren't suggesting that *I* try to—?"

"No. She'd never listen to you. But the girl—she might listen to her."

"What girl? Do you mean the Chosen One? Because take it from me, those two are not on the best terms—"

"No, not that one. The other . . . "

He was used to the caller speaking in cryptic terms like this. He'd learned long ago to ignore it. He himself preferred action—but he didn't often get what he wanted.

"Fine," he said, with a certain amount of sarcasm. "Then I'll continue protecting the Chosen One from our own people—and the weather."

The caller's voice warmed. "You're a good boy. Have I told you that lately?"

"You think so? Well, in that case, give me a raise. A big one."

This was followed by laughter. Then the caller hung up—without saying goodbye, as usual.

He put his phone away, then turned around and went inside. Not much had changed. The mother of the toddler had disappeared into the dressing room, presumably changing back into her street clothes, and Grandma was still waiting in the second Friends and Family chair, her phone neatly tucked away.

"Well," she said conversationally, as Derrick sat down again. "How was your call?"

"Fine." His coffee cup was empty. It was after five. He really couldn't drink another one, or he'd never sleep tonight. But with what he knew now, could he afford to sleep?

"It doesn't look like it was fine." Grandma played with the baby some more. "Who was it? Your boss?"

"Sort of," Derrick said, and settled back into his chair for what he presumed would be many more hours of waiting. "It was my mother."

Jessica

To stop those who speak ill of thee, dip their names in honey. Henceforth the only words they speak of thee will be sweet.

Goody Fletcher,
Book of Useful Household Tips

It was hard to focus on work with Derrick Winters sitting in my shop.

It wasn't only because every time I glanced in that direction, there he was, reminding me of West Harbor's impending doom—not to mention that kiss we'd shared.

It was also because of how fast word had spread that he was there. West Harbor was a small enough town that everyone knew everyone else's business (and what they didn't know, they made up).

I realized that the moment I felt a tug on my sleeve as I was trying to refold a decimated pile of summer stretch capris just before closing, and saw Dina standing beside me, her dark eyes huge.

"Oh my God, Jess," she said. "Tell me it's true."

For some reason I thought she was talking about the hailstorm

Rosalie had created to demolish my car. "Oh, it's true. She nearly killed me this time."

"What? Who nearly killed you?" Dina was confused. "What are you talking about?"

Dina wasn't the only one who was confused. "What are *you* talking about?"

"I'm talking about the fact that that's him, isn't it?" She nodded toward Derrick, still sitting in the Friends and Family Chair with Pye curled in his lap, his gaze on a pair of older women lingering by the crystal display near the door, but who actually had eyes on only one item: him. "Has he really been sitting there all afternoon?"

"Um. Yes."

When Derrick had pulled into a parking space close to Enchantments to drop me off, I'd removed my seat belt and reached for the car door handle, saying brightly, "Well, thanks for the ride. The shop closes at seven, so I'll see you at home around then."

I probably shouldn't have been surprised when he'd replied, "I'm coming in with you."

"You are? Why?"

"In case you've forgotten, you were seriously injured a few hours ago." He undid his own seat belt. "I'm not going to allow that to happen again. I'm staying with you until the Bringer of Light has been trained and you've both saved this town."

"But you can't just *hang around* inside a women's clothing shop."

"Watch me."

He'd then proceeded to do just that.

I had to admit, his presence didn't seem to adversely affect transactions—if anything, they went up. I had to call in my assistant sales manager, Zahrah—even though I'd given her the day off—for emergency reinforcement since so many people were

showing up and actually making purchases. The only thing Derrick's being at Enchantments seemed to negatively affect was my
ability to concentrate.

"Let me guess," I said to Dina. "Mama G."

"You got that right. I think she called every single person in
her contact list." Dina took half the pile of capris I'd been folding
and began neatly stacking them back into their rack. "Pretty good
for business, though, huh? It looks like you have as many customers in here on the Monday after the big sale as you had over
the weekend during the sale. And they aren't all looky-loos." Her
gaze landed on the two older women by the door. "Well, maybe
some of them are."

"That's all anybody is talking about?" I asked. "The fact that
there's some guy sitting in my shop? Nothing else?"

"What else would they be talking about?" Dina asked, puzzled.

She hadn't heard. No one was talking about the freak hailstorm at the high school.

She'd find out about it eventually. Sal was bound to mention
it. His own car might not have been damaged—faculty parking
was in the back—but others certainly had.

So she'd find out. I'd tell her about Bluebell—and Billy—
eventually. But not now. Too many people could overhear.

"And he isn't *some guy*, Jess," Dina went on. She shook her
head as she gazed at Derrick. "I don't blame those two over there
for staring. Why didn't you tell me about those shoulders? And
those cheekbones! You could grate parmesan on those, they're
so sharp."

"Dina." I turned to put the rest of the capris back where they
belonged. "Do me a favor?"

"Anything."

"Tell Zahrah to go ahead and close the register. I've got to
start shutting this place down or we'll never get out of here."

Dina grinned. "Sure. But first tell me how it went with your new mentee."

My visit with Esther seemed to have happened in a different lifetime. "It went fine. Can we talk about it later?"

"Sure. Meet me and Mark at Mama G's for dinner." Her voice rose to a teasing lilt. "You can bring your new boyfriend."

"He's not my——"

"That's not what he told Mama G!"

"Dina. It's not real. We're fake dating. It's all part of his plan to save West Harbor from sinking into a demonic rift."

"Ooo-ooh, now there are demons?" She laughed with delight. "That's great. But come on. Look at him. Something *should* happen between you two. And I think he and Mark will really get along. They have a lot in common."

I looked from Derrick—now openly glaring at the two women who'd been staring at him—to Dina and then back again.

"Because they both wear motorcycle jackets?" What else did dark-haired, Italian restaurateur Mark have in common with my blond, fake witch boyfriend Derrick?

"No!" Dina laughed some more. "Because they're both mama's boys."

I was confused. "What do you mean?"

But before I had a chance to find out, the bell over the shop door tinkled. I glanced over to see that Derrick was holding open the door with one hand, while sweeping his other out toward the darkness that had fallen over the Post Road, giving his two fans a courtly bow.

"Sorry, ladies," he said, in response to their surprised glances. "It's seven o'clock. Closing time. Please, allow me."

The women, blushing and tittering, left the shop. Once they were gone, Derrick closed the door, locking it behind them, then flipped the *Come In! We're Open* sign to the side that said *Sorry! We're Closed*.

"Finally," he said with satisfaction, locking the dead bolt. "I thought they'd never leave."

Becca and Zahrah, behind the cash register, burst into giggles, but I gave Derrick a disapproving look.

"What?" he demanded, noticing my glare. "Those two were never going to buy anything anyway."

"He's right," Zahrah said. "They were only window-shopping."

"And not for anything we actually sell," Becca added, and then she and Zahrah collapsed into snorts of laughter.

I was giving them a disapproving look when—*thump!* Something struck the front display window.

Expecting to see a dazed bird—they sometimes flew into the windowpane during migration season—I was startled when instead I saw that a curvy purple-haired Latina girl had suddenly thrown herself against it. There was a small, frantic-looking dog clutched in her arms.

"Wolf!" we could all hear her crying frantically through the glass. "There's a wolf!"

Zahrah and Becca stopped laughing, and Dina, flinging her hands to her cheeks, cried, "Mark's wolf! Oh my God! It's real."

It made no sense. How could there be a wolf in West Harbor? Especially downtown West Harbor, where people were still hurrying along the sidewalk in order to make it to the Country Gourmet to pick up their prepared food for dinner before it closed.

Still, Derrick and I reacted at the same time, and so similarly that we almost collided into one another:

We both ran for the door.

"What are you doing?" I cried as Derrick's hard fingers sank into my soft shoulders.

"Stay. Here." Then he pushed me behind him before throwing back the dead bolt and opening the door.

"Sweetheart?" he said to the girl in a voice I'd never heard him use before, it was so gentle. "Come here."

It's weird how our brains respond in moments of peril. Mine registered the softness of his voice and thought, *That must be how he talked to the animals on the farm. No wonder his dad wouldn't let him go to school. He needed him.*

The gentleness of his voice seemed to work. Before I knew it, the teenager was inside the shop, panting breathlessly and squeezing her little dog nearly to death as her gaze scanned the night-darkened sidewalk outside. I saw no signs of a wolf—or anything else, except a normal chilly night in October, with normal West Harbor residents hurrying to get home to their loved ones.

But there was no denying the terror in her gaze.

"Wait!" she cried, as Derrick threw the door closed behind her and prepared to lock it. "My friend! She's still out there, in the parking lot, around the back!"

Derrick looked at me, his silver eyes so bright they might as well have been stars. "Lock the door behind me," he said to me, then plunged out into the darkness.

What was going on? Wolf attacks didn't happen in West Harbor—at least, none that I'd ever heard of.

Except that here I was, locking my shop door against one.

"Holy shit," Dina cried, rushing forward with Becca and Zahrah to surround the terrified girl. "Are you all right, honey?"

"Did the wolf bite you?" Becca asked. "What about your puppy?"

"Do you want some water?" Zahrah wanted to know. "What's your name? Can we call your parents?"

The girl, overwhelmed, could only gaze out the glass door after Derrick. "No. I think I'm okay. My name is Gabby."

I gasped as I turned around after throwing the dead bolt into place. "Gabby? Are you Esther's friend?"

She nodded, gazing up at me with mascara-smeared, tear-filled eyes. "Yes, Gabriella Aquino. We were just out walking Willa—that's my dog—after the Harvest Princess meeting, and I was saying how lucky Estie is to have you for a mentor. I love this shop. I would give anything to work here. So we decided to walk by. Not to *spy* on you, or anything," she added, hastily. "I would never do such a thing. But I wanted to see if you'd discounted anything even more since the Fall into Fall sale. I got these shoes here." She pointed to the purple clogs she was wearing. "But just as we were cutting through the parking lot out back, this wolf—at least, I think it was a wolf—appeared out of nowhere, and—"

She broke off, shuddering, which was just as well because it was at that point that I saw Pye slink into view. He'd realized there was a dog in the shop—wolf or domestic pet, it didn't matter, Pye hated all dogs equally—and had leaped silently up onto the sales counter, his tail puffed.

"It's okay," I said soothingly, slipping an arm around the girl and turning her so that her back was to Pye. The dog, unfortunately, now had a perfect view of the cat, and began to whimper—and rightfully so. Pye was harmless—unless you were a mouse, chipmunk, or small lap dog. "My friend Derrick will find Esther and bring her here, good as new."

"Really? Do you think so?" Gabby sniffled. "I'm so worried. I shouldn't have left her out there, but I was just so worried for Wil—"

Bang. We all jumped as a fist struck the glass door. It was Derrick, standing beside a smiling Esther. "Heeeyyyy!" she called, waggling her gloved fingers at Gabby. She was dressed in the same clothes she'd been wearing when I'd seen her at school, including her backpack—which meant that, unless she'd found and removed it, she still had my protective amethyst with her.

"Look," I said to Gabby, relief flooding over me as I hurried to unlock the door. "There they are, just like I told you."

Weirdly, it wasn't only Esther I was happy to see. Obviously I was glad to see Esther. She was my mentee, and even more than that, she was a sixteen-year-old girl. Who wouldn't be relieved at seeing a sixteen-year-old girl alive and well and unharmed by some random escaped wolf in Connecticut?

But I was glad to see Derrick, too, a man I'd known only for a few days—and whose presence in my life had turned it completely upside down.

What was up with that?

"*Gabs*," Esther cried as soon as she got into the shop. "You completely missed it!"

"Missed it?" Gabby, exasperated, put her dog down on the floor just in time—Pye had been about to take a swipe at him from the sales counter. "It was a *wolf*. A wolf, Estie. Where even were you? I was scared to death for you!"

"Yeah, I know. Sorry." The two girls hugged tightly—a pleasing sight to see, at least to me, since Esther was so tall and thin, and Gabby so small and round, and yet they seemed to fit so perfectly together somehow. "But it was *so* cool. This guy here chased it up onto the railroad tracks. It disappeared into the bushes."

"Wait." Dina was leaning against the sales counter, one hand curled around Pye to keep him from launching himself at Willa. "There really was a wolf?"

"Hard to say." Derrick wasn't meeting anyone's gaze. "It's pretty dark out."

"It was a wolf," Esther said firmly. "A great big gray wolf."

"It was following us," Gabby said. "It followed us all the way from the Harvest Princess meeting at the Yacht Club down the jogging trail to the back of Enchantments. I think it was after Willa."

"I did a report on wolves once in the sixth grade," Esther said, "and while deer are their preferred source of food, they'll prey on small mammals, as well."

Gabby squealed and buried her head in the much taller Esther's neck.

"Well, it's gone now," Derrick said in a voice that was unusually cheerful. "Everyone is safe."

"Yeah," Esther said, and gave Gabby one last squeeze before letting her go. "We're good now, right?"

Gabby nodded uncertainly. "I guess so."

Derrick gave me a penetrating look. He seemed to think telepathy was one of my gifts.

And if I could have read his mind, it would have been great because I would have been more prepared for what he said next, which was, "But I think to be on the safe side, Jessica and I should take you girls home."

Wait. *What?*

"Oh, you don't have to do that," Esther said, at the same time that her best friend beamed and said, "Oh, thanks. That would be great."

Apparently being chosen meant I was also part of a rideshare service for the Bringer of Light.

Which was fine, except that because Gabby was in the car with us, we couldn't actually use the time to discuss the real reason I'd contacted Esther earlier that day—or why it was that wolves had begun appearing in downtown West Harbor lately.

Instead, I found myself in the front seat of Derrick's rental car, an indignant Pye in a cardboard box on my lap, listening to Esther—in the back seat with Gabby—explain why they'd been at a meeting for Harvest Princess volunteers in the first place.

"I only went along to support Gabby," she said. "She really needs the extracurriculars for her college apps. She doesn't have any, except band. And also because the meetings are at the Yacht Club, and they give out those cookies—"

"Oh my God, yeah." Gabby sounded wistful. "Those chocolate chip cookies are the *best*."

"Right?" Esther opened her backpack. "Do you guys want one? I stole, like, twenty of them."

"No, thank you." I really wanted one of the cookies, but one glance at Derrick's stern profile told me that I needed to keep the conversation on track. "So you don't want to be a Harvest Princess, Esther?"

"No." Esther leaned back, munching. I respected how her devotion to veganism was dependent on the level of chocolate in the available snacks. "I don't care about princesses. Gabby's the one who loooooooves them—"

"I do not!" Gabby cried, faux-outraged. "I mean, okay, I do. But actually, the Harvest Princess thing is pretty cool. If you get picked—"

"Big *if*," Esther interrupted.

"Yes, okay, *if*. But if you get picked, you get free tickets to the ball and the pre-ball banquet at the Yacht Club. And you get scholarship money to college and stuff. The only problem is, more girls signed up than there are places available. There are twelve of us and Mrs. Hopkins says they only have room for nine girls—"

"*And* one of the girls who signed up happens to be Mrs. Hopkins's daughter," Esther interrupted again.

"That doesn't necessarily mean Lizzie's going to get selected,"

Gabby said defensively. "There are a lot of conditions. Like I know for a fact at least one of the girls isn't going to make the cut based on her GPA alone. And if you count having to be comfortable conversing with strangers and being free all weekend so you can go to all the Tricentennial events in the town square, that eliminates at least one of the others because she works at Dairy Queen and doesn't have anyone yet to cover her shift."

"Right. But Lizzie Walker-Hopkins's mother is running the whole thing, so she's more than likely going to get picked—"

"Not the *whole* thing. There's someone else. He's coming on Wednesday from New York City for the final judging."

"That's my problem with it." Esther leaned forward so that she could speak to Derrick and me more intimately, even though Derrick was taking care not to contribute to the conversation at all. Instead he kept his gaze straight ahead as we wound our way down the night-darkened coastal road toward the girls' homes. "I mean aside from the fact that I think with things like this, who gets selected is always based on looks—"

"Not *always*," Gabby insisted.

"Okay, and I'm not saying I don't think you're beautiful, Gabs, you know I do. But then why do the princesses have to wear ball gowns?"

"Because it's for the Tricentennial *Ball*."

"Then why can't they wear suits? Ms. Gold carries that whole line of evening tuxedos for women."

I brightened at this. "Thanks," I said. "I do. And I'd be happy to find one for you, Gabriella. But please call me Jessica."

"Thanks, I know, I love your suits, Jessica," Gabby said. "But I want a gown. I can't really afford one from Enchantments, though. My mom said if I want to do this princess thing, I have to pay for it myself, and I don't have a credit card."

I considered this. I was certain I had the perfect gown for her.

"How about if we worked out a payment plan?" I asked. "You could pay me in installments, either with cash or by helping out in the shop."

Gabriella let out a gasp. "Could I really? I would *love* that!"

"Of course. We need the help. What's your weekend and after-school schedule like?"

"She's free," Esther said drily. "That's why she signed up to be a Sacrificial Princess."

Gabby playfully struck her friend in the arm. "Stop! You're making me sound like a loser."

"Sorry." Esther didn't sound particularly sorry, however. "It's not that I'm against the whole thing. I just have questions I don't feel have been adequately addressed. Like what kind of guy would take the time to come all the way to West Harbor from New York City just to crown a bunch of girls Harvest Princesses? Unless he's got a line of cosmetics he wants you to endorse, or something, I feel like he has to be a perv."

I did my best not to look at Derrick, who'd come all the way to West Harbor from Montana to do something extremely similar.

"He's not a perv, Esther!" Gabby insisted while Willa, sitting in her lap, whimpered a little. She either sensed the hostility radiating from Pye, in her box on my lap, or that we were nearing her house. It was hard to tell. "Mrs. Hopkins says he's a very important academic, published author, and historian."

"Ugh, that's so *gross*," Esther asked. "What's a *published author* doing, judging a beauty contest? When are we going to find out his name so that I can research him and make sure he doesn't have a criminal record?"

"Oh my God." Gabby rolled her eyes. "Here we go again."

"You know I love you and support you no matter what, Gabs. I just worry that you're going to get emotionally invested in this and it's not going to turn out the way you hope."

"Just say it: you don't think I'm going to get picked."

"Actually, I think you *are* going to get picked, and something worse is going to happen."

"Like what? They're going to pour pig blood on me while I'm onstage?"

"No. Like this author guy is going to turn out to be a vampire who feasts on virgins, or something."

I threw Derrick a knowing look. *Vampires? See?* I wanted to scream at him. I wasn't the only one who thought vampires might be showing up in this town eventually.

But Derrick ignored both my look and Esther's vampire comment, saying only, "Oh, look," in a mild tone as he slowed the car to a stop. It was the first time he'd spoken since getting into the vehicle. "We're here."

I glanced at the house we'd pulled up in front of. Only a few blocks over from my own, it was nearly twice as large. New construction that straddled two lots, Esther's house had a wide wraparound porch, a four-car garage, no less than three jack-o'-lanterns grinning maniacally down at us from the front porch, each with a flickering candle inside, and a small sign at the end of the driveway that said *This Home Protected by AlarmSafe.* Every light in the house seemed to be on.

"Thanks for the ride," Gabby said, brightly, her argument with Esther completely forgotten. "You can let me out here, too. I live next door, but we're going to do our Spanish homework together."

"Are your parents home?" Derrick asked quickly.

"Yeah." Esther undid her seat belt. "My little brother finishes soccer practice about now, so we all eat dinner together late."

"Good," he said. "Go inside and tell your parents to set their home alarm. And don't go out again until daylight."

"Because of the wolf?" she asked, looking thrilled.

"Because Halloween is on Friday. You never know what might be out there, lurking in the dark."

"Cool." Esther sounded delighted. "I'll text you about meeting up later for mentor stuff, okay, Ms. Gold?"

"Jessica," I corrected her. "And sure, that would be great. Gabby, get my number from Esther, too, so we can set up a time for you to come in and try on a dress and figure out a work schedule."

"Oh, my gosh, thank you *so* much, Ms. Gold!" Gabby gushed.

Both girls and the dog leaped from the car as Derrick said, "Good night—and be safe!"

"We will!" they cried, and raced hand in hand up the lawn to the home's front porch.

"Spanish homework," Derrick said, as we watched them disappear into the house. "So that's what the kids are calling sex these days."

I grinned. "You got that feeling, too, huh?"

"They're like an old married couple."

"But more attentive to one another's feelings. What do you think about Esther? You agree she's the One, right?"

"No."

When I threw a startled glance in his direction, speechless with astonishment, I saw that he wasn't even looking at me. He was concentrating on navigating the night-dark road.

"*You're* the One," he went on, his gaze still on the road. "Esther is the Bringer of Light." I felt my shoulders, which had tensed up at his *No*, relax. "I'm here to support and protect you. If you think it's her, then it's her. But I will say"—my shoulders tensed up again—"from the moment I met her, she's shown the same kind of calm presence I've seen in previous Bringers of Light I've encountered. She wasn't the least bit concerned about the wolf. More delighted, really."

I felt my shoulders relax again. Not that I needed his approval. But it was always nice to know your coworkers had your back.

"And do you think Esther's right?" I asked. "About this guy who's coming in to judge the Harvest Princesses possibly being a vampire?"

"No, because there's no such thing as vampires."

"Oh, okay. So demons exist, but not vampires?"

"Of course demons exist. I've seen them. I told you: they're the tortured souls of those looking to right what they see as their unjust death. But I've never seen a vampire. I think they were made up by old Eastern European grannies to frighten children into eating their garlic."

I rolled my eyes. "Okay." I'd never encountered a vampire before, either, and Goody Fletcher made no mention of them in her book. But she had plenty to say about evil spirits and demons. "So there's no significance to the fact that Rosalie Hopkins is looking for nine Harvest Princesses, and nine is such a powerful number in the witching world?"

He raised his eyebrows as he pulled away from the Dodge home. "What are you suggesting?"

"Well, could Esther be right? Maybe not about the judge for the contest being a vampire but . . . is Rosalie up to something? Could she even—I don't know—know about the prophecy, and be trying to find the Bringer of Light herself?"

He was shaking his head before the words were fully out of my mouth. "No. Absolutely not."

"Why not? She's a council member of the World Council of Witches. Why wouldn't she have heard about it?"

"Because even if she did, her research would have led her to the same conclusion mine did: that *you're* the Chosen One."

"Yeah, research was never Rosalie's forte in school. And I don't think she'd like it if she found out I was chosen for anything and she wasn't. But it wouldn't be the worst thing if she was looking for the Bringer of Light, too, would it? We're all on the same side." When he didn't say anything right away, I prodded him in the shoulder. "*Aren't we?*"

"We are." He didn't take his gaze off the road, but I had a feeling he wasn't really seeing it. "Of course we are. But it doesn't matter what Rosalie wants." That was when he finally turned to look at me, and I saw that the muscle in his jaw was leaping. "Only you and the Bringer of Light can stop what's coming. Do you understand?"

"Yeah, about that, I've been meaning to ask you. How are we supposed to do that? Did you bring along any weapons we should be training to use against these demons, stakes or crossbows or anything? Because it's getting kind of late to order some. I guess we could try Walker Hardware tomorrow, but I don't know if they even carry—"

"All you need are yourselves." He turned his face back toward the road, his lips pressed together, his expression grim. "Together, you and Esther *are* the weapons. That's why I can't imagine that Rosalie, even if she knew about any of this, which I doubt, would be thinking about selecting another Bringer of Light. If anyone else were to attempt it, it would end in . . ."

"What? It will end in *what?*"

"Exactly what we're trying to stop."

"Oh. Great. So the end of the world."

"Not the world," he said. "Just—"

"West Harbor," I said, at the same time he said it. "I know, I know, you don't have to keep telling me. So was there really a wolf?"

"A wolf, or a really big dog that looked just like one."

"Damn. You know, Mark Giovanni said he saw one while he was out jogging a few weeks ago."

Derrick threw me an incredulous look. "Why didn't you tell me?"

"Because there hasn't been a wolf sighted in Connecticut in three hundred years!"

"Exactly," he said. "And yet just in time for the Tricentennial, one makes a reappearance."

"What does that even mean?"

"I don't know," he said, tightening his grip on the wheel. "But I intend to find out."

Jessica

To enhance thy beauty in his eyes, serve him garlic.

Goody Fletcher,
Book of Useful Household Tips

Walking around train tracks in the semidarkness, looking for wolves, was not my idea of a fun night out.

But when Derrick reminded me of the window in my office that was stuck open—the one Pye used to get in and out of my shop—and how much a cat would look like prey to a wolf, I agreed to a short walk along the tracks.

Not that I thought Pye was in any actual danger, especially given that he was currently trapped in a box in Derrick's rental car. I didn't believe there was a wolf, and if there was, I knew Pye could take care of himself. I'd once seen him defend himself against an entire pack of raccoons.

But it never hurt to be sure.

Fortunately there was no sign of wolf paw prints, something Derrick was apparently an expert in.

"So are you going to call them?" I asked him as I used the flashlight on my phone to pick my way through the rocks and weeds back to where he'd parked at the West Harbor train station (designed to look like a quaint Colonial farmhouse, even though thousands of commuters used it every day to get to and from the city).

"Call who?"

"Your supervisors, or whoever, and tell them about the wolf, and Rosalie and the Harvest Princess thing."

"Oh." He was using the flashlight on his own phone to scan the brush on the other side of the tracks. He hadn't said what, exactly, we were going to do if we found the wolf. Call Animal Control? Cast a spell over it? Unclear.

What was clear, however, was that he was sticking close to my side in case the wolf did reappear. That kind of old-fashioned chivalry was definitely something that had been lacking in the guys I'd met lately through dating apps.

"I might. But I think Esther is right about the Harvest Princess. It's only a beauty pageant," he continued. "Harmless."

When I snorted in response, he glanced my way. "You think I'm wrong?"

"Beauty pageants are never harmless—especially a beauty pageant run by Rosalie Hopkins. Free cookies aside, I think she's up to something."

"The timing is a little concerning," he agreed, "especially with it being the same night as the Hunter's Moon."

I shivered involuntarily. "Would you please stop calling it that?"

"Why? That's what it's called. The Hunter's Moon symbolizes abundance—a time when people celebrate the harvest and all they've reaped as they prepare for the change that's—"

"Okay, now you're just creeping me out."

"How can that creep you out? You're a *witch*."

"I'm a *cottage* witch," I reminded him. "I make things look nicer, and people feel better about themselves. I don't mess around with reapings . . . or wolves."

"I think you underestimate yourself."

Even though it was so dark, I saw his eyes flash at me—just for a moment—almost as intensely as the few stars that were winking above.

Then he said, "Watch out for that gravel there," and reached out to take my wrist and guide me over the deadly gravel. "I wouldn't want you to turn an ankle in those boots."

"Yeah, thanks." My voice was as unsteady as my feet since I was still a bit shaken by the compliment—and the *zing!* of my heart-strings at the feel of his fingers, though this time he was touching me through the fabric of my coat, and I knew the sensation was all in my head. "Next time we go tracking a wild animal, I'll try to dress more appropriately."

"At least don't wear such high heels. You know, I don't think we're going to find anything out here." Derrick looked out across the darkness surrounding the train tracks and heaved a sigh. The temperature had fallen since the sun had set, so his breath fogged up in front of him. "We should probably call it a night and head home."

"Sounds good to me," I said. I'd been yearning for a hot shower and a glass of wine for hours. And maybe a little something more. "Do you want to stop for something to eat along the way? My friend Dina asked us to join her and her boyfriend, Mark, at his family's restaurant."

What Dina's most recent text had actually said was:

LegalBeagle: Get over here! The special tonight is branzino. It's selling out fast, but Mark says he can hold some for you and your fake boyfriend if you can get here by nine.

"Not sure going out is the best idea," he said. "Especially given that your cat is in a box on my front seat."

"Yeah, you're right."

Hmmm. Was he really worried about Pye, or was this a sex invite? It had been a long time since I'd made it to the sex stage of a relationship with a guy. Usually we didn't make it past Getting to Know You coffees because it became so glaringly obvious one of us had lied on our dating profiles (Me. Always me. About not being a witch).

"I have some lasagna I can heat up," I offered. "From Sunday night. Mama Giovanni always makes sure I go home with some, in addition to her gravy."

"That sounds good," he said.

Yes, it did. It did sound good. So did the idea of those lips and fingers of his on my naked body.

Which was how we found ourselves a little while later back at my place, after me having texted Dina back:

Nix the branzino. Fake BF wants to stay in.

Her reply was classic Dina:

LegalBeagle: Wooo, girl! Ride that biker boy!

The world works in funny ways. If you had told me a week ago that I'd be getting dinner ready for myself and my fake witch boyfriend, I'd have fallen over laughing.

But here I was, the height of domesticity, giving Derrick a tour of the upstairs of my house as Mama Giovanni's lasagna warmed up in the oven (I said "the height of domesticity." Just because I'm a cottage witch doesn't mean I can actually cook).

"So this is my parents' old bedroom," I said, flicking on the light. "You're welcome to stay in here, but you might find it a little . . . crowded."

That's because even though the second-floor bedroom was huge, I'd converted it instead to a sewing room, since the thought of banging guys in my parents' bedroom was deeply unsexy.

Now, in addition to the floor-to-ceiling shelves where my dad had once kept all his nonfiction World War II books, and on which I now stored containers of all my best buttons, lace, elastic, ribbon, and thread, the room contained my sewing machine and a half dozen dressmaker's dummies, each garbed in a nearly finished gown that I intended to deliver to its owner sometime this week.

"The sofa folds out into a bed," I said, as Derrick stared skeptically into the chaotic sea of pale pinks, purples, and black sequins. "It's really comfortable. I sleep on it when my parents come back to town to visit."

"Thanks," he said, looking dubious. "But the couch downstairs is fine—"

Ouch. I could see I'd made a strategic error by showing him this room first. But I hadn't wanted to seem too eager.

"Or there's my brother's room." I led him across the hall, Pye following at our heels, because Derrick was his new favorite person.

This was not only because I'd thrown him into a box to transport him home, but because I'd also locked his cat door so that he was now trapped inside for the night. Although I doubted the existence of the wolf, and trusted Pye to win in a battle with it if it turned out I was wrong, I wasn't going to risk it.

I threw open the door to Ethan's room. "My little brother's in grad school overseas and doesn't really have anywhere to store his old stuff, so I told him I'll hold on to it until he lands somewhere permanently."

Derrick glanced appraisingly at Ethan's old soccer trophies and plaid wallpaper. "I'll leave my things here," he said, and slung his duffel bag down onto the single twin bed. "But I'll still probably sleep on the couch downstairs. That way I can keep an eye on the doors."

"I hardly think that's necessary, but okay." I was trying not to show how nervous I was that he was standing so near the door to the one room in the house I hadn't shown him—my bedroom.

It wasn't like I hadn't entertained other male guests in there before. But none of them had ever carried me over my threshold because my knee hurt, or cured that hurt with his touch.

And he'd just announced he'd be sleeping on the couch.

Which was fine, just fine. I wasn't at all stressed by that fact, or the fact that Dina kept texting, along with various fruit- and vegetable-shaped emojis:

LegalBeagle: Any action yet????

Why did I have such nosey friends?

"Well, I'm sure you'll want to get washed up before dinner," I said, showing him the Jack and Jill bathroom I'd battled over my whole life with my brother, and that, since I now owned it, I'd had renovated into a luxurious spa complete with a rainfall showerhead.

Derrick didn't look the least impressed by my newly installed radiant floor heating or subway tile, however. He only said, "Thanks," and disappeared into Ethan's room, closing the door behind him.

Okay, then.

By the time he reappeared downstairs, I was in my best silk pajama set and kimono, having had my own quick shower in my parents' old bathroom. I'd also set the dining table with the

Limoges dinnerware my mother had left behind, lit the candles in the silver candlesticks my great-aunt Ruth had bequeathed me, put a Nina Simone record on my father's vintage turntable, and reapplied my lip gloss half a dozen times.

When Derrick saw this, he looked stunned—though I wasn't sure if it was because of my incredibly shiny lips or the romantic tablescape I'd created.

"What's all this?" he asked.

"Dinner." I made the same motion with my hand that Vanna White made when she turned over the letters on *Wheel of Fortune*. I wasn't sure if I was showing off the table or myself. Either way, Derrick looked impressed.

"You didn't have to go to all this trouble."

"It wasn't any trouble at all." I always eat off of 24 karat gold-trimmed vintage plates from France that you have to wash by hand. "Did you find everything you needed up there?"

"I did, thanks."

He certainly looked as if he had. He'd changed out of his black jeans and henley into . . . another pair of black jeans and henley. But these, just like the last, fit him like a glove.

"Would you like a cocktail?" I asked, in a huskier voice than I intended to. I cleared it. God, I sucked at seduction. "Wine? Beer?"

"What I'd really like is to get a look at your security system."

"Security system?"

The expression on his face might have been a smile, if he ever smiled. "I know. Why would you have a security system? People in this town don't bother locking their doors. But I thought I'd ask."

"I told you, there's no crime in West Harbor—except for the usual stuff in the summer, kids drinking on the beach and breaking into vacant homes. That kind of thing."

"Jessica. You live a block from the beach."

"Yes, but my home's not vacant. And I *do* lock my doors. I even sprinkled salt across my threshold, like any decent witch—"

"What about protection against nonsupernatural entities?"

"Who would want to break in here? I don't have anything worth stealing." No one wants Limoges anymore. Great-Aunt Ruth's candlesticks, maybe . . .

"What about the book?" he asked.

"What book?"

"The one written by the local woman. The grimoire the love spell came from."

"Oh, *that* book. Don't worry, I keep it in a safe space. No one will ever find it."

Now Mark was texting me as well as Dina:

Scungilli: Use protection! You don't know where that filthy warlock has been!

"Besides, I don't know that Goody Fletcher was a local woman." I really needed to switch off my phone. "My mom bought her book at an estate sale in East Harbor, but who knows where it was from originally."

LegalBeagle: Mark, how many times do we have to tell you that the term witch is gender neutral?

Scungilli: You better hope for Jess's sake he's not gender neutral.

"Have you ever researched her?" Derrick asked.

"No, I never bothered. Records from that time period are impossible to find. There was a flood that destroyed most of the town records—"

"Yes, I know, in the early eighteenth century. Then there was the fire that took out most of the town in the early nineteenth century. And I'm not even going to mention the smallpox epidemic in the seventeenth century, or the influenza that wiped out half the population just after the First World War——"

I hesitated as I headed for the wine refrigerator. "What are you saying? You don't think——"

"That every ninety years or so since it was settled by Europeans, a disaster of epic proportions befalls West Harbor? Yes, I do. And it's overdue for another one, unless you and Esther can stop it."

But if that was true, did that mean the rift had nothing to do with me? What about all of those people who'd nearly frozen to death out on the interstate during the blizzard Rosalie had summoned?

Pop! I'd been tugging on the cork of a bottle of pinot noir, and startled myself when it suddenly came free.

"But why?" I asked, trying to sound casual. "What did West Harbor's early settlers do to put a curse on the town?" I poured two glasses of wine. "If it's because they slaughtered or enslaved Native Americans, lots of towns in New England did that. Why aren't Hartford or Greenwich facing a supernatural threat?"

"How do you know they aren't?"

Thanks to the wall I'd had removed, I had a perfect view of him from my kitchen, prowling around the living and dining rooms, going up to each of my windows and making sure they were completely closed, the locks secured. What he didn't know, of course, was that half the windows didn't open at all. The frames were so old, I couldn't find a carpenter who knew how to fix them.

"Well, obviously I don't know. But I think I'd have heard about it."

"Why? You never heard about this one until I told you."

"Yeah . . . you have a point."

Another text:

LegalBeagle: WTH, Jess, why am I only hearing just now from my brother that your car got destroyed by hail at his school today, and towed away by Hopkins Motors?

Scungilli: Jess, did you make a certain someone mad again?

I texted back:

Can't talk right now. I'll call you later.

LegalBeagle: Jess, I don't like this. What do you know about this guy? Who is he even working for?

Scungilli: Yeah, at least before he showed up, Rosalie wasn't actively trying to kill you.

"Is this usable, or is that woodpile outside just for show?" Derrick was kneeling down in front of my fireplace and looking up the flue.

I crossed into the living room holding both the glasses of wine I'd poured. "Yes, of course the fireplace works. Why? Don't tell me you think a demon is going to come flying down the chimney."

"No," he said, and began to push up his sleeves—enough to reveal that he had a tattoo on the inside of his right forearm, but not enough so that I could see what it was. "It's cold outside. I thought I might build a fire."

Drinks in front of a crackling fire with Derrick Winters? This was better than anything that had ever happened in my bedroom—better than anything I'd ever *fantasized* about happening there.

Even if my friends might not be particularly thrilled with the idea.

"Be my guest," I said, trying my best to sound casual as I handed him one of the wineglasses. "Red okay?"

"Yeah, thanks."

"Well, then." I raised my glass, still trying to control my facial muscles. Be cool. Do *not* smile too much. "To the Bringer of Light."

He clinked his glass to mine. "May her Spanish homework go well."

Dammit. I not only smiled, I *laughed*. "Cheers."

Derrick

Witches value consensual sex as pleasure, one of the sources of energies used in the practice of magic, and the embodiment of life.

Rule Number Five of the Nine Rules
World Council of Witches

For a second, Derrick's gaze met hers above the rim of their wineglasses. He was struck, once again, by her eyes—twin wells into which he felt he could fall and lose himself forever.

He'd be happy to spend the rest of his days swimming in those warm dark pools, and living in this warm, cluttered house. He had never been in a place that felt more colorful, more comfortable, more *home*. He wasn't sure if it was the house itself or Jessica, in her body-skimming, shimmering silk robe, with her laughing mouth and damp black curls hanging down her shoulders, that made him feel so relaxed. He wasn't sure about anything anymore.

What was he even doing here? He'd been told to protect her, not move in with her, and certainly not sleep with her. Was he going to be able to stop himself?

Not if she kept looking at him that way.

When the first side of the record she'd put on came to a sudden end, he became disturbingly aware of how quiet it was. Her neighbors, he knew from his earlier research, were mostly retirees who went to bed early—but rose early, as well. He imagined they'd have pointed questions for her tomorrow morning about the whereabouts of her car—and the owner of the severely dented Fiat parked in her driveway.

Bzzz. The room was so silent, Derrick heard the phone in the pocket of her robe alert her to a text, even though she'd set it on vibrate.

"Do you want to check that?" he asked politely.

She smiled widely and took another sip of her wine. "It's probably not important."

"What if it's Esther?"

The smile disappeared. "Right. Of course." She fished the phone from her pocket.

Derrick, to be courteous, turned toward the fireplace, even though he knew who it was. He hadn't meant to look at her phone, but she'd left it out on the counter earlier, and he hadn't been able to keep from glancing at the screen when it lit up with a text from someone called Scungilli referring to a "filthy warlock," and urging her to use protection.

Was *he* the filthy warlock? "Eavesdroppers get what they deserve," his father always said, and in general Derrick agreed. But did Scungilli mean filthy in a good way or a bad way?

It was natural, of course, that her friends would be suspicious of him. He was suspicious of *himself.* How was he going to do his job when all he could think about was what was behind the one door in the house she hadn't opened for him . . . Jessica Gold's bed?

"Sorry," she said, putting her phone away again. "Nothing important, just a friend. Do you like vinaigrette? I was going to whip one up to go with the salad."

"You really don't have to go to all this trouble for me."

"Oh, it's not for you. It's for me." She smiled again, and bounced away to the turntable to flip the record over.

He pretended not to notice that she was also quietly answering the text.

"Are these your parents?" he asked. He'd got a fire started, and had begun scanning her bookshelves as she busied herself in the kitchen. Now he held up a framed photo as, on the record player, a woman crooned about how much she loved her man.

"Yes," Jessica said, glancing over from the kitchen. "That's my mom and dad's wedding photo."

He squinted down at the photo. It showed a deliriously happy-looking dark-haired couple in formal wear, standing under a Jewish wedding canopy. "Do they know?"

"Know what?"

"About you being a witch."

"Oh, God, no. Do yours?"

"Yes," he said shortly. He wasn't going to discuss *that*. Better to keep her on the subject of her own family. "Why haven't you told yours? Would they be upset?"

Jessica had come over from the kitchen to gaze down at the photo in his hand. "Upset? No. Concerned? Yes. My ancestors did a lot of running because of their beliefs—from the Cossacks, Nazis, Mussolini. You name it. So I guess I'd rather spare my parents from any news that might make them feel like I'm going to have to run someday, too, like our ancestors had to. What about your parents? Are they—what did you call it? Magically inclined?"

"More or less." It was dangerous to talk about himself, so he turned his attention back to the photos on the bookshelf to distract her—and himself. She was standing so close to him that he could smell the grapefruit-scented shampoo she'd used on her hair. He reached quickly for a photo of an awkwardly tall boy wearing a graduation gown. "Is this your brother? Does he know?"

"I never told him, but I think he suspects . . . *something*." His strategy wasn't working, because she came even closer, grinning down at the photo and enveloping him with the scent of citrus and a feeling of longing. "What about you? Any siblings?"

He didn't like talking about his past. But because it was her, he grudgingly admitted, "Half-siblings. We weren't raised together."

"So you were basically an only child. That makes a lot of sense."

He glanced at her as he put the photo of her brother back where he'd found it. But glancing at her was a mistake, since it only caused him to notice, once again, how kissable her lips looked. "Why?"

"Only children often have to mediate between their parents, smooth things over, make things nice, take care of them. That's what you do."

He was astonished by this description of himself. "No, I don't."

"Yes, you do." Her laughter tinkled like the piano keys in the music she'd put on. She seemed to find his response very amusing. "What about when you rushed off to save Esther from that wolf? Or what you did when Rosalie attacked me, and I hurt my knee this afternoon?"

"That's—" What was she even talking about? It's true that he'd never learned to handle compliments well—possibly because his father had hardly ever given them, and his mother had rarely been around. But this was ridiculous. "Anyone would have done that."

"No, they wouldn't." She smiled up at him with those shining lips. "You said every witch is a healer—or has the capacity to be, anyway. Well, you're something more. I think you're a caretaker."

"No, I'm not."

What was happening? This conversation had gotten way off track. He desperately needed to steer the subject away from himself.

He also needed her to move away from him, since she was standing far, far too close to him. Just to be on the safe side, he set his wineglass on the mantel and reached for the fireplace poker, keeping his hands away from the temptation of reaching for her.

"Do you think the food is ready?" he asked, stirring up the flames. Yes. This was good. Steer the conversation back to dinner. "It smells great."

"I have the timer on," she said. "It will ding when it's ready. So, is there anyone you're currently caring for?"

He paused in poking the fire, not certain he understood her. "What?"

"Besides me. Back at home. Do you have anyone special waiting for you back home?"

"Not currently, no." He kept his attention resolutely on the fire . . . which was difficult, since she'd taken a step closer to him in order to set her wineglass on the mantel alongside his.

"Wow," she said, with another peal of that musical laughter. "You really do hate talking about yourself, don't you?"

Suddenly the fire felt too hot.

Or maybe it wasn't the fire. Maybe it was her.

"There's nothing about me that's very interesting," he said.

"Now you're the one underestimating yourself. What about what got you into this line of work?" She looked up at him through her dark eyelashes. "The town-saving business. I bet that's a pretty interesting story."

"It's not," he said quickly. "Trust me."

This was agony. Why had he agreed to this job in the first place? He should have said no the second he'd read her bio and seen her photos. At the very least, he should have left West Harbor the moment he met her and felt her magnetic pull. . . .

But then who would have helped her?

She reached out to lay a finger on his chest. Just one fingertip, on the bare patch of skin that showed through the V of his shirt.

It felt like . . .

Home.

"I think that might be what you're not getting," she said, and this time there was no laughter at all in her voice. There was a sincerity that caused his heart—the heart he'd been certain for so many years didn't exist—to twist. "I do trust you, Derrick."

Screw it.

He tossed the fire poker aside, pulled her roughly into his arms, and covered her mouth with his.

Jessica

A woman who under a waxing moon first chooses to bed
Will soon be happy, healthy, wealthy, and wed.

Goody Fletcher,
Book of Useful Household Tips

Was I surprised when Derrick Winters started kissing me?

No.

Was I happy about it?

Yes.

It's what I'd been willing him to do all evening. I couldn't understand why he wasn't reading my signals. How much more obvious did I have to be?

But once he finally got the message, he got it *good*.

For once I was glad that all of my neighbors went to bed right
after *Jeopardy!* They'd be shocked enough if they found out I was
entertaining a strange male witch in the house.

They'd have been even more shocked if they'd happened to
look through my living room windows and seen what he was doing to me.

And what he was doing to me was filthy . . . which was exactly what I wanted. No sooner had he pulled my body to his

and brought his lips down over mine then he was dragging those same lips along the side of my neck, shoving away the silk of my kimono in order to expose the tender skin just above my breasts and then greedily kissing that, too, causing all the nerve endings in my body to detonate. My nipples became hard as rocks, and he knew it. I knew he knew it because I felt a sudden corresponding hardness under the fly of his jeans.

Oh, yes.

If any of my neighbors *had* happened to be out past their bedtimes walking their dog and glanced through my window at that point, they'd have seen Derrick tugging at the buttons on the front of my pajama top in order to get at those nipples. Eager as I was to have his hands and lips all over me, I had to object.

"Dude, I just bought this," I said. "Don't rip it."

"Sorry," he muttered, but he wasn't that sorry. I know because he couldn't even wait for me to take it off. He was already reaching up beneath my shirt before I'd gotten a single button undone.

Boom! That's what the eruption felt like in my head—and between my legs—when his hand found my breast. If I'd thought his callused fingers on the bare skin of my knee that afternoon had felt amazing, that was nothing compared to the sensations that coursed through me when his callused palm closed over my nipple.

My knees buckled. I couldn't hold myself up. This was a first for me: I've never been brought to my knees by the touch of a man.

But I didn't mind, and he didn't seem to, either. Always the protector, he had an arm wrapped around my waist, which kept me from falling to the floor. Instead, he sank gently with me. Thank God we were now below windowpane level.

And thank God for the blue hand-knotted rug I'd bought so many years ago and laid in front of the fireplace. I hadn't realized how soft the wool was—soft enough for my purposes, anyway. And his, too, it turned out, which appeared to be leaning my body back and caressing and kneading and stroking every inch of it, first through my pajamas, and then, quite suddenly, without them . . . though I had no idea where they'd gone, or how they'd been removed.

I heartily approved of their removal, however, and showed him my appreciation by twining my fingers into his long, thick hair and bringing his mouth down where his hand had been seconds before.

For a moment or two, I thought I was going to pass out from the sensation of his tongue on my bare nipple. I don't think I'd ever felt anything so good as that searing heat . . . until, a second later, his fingers dipped between my legs.

I died and went to heaven.

Okay, not really. But it felt like it. It felt like my birthday, a gigantic bag of Halloween chocolates, and my first taste of ice cream on a hot summer's day all rolled into one. Only better.

Especially when I lifted my head and saw that his clothes were gone, too, and that in the warm golden glow of the firelight I could make out every detail of his strong, muscular body, from his long, solid legs to the tattoo I'd been so curious about on the inside of his right arm. It was the symbol of Gaia, the same one we each wore around our neck. Only the one on his arm was entwined with colorful flowers: a bright yellow dandelion for healing, a white orchid for strength, purple periwinkle for protection, silver rue for witchcraft, and deep red poppies for love.

Nice.

But that wasn't all. His chest was covered with crisp golden hair that tapered down to a V where, oh my God, I very much approved of not only what he had going on where that V tapered to, but also what was happening above it, too, because instead of the ultraflat six-pack too many of the guys I'd dated worked out for, Derrick had something that had become all too rare: a tiny belly. Not a beer belly. Just a sweet little ledge in the exact right place where a witch such as myself might need a little friction . . .

"Wait," I said breathlessly. I was straddling him, my hair enveloping both our faces in a tent of dark curls. Suddenly Dina's text was chiming in my brain like an alarm. *What do you know about this guy?* "We have to share our STD status with one another."

"Is that a thing people do?" His eyes, as he looked up at me, had the glazed look of a man just waking from a dream.

"Yes, God, where have you been? And don't say—"

"Montana." He said it at the same time I did.

"I don't care." His eyes were the same silvery color as the rue tattooed on his arm. Healing. Strength. Protection. Witchcraft. Love. "Do you?"

"No." I bent my head to lower my lips down to his—but he put up both hands to stop me, gripping my bare shoulders.

"Wait," he said. Now the glazed look was gone. "With humans you normally do use protection, though, right? *Real* protection, not salt like you use with your house—?"

"Of course not!" I couldn't believe it. "My house is just a house. I can get a new one anytime. But we're only given one *body*. I would never—"

"Good." To my surprise, he flipped me over onto my back, so that suddenly I was the one with the soft blue carpet beneath me.

But this was fine, because a few seconds later, that mouth of his had slid down . . . *way* down, until I felt his whiskered cheeks between my thighs.

And if I'd thought the sensation of his lips on my nipple had felt like heaven, well, that was *nothing* compared to what I felt when his tongue began to explore the softest—and now wettest—part of me. Gasping, I gripped twin handfuls of the rug, heat from the fire beside us and a fire he seemed to be igniting deep inside me making me certain my heart was about to burst into flames.

But what burst instead was a dam of pure sensual delight. It poured over me like a tidal wave, sweet and cooling . . . and continued to sweep me up in its soft blue peaks as Derrick clung to my thighs with both his lips and his hands.

It wasn't until a few moments later, when the tsunami had receded, that I became conscious of a chiming. It was the first time a man I'd slept with had rung my bell so hard, I could actually hear it tolling inside my head.

Then I opened my eyes and saw him looking down at me with an amused expression on his face.

"I think dinner's ready," he said. "The timer on your oven is going off."

Jessica

Milk is sacred to Gaia. Like the Mother Goddess, milk comforts and it calms. Drink milk to soothe and to fall asleep at night—but use caution. Like Gaia, milk can also harm.

Goody Fletcher,
Book of Useful Household Tips

We ate our lasagna from cereal bowls in front of the fire instead of on the Limoges plates at the dining table.

It worked out great. Casual dining nearly always does—especially when you've already seen the other person naked and made them orgasm a bunch of times.

And honestly, my dining room chairs aren't really that comfortable anyway.

I still couldn't convince him to tell me who he actually worked for, though. I could barely even get him to tell me what he did for a living.

"So do you get paid to do this?" I asked him much later, as he climbed into my bed. Yes, I'd lured him into my bedroom. All it had taken was a nonchalant mention that I had ordered one of those mattresses that came out of a box, and that it was king-sized and supercomfortable, and that he should try it.

He did.

"Sleep with women?" He was sitting on the edge of my new mattress, giving it a few experimental bounces. Pye had, of course, followed him up the stairs, and now sat on the edge of the bed giving his paws a wash.

"No. Travel to small towns to help save them from demonic ruin."

That actually earned a rare laugh from him. "Oh. Sort of."

He evidently liked my bed, however, since he lifted his feet onto it, pulled my duvet up over his wide, bare shoulders, and sank his head into my pillows (in deference to the power of nine, there were exactly that many of them, each of varying degrees of fluff).

"I agree," he said, stifling a yawn. "This is surprisingly comfortable."

"I know, right?" I lay down beside him. I'd completely redone my room from when I'd been a girl, changing the pink to muted tones of seafoam and getting rid of all the Fiona Apple posters. It was a temple to serenity now. "So do you *sort of* go around saving small towns from demonic ruin full-time?"

My room was so serene now, it apparently put my sex partners immediately to sleep—at least this one, who'd been well-satiated by me—since his eyes had drifted closed. "Pretty much," he murmured.

I rose up on one elbow to jab a finger at his naked chest. "Are you serious? What are you, some kind of paranormal handyman?"

"Exactly." I couldn't tell if he was kidding, or even if he was awake. His eyes were still closed. Then he rolled over onto his side—being careful, I noted, not to jostle Pye, who'd predictably curled up at his feet. "Lots to do tomorrow," he muttered.

"Seriously?" I sat up. Unlike him, I was wide-awake. "*This* is what you do for a living? You travel around to different towns, helping them out of otherworldly jams?"

He murmured something. It was hard to tell what because his head was buried in so many pillows, and he was drifting off to dreamland. But it sounded to me like a *Yes.*

I couldn't believe it. "And you get *paid* for it?" When he didn't respond, I nudged him in the shoulder. "Hey. I'm asking you a question. Do you seriously get paid for this? Because if so, can I get paid, too? I think it's only fair, since I'm the Chosen One. Who do I talk to about that?"

But he was out like a light.

Which I guess I could understand, given that he'd spent the last few days sleeping in his car, showering at the gym, and attempting to protect me from malevolent attack. I was pretty tired myself and, knowing tomorrow I had to finish up the hems of all the dresses I still hadn't delivered for the ball, plus train Esther to battle the forces of evil, I crept into the bathroom to brush my teeth, trying not to wake him.

Fortunately my phone was still on vibrate, so when Dina's text came, he didn't hear it.

LegalBeagle: Mark and I drove by your house to make sure you were all right and none of your lights were on. Are you okay? Did that guy give you a sleeping potion and steal all your stuff?

Thank God they'd driven by after Derrick and I had made love—or possibly during—or they'd have gotten quite an eyeful through the windows. I wrote back:

I'm fine! We just went to bed early.

This wasn't a lie . . . except the bed part. I wondered if Derrick would wake up with rug burns from when I'd pinned him to the floor and straddled him.

LegalBeagle: TOGETHER?????

After sending me so many eggplant emojis, she was shocked I'd actually taken her advice? I texted her several devil face emojis in reply. She responded with flaming hearts.

Grinning down at my phone, I came out of my bathroom to a sight that stopped me in my tracks: a naked man sleeping in my bed, my duvet half on, half off him, my cat curled between his legs, purring like mad.

There really wasn't anything hotter than a guy sleeping shirtless with a cute cat curled up next to him.

Except maybe a guy who made breakfast the next morning. Though I would have appreciated it if he'd waited a few hours later to do it.

"What are you doing?" I asked, after I woke to the sound of my coffee grinder churning and came downstairs to find him in black sweats and a low, messy ponytail in my kitchen.

He beamed at me like I was the most beautiful sight in the world in my bedhead, pajamas, and robe. "Making coffee. Want some?"

I pointed toward the windows. "It's still dark outside."

"It's morning. I thought you might want some breakfast." He wasn't only making coffee. He was making toast, as well as frying bacon and eggs. The smell had hit me as soon as I staggered down the stairs.

"I know it's *technically* morning," I said. "And don't get me wrong, I'm a big fan of breakfast." I was an even bigger fan of men making breakfast for me in my own kitchen after having defiled my body half the night, although to be honest this was the first time it had ever happened. "But don't people normally eat after the sun rises?"

"I just went for a run." He smiled, poured a cup of coffee, then walked over to hand it to me, slipping the mug into my hand and landing a kiss on my cheek. "I put a Nordic protection spell around the house while I was gone, though, so you were never in danger."

"Oh, a Nordic protection spell. Thank God, you had me worried."

His smile widened at my sarcasm. "Hungry?"

"I am," I admitted, then put down the cup and headed straight for my electric kettle. "It's just that I normally eat at a more civilized hour."

He looked puzzled. "What's a more civilized hour?"

"After the sun is up?"

The smile disappeared, and he went back to looking like his normal doom-foretelling self. It was hard to believe that stern face had been buried between my legs last night, sending me to the heights of ecstasy. "We can't afford such a late start."

"Oh, no." I'd filled the electric kettle and turned it on. "Don't tell me there's more wolf hunting on the agenda."

"No. But there are a lot of other things we need to get done."

"Like what? We can't pull Esther out of school and start training her in the art of the Craft, much as she'd doubtlessly enjoy that. I'm pretty sure her parents would object. And Sal's not exactly a believer, so he isn't about to write her a pass."

"Right." He took jam and butter from my refrigerator and set them out on the pass-through. "But before we even get to that, we need to secure this place."

"Secure it? Your Nordic protection spell isn't enough?"

He ignored me. "I have to fix all of your windows so they actually open, and install a security system that works against humans as well as supernatural forces."

I blinked at him. "You *want* the windows to open? I thought you were worried about people breaking in."

"I am, but it's just as big a problem if you can't get out. What are you going to do if there's a flood?"

"Open the door and leave like a normal person."

"And what if the door is blocked by detritus?"

"Can we not talk about detritus before I've had my morning caffeine?" I poured hot water from my electric kettle into a teacup. "It's really a downer."

"You don't drink coffee?"

"Of course I do. But every cottage witch knows you're supposed to drink a cup of Earl Grey tea first thing in the morning." When he only looked at me blankly, I explained, "Earl Grey has bergamot in it. Bergamot is a type of orange grown in Bergamo, Italy, that for centuries has been thought to promote prosperity and success. And I think so, too, because ever since I started drinking it, the shop's done really well." I poured a generous dollop of milk into my tea, then took a big gulp. "Maybe it will help defeat demonic rifts, too."

Derrick looked skeptically down at the tea. "I think you're wrong."

"About bergamot helping to defeat demonic rifts?"

"No." He raised his gaze, and I was unnerved all over again by how bright his eyes were. "I think you've earned your success through hard work and good choices."

I could have argued with him about that one—Billy Walker had *not* been a good choice. But instead, I slid onto one of the stools at the pass-through and said only, "Thanks. You could be right. I think luck had a lot to do with it, too, though. Which is why I think you should at least *try* the tea. Aside from its magic properties, bergamot is rich in flavonoids."

"I'll stick with coffee, thanks. Here you go." He slid a plate down in front of me. It was kind of like sitting at the counter of your favorite diner, only the cook had given you a bunch of orgasms the night before.

I rotated the plate to get a better look at it, then grinned in spite of my sleepiness. "Aw, did you make an egg and bacon smiley face all for me?"

"Yes." He didn't return my grin. He settled onto his own stool across from mine, with his own plate, and began eating voraciously. Pye, whose normal morning routine was to demand to be let out as soon as I woke, sat patiently at his feet, gazing up at him adoringly and showing no interest at all in going outside—or in me. "Another thing I'd like to do today is get a look at that book."

"Goody Fletcher's book?" I took a bite of bacon. It was exactly the way I liked it. Not too crispy, but not too floppy, either. This man seemed to be able to do anything, including cook the perfect piece of bacon. "Okay. But why? I've read it so many times I have it memorized by now, and there isn't anything in it about a rift. It really is just a collection of recipes and household tips."

"Even so. Why do you think Rosalie Hopkins wanted to get her hands on it so badly, back in the day?"

I shrugged. "Aside from the love spell, which didn't work for either of us, she always hated it when anyone had something she didn't. Which wasn't that often, because her family is so wealthy. I'm not sure she ever even liked Billy that much. She was just mad that I had him and she didn't."

"I'd still like to take a look at it."

"Be my guest," I said. "It's in the living room."

He regarded me over his now nearly empty breakfast plate, one golden eyebrow raised. "The living room?"

"Yes. On the bookshelf."

His other eyebrow rose. "You told me you had it in a safe place."

"It *is* in a safe place. Who would think to look for a book like that on a bookshelf? And even if they did—"

"Jessica. It's a handwritten book from the sixteen hundreds. I'm not saying you haven't done a great job keeping it safe for all these years, but I'm sure it's fairly easy to find."

"Okay," I said, scooping up egg yolk with my toast. "Go ahead and look."

"Fine." He rose from the counter. "I will."

I swiveled on my stool to watch as he crossed the dining room and then went into the living room to look for the book. For once Pye, perhaps knowing what was coming, didn't follow him, but stayed near me. I looked down at him and winked. He slow blinked back at me, a sign, I'd read, that cats reciprocated their owner's love, and accepted them as their cat equal.

"It's in here?" Derrick was standing in front of my bookshelves, looking up at my many cookbooks, celebrity memoirs, books on herbology and the Craft.

"It sure is," I said.

"You have a lot of old books in here."

"Well, my parents did own an antiques shop."

"Did they leave a lot of books behind?"

"No. These are all mine." Despite the early hour and seriousness of the situation, I was enjoying myself. "Why? Is only Plutarch good enough for you?"

"No, I enjoy reading a wide variety of books," he said, still scanning the shelves. "I just don't keep them around after I've finished them."

"Oh, right, because you travel too much for work. Your work going around, informing witches that their towns are under demonic attack."

He gave me a sarcastic look. Then he reached up and expertly pulled down a large book covered in a lurid black-and-yellow dustjacket. *Best Movies of the 1980s, 1990s, and 2000s,* the dust jacket exclaimed.

"Watch out!" I cried in alarm as he turned the book toward him and opened it.

But it was too late. A thick cloud of black powder erupted from inside the book, covering his chest, arms, and hands.

I couldn't help it. I dissolved in laughter.

"Yeah," I said, grabbing a handful of napkins and then hurrying over to him. "I forgot to mention that I do have a security system. It's called my exploding incense powder spell."

He stood perfectly still as I dabbed at him with the napkins. He wasn't laughing with me, but he didn't look upset, either.

"I told you I'd find it," he said, still holding on to Goody Fletcher's book.

"You did." I was blinking back tears of laughter. "Congratulations. What was the tip-off?"

"You have a lot of books, but you don't really seem like the kind of person who'd hang on to an outdated 'best of' movie guide."

"You're right about that."

"That incense powder doesn't really seem to be coming off, does it?"

"You're right about that, too." But he didn't seem to mind. In fact, the more I rubbed at him, the more he seemed to like it. "I think you're going to need a shower."

"Yeah. Maybe you'd like to join me?"

I looked up at him. I don't think I've ever seen a more intensely glowing pair of eyes—or a more invitingly upturned mouth.

So of course that's when there was a knock on the front door.

If Derrick had had a weapon, I swear he'd have whipped it out and leaped in front of me to defend me from whatever danger he imagined was out there on my porch—or was keeping us from "showering" together.

But since he didn't have one, he simply used his body to shield me.

"Are you expecting anyone?" he asked, those gleaming eyes narrowing dangerously.

"At seven in the morning?" I had to admit, my heart was hammering. Maybe I hadn't quite fully recovered from yesterday's hailstorm. "I'm not a barbarian."

Then I heard Dina's familiar—and very loud—voice call from behind the door, "Jess? It's me! I saw your lights on. Why aren't you answering your phone?"

I was already at the door and opening it before Derrick could move a muscle.

"Oh, hi," she said, bursting in and not even pretending to be surprised to see me standing there in my pajamas with Derrick covered in incense powder right behind me. She held up two large coffees from Wake Up West Harbor. "These are for you two. Jess, why aren't you answering your phone?"

"Because it's seven in the morning. I haven't even looked at my phone yet."

Although Mark and Dina were both early risers—dog owners generally were—they knew that swinging by my house with coffee before eight in the morning under normal circumstances was pointless, since I wouldn't be out of bed by then.

But these weren't normal circumstances. So there they stood, with carefully neutral looks on their faces, and steaming hot beverages in their hands. Mark, in his black leather jacket, was even waving a box of pastries.

All because they wanted dirt on my private life.

Or maybe not. . . .

"So you haven't heard?" Mark asked.

"Heard what?" I asked, despite my own misgivings and the disapproval I could feel radiating off Derrick.

But it was too late. Dina had already thrust her coffees at us, and Mark was hurrying into my kitchen.

"There was a king tide last night." Dina couldn't spill the beans fast enough. She began shedding her coat and scarf, throwing her things everywhere, as had been her custom since we were tweens. "Water went all the way up to the Post Road." Seeing my face, she added, "Don't worry, it didn't reach Enchantments. It stopped before it got to downtown. But there's driftwood in front of the library."

Derrick was so concerned, he didn't even seem to notice the new coffee in his hand. "I saw that there was seaweed and sand on the road when I went for my run this morning. But I thought maybe that was normal here this time of year."

"You run, bro?" Mark came back from the kitchen, an assortment of pastries laid out on one of my plates. "Me, too. What's your daily?"

"I like to get in six miles, if I can," Derrick replied.

Mark shook his head. "Six is murder, bro. You spend the first two getting warmed up, then you just get your groove going, and you gotta start cooling down. Gotta do ten."

"Six works for me," Derrick said.

"Hi, we weren't properly introduced last night in all the fuss over the wolf." Dina walked over and held her hand out toward Derrick. "I'm Jess's friend, Dina DiAngelo."

"*Best* friend," Mark said. "Don't forget. *Best* friend since middle school. Get ready, bro. If you tell one of these witches something, she's going to tell the other one, and vice versa."

"Well, it's true," Dina said, as Derrick extended his hand toward her. "Isn't that what best friends are for?"

Derrick looked bemused. "Thanks," he said. "I'll keep that in mind. Oh, er, sorry, I——" He noticed the uneasy glance she gave his blackened hand, then said, apologetically, "Incense powder. Jessica and I were just——"

"Oh, Goody Fletcher's book!" Dina laughed. "You found it. Congrats."

He grinned. "Thanks."

I carefully watched Dina's face to see if it registered anything—shock, pleasure, pain—when Derrick's fingers touched hers.

But it didn't. Dina looked like her normal self—granted, in full makeup even at such an early hour, ready for a day at the office in her skirt suit, high heels, and pearls—as she dropped his hand. "It's very nice to officially meet you. Derrick, right?"

"Yes," Derrick said. He still seemed bemused . . . for which I couldn't really blame him. Dina and Mark were a lot even at a normal hour. At seven in the morning, especially when you threw in the cannoli and the news of the king tide, they were extra.

"So how bad is the flooding this time?" I asked.

"Bad." Dina shook her head. "I heard from Sal this morning. He had to call an in-home learning day for the high school. The cafeteria flooded. The entire first floor, really."

"But it didn't even rain last night." I couldn't believe this. "And the full moon isn't until Thursday."

"I know." Dina was eyeing Derrick as he sipped the coffee she'd brought him. "Is this part of the rift thing Jessica said you're here to help us with?"

"It could be," Derrick replied, carefully.

"I knew it." Dina shook her head. "I *knew* something weird was going on."

"Something weird is *always* going on around this town." Mark was also eyeing Derrick, only he was doing so suspiciously, making it pretty clear that he included him in the list of the many weird things going on around town. "Jess says you saw the wolf? Because I saw it, too, weeks ago, but nobody believed me. Everyone said it was only a dog."

Derrick shook his head. "That was no dog."

"Right? I know what I saw." Now that Mark could see Derrick was on his side about the wolf, he began to warm up to him. "Hey, is that your ride out there in the driveway, bro? Dina's brother told us about that hailstorm over at the high school yesterday. Sal's a skeptic, so he doesn't think it was paranormal, but I can tell you it didn't hail over on my side of town. First the wolf, then the hail, now this crazy tide. What the hell is coming next?"

Derrick sent me a silent look, halfway between a plea for help and a rebuke—whether for letting Mark and Dina into my house in the first place, or telling them who Derrick was and what he was doing here, I didn't know. All I knew was, a second later, Mark had his arm wrapped around him, and was steering him toward the front door.

"This is scary shit," Mark was saying. "Your car looks like hell. Listen, I know a guy—"

"It's a rental."

"Oh, man, I hope you took out the supplemental. I can't believe—"

The rest of what Mark was saying was lost as he herded Derrick out the door to go look at his dented rental car.

As soon as they were gone, I grabbed Dina by the arm. "Did you feel it?" I asked.

She shook her head, looking confused. "Feel what?"

"His *fingers*, when you shook his hand."

"No. What are you talking about?"

"Like an electric charge from his skin—every time he touches me, I feel it. It's like being hit by a shock. But in a good way. Are you telling me you didn't feel it?"

"No, I didn't feel a thing. His fingers just felt—normal. Wait—what do you mean *every time*?" Her eyes widened as her voice dropped even lower. "Like during sex, too?"

I nodded, unable to keep a smile off my face as I thought of the previous evening's activities. "It's so amazing, Dee. I don't know if it's a spell or a technique he learned somewhere or just a natural gift. But let me tell you, whatever it is, it's *hot*. I have never, in my life—"

Both Dina's hands flew out to grip my wrists. "Wait. Jess." Her face looked graver than I'd ever seen it.

"What?" I asked, alarmed. "What is it?"

"What he's doing," she said. "That thing with his hands?"

"And his tongue," I added. "And his—"

"Yeah," she said, quickly. "That. That isn't because of a spell, Jess."

"It isn't? What do you think it is, then? Reiki? Hypnosis?" I gasped. "Wait. You don't think—not *crystals*?"

"No," she said, shaking her head. "Worse."

"Why?" I asked, already dreading the answer. "What is it?"

She grinned at me. "You like him."

Jessica

To make a friend of anyone, simply go and bake a bun:
Butter, cream, sugar, and flour worked together for an
    hour
If mixed with yeast, then left to bake the heart of anyone
    will take.

Goody Fletcher,
Book of Useful Household Tips

It was completely ridiculous of Dina to suggest that the reason my skin felt as if it were bursting into flame—in a good way—every time Derrick Winters touched me was because I *liked* him.

I know all about the love hormone oxytocin and how it works. I was there that day we learned about it in tenth-grade health class.

What was happening with Derrick was something else.

But I was fine with letting Dina think what she liked. All she'd ever wanted was for me to find the same kind of domestic bliss with someone that she had with Mark.

But how could I tell Dina that—especially after what had gone down with Billy—I wasn't sure that's what I wanted for myself?

Then again, I didn't know what I wanted for myself.

But it certainly seemed like everyone else in town thought they knew what was best for me.

This became pretty obvious after Dina and Mark had left, and Derrick and I finally got to that shower (and what followed after, which was just as interesting as what had gone on between us last night). I was in my sewing room, finishing up some hems on a few gowns for the ball, when Derrick called up the stairs to me.

"Jess?"

He was already hard at work on the wireless home security system he'd run out to pick up from Home Depot. Not surprisingly, the man knew how to work a drill. I kept going downstairs on the pretense of getting more tea when really I was sneaking glimpses of him. I was going to be so overcaffeinated by the time I showed up at the shop, my customers were going to be afraid. And so were Gabby and Esther. The two of them had already texted that they wanted to come by after online school.

Gabby: I can pick out a dress and also start training to work there! And you can start mentoring Esther!

I texted back:

Great. See you both this afternoon.

Wait until Esther found out what I *really* intended to mentor her in.

I trotted down the stairs to see what Derrick wanted. I pretended like I didn't notice how good his arms looked in his short-sleeved T as he held my drill.

"A woman just pulled up in front of your house." Derrick was peering suspiciously out the window he was attaching sensors to. "Do you know her?"

I followed the direction of his gaze. Despite the gloomy start to the morning, it had turned into a beautiful fall day, the sky a cloudless blue against which the autumn leaves were blazing red and gold. A flock of birds, a little late in heading south for the winter, formed a perfect V in the distance.

But the second I saw who was getting out of the cherry-red Mercedes coupe in front of my house, it felt like the sky had turned dark.

"Oh, no." I ducked behind my curtains.

"Who is it?" Derrick didn't duck. He just stood there in the window, staring at the woman who was flouncing down my front walk, her perfectly straight blond hair flowing gently in the breeze. "Is she from your homeowners association, or something? Did I need to get a permit from them first before installing these cameras?"

"How can you not know who that is?" I reached out to pull him behind the curtains with me. "It's Rosalie Hopkins. She practically runs the WCW!"

"Oh." He looked blank-faced for a second, then said calmly, "I've never met her."

"Yeah, well, lucky you. What do we do? Do we let her in?"

"Of course we let her in. Why not? We're not doing anything wrong." He raised his eyebrows at me meaningfully. "Right now, anyway."

"Funny. Very funny." Although it was sort of funny. Rosalie, in her stylish ensemble of puffy vest, slouchy camel sweater, riding jodhpurs, and boots, did look a little like she was striding down my front lane to either lodge a complaint or welcome me to the neighborhood. There was a determined expression on her face, and a cellophane-wrapped basket of what looked like muffins in her hands. "Billy must have told her about you. What are we going to—?"

But it was too late. Rosalie's knock was brisk. "Hello, Jess?" she called. "Hi, it's me, Rosalie."

"Coming," I called. There was no point in pretending I wasn't home. I was sure Rosalie had seen me through the window. Besides, she, like Billy from the day before, would have heard us talking through the door.

"Well, hello, Rosalie," I said, giving her my biggest, fakest smile as I swung open the front door. "What a surprise. How are you?"

"Well, I'm just great, Jess! It's good to see you looking so . . . *well*." On the word *well*, Rosalie's gaze strayed to Derrick, standing behind me with his drill, and stayed there.

"Thanks so much," I gushed. "Won't you come in? Rosalie, this is Derrick." I didn't bother telling Rosalie Derrick's last name. I knew she'd have already learned it from Billy. "Derrick, this is my old friend from high school, Rosalie. Derrick's visiting for a few days from the city, Rosalie."

"Oh, how lovely." Rosalie was quick to take in everything, from the tool in Derrick's hand to his tattoo to his motorcycle boots. "It's always nice to get out of the city this time of year, isn't it?"

"It is," Derrick said, casually swinging an arm around my shoulders. "The weather's been just beautiful. Except for a little hail yesterday, right, sweetheart?"

"Oh, right, yeah, the hail." Why did the way he said *sweetheart* make my heart stutter, even though we were in a fake relationship? Well, fake-ish. "The hail wasn't so great."

"Oh, that hail." Rosalie shook her head as she swung her basket of muffins onto my coffee table, the autumn-colored cellophane crinkling like crazy. "Wasn't that nuts? Bill told me what happened to your car, Jess. Such a shame. You know he's had it towed over to Hopkins, and they're doing everything they can to get the dents out. And of course if you need a loaner until it's fixed, well, you only need to ask."

Wait. What was happening? Rosalie was actually being . . . *nice*?

"Um," I said, confused. "Thanks."

"And, here, Jessica, I brought this for you." She pointed at the basket. "My world-famous pumpkin spice muffins with streusel topping. Ha ha, I say world-famous, but really it's only my kids and Bill who love them. I hope you will, too, though."

"Gee, thanks, Rosalie." I looked through the orange-and-red cellophane into the basket. There really were a ton of muffins inside, each with a piece of raffia tied in a bow around it, along with a gift card with a gold rose on the front—Rosalie's long-time chosen personal insignia. "How thoughtful of you. You really didn't have to."

She batted her faux mink lashes. "But I *wanted* to. I just felt so bad for you. I know how much you loved that car. You've had it forever. Still, maybe this is a blessing in disguise. Maybe now is the time to test-drive something new. It's always good to try new things, isn't it?"

When she said "try new things," she glanced over at Derrick.

So *that's* what this was about: a peace offering because she thought I'd finally moved on from her husband. Like I hadn't moved on from Billy more than a decade ago.

But it turned out that wasn't all she was talking about.

"I heard you're a Reach for the Sky mentor for one of my Harvest Princess candidates." Her smile was bright. "Gabriella Aquino?"

"Uh." Rosalie had gotten her information wrong, but that was no surprise in a town as small as West Harbor. Gossip here flew as fast as birds, and was about as reliable.

But I saw the quick warning glance Derrick sent me, and so I didn't correct her. Besides, I was curious myself to see where this was going.

"I did sign up to be a mentor," I admitted. "But I haven't really had much time to—"

"Gabby's such a darling," Rosalie purred. "We all just love her to death."

"Yes," I said. "Gabby is great."

"So I wanted to make sure to extend an invitation to you to come to the selection ceremony tomorrow night. It's at the Yacht Club. I really think you'll enjoy it. We're trying to make it very special for the girls. It's a shame they can't all be princesses, but we just don't have enough scholarship money to go around."

"Sure," I said, instead of what I wanted to, which was, *You are so full of crap.* "That's understandable. I'll try to make it."

"Oh, that would be so great. It would mean so much to Gabby, I know. And will you be staying through the weekend, Derrick? It's going to be very special this year. We're going to have a ball in the village square to celebrate West Harbor's Tricentennial."

"That's what I've heard." Derrick had made no move to remove his arm. "I'm staying . . . and looking forward to it."

Rosalie looked as delighted as if Derrick had said he was going to back a truckload of garbage onto her lawn and dump it there.

"How great!" Her smile wasn't reaching her eyes now. "It's going to be *such* an important night for our town's history. Not many towns can boast that they've been around as long as we have. That's why it's so important we celebrate it. Speaking of which—" Rosalie reached into her Gucci handbag and took out an envelope that she handed to me. "I happen to have two extra tickets to the ball on Thursday. I noticed you hadn't signed up yet, and I thought, well, there has to be some kind of mix-up, because I can't imagine this event without Jessica Gold!"

I looked down at the envelope, which had my name written across it in fancy calligraphy. There hadn't been a mix-up. I hadn't purchased a ticket to the ball for myself—though I'd purchased them for all my employees and their significant others. They deserved to go, if they wanted to, after all the hard work they'd put in at the Fall into Fall sale, and the work they were going to do the next day, giving candy to trick-or-treaters outside the shop. I myself had been intending to do what I did every night during Halloween season in order to protect my mental health: go straight home after work, turn out all my lights, get in bed with Pye and some takeout, and watch the Food Network.

Or at least, that had been my plan before Derrick Winters had shown up.

"Gosh," I said. "Thanks so much, Rosalie."

"Oh, it's my pleasure." She beamed at me—but mostly, I couldn't help noticing, at Derrick. "Well, Jess, I know you're busy, so I won't hold you up a second longer. I really only wanted to stop by to introduce myself to your new beau, and to let you know that Bill is doing everything he can to repair your car—and of course to make sure the two of you got those tickets, and invite you to our selection tomorrow night!"

"Thanks again. We'll try to be there." I hoped she hadn't developed the ability to read minds in the years since high school.

She hadn't—at least if her smile was any indication. "Great." She shouldered her bag and waved at us. "Well, bye for now!"

And then she hurried off, as suddenly as she'd breezed in.

"What was *that*?" I turned to ask Derrick as soon as she was in her car and out of earshot.

"I don't know." He was looking after her, too, lost in thought. "I take it she's not always that friendly?"

"No, I told you, she hates my guts. She's the witch who destroyed my car, remember?"

"Yeah." He looked after her for a moment longer, then shrugged and turned back to my window. "Maybe she's changed. People do, you know."

I stared at him. "In twenty-four hours?" I held up the envelope. "Why is she so anxious for me to go to her selection thingie? And for us to go to the ball? And why did she keep giving you the side-eye?"

"Well." Grinning, he lifted the drill and gave the trigger a press. *Zing!* "I've been told I *am* pretty good with power tools."

I didn't smile back at him. "You do realize *she's* probably what's causing the rift in West Harbor, right? Rosalie Hopkins looks beautiful, but her intentions aren't. I'm willing to bet my shop that she knows what we're doing, and the live entertainment at the pre-ball dinner is going to be the sacrificing of the virginal Harvest Princesses, just like Esther said."

He stopped grinning. "I think you've had a bit too much of that tea."

"Really? You don't think I was chosen because I can tell when evil is walking around right under our noses?"

Derrick shook his head. "That's not actually how——"

"I'm telling you, *that* was the evil, right there." I pointed in the direction Rosalie had driven. "Forget stupid wolves. The evil is Rosalie Hopkins. She's up to something and she wants us to go to the ball on Thursday night to keep us out of the way while she does it, which is why she gave us these." I waved the envelope with the tickets. "So what are we going to do about it?"

He took the envelope from me, slid it into the back pocket of his jeans, then took my hand and pulled me close. Instantly, I felt soothed—but also a little turned on. "We're going to carry on with our plan," he said. The rumble of his voice inside his chest felt reassuring against me. "You're going to train Esther, and I'm going to protect you both. I do think, however, that it would be a grave mistake to eat any of those muffins."

I couldn't help letting out a snort of laughter. "Agreed."

Derrick

Witches most revere those who teach, and unselfishly give of their greater knowledge and wisdom to those who ask respectfully, in order to help make the Earth a better place for all.

Rule Number Six of the Nine Rules
World Council of Witches

Derrick had a problem.

Derrick had multiple problems, actually, but the one that seemed most pressing was that he had slept with the Chosen One. Not just once, but multiple times.

And he didn't plan on stopping anytime soon. If anything, he hoped he and Jessica continued sleeping with each other until one or the other of them put a stop to it. And the only thing he was certain of at this point was that that person wasn't going to be him.

He'd known he should have turned down this job. He'd helped dozens of witches in dozens of villages exactly like West Harbor. Many had been saved. A few had not.

But none of those jobs had ever gotten personal . . . until now.

The obvious difference was Jessica. He could have laid the

blame on her warm laughter and darkly shining eyes—not to mention her deliciously soft body and even softer mouth.

But he knew it was more than that. More even than her sarcastic sense of humor and skeptical attitude—both clearly worn as armor to protect a heart that was as vulnerable to mishandling as her home was to the elements. More even than that cheerful home and warm, inviting bed.

It was her. Just her.

That's why he had to protect her, and why he was willing to risk everything to do so, even though he knew that when she found out the truth, it was probably going to get him banned from that bed forever.

But until that time, he could make himself useful. He'd been in her office in the back of her shop, using a putty knife and a hammer to try to unstick the window there, but now he was leaning in the open office door, watching while she fitted Esther's friend with a gown. Or tried to, at least, since the kid wouldn't come out of the dressing room.

"I'm sure it looks lovely on you, Gabby," Jessica called to the girl.

"It doesn't." The reply from behind the velvet curtain sounded hopeless.

"Just come out and let me see. Or let me come in. It's a tricky gown. It might need some adjusting."

"It's not the gown. It's me. I look terrible."

Derrick saw Jessica exchange glances with Esther, who was sitting in his old spot in the Friends and Family Chair, doing her homework. Jessica's look was pleading. The kid rolled her eyes and called, "Come on out, Gabs. There's no one else here." At this, she exchanged an apologetic glance with the salesgirl behind the register. But the salesgirl only smiled and went back to whatever she was doing on the computer. "I'm sure you look amazing."

"I don't."

But finally the girl flung the curtain back and came out of the dressing room. And . . . she was right. She looked terrible. Derrick couldn't believe that Jessica, of all people, would have put her in such a hideous garment. A pastel nightmare of some kind of shiny material, covered in fake flowers, the kid looked like a wedding cake someone had left in the sun to melt—and from the expression on her face, she knew it.

"Okay," Jessica said, her tone way too chipper. "That's not so bad."

Not so bad? He darted a look in Esther's direction to see what her opinion on the matter was, but she'd wisely ducked her head back over whatever she was writing. Smart kid.

"*Not so bad?*" Gabby stared at her reflection in the full-length mirror in dismay. "What are you talking about? I look *awful*."

"You don't look awful." Jessica reached out to do something to the gown. "You just need a little . . ."

And suddenly, with a twist of Jessica's fingers, the fake flowers fell into place, and turned to silk blossoms in the palest of purple that gently kissed Gabby's shoulders, and then floated together to form a heart shape at the center of her chest. The shiny material seemed to transform into shimmering gossamer, nipping in softly to cling to Gabby's curves in all the right places, then billowing out gently at others.

"There." Jessica took a step back to admire her handiwork. "That's more like it."

Suddenly, instead of a melting wedding cake, Gabby looked like a woodland sprite. An enchanted fairy. Something otherworldly and ethereal. Definitely beautiful, anyway.

And she knew it. She was blinking back tears of astonishment at her own transformation in the mirror.

And she wasn't the only one.

"*Whoa.*"

Esther had lifted her head from her homework and was staring in wonder at her friend. "Gabs. You look *awesome!*"

Gabriella smiled—a small, tentative smile—and reached up to wipe her eyes. "Do I?"

"Yeah." Esther set her homework aside and rose from the Friends and Family Chair to cross the shop to admire her friend. "Totally. Dude, you might even *win*. Ms. Gold, how did you do that?"

"Me? I didn't do a thing." Jessica leaned down to fluff up the gown's light, airy skirt. "It's all Gabriella."

Gabby, clearly delighted, laughed and twirled in the mirror. The skirt of the gown ballooned out, shimmering in a rainbow of colors, all the palest tones of pinks and lavenders, like a spring sunset. The kid laughed, and twirled some more.

Derrick couldn't help grinning at Jessica's pleased expression. It was heartwarming to watch her perform her very specific kind of magic, and even more heartwarming to see the joy she got from doing it. It gave *him* joy to see her doing it.

Goddess help him. He looked down at Pye, who was sitting by his feet, daintily licking a paw. He had it bad.

"But Ms. Gold," Gabriella said, stopping midtwirl, a look of anguish crossing her face. "I can never afford this."

Jessica nodded. "I know. It's a good thing you don't have any extracurriculars, because you're going to be working here every weekend for the rest of the year to pay me back."

The girl squealed and threw her arms around Jessica's waist. She was too short to reach her neck. "Oh, thank you, thank you, thank you!"

"You're welcome." Jessica, noticing Derrick's gaze on her, smiled at him over the top of Gabby's head, then patted the girl on the back and said, "Now go take it off so I can adjust the hem.

It's way too long. And don't worry, I'll have it done by tomorrow night."

As Gabby floated on a cloud of happiness back into the dressing room, Jessica crooked her finger at Esther. "Come here."

The kid's eyes grew twice their size behind the lenses of her glasses. "Oh, no, not me. I told you, I'm not into princesses. Or dresses."

"I know. That's not what I want to talk to you about."

Reluctantly, Esther followed Jessica, who led her back into her office where the window was still stuck half-open, Derrick's hammer and putty knife on the sill. Jessica sank down behind her desk, gesturing for the kid to sit in the chair opposite. Derrick leaned in the open doorway, curious to see how this was going to go. This wasn't his show, after all. Jessica was the Chosen One.

Jessica opened with, "Chocolate?" and offered Esther candy from the open bag on her desk.

"Oh, cool," the kid said, and grabbed a handful of mini chocolate bars. "Thanks."

"So, Esther." Jessica was unwrapping a Snickers bar of her own. "Remember the wolf?"

The kid nodded, chewing. "From last night? Yeah, how could I forget?" She glanced up at Derrick. "Did Animal Control catch it yet?"

"No," he said. Like the Animal Control Department of West Harbor wouldn't wet themselves laughing if someone called in to report a wolf sighting. "Not yet."

"Oh." The kid glanced a little nervously at the open window behind Jessica's head. It was only late afternoon, but the autumn sun was already sinking. It would be dark in less than an hour. "So it's still out there."

"Yes," Jessica said, leaning forward so that her elbows were on her desk. "That's what I wanted to talk to you about. Derrick here thinks that the reason there are suddenly wolves in West Harbor—not to mention the king tides that keep flooding the school and stuff—is because a demonic rift is opening up beneath the town."

The kid, instead of laughing or rolling her eyes, nodded. Apparently, this was no surprise to her.

"And in order to close it and save West Harbor," Jessica went on, "we're going to need you. Because according to an ancient prophecy, I'm the Chosen One, and you're the Bringer of Light— which means only we can stop the evil."

Esther looked from Jessica to Derrick and then back again. Then she took a bite of the mini chocolate bar she was holding, chewed for a moment, swallowed, and said, "Okay."

Derrick wasn't sure the kid understood.

"Esther," he began. "What we're saying is—"

"No, I get it." The kid reached into the bag on Jessica's desk for another candy bar. "There's a big bad in town, and you need me to fight it."

Derrick glanced uncomfortably at Jessica. "No, that's not what we're say—"

"Yeah, it is." The girl shrugged. "Don't worry about it. I knew this day was going to come. I'm a Scorpio. Spooky stuff is my jam." Settling farther back into her chair—so comfortable that she might almost have put her sneakered feet up onto the desk if it had been her own and not Jessica's—she continued. "So, what do you need me to do?"

Derrick exchanged glances with Jessica. She was smiling, her eyes warmly prideful and easily read. *See? I told you this was the girl. Isn't she amazing?*

He couldn't help feeling a little more cautious, however. He'd been through this before.

"We don't actually know yet," he said. "But we do think whatever is going to happen, it will be during the full moon on Thursday."

"Makes sense." Esther was nibbling the chocolate sides off her candy bar and leaving a gooey mess of caramel and peanuts in her fingers. "So, during the Tricentennial Ball, when everyone is at the village square."

"Exactly."

"And I personally think you might be right about this Harvest Princess thing," Jessica said. "I find Mrs. Hopkins's plan of selecting nine girls for it a little suspicious."

"But we don't know anything for sure," Derrick hurried to say.

Esther squinted up at him through her glasses. "Sagittarius," she said, pointing at him. "Am I right? On the cusp of Capricorn?" When he only gaped at her, she nodded. "Yeah. Definitely a workaholic who likes to keep the peace."

Jessica burst out laughing. "Uh-oh, Mr. Winters. She's got your number."

Derrick couldn't believe it. He *was* a Sagittarius, but born just before Christmas. His mother had always complained it was difficult to find him two gifts, one for his birthday and one for Christmas, and so every year he'd received only one from her, though it had always been a big, absurdly impractical one.

He'd never complained, however, because he'd wanted to keep the peace between his separated parents.

Esther had been absolutely right . . . not that he believed in any of that astrological crap.

"Very funny," he said to Jessica. "Listen, Esther, this is serious. We have no way of knowing what to expect. We simply have to be alert. And you, especially, have to be careful. I don't want you going out by yourself after dark. I understand that spooky stuff is your, uh, jam, but that wolf could be the least terrifying thing to come after you in the next few days."

She looked just as she had the night before: absolutely thrilled. "Cool!"

"No, not cool." May the Goddess give him patience. "I'm serious. Halloween is the day after the full moon, and is traditionally believed to be when spirits roam the earth, looking to avenge their death. So in addition to dealing with the rift and the threat from any living beings who might be on the side of the demons, we've also got to be wary of that, as well."

"Oh, no worries, Mr. Winters." Esther pulled her homework from her backpack. "I've got it covered. I've written all about it in this letter to the mayor."

"The mayor?" The Goddess clearly wasn't listening to his pleas. "I don't see how that's—"

"It's complicated, but I'm pretty sure the mayor can help with our demons."

Derrick didn't want to be the one to break it to her that only Esther herself—with the aid of Jessica—could rid her town of its demon problem, especially when the kid was looking down at her letter, her brow slightly creased—the first sign of real anxiety she'd shown so far.

"I'm just not sure how to get this to her," she went on. "If I mail it, it won't get there in time. And if I ask my mom to give it to her—because the mayor and my mom are friends—she's going to want to know what it is. But I don't want my parents to know about this stuff. They . . ." Her brow creased even more. "They don't know about my magic, and I don't want to tell them. It would only worry them."

Jessica's voice was warm as she stretched her hand out across her desk. "I feel the same way about my parents, so I understand. Give the letter to me. I know the mayor's wife. I'll make sure she gets it."

Esther brightened with relief, all the lines gone from her face. "That would be great." She laid the letter in Jess's hand. "Thanks."

Derrick was about to say something—what, he hardly knew. Maybe, *I don't think a letter is going to work*—when Pye, tired of all of this conversation, leaped from Derrick's feet to the window-sill. The cat was obviously intent on going outside for a prowl just as the sun was beginning to set.

"No!" Jessica cried, springing from her chair. She lunged to grab hold of Pye's sleek black body, but the cat moved too quickly for her. His paws were on the sill, poised to push him-self out of the window, when the entire office shook—from the floor to the ceiling—as if from a small tremor beneath the earth. Samples of candles and crystals tinkled on the shelves above their heads, and piles of stock—fortunately mostly only colorful clothing, still in plastic wrapping—came tumbling down upon their heads.

But that wasn't all that fell. The office window came crashing closed with a bang, trapping a very startled Pye inside. The cat jumped from the sill to crouch at Jessica's feet beneath her desk, his back arched in indignation.

Derrick—who'd gripped the sides of the doorframe in which he'd been standing at the first sign of what he'd assumed was an earthquake—sprang across the desk to reach the window. Be-cause just as the frame had come crashing down, he could have sworn he'd glimpsed a shimmer of light behind the glass. The glow of a flashlight belonging to some teenagers, performing a pre-Halloween prank?

Or the eyes of the demon who was behind what Derrick now realized wasn't an earthquake or prank at all, but a concentrated effort to trap them inside, and then destroy them?

But when he got to the window, he saw nothing outside except

the parking lot behind the store. There was no one there—
pranksters, demons, or otherwise.

"Are you all right?" he turned to ask the women as they both
pushed clothing from their laps. "Are either of you hurt?"

"I'm fine." Jessica had dug Pye out from beneath her desk and
was stroking the affronted creature. "Esther?"

"Yeah, sorry about that." Esther picked a piece of fuzz from
her lips that a cashmere shawl had left behind as it fell on her. "I
didn't mean to slam the window down so hard. I just wanted to
make sure the cat didn't get out."

Derrick stared. "Wait . . . *you* did that?"

"Yeah. Sorry. I've never moved anything that heavy before. I'm
surprised it even worked. Either that window was stuck harder
than I thought, or . . ." She trailed off with a shrug. "I don't know."

Derrick knew. Derrick knew exactly why it had worked. The
reason it had worked was sitting next to him, holding her cat
close, and stroking the thoroughly unimpressed feline.

The Chosen One. The Chosen One had found her Bringer of
Light.

And Esther had brought the light, all right.

Derrick felt like he needed a drink—a strong one, and not
coffee, either. He had never in his life seen someone with powers
as strong as Esther's.

And she was only a kid.

Jessica

Offerings should be made to the Mother Goddess during the time of reaping to show thy thankfulness for a successful harvest.

Goody Fletcher,
Book of Useful Household Tips

Derrick wanted a drink. I told him there was no better place to get one than Tuesday Night Trivia at the Brewport.

"That isn't exactly what I had in mind," he growled.

"Look, I don't want to go, either," I said as I locked Pye up into my house, an act he was expressing his outrage against by meowing loudly behind the front door. "But I never miss Tuesday Night Trivia, so if I don't show up, it's going to look weird—like something is up."

"You mean like you just got a new boyfriend and you want to stay home so he can ravage you?"

"Um . . ." I paused before dropping my keys into my bag. Maybe I was making the wrong decision. "I wasn't aware that was an option."

"It is. It would be safer and therefore more sensible. Also vastly more pleasurable."

He still seemed a bit shaken by what he'd seen back at the shop. Not the part where I'd found the absolute perfect dress for Gabby—the part where Esther had performed her telekinesis.

That had shaken me, too, though not as much as it seemed to have shaken him, since I'd seen her do it before.

"I agree," I said. "But Esther's going to be there. Her parents own the place and are making her work at the hostess station. Don't you think we should go and keep an eye on her? Especially since Rosalie and Billy might be there."

He looked almost physically pained. "Might be?"

"They're on a team, yeah," I said. "They don't always show up. I wouldn't expect them to this week, with all the Tricentennial stuff going on. But if they do, do we really want them around Esther without us being there to keep an eye on—?"

"Trivia it is." He held out his arm to escort me down my porch steps.

I smiled and laid my hand upon his arm, like he was a gentleman and I was a lady. "Thank you, kind sir."

"But I'd rather stay home tonight and ravage you."

My pulse quickened. So much for him being a gentleman.

"Obviously I'd prefer that, too," I said. "But I think we'll have plenty of time for that after Trivia. Should we walk? It's a nice night, and the restaurant's not that far—"

Derrick cast an aggrieved look in the direction of his rental car. "Walking is fine by me."

We had to go almost half a block before I could no longer hear the sound of Pye's piteous wailing at being left inside on such a cool, clear night.

"So do you feel a little better about our chances of beating this thing—whatever it is—now that you've seen what Esther can do?" I asked as we turned onto the coastal road. Though I couldn't yet see them, the sound of the waves grew louder. And the night air, which I'd thought pleasantly cool before, grew colder.

"I don't know what to feel now," Derrick said. "I've never seen anything like that."

I laughed—but more with uneasiness than anything else. "Oh, come on. You must have. You've traveled all over the world doing this, haven't you? Surely—"

He cut me off. "No. Never. Not like that."

"Well." I was hugging myself, but I wasn't certain if it was because of the chill of the wind coming off the Sound—or fear. "That bodes well for us, doesn't it? She's on our side, so if she's the most powerful witch you've ever seen, that must mean we can't lose."

He stopped walking and looked down at me in the amber light from the streetlamp. The nearly full moon was hidden be-hind swiftly moving dark clouds. A mist was beginning to roll in from the sea, and I could smell its briny scent, like shucked oysters—only these oysters smelled as if they'd sat out a bit too long in the sun.

"We can most definitely lose," he said, his gaze hooded and unreadable in the half-light. "And more than just this town's ranking as a cute stop for leaf peepers. We could lose our lives. She nearly brought the ceiling of your shop down on our heads."

"Oh, come on," I scoffed. "Esther would never—"

"Of course she wouldn't—not on purpose. But she's a kid. And like most kids, she doesn't know her own strength. If she gets emotional, there's no telling what kind of damage she could do." He nodded toward my bag. "What does her letter to the mayor say?"

I grasped my tote. "Are you kidding me? We can't read her letter. That's private."

He frowned. "The fate of your town might rest on what that kid has written in that letter, and you're not going to take a peek?"

"No. I would never!"

Then, just as I'd begun to worry that I'd put all my trust into someone who would open letters that weren't addressed to him, he snaked out an arm, pulled me close to him, and buried his lips in my neck.

"That's why you're the Chosen One," he murmured, and the feel of his skin against mine sent shivers of a completely different—and entirely pleasurable—kind through me.

"Get a room, you two!"

Derrick and I broke apart as a car swerved up close to the sidewalk where we stood. I looked over to see Dina leering at me from the passenger seat, while Mark sat behind the wheel.

"Hey, lovebirds," she called through the window she'd put down. "Headed our way?"

I hoped the light was dim enough that neither of them would notice my flaming cheeks.

"Oh, hi," I said. "I don't know. Where you headed?"

"You know where we're headed, byotch." I heard the rear passenger door closest to us pop as she unlocked it. "Get in, losers!"

I smirked and reached for the door handle, until I noticed Derrick's hesitation to follow me—and his confused look. "Oh," I said to him, remembering his upbringing, and that he'd probably never seen *Mean Girls*. "That's a line from a movie Dina and I liked as kids."

"Oh." He didn't look particularly comforted—especially when he followed me into the car only to hear Mark cry, only half sarcastically, "Dude! How's it hanging?"

But I'm not sure anything could have prepared Derrick for the shock of the fact that Get In, Losers was our trivia team's name, and was shining down from all the flat-screen TVs (of which there were dozens) in the Brewport, along with our team stats (which weren't great).

A large family-style restaurant built on a deck right over the Sound, with a dock leading from it, the Brewport offered every-thing from craft beers and burgers to a video game arcade guar-anteed to keep the kids occupied while their parents watched their favorite sports team (or played Trivia). Packed with beach-goers in the summertime, business was no less slow in the golden glow of autumn. The beginning of hockey and end of baseball season always left the place slammed, right on through to the Superbowl and basketball playoffs.

But everything stopped for Tuesday Night Trivia.

Esther's parents' team, the Brewport Bruisers, included their friends as well as waitstaff and bartenders from the restaurant. They won nearly every week.

But that never stopped Dina and Yasmin—who were both competitive by nature—from strategizing over how Get In, Losers might steal the Bruisers' crown.

Dina was quizzing Derrick as Mark and her brother, Sal, were up at the bar, securing beer and wine for our high top.

"So what are your areas of expertise?" Dina asked Derrick.

Cunnilingus, I thought.

But Derrick only said, "I don't know. I've never played trivia before."

"Never played trivia before?" Yasmin echoed. She had been at the restaurant for an hour already with Sal and the kids—who, having finished their burgers, were off in the video arcade sec-tion, happily assassinating digital aliens with their friends—and was on her third glass of pinot grigio. "Not even Trivial Pursuit?"

"No." Derrick smiled at her, definitely giving the appearance of paying attention to their conversation.

But I could see his gray-eyed gaze quickly sweeping the room, taking in the other tables and teams, trying to figure out if there were any supernatural—or otherwise—threats he needed to worry about.

He'd already clocked Esther at the hostess booth. She'd seated us, assuming a politely distant professional demeanor as she brought us to our table and handed us our menus. I'd complimented her on how she looked in her Brewport uniform of khaki pants and navy polo shirt, and received in return an icy "Thank you."

Esther hated her new job.

"Well, it's simple," Yasmin was saying to Derrick as she pointed to the flat screens overhead. "Dr. Steve—he's our local veterinarian, but also the trivia master—will project the questions up on the screens, and then we write our answers on here." She showed him our answer sheet. "When we're done, each team hands their answers in. Then Dr. Steve tabulates them, and the team with the most right answers wins a really great prize."

I smiled at Derrick. "A Brewport T-shirt in the color of your choice."

"Every team member gets one!" Yasmin cried excitedly. "So far we've never won."

"Well," Derrick said with mock seriousness. "Then I guess we'd better win tonight."

I grinned at him, and tried to ignore the flutter I felt in my heart when he grinned back. This was bad. This was so bad. Dina couldn't be right. I couldn't *like* Derrick—not that way. It never worked out when I liked a guy. It always ended in disaster— occasionally spectacularly. I couldn't let this end the same way, especially with innocent teenagers involved.

But surely it wouldn't—not this time. Derrick was leaving soon anyway, regardless of how things turned out. He had to get back to his important job of saving other towns from demonic

ruin. So probably I was worrying unnecessarily. Probably everything was going to be——

"Jumbo nacho platter for the Sisters In Law?" a server asked,
before sliding a heavy plate in front of us. "Compliments of the
house."

"Yay," Yasmin cried. "Yep, that's us!"

"Oh, it's so sweet of them to remember," Dina said, before
digging in. "Thanks!"

Derrick looked down at the heaping plate of gooey deli-
ciousness before us and raised a questioning eyebrow. Before I
had a chance to explain, an attractive Black woman appeared at
our table, her hands resting on the slim shoulders of a very embarrassed teenaged girl. It was Esther and her mother, Virginia
Dodge.

"Oh, good," said Mrs. Dodge. "They brought your nachos."

"Thanks so much, Virginia." Yasmin's mouth was full, but
that didn't stop her from gushing, "You really don't have to keep
doing this every time."

"Are you kidding me?" Mrs. Dodge, soft and curvy in all the
places her daughter was sharp and angular, also shared the same
intelligent eyes and warmly generous mouth as Esther. "After
what you did for us? I think we would have had to move if you
two hadn't cleared up that fence line situation. And now you,
Jessica Gold, agreeing to be Esther's mentor? Do you know how
much money that's going to save us? College tuition has gotten
outrageous, and of course this one wants to go to one of the most
expensive universities in the country. And we have her little
brothers to send, as well. We owe you a lot more than nachos!
Please order anything you like, on the house."

I smiled while Esther said nothing, merely looked as if she
wished the floor of the restaurant would open and drop her
straight into the sea.

"You don't have to do that, Mrs. Dodge," I said. "It's my pleasure. Esther is a remarkable girl." In more ways than her mother knew. "She really doesn't need any mentoring. But I'm glad to do it, just the same."

"We'll just be happy if you can get her out of her shell." Mrs. Dodge wrapped her arms around her daughter and squeezed her tight, while Esther rolled her eyes. "She's so shy. We're hoping her working here a few nights a week will help."

Derrick glanced questioningly at me. *Esther, shy?*

I grinned back. *I know.*

"Mom." Esther wiggled out of her mother's arms. It was amusing to see how the normally poised and confident girl reverted into someone completely different when her parents were around. "Can I go back to work now?"

"Oh, yes, go." Mrs. Dodge patted Esther on the shoulder as the girl returned to the hostess booth. "And please, Jessica, call me Virginia—or better yet, Ginny. Reggie"—Reginald Dodge, Esther's father—"is around here somewhere, I know he's going to want to stop by to thank you as well, but there's a problem with one of the ATMs. Are you all ready to get your butts beat tonight by the Bruisers?"

"Not gonna happen!" Yasmin drained her wineglass. "Tonight's the night for the Losers!"

"Sure, it is," Ginny said, smiling sweetly. "Have you checked out the categories?" She pointed to the largest screen above our heads just before hurrying back to her own table. "I have a feeling we all might be in trouble!"

I did not agree. Tonight, Dr. Steve had selected his categories based on a holiday theme, and the holiday he'd chosen was Halloween.

So with categories like Haunted Houses, Ghosts and Ghouls, Spooky Music, I Want Candy, and Witches, it seemed like the

Losers might have an unfair advantage over everyone else, even if none of them knew it.

"Thank God," Yasmin said, confidently scrawling our team name at the top of our answer sheet. "Things might finally go our way for once."

"Have you ever considered changing your team name to something that doesn't have the word *loser* in it?" Derrick asked.

"Why would we do that?"

"Because it could be a self-fulfilling prophecy. Maybe it's why you never win."

Yasmin shot him a dirty look. "Jess, I'm not sure about this guy. If you want to keep hanging out with him, you might have to leave him at home next time."

She was only half joking. Yasmin took her trivia very seriously.

I was giving Derrick a mock-reproachful look when Sal and Mark appeared with the beer and wine.

"You girls are never gonna guess who I ran into at the bar." Mark slid wineglasses and frozen beer steins in front of us.

"If you're going to say the mayor, don't." Dina was pouring pinot grigio from the carafe Sal had brought over into our glasses. "I already spotted her over at the table with the rest of the Right Honorables."

"The mayor's here?" I looked around and saw her sitting with her wife and several of West Harbor's judges, along with the city attorney and a couple council members.

Would this be a good time to sneak Esther's letter to Margo Dunleavy? Probably not, with Esther so close by at the hostess booth. She hadn't wanted her parents to know anything about her magic.

But if I could catch Margo alone . . .

Sal looked, too. "Oh, damn. Half of city hall is here. They're great at this. We're gonna get creamed."

"No, we're not." Yasmin was exuding confidence. "What do they know about witches? We've got two of the witchiest witches in town sitting right here next to us. We're going to ice those nerds."

"The mayor's not who I was talking about," Mark said. "I meant Rosalie Hopkins."

"Rosalie really is here?" The hair on the back of my neck rose. I'd known she'd be there, of course, even hearing her name caused me anxiety. That woman had given me paranormal PTSD.

"Yeah. She just went back to her seat at that table over there with the Veuve Clique Ohs."

I swung around to look, then let out an inward groan. Rosalie was there, all right, sitting in one of her many pastel-colored cashmere sweater sets and sipping champagne while idly chatting with her friends from the Yacht Club. Billy—who'd evidently come straight from work, since he was wearing a suit—seemed to sense my gaze and began turning his head toward me.

"Oh, God." I ducked behind a menu, pretending to be searching for something to order.

"Subtle," remarked Derrick.

"I don't care." I kept my face buried in the menu. "Is he still looking over here?"

"Uh." Derrick shook his head. "No. One of his kids just came up and is talking to him. At least I think it's his kid. A young girl in a cheerleading outfit?"

"Lizzie." I lowered the menu and peeked. Billy was engrossed in conversation with his daughter, who was a smaller, perkier version of Rosalie. Dressed in a West Harbor High junior varsity cheerleading uniform, her blond hair was swept into a high ponytail tied with a large maroon bow. Lizzie had a sweet face and, from all I'd heard on the teen circuit, an even sweeter disposition.

But it was the adoring look on Billy that got to me. Billy clearly cherished his kids. Rosalie had given him exactly what he'd always wanted: a family of his own to love. Maybe she wasn't as bad as I thought.

Or maybe the spell Dina and I had cast had actually worked.

"*Good*," I said, as I turned back to my menu and began to read it, though I mostly knew it by heart.

Derrick raised a quizzical eyebrow. "Good what?"

"I mean . . . the food is good here." I hadn't meant to share my musings on Billy out loud. "Do you want something more to eat than just nachos? I really like the burger."

"Sure," he said, grinning at something he seemed to find amusing. "Let's make it two."

I signaled our server and put in our order for two cheeseburgers with fries just as Dr. Steve, the trivia master, began welcoming everyone over the microphone. The game was starting.

Meanwhile, Mark was complaining. "I really don't know what you all have against Rosalie."

"Shhh." Dina was almost as intense during Trivia as her sister-in-law, because it was one of the only nights Mark took off from the restaurant. "Dr. Steve is speaking."

"She's just a very nice person when you get to know her," Mark said.

"Mark, what are you talking about?"

"Rosalie."

"*What?*"

"Rosalie Hopkins."

Dr. Steve had uploaded the first question. It flashed onto the screens above our heads in the Haunted House category. Dina spun around on her stool and hissed, so she wouldn't be heard by nearby teams, "Sleepy Hollow. It's Sleepy Hollow, isn't it?"

Derrick agreed. "I was going to say Sleepy Hollow."

"Write that down," Dina commanded Yasmin, who had the pen. "Sleepy Hollow!"

"Wait a minute," I said. Something was bothering me. "Mark, what were you just saying about Rosalie?"

"I said she's actually very sweet once you get to know her." Mark chewed thoughtfully on a mouthful of nachos. "And Billy. He's such a great guy. I don't know how we've overlooked that for so long."

"Mark," I said. "Are you all right?"

"Yeah," he said, smiling at me. "Never better. I was just thinking. Don't you agree that Rosalie and Billy are great? Just a really cool couple. I don't know why we don't hang out with them more."

Dr. Steve posted another question, and Dina whipped around. "Who is the earliest recorded witch? You guys? First recorded witch? Hecate?"

"Actually," Derrick said, "it's the Witch of Endor in the Bible, First Book of Samuel."

Dina gasped. "It is! You're right. Yasmin, write that down."

"Uh," I said. "Mark, can you ask Dina what you just asked me? About Rosalie and Billy."

"Sure." Mark turned toward Dina. "Honey, how come we don't hang out with Rosalie and Billy?"

Dina looked away from the screen above our heads long enough to stare at him. "What the hell are you talking about?"

"They're such a nice couple. We should really have them over sometime."

"Are you kidding? *Now* you decide to mess with me?"

"I'm not messing with you." Mark's eyes were wide—but I noticed they also had a slightly glassy haze to them, like the streetlamp outside, as if the mist from the sea had rolled in and was obscuring their light. "Maybe we should invite them to the restaurant for Sunday Gravy."

"Rosalie and Billy. *Billy Walker?*"

"Yeah." He shrugged, smiling pleasantly. "Why not?"

Dina's gaze flicked over toward me. "What's wrong with him?"

Concerned, I shook my head. "I don't know. Mark. *Mark.*"

It was loud in the restaurant, with the buzz of all the teams, the drone of the baseball playoffs on the TV screens that weren't projecting the trivia questions, the bing-bong of the games over in the video arcade, and Dr. Steve's voice over the microphone. Plus loud rock was being pumped out over the Brewport's sound system: I recognized their classic rock station as being from the same music streaming service I used at Enchantments, only mine was set to Coffee Shop.

But Mark was only sitting a foot or two away from me. He should have been able to hear me. It still took a few moments for him to respond. When he did, it was with the same slow, glassy-eyed look I'd noticed before.

"Yeah?" he asked, and took a tiny sip of his beer.

"Mark," I asked. "How long have you felt this way about Rosalie and Billy?"

"Oh, I don't know," he said, thoughtfully. Mark never did anything thoughtfully. He did it quick, and thought about it later. "I guess it's been coming on slowly over time. But it really struck me just now, up at the bar, when I ran into Rosalie, and she gave me one of her homemade muffins. Those things are *delicious.*"

Derrick

A True Witch acknowledges that evil exists, and does
their best whenever possible to combat it.

Rule Number Seven of the Nine Rules
World Council of Witches

Derrick had witnessed magic in all of its many forms around the
world. Nyama in West Africa. Kotodama in Japan. Seiðr in Ice-
land.

But he'd never witnessed anything quite like what was happening in West Harbor, a place where magic seemed to be emanating from everywhere and everyone—even from the people he
least expected.

The second Jess's friend Mark mentioned the word "muffin,"
Derrick glanced back toward the high top at which Rosalie and
her husband were sitting and saw what he'd failed to notice before: the basket sitting on the floor beside them . . . a basket
that was the twin of the one Rosalie had dropped off at Jessica's
house.

Only the cellophane wrapping around this one had been broken open.

And on the table in front of the people sitting around Rosalie were crumpled cellophane wrappers and strings of raffia . . . the remnants of the muffins they'd consumed.

"What the *hell*," he heard Jessica mutter. She'd just noticed the same thing.

"You guys." Yasmin turned around, pen in hand, to whisper to them urgently. "You guys, which country executed the most people for practicing witchcraft, and how many people was it?"

"Germany," Derrick said. "Forty thousand." But the response was automatic. To Jessica, he said in a low voice, "Rosalie's used a friendship spell."

"Love muffins." Jessica's normally warm brown eyes were blazing with anger. "I can't believe it. She's handing out love muffins. What is she *thinking*?"

"That she wants people to like her."

Jessica snorted. "She's not a kid anymore. What kind of *adult* would resort to a friendship spell to get people to like them?"

One who is up to no good. But aloud, he only asked, "Has she ever done anything like this before?"

"Aside from the love spell she tried to do on Billy? Not that I know of. Baking is more Dina's thing, really."

Dina, meanwhile, was still trying to figure out what was going on with Mark.

"What do you mean, Rosalie gave you one of her muffins?" If Jessica's eyes were blazing, Dina's were twin nuclear warheads. And detonation was imminent.

"It was so good." Mark was smiling amiably in the direction of the Veuve Clique Ohs. "How come you never make muffins that good, hon?"

"That's it." The legs of Dina's stool scraped noisily against the cement floor as she pushed herself away from the table. "Where is that witch? I'll show her what happens when you give my boy-friend a muffin—"

But when the diminutive brunette jumped off her stool to storm away in Rosalie's direction, Derrick caught her arm.

"Hold on," he said. "Violence is never the answer."

"Are you serious?" Dina wrenched her arm from his grasp. Her gaze had gone from DEFCON Five to One in seconds. "*Look at him. She's going to have to pay for this. My boyfriend is high on magic.*"

"He isn't high." Derrick steered Dina gently back into her seat. He was trying very hard to make it look as if everything was normal over at the Get In, Losers table, even though of course everything was far from normal—starting with the fact that their team name was so terrible. "It's only a friendship spell."

"A *friendship* spell?" Dina spat. "I'll show that witch some friendship. My foot's about to get *real* friendly with her—"

"I don't know where all this hostility toward Rosalie is com-ing from," Mark said, holding out his hands in a helpless gesture. "She's never been anything but nice to us."

Dina stared at him in horror. "What the *actual* f—"

"Hey." Yasmin tapped urgently on the carafe of wine to get their attention. "How many people accused of witchcraft were burned at the stake in Salem?"

"None," Sal said, and all eyes went to him for a change.

"What?" He shrugged his large shoulders. "It's a trick ques-tion. I saw it on the History channel. No people accused of witch-craft in Salem were burned at the stake. They were either hanged or crushed to death beneath stones."

"Gross," Yasmin said, and wrote down *Zero*.

"Dee." Jessica had left her own stool, and now laid a hand on her friend's arm to keep her from physically launching herself at Rosalie. People were beginning to glance in their direction, mostly because of the agitation emanating from Dina. "You know friendship spells wear off in a few days."

"In a few days it will be the Tricentennial Ball." Dina slid back into her seat, but she didn't look happy about it. "She's trying to get everybody on her side so they'll write extra nice reviews of her event online."

Derrick had the feeling that Rosalie's motives for handing out the muffins were a bit darker than a desire for positive online feedback.

"Is this kind of thing okay with whoever you work for?" Dina asked Derrick bitterly. "Slipping people happy muffins without their consent?"

"No," he said. "It is not."

"Well, then what are you going to do about it?"

"This," Derrick said, and he held his right hand out to Mark. "How are you doing, Mark?"

Mark slipped his hand automatically into Derrick's, giving him a hearty handshake. Not as hearty as the one Mark had given him when they'd met. But Mark hadn't been strung out on Rosalie's love muffins then. "Hey, man," he said. "Thanks, I'm doing good. How are—"

Mark broke off with a perplexed expression. He seemed to be hearing something the rest of them couldn't. He cocked his head, listening, while Derrick continued to gently clasp the other man's fingers.

It wasn't something Derrick ever learned consciously to do. It wasn't something he'd ever even known he *could* do until one day, when he'd been a kid, a favorite horse had run afoul of some barbed wire, and Derrick, in a panic, had laid his hands upon the wounds.

Like magic, the horse had calmed, the pain disappearing. The wounds themselves had healed up by the time the vet arrived.

A miracle, anyone else would have called it. But his father had taken one look, shook his head, and sighed.

"Your damned mother," he'd said to Derrick—not without affection.

Maybe Derrick had inherited the ability from her. Or maybe it had been another one of her gifts. Since she only gave him one a year—which was also the number of times per year she visited him, since other obligations kept her busy traveling all over the world—she tried to make her presents especially impressive.

True, as a boy he'd have preferred a Nintendo, particularly since, after that, it was Derrick who got called anytime an animal—or ranch hand—fell ill or was injured on the farm.

But the gift of healing is what his mother gave him, and so it was what he gave back to others . . . like now, in the restaurant, holding Mark's hand as he waited for the foggy glaze in the other man's eyes to lift.

"What . . ." Mark blinked a few times. Then Derrick saw the clarity return, seeping back like the tide beneath the dock. Mark hastily snatched his fingers from Derrick's.

"Hey, bro." His voice sounded once again like his own, his diction crisp and rapid-fire. "What's going on?"

"*What's going on?*" Dina struck her boyfriend in the shoulder. Her gaze was still fiery, but now her eyes were lit with the warmth of affection and worry, not rage. "*What's going on?* What's going on is that Rosalie gave you one of her homemade happy muffins and *you ate it*. What the hell is the matter with you?"

Mark shook his head, his long dark hair brushing his shoulders. "What? No, that didn't happen."

"Yes, it did. You were going on and on about how good it was and how great she and Billy are."

"No." But Mark looked vaguely troubled, as if he did have

some distant memory of . . . something. "I don't know what you're talking about. I hate that stupid witch and her dopey husband. I always have."

"That's not what you were saying two minutes ago." Dina pointed at Derrick. "If he hadn't done his little magic trick with his fingers on you, you'd probably still be all, *Oh, Rosalie and Billy, they're so great, why don't we get together with them for Sunday Gravy?*"

Mark laughed—but nervously. "I literally never said that."

"You *literally* did."

Derrick felt a hand slide into his. He looked down and saw Jessica looking up at him, her face very pale under the bright lights of the brew pub.

"Thank you," she said, in a voice so quiet he wouldn't have heard her if his very being hadn't become attuned, over the past few days, to her every word, her every movement, her every breath.

He squeezed her fingers in his. "I didn't do anything."

"You did." Her eyes, in all the wild lights around them, looked larger and darker than ever. Her hand, so warm and alive in his, felt oddly reassuring. "Even Mark knows it, deep down. I don't know how you did it, but you did. Thank you."

"You don't have to thank me. It's my job." The words were automatic, and came out sounding more gruff than he meant them to.

But that's because he was filled with sudden emotion—emotion he couldn't identify. All he could think was, *Why is she thanking me? Doesn't she know? Doesn't she know how I feel about her?*

But evidently she didn't, since she began to pull her hand away, her voice going tart as the essence of bergamot.

"Oh, so you were only doing your job? Well, in that case—"

He tightened his grip on her fingers, keeping her anchored beside him.

"There might be mitigating circumstances in this case that may have caused me to go a little above and beyond my job," he admitted.

The smile returned to her eyes—and her lips. "Mitigating circumstances? Would *I* qualify as one of those?"

He couldn't help smiling back. "It could be—"

"M&M's!" Yasmin cried, startling everyone. Her gaze was totally focused on the screens overhead. "They're the candy that melts in your mouth and not in your hand, right?"

"Honey." Sal shook his head at his wife as she happily scrawled her response onto the answer sheet. "Read the room."

It was good advice. Pay less attention to the attractive woman sitting beside him, radiating sexual energy—at least, to Derrick—and more to what was going on in the room around him. That's how he happened to notice that Rosalie had left her table. A quick scan of the restaurant showed him that she was over by the entrance to the video arcade, talking to a boy who could only be her son. He was the spitting image of Billy, only much younger, shorter, and dressed in skinny jeans.

"Excuse me," Derrick said, releasing Jessica's hand and reaching for the empty beer pitcher and wine carafe. "I have the next round."

"Oh." Jessica hadn't noticed Rosalie. "You don't have to do that. We can ask the server—"

"It's no trouble." Derrick made his way through the throng gathered around the bar and set both containers down. "Two more for that table over there, please," he said to the first server who acknowledged him, and pointed back toward the Get In, Losers table. When the bartender nodded, Derrick turned toward the entrance to the video arcade.

Rosalie's back was to him. She had her wallet open and was handing a fifty-dollar bill to her son. Derrick was close enough that he could hear her, despite the thrum of the bar and music from the games inside the video arcade.

"Now, I want you to share this with your sister," Rosalie was saying to the boy.

"Aw, Mom," the kid said, looking annoyed. He had his father's dark hair, only he'd slicked it down in the front with some kind of product to make his bangs resemble those of a member of a boy band Derrick had seen on the front of a magazine at the airport. "That's not enough!"

"Use your allowance, then." Rosalie's voice was crisp. "That's what it's for."

The boy made a face, then spun away from his mother in irritation. Derrick reflected that if he'd ever responded to either of his parents in such a manner, he'd never have seen an allowance again, but Rosalie seemed unfazed. She closed her wallet and turned around to head back to her table . . .

But instead she walked straight into Derrick, who was standing behind her, his arms folded across his chest.

"Hello," he said with a smile. "I think it's time we have a chat, don't you?"

Rosalie paled visibly under the bright lights of the flat screens above their heads. But he didn't miss the way her gaze dropped down to the amulet at his neck.

"Oh, I . . . uh . . ." She glanced toward her table, but neither her husband nor any of the Veuve Clique Ohs were looking in her direction. "I'm sorry, but I don't know what you mean. I really should get back to—"

"Oh, you know exactly what I mean. That's why you came over this morning with your magic muffins—and why you're passing them out here, as well. Billy may have gone home yesterday and told you Jessica got a new boyfriend, but when you met me this morning, you suspected there was something more going on, didn't you?"

Her blue-eyed gaze was darting all over the place. She really wasn't very good at this. "I don't—I really don't—"

"Oh, I think you do. In fact, after that stunt you just pulled, I think I deserve five minutes of your time." Derrick motioned toward the exit. "Shall we go outside to discuss this? Or do you want to do it in front of your husband who, from what I gather, isn't aware of your . . . extracurricular activities?"

Her gaze flew toward Billy, who was laughing with one of her friends. Then, before Derrick could say another word, Rosalie spun on one of her high heels and marched toward the nearest door, which happened to let out onto the pier. He followed, reflecting that everyone had their secrets . . . but the one Rosalie was keeping from her spouse had to be one of the biggest.

The burst of wind that hit him the moment he stepped outside was so strong, it snapped the door shut behind him. It was cold, too, but not as cold as the spray of salt water that crashed against the side of the decking where they were standing. It had been noisy inside—a rude onslaught of music and seemingly endless chatter from both the television screens and the patrons—but the moment the wind knocked the door shut, all of that ended.

Now there was a different kind of noise: the howl of the wind and the splashing of water surging around the pylons beneath them, the hard rhythmic slap of the waves hitting the seawall beyond. The moon was still busy playing hide-and-seek with the dark storm clouds overhead that were being sent skidding fast across the sky by the wind.

The foul weather wasn't courtesy of Rosalie's gift, however.

He knew even the most powerful storm witch couldn't whip up a gale this fast.

That didn't mean that Rosalie was happy, though.

"This is harassment," she protested, hugging her arms to her chest as the wind buffeted her blond hair around her face. "I don't even know who you are."

"Don't you?" Derrick lifted an eyebrow. "We were introduced this morning."

"Who you *really* are." She pointed at the amulet he wore around his neck. "Where did you get that? And why does Jessica have one? I reported you, you know, for stolen—"

"I didn't steal anything," he said. "And speaking of reporting, does your precious World Council of Witches know that you're handing out magic muffins to members of the general public?"

In the fluorescent safety lighting the Dodges had installed along the pier outside their restaurant, he saw her make a face that was remarkably similar to the one her son had made when she'd told him he had to share the fifty-dollar bill with his sister.

"I didn't do anything wrong." The wind and sea were churning so wildly, her voice was barely audible.

"Didn't you?"

"No!" Rosalie shoved loose strands of hair from her mouth, where they were sticking to her lip gloss. "Rule number three: 'A true Witch does not seek power through the suffering of others.' Friendship spells don't cause suffering. People enjoy my muffins."

"I think that might be an overly generous interpretation of the rule."

Rosalie didn't like hearing this. Her glossy lips twisted. "I don't know why you think I have to stand here and listen to anything you say. I called the World Council of Witches, and you're not a member. No one there has ever heard of you. No one. Not even Bartholomew Brewster himself."

Derrick's grin broadened. "So the old Grand Sorcerer said he didn't know me, did he? Well, isn't that a kick in the pants."

Rosalie was so focused on her own indignation, she wasn't paying attention to Derrick's smile. "And he said I should warn Jessica that you're not a Council member, and that you never have been!"

That made his smile disappear. "She already knows."

This set her blinking, and not just at the salt spray the wind was still kicking up at them. "She . . . she does?"

"Of course she does. Do you think this is a game? The fate of this town rests on what happens Thursday night. I think you know that. I think you're well aware of it, as a matter of fact. And what are you doing to help, except going around, phoning Bart Brewster to complain, and giving out magic muffins?"

"How—" She looked stunned. "How do you know about Thursday? Unless . . . unless you're here to stop it!"

"Trying to stop whatever it is *you're* doing? *Absolutely.* You don't seem to have the slightest idea what it is you're playing at here, Rosalie. If the witching community doesn't work *together* to try to stop this rift, people are going to die, or at least get hurt—like Jessica Gold got hurt yesterday, when you chose to nearly kill her"—Rosalie sucked in her breath to object, but Derrick continued relentlessly—"*and* destroyed her car. Honestly, how did you think that was going to help? Now, you may not like that I'm here, but you have to admit that it's a good thing I am. Because otherwise, you would still be worrying about how people feel about the party you're throwing for your town instead of focusing on what's actually important right now: keeping that town from being destroyed by a very real, very deadly threat."

Now Rosalie didn't look stunned. She looked frightened.

He wasn't sure it was because of what he'd said, however. The waves around them were growing stronger. They were beginning to breach the concrete seawall at the end of the pier, near the front of the restaurant. Some diners trying to enter the place got splashed, and screamed in both delight and terror.

Rosalie, seeing this, blinked rapidly.

"I—I *am* focusing on keeping this town from being destroyed," she stammered. "That's why I'm the board chair of the West Harbor Tricentennial Committee. I want to bring people together to celebrate our history and heritage. And I had nothing to do with what happened to Jess. That was—that was—"

"Sure. Whatever you say. Look, here's what's going to happen," he said, very calmly—more calmly than he felt. "You're going to take the rest of those muffins home tonight and destroy them, and any other baked goods you might have that could, in any way, alter anyone's feelings about you. Is that understood?"

Rosalie didn't nod. Her face—her entire being—seemed frozen, but whether with cold, fear, or anger, it was impossible to say.

"And then," he went on, "for the rest of this week, and every week after this for the rest of time, if West Harbor continues to exist, you're going to do everything you can to make Jessica Gold's life easier, not harder. Do I make myself clear?"

"*Who are you?*" Rosalie asked, looking not at him but at a rogue wave to one side of the pier that was so enormous, it managed to surge over the seawall and into the restaurant's parking lot, deluging the cars there. Her eyes flashed wide in the safety lighting. "How are you doing this?"

"I'm not doing anything," he said in a tired voice. "Except standing here trying to talk to you like we're two good witches. Because that's what we are, right?"

Another wave, this one even bigger than the last, heaved

relentlessly toward the shore, seeming to head straight for them. The wind's howl grew louder, as did the thrum of the sea.

"Now," Derrick said. "Are you going to leave Jessica—"

"Yes!" Rosalie threw her hands over her face to protect it from the onslaught of ice water she was expecting. "I'll leave her alone! I swear!"

But instead of breaking over the pier railing, the wave suddenly collapsed, dipping down beneath the planks upon which they were standing, and causing only their feet to get sprayed.

"And?" Derrick asked.

"And make her life easier," Rosalie said. The words seemed to have been wrung out of her. "From now on."

"Perfect." Derrick drew his cell phone from his pocket to check the time. "Oh, look. It's late. We'd better get back inside."

"Please." Rosalie's voice was weak. "Please tell me. Who *are* you?"

He blinked at her. "You already know. I'm Derrick Winters."

He left Rosalie staring after him, her eyes burning with resentment— and maybe a little bit of fear.

Back inside, a new pitcher of beer and carafe of wine had been delivered to the Get In, Losers table, as well as two cheeseburgers. Jessica was digging into hers, and looked up reproachfully when he appeared.

"Where have you been?" she asked. "Your food's getting cold."

"Sorry," he said, and slid onto his stool. "Had to make a quick call. This looks delicious."

He realized he was starving. The food smelled especially good after the small victory he'd scored.

"Here," Jessica said. He could barely hear her over the din from the baseball and hockey games, the music, and the other customers. "Have some ketchup. Or are you a mayo and fries kind of person?"

"Both. Thanks."

She grinned a little wickedly at him. "Both, huh? I like that in a man."

He grinned back at her.

Mark and Dina had stopped arguing. They now had their arms around each other and were murmuring lovingly to one another.

"You guys." Yasmin whipped around on her stool. "You guys, look. Dr. Steve has finished tabulating the results."

And then she and Dina both let out ear-piercing screams. Because there, on the flat screen above their heads—and all the other flat screens in the restaurant that weren't showing sports— was the trivia team with the most points that evening: *Get In, Losers*.

"We won!" Dina and Yasmin leaned across Sal to hug one another, while he protectively snatched his beer out of their way.

"Yay," Jessica said, raising her glass. "Finally! To the Losers!"

"To the Losers!"

Everyone at the table raised their glasses in a joyful toast as Derrick noted Rosalie hurrying back into the restaurant from outside. The salt spray had nearly flattened her hair to her head. She had to have been cold and uncomfortable. But no one would have been able to tell from the way she was smiling and chatting with her friends and husband, looking everywhere but in Derrick's direction.

He and Jessica and her friends were picking out their West Harbor Brewport T-shirts and accepting the congratulations of Dr. Steve when Esther's father walked over and asked if he could borrow the trivia master's microphone. When Dr. Steve told him of course, the restaurant owner's voice came booming over the sound system.

"Sorry to interrupt the fun, folks," he said. "But anyone with a car parked near the seawall might want to think about moving it. The tide's acting up again, and the weather service just issued another coastal flood warning."

A number of patrons stood up and reached for their coats, and even more groaned, but Esther's father put out a hand to calm them.

"Come on, it's not that bad. There's plenty of room in the back parking lot. Sorry again for the interruption, and thanks, as always, for dining at the Brewport!"

"Well," Sal said. "That's us. I'll go round up the kids. It's past their bedtime anyway."

"Yeah, we'd better leave, too," Dina said, sliding an arm around Mark's waist. "I have to go bone this one's brains out."

"Ew, Dina." Jessica winced.

"Why?" Dina asked, a bright glint in her eyes. "It's not like you two are going to go home and do anything different."

"On that note," Jessica said. "Good night, Losers."

They were strolling arm in arm toward the door when Derrick's gaze fell upon Rosalie. She was gathering up her family, too. The son was resisting, whining that he still had money left on his game card, but the daughter was coming along willingly enough. Billy was waving farewell to the other Veuve Clique Ohs like he didn't have a care in the world. Rosalie was giving a very good imitation of the same . . . until her gaze happened to fall upon Derrick. Then she looked quickly away.

But he didn't miss how the smile on her face went from looking genuine to fixed, like a mannequin's.

He wasn't the only one who'd noticed.

"What's up with Rosalie?" Jessica asked him. "I've never seen her smile so fake. Do you think she knows we're on to her about the muffins?"

"Oh," Derrick said, taking her hand. "I think she knows."

"Is that why the weather's turned? Is she trying to punish us?"

"No," Derrick said. "This weather is courtesy of someone else."

"Who?"

He smiled and squeezed her hand. "Mother Nature."

Jessica

Grow basil in a pot inside thy home to promote prosperity and keep thy lover true. Use its leaves to thicken pottage stew.

Goody Fletcher,
Book of Useful Household Tips

I did, in fact, go home and bone Derrick's brains out. Or at least I tried to. When I woke up the next morning, his side of my bed was empty.

If he was able to put his clothes back on and leave, he probably still had some brain cells left.

Plus I saw that the clothes he'd put on were his running gear. If he was out exercising, I definitely hadn't fulfilled my duties.

But that was the least of my problems, it turned out. The reason I woke up was the insistent *beep beep beep* of a truck reversing in front of my house.

I live on a small street, so it's not like we get that much traffic.

And having lived there most of my life, I of course knew everything about my neighbors. So I knew it was highly unusual for any of them to get a delivery they hadn't told me about in advance.

So of course I leaped from the bed—disturbing Pye, who was curled at the end of it—and ran to the window.

I don't think I could describe my shock at seeing a bright blue Mini Cooper Electric Hardtop being unloaded from an open car hauler that had the Hopkins Motors logo written across the side. There was a large white bow on the roof of the car.

"What the—"

Billy had promised me a loaner. But he'd never said he was delivering it. He'd said I should stop by to pick it up.

Flinging on a robe and a pair of boots, I hurried downstairs and threw open the front door just as a man with a clipboard in his hand was about to knock on it.

"Oh, hey, there," he said, affably. "You Jessica Gold?"

"Yes."

I could see that behind him, my neighbors were already gathering at the edge of their yards, some brandishing rakes to make it look as if they had a reason to be outside at such an early hour on such a chilly October morning. But most hadn't bothered, and were simply holding mugs of steaming coffee in their hands, enjoying the show.

"Car for you." The man handed me the clipboard and a pen. "You need to sign for it."

"I think there's been a mistake." But there it was: a bill of sale signed by William Walker, CFO of Hopkins Motors, listing the car as having been paid in full. "I was supposed to come to the lot and borrow a car—"

"This ain't a loaner," the man said with a chuckle. "It's for you to keep, soon as you sign for it." He indicated where my signature was needed, down at the bottom, beneath Billy's. Like someone in a dream, I signed. "That's good. And on the next page, too."

"That's why I think there's been a mistake," I prattled on. "I haven't bought a new car. Billy Walker said that Hopkins Motors was going to fix my old car."

"Well, I guess it couldn't be fixed." The tag on the man's coveralls said that his name was Earl. Pye seemed to like him—though Pye liked almost everyone—since he was rubbing his head against Earl's legs. "'Cause he got you a whole new car instead. Even the taxes been paid. Mr. Walker told me to tell you that all you need to do is have a charging station installed, and call your insurance company to add this car to your policy. Oh, and I'm supposed to give you these."

Earl reached into the pocket of his coveralls, then withdrew an envelope and set of keys, both of which he dropped into my hand.

"But . . ." I stared down at the items in my hand. "Sir . . . I don't—"

It was too late. Earl waved away my protests. He ambled back to his truck, climbed in, and drove away, leaving the Mini gleaming in my driveway beside Derrick's beat-up rental car, and Pye meowing after him in farewell.

"Uh," I said, looking down at the keys. What was happening?

I assumed that as owner—co-owner—of Hopkins Motors, Billy got a significant discount on the cars he sold.

But even so. This was ridiculous.

"Isn't your birthday in February?" my neighbor Annalise asked, as she sipped her coffee. Annalise and her husband, Ronnie, had lived next door since before I was born. They knew everything about me, except of course the most important thing, that I was a witch.

"It is," I said.

"So why is Billy Walker giving you a new car when it's not even your birthday?"

"That's a good question." I tore open the envelope Earl had left me.

Inside was a card with a gold rose on the front. When I opened it, I was flabbergasted to see only two words, scrawled in bubbly cursive, followed by a single letter.

I'm sorry.
R.

Rosalie. It was the same card that had been inside the basket of muffins she'd given me (and that I'd thrown into a dumpster behind Office Depot yesterday on my way into work, even before I'd known they were love muffins. No animals or freegans were likely to find and ingest them there).

But why would Rosalie be apologizing to me? And why would she give me a car—or rather, force her husband to?

"It sure is pretty," remarked Val, who was retired from the post office.

"Yes," I said. It *was* a pretty car. Prettier than Bluebell by a mile. And much more energy efficient. "But I can't possibly keep it."

"Why not?" Val shrugged. "Take that boy for all he's worth."

The rest of my neighbors nodded in agreement. Although it had been more than ten years earlier, all of them seemed to remember Billy's screaming of my name outside my bedroom window late at night when I'd refused to come down.

Awkward that none of them had thought to call the police or even tell my parents about it at the time.

Oh, well.

I heard the steady slap of footsteps, and looked up from the car to see Derrick running down my street. On such a chilly gray

October morning, with his long blond hair, silver eyes, and wide shoulders, he looked like a Viking racing through the mist across a battlefield, toward his ladylove.

I won't lie: it was hot.

My neighbors must have thought the same thing, since when Derrick reached me, panting and sweaty, and bent to kiss my cheek, I saw all of them smile, even grumpy Val.

"Good morning," Derrick said. "Is everything all right?"

I could see why he'd ask. I was standing outside in my robe. He must have thought his Nordic protection spell had failed, and some kind of supernatural threat had forced me from the house while he'd been out running.

But all of my neighbors only nodded their heads. Everything was all right.

Then Derrick's gaze fell on the car. "Where did this come from?"

"Where do you think?" I showed him Rosalie's card.

He raised an eyebrow while reading it, then took a swig from the battered metal water bottle he carried when he ran. "How unexpectedly generous of her."

"Isn't it?" I glanced back at my neighbors, all of whom were still watching us with rapt attention.

But when they saw my gaze swing their way, they pretended to be busy doing something else, now that Derrick was around. Val went back to raking, and Annalise suddenly had an important text in her phone that needed her attention.

"Maybe," I said, "we should talk about this inside."

"Yeah." Derrick gave the car an appreciative sweep with his hand, admiring its smooth curves. "Let's do that."

"See you later," I said to my neighbors, who all called cheerful goodbyes back to me and returned to their pretend yard work.

No sooner had I shut the door behind us and spun around to

tell Derrick what a duplicitous piece of garbage Rosalie was—
because I didn't for a second believe that her gift hadn't come
with some kind of strings attached, or at least faulty brake lines—
than I found that he'd stripped off his shirt and was headed for my
washer/dryer, which were located in the mudroom.

"What . . ." It was difficult for me to concentrate on my outrage over Rosalie's blatant attempt to manipulate me when there
was a half-naked man striding through my living room.

"Yes?" He paused to sit on one of my dining room chairs to
pull off his running shoes.

"I mean, it's not like she can just give me a car and think I'm
going to forgive her."

"Of course not." His socks came off next.

"It's probably booby-trapped in some way. Like when I go
down a hill, the transmission will burst into flames and I'll crash
into the Sound and drown."

He cocked his head thoughtfully. "I don't think so. Because
number one, that isn't how transmissions work, and number two,
that would reflect badly on Hopkins Motors. And if Rosalie is
anything, it's proud of her family name."

"Okay, but—I can't just accept it. With my history with Billy,
it wouldn't be right."

"After the way Rosalie has treated you," he said, standing up,
"I think it's more than right. I think you not only can't turn it
down, you deserve it."

Then he pulled his joggers down. Beneath them he was only
wearing a pair of briefs. A very tight pair of briefs, which he casually peeled off as he spoke and tossed into the washer.

"Why don't we take a shower together," he suggested, "then
get changed and take the car for a test-drive over to Wake Up
West Harbor for breakfast? Then you can decide."

What magic was this? I wondered, as I found myself nodding

and then heading toward the stairs with him, as if he were a light-house and I was some storm-tossed vessel, allowing him to lead me to the safety of shore?

But of course the witch in me knew it wasn't magic at all. It was him.

And that might have been more frightening—and yet exciting—than any enchantment.

Derrick

A True Witch keeps the existence of magic and witchcraft a secret from the non-magical, knowing that their minds are too fragile to handle the truth.

Rule Number Eight of the Nine Rules
World Council of Witches

Derrick was in trouble. He'd known it when the server at Wake Up West Harbor looked at him as soon as he and Jessica sat down and said, "Cheese Danish and an Americano, black. Am I right?"

But he'd had an inkling even earlier, when he'd been on his run and someone living blocks away from Jessica opened their front door to pick up the newspaper, saw him, waved, and called out, "Congratulations on the win last night!"

At first he hadn't understood what she was talking about. Then he'd remembered: Tuesday Night Trivia.

They knew him. The people of West Harbor were beginning to recognize him on sight.

Not just recognize him, but smile and wave to him, and recall his favorite breakfast order.

None of this was good. None of this was good at all.

It confirmed what he'd already realized that morning, waking in Jessica's bed—Pye a dead weight on top of him, a gentle rain pattering down on the roof above him, Jessica sleeping there so peacefully beside him. This was the happiest he'd ever felt in his life.

All signs pointed to the fact that West Harbor was about to suffer another of its ninety year calamities. In forty-eight hours—maybe less—this town would be underwater, on fire, or possibly simply a gaping hole. And because the population of this sleepy village was now so dense, this time the death toll would be staggering.

Yet he could not remember ever feeling this happy.

How was he supposed to do his job if he couldn't be impartial?

He'd thought that dragging himself out for a run in that cold, stinging rain would cure him, smack some sense into him, bring him back to reality.

But the only thing that happened was the rain stopped, he saw the neighbor, and then he saw the object of his happiness herself, standing outside her house in her robe, and his heart seized up—until he realized she was safe.

That's when he knew that he wasn't going to be able to run away from the happiness he was feeling. Worse, that he wanted to stay. He cared. He actually *cared*. He wanted to come home to her like this every day.

Except that unless something extraordinary occurred, she soon wouldn't have a home.

This awareness pressed down on his heart more heavily than a hundred Pyes.

Not that there was anything he could do about it at the moment. Jessica had gotten over her perfectly legitimate fear that Rosalie had somehow booby-trapped her new car almost as soon as she got behind the wheel.

"I never thought I could love any car as much as Bluebell," Jessica said later, after their shower (and subsequent return to bed). They were sitting inside Wake Up West Harbor, at a table where she could gaze at her new car through the window. "But I think I could learn to."

This became even more evident when the server who'd brought them their breakfast suddenly let out an expletive after attempting to run Derrick's credit card to pay for breakfast—they were on paranormal business, Derrick reasoned when Jessica tried to argue with him that they should at least split the bill, so he should pay.

"Internet is down," Stacy, the server, groused.

Jessica reached immediately for her bag. "Ugh, again? I know how you feel. The Internet goes down at my shop all the time. But that's okay, I have cash. We really have to go." She wanted to get back into her new car as quickly as possible, to drive it some more. They were delivering more gowns she'd hemmed, including Gabby's.

"Yeah, but this time the Internet's down all over town." Stacy shook her head. She'd picked up her phone and was scrolling her texts. "Online school is canceled today. God knows what my kid is up to instead."

Jessica instantly snatched up her own phone.

"Oh my God. It's true." She leaned forward to show Derrick a text from Dina. "The king tide from last night took out a chunk of the road where, in their infinite wisdom, they laid the Internet cables."

Derrick knit his brow. "So what does that—"

"Sal's declared it a day of community service. He wants all the kids from the high school to go over to the village square to help clean and paint in preparation for tomorrow's festivities since they can't be in class." She shook her head so forcefully that her curls swayed. "Ha! Good luck with that."

Derrick considered this. "It might work to our advantage, though."

"How?"

"Now is the time for me to be training Esther—and you—for the fight ahead."

Anxiety creased Jessica's forehead at the word "fight," but she lifted her tea. "Let's go."

Which was how, a few hours later, they ended up standing in a barren field in front of a line of pumpkins Derrick had balanced along a wooden fence several dozen yards away.

"You can't be serious," Esther said, after Derrick had explained to her what he wanted her to do.

"Just try it."

Jessica was leaning against the hood of her car. Of course she knew the farmer who owned the field. She'd supplied his wife, daughters, and one son with clothes for all the important occasions in their lives—proms, graduations, weddings. Farmer Frank was more than willing to give her some of his more misshapen pumpkins that were unlikely to sell. He'd also allowed her to park on his back field for what she'd called "a little target practice."

"But I don't want to hurt you," Esther protested.

"They're pumpkins, Esther. And they're fifty feet away," Derrick pointed out. "And you didn't hurt anyone yesterday in Jessica's office."

"Yeah, but I could have."

Esther was hugging herself miserably. She'd been less than thrilled when Derrick and Jessica had shown up at her front door. Dressed in her pj's and fuzzy slippers, the kid had been watching a Marvel movie with her younger brothers, unbothered by West Harbor's lack of Internet. She surely wasn't the only teen in town who'd completely ignored the principal's plea to come to the village square to help clean it.

"Why would I want to do that?" she'd asked, when Jessica had whispered—unsure whether or not the girl's parents were within earshot—that today was the day to begin training for Thursday's supernatural battle with the powers of evil. "It's *cold* outside."

She wasn't wrong. It *was* cold. The sun continued to remain hidden behind a bank of gray clouds, and flocks of birds that hadn't already made their way south for the winter were darkening the sky as they fled for a warmer—and safer—location than frozen, doomed West Harbor.

The birds knew what was coming. Birds always knew.

But Jessica kept her tone upbeat, even as she turned up the faux fur collar of her coat against the icy gusts of wind that kept sweeping in from the Sound, tearing at the leaves that still remained on the trees at the edges of the field.

"Oh, come on, Esther," she'd said. "It will be fun! Don't you want to see what you could do with your powers if you really tried?"

The kid had glanced uncertainly back at the soft warm couch on which her brothers were piled with a bowl of popcorn, a blanket, and a big slobbery dog. "I guess. But I thought this whole thing was going to be more about learning how to do rune or tarot card readings. Are we actually going to be blowing people up?"

"Manipulating the energy around you," Derrick corrected her quickly. "No one is going to get blown up." He hoped.

For a moment the kid had looked disappointed. It was evident she'd have been more willing to come if blowing up people was on the table.

"Well," she'd said finally. "Gabby's at the salon all day, getting a blowout and spray tan for the stupid Harvest Princess selection thing tonight. So I guess I might as well come with you. I've seen this movie a hundred times before anyway."

Which was how they'd ended up in Farmer Frank's field, the kid having exchanged her pajamas for her usual Converse, sweatshirt, and leggings, this time paired with a down parka and a knit cap with a rainbow pom-pom on the top.

"So," she said, squinting through the lenses of her glasses at the pumpkins on the fence. "What is it that you want me to do again, exactly?"

"First I want you to feel the magic," Derrick said.

The kid looked skeptical. "There's magic at Farmer Frank's? My parents have been making me and my brothers come here to pick pumpkins since I was a little kid, and I've never once felt anything magical about it."

"There's magic everywhere," Jessica said from the warm hood of her new car. Derrick could tell by the dimples at the sides of her cheeks that she was trying not to laugh. "Its energy is present in every grain of salt, the leaf of every tree, every animal, and every person that inhabits the earth."

Esther scratched her nose. "You mean like the Force?"

"If that's how you want to think about it," Jessica said. The dimples deepened. He couldn't believe he'd never noticed them before. "The ability to manipulate that energy is one that every witch possesses."

Derrick was startled to hear his own words—or a version of them, anyway—coming out of Jessica's mouth.

"Magic is similar to the Force," she went on, "but it's more complicated than that. Magic is in the sun, the moon, the stars, and the rhythms of the sea. And a good witch learns to harness that magic and create positive things from it—kind of the way a seamstress creates something beautiful out of a bunch of cloth.

In some ways, a witch—a good witch—is a seamstress of the universe."

"You're already very good at harnessing magic, Esther," Derrick said. "But I—*we*—need you to get even better."

The kid nodded. "Because of the prophecy?"

"Right. Because of the prophecy."

"Okay. I'll try." Esther pulled her hat down more snugly over her ears, then turned toward the pumpkins. "What do you want me to do?"

"Try knocking down one of the pumpkins," Derrick suggested. "Like when you shut the window in Jessica's office."

"All right." Esther shrugged. "But I'm just letting you know, I'm pretty bad at sewing. You guys probably have the wrong girl."

A second later, she glanced at the misshapen pumpkin sitting on the fence post to the far right, then lifted a single hand. . . .

There was a flash of light, and then an explosion. Bits of orange pumpkin went flying everywhere, causing crows, perched high in the bare treetops, to take flight with loud, indignant cries.

Even though they were standing carefully out of range, Jessica let out a cry as well, and ducked behind her new car.

Derrick stared at the pumpkin carnage before them. Then he looked at Esther, who had her gloved fingers over her face, clearly as shocked as he and Jessica were by what she'd done.

"See?" she said, when she noticed his stare. "I told you. You have the wrong girl."

"Oh, no," he said. His smile was wide. "We absolutely have the right girl."

Jessica

A crow flying south means good fortune is about.
A crow flying north means trouble comes forth.

Goody Fletcher,
Book of Useful Household Tips

"I don't understand it," Esther said. "I've never been able to do that before. Not like *that*."

"It's because of her," Derrick said.

It was a minute or so before I realized he was talking about me. Both he and Esther were staring in my direction.

"*Me?*" I shook my head. "Oh, no. I had nothing to do with *this*."

I looked down at the bits of shattered gourd on the cold, hard ground. There were pumpkin seeds everywhere. It was going to be impossible to clean up. I hoped Farmer Frank wouldn't mind the mess we'd made. Maybe crows liked pumpkin guts?

"You have *everything* to do with this," Derrick said. His voice sounded unnaturally loud, but only because it had grown quiet in the field. The crows had stopped their outraged shrieking and, strangely, there were no other birds flying overhead. Even the wind seemed to have died down. "'When the Bringer of

Light is joined by the Chosen One, her power will increase ten-fold.'"

I glanced at Esther to see what she thought of this, and saw that an enormous grin had broken out across the girl's face.

"Cool," she said. "Let's do it again!"

And so she did.

With the exception of Rosalie Hopkins, I'd never seen anyone with powers as strong as Esther's.

But she was so casual about it. Just a wave of her hand, then *boom!* A flash, and a pumpkin exploded to bits.

"Was that okay?" she'd ask. "How was that? Want me to do another one?"

Boom! There went another one.

When Derrick asked her to levitate a pumpkin instead, no problem. Suddenly one of the pumpkins was floating across the field, three feet in the air, seemingly without any effort on Esther's part at all. It was a good thing Farmer Frank didn't choose that moment to wander over to see what we were up to, since what Esther was up to might have blown his middle-aged, firmly-rooted-in-reality mind.

What Esther couldn't seem to do, however, was concentrate on what she was doing for very long. The second her cell phone chirped—which it did constantly, because though the Internet was down, there was nothing wrong with the local cell towers—she pulled it from her pocket to look at the screen. While I didn't exactly blame her—I was getting constant calls from Becca since we couldn't do any credit card transactions at Enchantments—this did cause anything Esther was levitating to fall to the hard ground with a *splat*, or nearly collide with my new car.

Most of the time, the texts she was getting were from Gabby, asking Esther if she liked Gabby's hair, her spray tan, her makeup, her nails, all sent with accompanying photos that Esther was required to scroll through and like or otherwise express an opinion on. Everything we were doing in the field had to shut down until these replies were made.

"Can't you do anything to stop this?" Derrick whispered to me when Esther began recording herself telling Gabby about how gorgeous she looked in the dress I'd dropped by for her that morning.

"Stop what?" I was texting my brother a photo of my new car.

"The chitchatting about the hair and clothes and makeup. What we're doing here is actually important."

"Um, excuse me, what those two are doing is actually important, too. First of all, they're a couple. People who love each other share things. And secondly, people are always trying to brush off the things that women love, like fashion and makeup, as superficial or frivolous. But they're not, because for some people, those things are armor they put on to feel more confident in a world that can sometimes feel cruel. They're transformative and empowering."

Derrick's eyebrows were as furrowed as the field we were standing in. "I'm sorry. I get it now. But can you not see that maybe *right now* isn't the best time for those discussions? In a day or two, all of this land will most likely be underwater. And then it isn't going to matter what color Gabby's hair is."

"Um." I lowered my phone. "Good point. Esther?"

She looked up from her screen. "Yeah?"

"We need to concentrate on doing magic stuff right now."

"Sorry." Esther slipped her phone back into her pocket. "Gabby has an anxiety disorder. Sometimes she freaks out if I don't respond right away."

"It's fine for you to call your friend," Derrick said. I could tell from his conciliatory tone that he felt bad for his earlier complaint about their chitchatting and was trying to make amends. It was so cute. "But we need to know that if things go to hell—and I mean that literally—in the next forty-eight hours, you'll be able to defend yourself."

Esther's face puckered with worry. "Why? Where are you going to be?" She was looking straight at me.

"I'll be around," I said quickly. "Of course. But I'm not the Bringer of Light. You are."

"*You're* the one they're going to come after, Esther," Derrick said. I noticed how tactfully he avoided explaining who *they* were. Demons? Or Rosalie and her friends? I still tended to favor Rosalie, despite her generous gift from this morning. "So we need to know you can protect yourself."

"Oh, I can protect myself, all right," Esther said, her worried look suddenly replaced with a confident grin. She nodded at a stray pumpkin that had fallen dangerously close to my new car as she'd been levitating it. "See that right there?"

"Esther." The pumpkin was also dangerously close to me. Derrick flung a protective arm around me. "Don't—"

"Get ready," she said. "Get set . . ."

"Wait, Esther!" I cried.

"Go!"

I didn't see what happened next, because the flash of light was so bright, it seemed to fill the entire field. Plus, Derrick had thrown both arms around me, blocking my view. For a second, all I could see was the interior lining of his jacket, and all I could smell was leather . . . and burnt pumpkin.

When he finally dropped his arms and straightened, the light was gone . . . and so was the gourd. All that was left was a small gaping hole in Farmer Frank's field, with a stream of smoke rising from it. There wasn't even a single seed to be found.

My new car was fine, though, and so was I. And so was Esther, who was grinning ear to ear at her accomplishment.

"Okay," Derrick said, looking resigned. "I think it's time to call it quits for the day."

Esther was already sliding her phone back into her pocket. "Good," she said. "Because I need to get home and change. Gabby's parents reserved a table for tonight at the Yacht Club. I'm supposed go with them to be at this selection thing and support her, since there's no way she's gonna get picked. Then hopefully this whole Harvest Princess thing will be over, and stuff can go back to normal."

"I wouldn't be so sure." Derrick was staring at the horizon. When I followed the direction of his gaze, I saw that he was looking toward the treetops. Almost all of the bright red and yellow leaves had been stripped away by the cold ocean breeze.

In their place sat hundreds—maybe thousands—of crows. Their black feathers hunched against the wind, they clung to the naked branches, peering down . . . at us.

"Why are there so many of them?" Esther whispered—although neither of us had told her to lower her voice. "What are they *doing* up there?"

"Waiting," Derrick said.

"For what?"

"Crows are scavengers." He put out both his arms and began slowly inching Esther and me toward the car. "They'll eat just about anything. But their favorite food is carrion."

Esther wrinkled her nose. "What's that?"

"Decaying flesh."

I swallowed nervously. "So they think there's going to be a lot of that lying around West Harbor soon?"

"In my experience?" Derrick nodded somberly. "Yes, they do."

Jessica

Blue is the common color. Wear blue to win the trust—
and hearts—of others.

Goody Fletcher,
Book of Useful Household Tips

"*That's* what you're wearing?" I asked when Derrick came down
my stairs in his usual black jeans and leather motorcycle jacket.

"Why?" He looked down at himself. "What's wrong with it?"

"Nothing's wrong with it. But the Bringer of Light's girlfriend
might be getting crowned Harvest Princess tonight. I'd have
thought you'd get dressed up a little."

"I did dress up a little." He plucked at his black long-sleeved
henley. "I changed my shirt." Then his gaze fell on me. "*Oh.* I see."

He came the rest of the way down the stairs, took one of my
hands into his, then spun me around, causing my full skirt to twirl
around me. "You look beautiful. Now I feel stupid."

"No, you're fine. You look great." *I* was the one who felt stupid. He was just being nice, whereas I had snarked at him. One
of the unfortunate things about my gift was that it didn't work
on myself. Prosperity spells? Yes. My bank account was full, and
Enchantments, even without being able to take credit cards, was

doing record business, thanks to the crowds coming in for the Tricentennial Festival.

But the ability to design a gown that looked great on myself? Not a skill that I possessed. Everything I owned came off the rack from the discount outlets—including what I was wearing, a midnight blue velvet minidress with a corset-inspired waistline, long, drapey sleeves, and a full skirt.

I was great at making money by telling other people what to wear. What I wasn't great at was much of anything else.

"We'd better hurry if we want to get there on time," I said, dropping his hand and the subject, and reaching for my handbag and coat.

"How come you can't take a compliment?" He reached for me again, his fingers skimming the many buttons along the dress's waistline.

"Oh, I can," I assured him. Lie. "I'm just worried about the dress code."

"There's a dress code?"

"Yes, of course. It's the Yacht Club."

"How am I supposed to know what people wear to a yacht club?"

"I should have told you. It's fancy. It's for members only."

"Are you a member?"

"No. What would I be doing, joining a yacht club? Do I look like someone who owns a yacht?"

His gaze flicked over my black lace patterned hose and platform boots. I won't lie: there was some heat there. That was more flattering than any verbal compliment he could have given me. "Maybe."

"The answer is no. No, I do not. And neither do you. But it's too late to change now." And the truth was, I didn't really want him to. I couldn't wait to see what all the West Harbor yachties made of Derrick, with his long hair and black leather motorcycle jacket and boots. "Come on. Let's go."

Pye's cries at the unfairness of being locked inside the house for yet another night followed us to my car, but there was no way I was letting him roam freely. Not when the moon was nearly full, another king tide was predicted, and there were rumors of more wolf sightings. Someone claimed to have seen one in the Dairy Queen parking lot after midnight—a strange place for a wolf to hang out—while someone else insisted they'd seen several over by the high school.

Good thing Sal had given up and canceled school for the rest of the week after learning the newly resodded football field had been flooded. Nobody had been that enthusiastic about attending class during Tricentennial Week in the first place. Who was going to want to show up with a bunch of apex predators on the loose?

"So we're only going to this to support Esther," I said to Derrick as I steered Bluebell 2 into the Yacht Club parking lot. "And she's only going to support Gabby. As soon as the two of them are out of there, we're out, too. Right?"

"Of course." Derrick was frowning. "Why would we stay?"

"Because people will try to make us."

"What?" He looked as alarmed as if instead of *people,* I'd said *demons*. "Why?"

"They want me to join." I pulled into a parking space marked Visitor and switched off the engine. "They used to not allow memberships to Jews and obviously not witches, but I guess they can't afford to be choosy anymore. Memberships have gone way down, probably because they're asking for twenty grand a year to join."

Derrick's silver eyes widened. "What kind of place *is* this?"

"The one place on earth even worse than the World Council of Witches."

The Yacht Club was located right on the Sound—obviously, since people docked their yachts in the adjoining marina—and the scent of sea was strong enough to permeate even the new car smell inside Bluebell 2. I could hear waves sloshing against the nearby pier, as well as the more distant tinkle of the live jazz trio inside the single-story, mostly glass structure that housed the club. The original building had been destroyed by a nor'easter back in the 1950s, and the members had rebuilt in the style that was popular back then.

"So a hellscape," Derrick said. "We're about to enter a hell-scape."

I smiled and winked at him. "Come on. Let's go."

Obviously I've been to the Yacht Club before. Mark's parents joined for a red-hot second back when their restaurant first took off. Mr. Giovanni thought that giving his wife an evening out every now and then, with some dinner and dancing, would be nice, and Mark's sisters were delighted by the private outdoor pool.

Then Mrs. Giovanni tasted the food. The ensuing battle to get her family's membership fee back was like nothing Connecticut had seen since—well, possibly the witch trials of the sixteen hundreds. The West Harbor Yacht Club was still trying to recover from Mama Giovanni having gone scorched earth on it.

Ever since, whenever I entered the building, I felt a little chill down my spine. I had a feeling Derrick might have felt it, too, since when he held the door open for me and I shivered going into the warm building, he looked down at me with a quizzical expression on his face.

But before I could explain, Rosalie was there before us, a tablet in her hand and a hands-free Bluetooth headset curled over one ear.

"Jessica!" she cried, looking startled, her blue eyes as bright and shiny as the floor-length gown she was wearing. "You came! I'm so . . . happy to see you."

"Thanks. I'm . . . happy to see you, too." Before I knew what was happening, a glass of champagne had been thrust into my hand from the tray of a nearby waiter, who'd been passing by.

"What?" Rosalie asked.

"I said I'm happy to see you—"

"No, not you, sorry." Rosalie reached up to touch her earpiece and spoke to whoever was on the other end of the call she was receiving. "No, that's not where I said I wanted them. I want them front of the stage. *Front of the stage.*"

"Okay," I said, saluting her with the champagne. "Well, we'll just—"

But she reached out and gripped my arm. "No, wait." Into the headset, she said, "That's right." Then to me, she said, "Did you get it?"

For a second, I didn't know what she was talking about. Then I realized. "Oh, the car! Yes! Thank you." It was killing me, but I had to do it. "That was very kind of you. And Billy. It was kind of both of you. You didn't have to."

She did have to. She really did.

"I'm glad you like it." Rosalie smiled frostily—though for some reason I felt it was more at Derrick, standing behind me, than at me. "I'm so glad. It seemed like the least Billy and I could do after all of your recent . . . troubles."

Hmmm. Same old Rosalie.

"Yeah, well, it was really nice of you," I said. "Good to know we can let bygones be bygones."

"Of course we can." Rosalie was as chilly as the ice princess from *Frozen*. "And thank *you* for coming. I think you're both going to enjoy what I've got in store for you tonight."

I did *not* like the sound of that. I could tell by the crook of his mouth that Derrick didn't, either.

But before I could ask Rosalie what she meant, a tall older woman in a wine-colored jacket and wide-legged trouser suit—that I had sold to her—came hurrying over from the bar.

"Jessica!" she cried. "I wasn't expecting to see you here! How *are* you?"

"I'm fine, how are you, *Mayor*?" I raised my eyebrows at Derrick to make sure he caught my emphasis on the word *mayor*. He nodded subtly back. "Did your wife give you the letter I—"

Her bright eyes twinkled at me. "Of course she did. What a little go-getter you have in that mentee of yours! Next thing I know, she'll be gunning for my job."

I laughed. She had no idea. "Well, I don't know about that." Esther's aspirations were probably far higher. President, maybe. "Mayor Dunleavy, may I introduce you to Derrick Winters?"

"How lovely to meet you." The mayor's gaze ranged across Derrick the way Pye's gaze ranged across birds he saw out the window. He wasn't something she wanted to eat so much as thoroughly tear apart and internally explore. "I've heard so many good things about you. You've really thrown the people of this town into a tizzy, haven't you?"

Fortunately it was so loud in the bar, thanks to the crush of people and the very noisy jazz trio, that I was sure Derrick couldn't hear a thing she was saying. He only smiled politely, which seemed to please the older woman.

"Here, let me get you both a real drink," the mayor said. "Randy." The mayor waved in the direction of the barman. "Randy, two more vodka sodas, please."

"Oh, no need, Madam Mayor," I said quickly. "We're very happy with—"

But it was too late. Two vodka sodas appeared on the bar and were quickly snatched up by a broad-shouldered man in a tuxedo. Because he was standing with his back to us, I didn't see who he was until he turned around.

Billy.

"Your drinks, Madam May—" He froze upon seeing me and Derrick, the grin he'd been wearing vanishing completely. He seemed to pale beneath his spray-on tan. "Jess. I—I didn't know you were coming to this."

"Oh, well." I plastered a smile across my face. "You know me. I'll do anything to support the youth of West Harbor."

"Yeah. Sure. Of course." He handed one of the drinks to me, and the other to Derrick. "Hey, bro."

"Thanks, man," Derrick said, cheerfully.

The two of us stood there, a drink in each hand, still in our coats, me with an evening bag dangling from my wrist, while I struggled to figure out what to say. *Thank you for the car* seemed inadequate. *Do you know your wife is a witch who tried to murder me?* seemed like overkill.

Fortunately Rosalie, a few feet away, got a signal over her headset, and suddenly banged on her tablet.

"Everyone? Everyone!" Rosalie's years of cheerleading had taught her how to use her diaphragm to project her voice, so she could easily be heard over the jazz trio and all of the voices in the bar. "We're ready to begin. If you could all take your seats . . . "

I was more than happy to follow the crowd into the Yacht Club's dining room, where Esther, looking tall and elegant in slim-fitting black trousers, white blouse, and, for a change of pace, pink-sequined Converse, gestured to me from a table where she was sitting with a woman who looked like Gabby's older, plumper twin.

"Over here," Esther called, waving urgently, as if there was some way Derrick and I might miss her.

"Hi, Esther," I said, when we reached her. "We were just talking about you. The mayor got your let—"

"That's great. Could you sit here?" Esther patted the seat of the chair beside her, and then, when I lowered myself into it, hissed in my ear, "Gabby's dad is stuck on the train from the city. There's flooding on the tracks. He's trying to get here as fast as he can, but for now, only her mom could come. Gabby's really upset."

"Oh, no." I put down my drinks and my bag, then peeled off my coat and introduced myself and Derrick to Gabby's mother.

She shook both our hands, but seemed especially thrilled when Derrick's fingers gripped hers. I didn't have to be a genius to guess why. The poor woman looked lost and a little out of place in the big room where she seemed to know no one except Esther, and then suddenly, a handsome guy with a warm grip slipped her an electric mickey? Bliss.

Especially when he followed it up with a grave, "You have a lovely daughter, Mrs. Aquino."

"Oh, thank you," she fluttered. There were two bottles of wine on the table, red and white, to accompany the coming meal, but Mrs. Aquino hadn't touched either. She, like Esther, was only drinking cranberry juice. "And thank you, Miss Gold, so much for the dress. Gabriella loves it. It's just such a shame her father can't be here. But then again, if she doesn't win, I suppose it's just as well. I know how much he'd hate the idea of her being humiliated—"

"She won't be," Esther said firmly. I saw her hand, slender and brown against the stark white tablecloth, ball into a fist. "She's going to win. She'd *better* win, or—"

The flowers in the decorative centerpiece began to tremble, and the salt and pepper shakers tinkled against one another. I laid a hand over Esther's fist and said, quietly, "It's all right."

The flowers stilled. The tinkling stopped. Esther took a sip of her cranberry juice, like nothing had happened.

But something had happened, all right. I was the only one who'd noticed, since Derrick was busy scanning the room (probably for demons), and Gabby's mother was too nervous to focus on anything except the stage in front of us.

Which was why, when Rosalie stepped onto it a second later, Mrs. Aquino was the first to notice. She reached out to grasp my wrist with an excited squeak.

"Oooh," she cried. "It's starting!"

"Ladies and gentlemen." Rosalie seemed anxious. She was barely giving her guests a chance to take their seats, let alone the waitstaff a chance to pass out the first course—a mesclun salad so sad looking, it would have sent Mama Giovanni's head spinning—before taking the podium on the stage at the front of the room. "Welcome to our first annual Harvest Princess Pageant, in celebration of West Harbor's *Tricentennial*."

Rosalie paused for both emphasis and the smattering of applause she'd known was going to follow the word *Tricentennial*. I took the opportunity to lean over to say to Mrs. Aquino, "I'm sorry your husband isn't here yet, but I'm sure Gabby is going to do just fine. And please, call me Jessica."

Mrs. Aquino grinned and pointed at herself. "I'm Anna."

"Your donations are what's made all of this possible," Rosalie went on. "Because of you—and of course the generosity of both Hopkins Motors and Walker Hardware"—I saw Billy, at a table near the front of the room with both of his children, beam with pride—"nine of the truly remarkable young women who will be on this stage shortly will have more than a year's worth of college tuition paid."

It was a good thing the lights had been turned down low,

because otherwise someone might have noticed how far back into my head my eyes were rolling.

"But before I introduce them, please join me in welcoming the man who helped choose the recipients of tonight's scholarships, a true academic, published author, and historian, Professor Bartholomew Brewster."

Suddenly my eyes snapped open.

"Bartholomew Brewster?" I whispered to Derrick, as everyone around us applauded. "But he's—"

Derrick was frowning. He rarely smiled, but his expression looked grimmer than I'd ever seen it. In the dim light of the dining room, he looked positively murderous. "I know."

I had to say it anyway. "He's the Grand Sorcerer of the—"

"I *know*."

Derrick looked physically pained as a dashing dark-haired man leaped from a table near the front of the stage and then sprang up the three or four steps to join Rosalie behind the podium. For someone who'd founded the World Council of Witches in the 1980s, Old Bart didn't look all that old. In fact, in his red smoking jacket and black cravat, he looked a little bit like—

"Thank you," he said in a deep, cultured voice as he held up his hands to still the smattering of applause for his presence. How had I not known that Bartholomew Brewster—at least judging by his accent—was British? "Thank you so much. It's a pleasure, honestly, to be here. I don't know where this country would be without little towns like West Harbor—they really are the backbone of this great nation."

This earned even more applause than Rosalie's mention of the Tricentennial. Derrick, however, wasn't clapping. Neither was I.

"If we were being accurate, West Harbor would be celebrating its quadricentennial rather than its tricentennial because it was nearly *four hundred* years ago that Europeans established a settlement in this area—"

Esther, looking disgusted, folded her arms across her chest and muttered, "More like spread smallpox and waged war against the Native communities actually living here at the time."

Amen to that.

"But of course West Harbor itself wasn't founded until the seventeen hundreds, when it incorporated separately from the towns and settlements around it. And look how it's grown since! I'm honored to be invited to share in your well-deserved festivities. And what makes my being here tonight so much sweeter is that I get to share this great privilege with none other than . . . my brother."

Professor Brewster raised a hand to shade his eyes from the bright stage lights as he peered out into the dining room. "Derrick, will you come up here so I can introduce you?"

Jessica

Write the name of thine enemy on paper. Hide the paper in the icehouse. Thine enemy's power against thee will be frozen.

Goody Fletcher,
Book of Useful Household Tips

At first I didn't understand what was happening. Why was Bartholomew Brewster, the self-proclaimed Grand Sorcerer of the World Council of Witches, calling Derrick Winters his brother?

This was surely some kind of joke. Derrick couldn't possibly be related to the man who'd founded the most despicably elitist organization in all of witchkind.

Then again, Derrick *did* have the symbol for that organization tattooed on his arm. And he did hand out amulets belonging to that organization pretty freely.

And he'd told me that he had a lot of half-siblings.

He wasn't denying that Bartholomew was one of them, either.

True, he wasn't leaping onto the stage to join him. Instead, he was glaring daggers at Rosalie. In fact, if I were Rosalie, and Derrick was glaring at me like that, I'd have run far, far away.

But instead Rosalie was standing behind Bart, grinning like the proverbial cat who'd swallowed the canary.

It's possible she couldn't see Derrick, or his glaring silver eyes, since the lights on the stage were so bright, and we were sitting at the back of the room. Far enough away that when Esther whispered, sounding confused, "Derrick? Does he mean you?" probably not that many people heard her.

But Derrick did.

"Yes," he said, shortly. And then instead of offering any sort of explanation, he simply said, "Excuse me."

Then he reached into his pocket for his phone, got up, and left the room.

Everyone *definitely* saw that. Including Bartholomew Brewster.

"Ah," the professor said, with a flippant smile and shrug. "My brother seems otherwise engaged at the moment. Well, we can choose our friends, but not our family, as the saying goes."

This earned him a gentle and understanding chuckle from the crowd. *Oh, ha ha. Yes, families are such a pain.*

"Shall we carry on?" the professor asked, and pulled a stack of note cards from the breast pocket of his smoking jacket. "What can I tell you about the girls you're about to meet that you don't already know yourself?"

Esther touched my hand. When I looked at her, I could see that her dark eyes, behind the lenses of her glasses, were wide and troubled.

"Aren't you going to go after him?" she whispered.

I nodded. Of course she was right. I should go after Derrick. That's what a good girlfriend would do.

Except that I wasn't really Derrick's girlfriend. Our relationship was only temporary, while we worked together to try to save my town, after which he'd be moving on, and I'd be . . .

well, no longer the Chosen One. I was only Derrick's fake girl-friend.

How much of what I knew about him was fake, too?

I stood up and slipped from the room, leaving my coat and bag behind. I'd find Derrick, get a reasonable explanation out of him, and be back in time for whatever this ceremony was. What was it his brother had said? We can't choose family.

No, we certainly can't. None of this was Derrick's fault.

Was it?

Except that when I got out to the bar area, Derrick was no-where to be seen. There was no one there at all except the bar-tender, busily cleaning glasses, and the jazz trio, packing up to go home.

"Excuse me," I said to the musicians. "Did you see a man in a motorcycle jacket come through here just now?"

"Tall, blond, chiseled cheekbones?" asked the drummer.

"That would be the one," I said.

He pointed toward the double doors to the parking lot. "He went that way. He was on his phone."

Of course. Derrick was always on his phone. Who was he talking to? I had no idea.

Maybe it was time I found out.

I was about to hit the double doors to go looking for him in the parking lot when someone called my name. I turned and saw Rosalie standing behind me.

"Jessica." She no longer wore the cat-who-swallowed-the-canary grin. If anything, she looked somber. She still clutched her tablet, but she'd ditched her headset. "Can I talk to you for a minute?"

I turned back to the doors. "Now is really not a good time. And that was a very shitty thing to do, Rosalie. I don't know what's going on between those two, but there's obviously bad blood, and you just—"

"I know. And I'm sorry. Jessica, I'm pretty sure we've both been played."

That caused me to drop my fingers from the door handles. "What? How?"

"I think it has something to do with this." She lifted the tablet. "Does this look familiar to you?"

I knew I shouldn't. I had no reason to trust Rosalie Hopkins. Sure, she and her husband had given me a car, but honestly, after everything they'd put me through, they *owed* me that car. That didn't make us even.

But somehow I found myself crossing the bar to see what she wanted to show me, aware that the guys in the jazz trio and bartender were watching my every move. *Oooh, cat fight!* they were probably thinking. I didn't care. I had to see what Rosalie was talking about.

When I got to her side, I saw the last thing I was expecting on the tablet between her French manicured fingers.

It was the prophecy. A photo of the exact same page from the grimoire that Derrick had given to me a week ago, predicting the prevention of the destruction of West Harbor by the Chosen One and Bringer of Light.

"*What?*" I snatched the tablet from her hands in order to get a better look. "How did you get this? Who gave it to you?"

Rosalie glanced at the men in the room, all of whom were staring at me in alarm due to the intensity of my reaction.

"Uh," she said. "Why don't we step into the ladies' room to discuss this, so we can have some privacy."

Even though the last time I'd stepped into a ladies' room with Rosalie, it had not gone well, I agreed. I needed to know what was going on. Besides, back then I'd been a young and naive witch. Now I was older and, if not wiser, at least less willing to believe Rosalie's crap.

She started ladling it on the second the door closed behind us.

"Jessica, I'm so sorry," she said, taking the tablet from me, then gliding over to the nearest couch to sit down on it.

That's right. There were *couches* inside the West Harbor Yacht Club ladies' room. Two of them, in some kind of retro pink-and-green Laura Ashley floral pattern. I guess they were there for women to stretch out on in case they fainted from having seen a circumcised penis, or something. I don't know.

There were also baskets of Tampax, Halloween candy, and hairspray by the sinks. Those I remembered from the few times Dina and I had been there as tweens. A part of me wanted to inhale the candy, but I knew I had to focus.

"Rosalie, did Professor Brewster send that to you?" I demanded, pointing at the tablet. "And tell you that you're the Chosen One?"

Rosalie crossed her legs and rested her hands on her knee, looking prim. "Jessica, I know it's hard for you to understand since you're not a member of the WCW. But the fact is, he didn't have to send it to me. I have the original. *I'm* the Chosen One."

It was a good thing I didn't have Esther's particular gift of magic, because I for sure would have blown something up at that moment. Probably the couches.

"Rosalie, that's simply not possible," I settled for saying instead.

"Why? Did Derrick tell you that *you're* the Chosen One?" Something in my face must have given away the truth, since Rosalie went on, knowingly, "I was afraid of that. I suspected the moment I saw that you were wearing the amulet. That's why I called the professor. You know, he told me that Derrick isn't even a member. He's never had any affiliation whatsoever with the Council."

"I'm aware. Rosalie—"

"Well, if you knew all along, why on earth did you believe him?" Rosalie was gazing up at me, her perfectly threaded eyebrows constricted with phony concern. "Not that I'm blaming you. It isn't your fault. I know it must have been hard for you all these years, not qualifying for membership in the Council, and never having been part of a coven. You were easy prey to anyone who came along and said you were special."

I felt my blood beginning to boil. "Rosalie—"

"But don't worry." She had the gall to reach up and pat my hand, like I was Esther's age. "No harm's been done. And Bartholomew says his little brother really does *mean* well. He just has a bizarre antipathy toward authority figures. Something to do with how he was raised. No respect for tradition—which is why, of course, he hates the WCW. Funny, you two seem to have that in common."

I chose to ignore that last dig. "Rosalie, what did you mean when you said you have the original of this prophecy?"

"I'm sure Derrick told you about the witch to whom the grimoire belonged, the one who hid it inside a wall in a home in upstate New York?"

"Yeah. So?"

"So that witch was my eleventh great-grandmother, Elizabeth," Rosalie said. "The one I told you about, who was found guilty of witchcraft right here in West Harbor—well, what would become West Harbor, but was then just a settlement, like the professor said."

I stared at her. "You said she was banished instead of executed."

"Yes! But only because as a widow, she was wealthy enough to bribe a judge." Rosalie's gaze had moved so that it was on my reflection in the mirror instead of on me. What it was actually doing was moving between me and her own reflection as she delivered her news, enjoying watching herself as she talked. "She had just enough money left afterward to flee to New York. That's where she hid the book that prophecy came from—the one that said the Bringer of Light who would save this place would come from the thirteenth generation—my *daughter's* generation."

It took a moment or two for the information to register.

"Wait," I said. "You think the Bringer of Light is *your daughter?*"

Rosalie frowned. Now she wasn't looking at our reflection. She was looking directly at me.

"I don't think it," she said. "I know it. And Bartholomew does, too. So does Derrick, of course. He admitted as much to me last night."

"Last *night?*" None of this was making any sense.

"Yes, when he asked to meet with me during Trivia, and begged me not to tell you the truth."

She lifted the tablet and scrolled to another page, then handed it to me. On the screen was a photo of the deck outside the Brewport. It was difficult to make out because it had been taken at night, at an odd angle, and there appeared to be moisture of some kind on the lens.

But I could clearly see two people standing close to one another. The woman's back was to the camera, but her hair gleamed as gold as the rose on Rosalie's stationery in the fluorescent security lighting, and she was wearing the same sweater set that Rosalie had worn last night.

And there was no doubt whatsoever that the man glaring down at her in the photo was Derrick. I'd recognize those furiously lowered brows and that sarcastic frown anywhere.

Rosalie must have seen the dismay in my face, since she said,

"Oh, don't be too hard on yourself . . . or him. Apparently he's done this to dozens of women—convinced them that he's working for some secret organization, and that their town is in mortal peril, and they're the Chosen One and only they can save it. Bartholomew says he's been doing it for years. I guess he's always had issues. Their mother is supposedly a very refined and cultured woman. She obviously prefers spending time with Bartholomew, who's done so much with his life. Derrick will do anything to get her attention. His father is just a farmer, or something, whereas Bartholomew's father was a dean at Oxford. Look, I'm sorry. I know you like him, which is why last night I tried to get him to promise he'd tell you the truth. He said he would. But I'm guessing, from the look on your face, it didn't work."

I couldn't tear my eyes from the photo. When had Derrick snuck out of Trivia to meet with Rosalie? And *why*? Surely not because anything she was saying was true. Derrick and I were in a fake relationship, but not *all* of it was fake. You couldn't fake the light Esther made when she used her powers and I was with her.

And Derrick couldn't have faked what he and I had together in bed—or the glow in his eyes when he looked at me. Could he?

There was no way I was going to let Rosalie—or Bartholomew Brewster—know that I had any such doubts, however.

"Huh," I said, and handed the tablet back to her. "I guess he forgot to mention it."

I saw Rosalie's shoulders relax. She'd won, and she knew it. Her gaze swung back toward her reflection, reveling in the knowledge that once again, she'd defeated me—even though I'd never wanted to be in competition in the first place.

"I'm really sorry," Rosalie said, smoothing another invisible hair away from her face. "I can't imagine what you must be going through right now."

I eyed the Snickers bars in the basket on the sink. Never had I wanted so badly to cram something into my mouth. "That's okay," I said. "I'll get over it."

Rosalie reached for the hairspray. "You really do have the worst luck with men," she said, giving her head a couple spurts.

There was no point in denying it. "I do."

"If it's any comfort to you, Professor Brewster says Lizzie's one of the most gifted witches he's ever met. He's been working with her all week."

"Great. That is so good to know." Screw it. I grabbed a Snickers, unwrapped it, and shoved it into my mouth. "Can I ask you something?"

"Of course."

"What's his plan for tomorrow night? You know, to stop the rift?"

"Oh, Jess." Her gaze on my reflection was pitying. "You poor thing. You know I can't tell you that. But don't worry. It's a good one. Do you really think I'd put the lives of the people I love at risk otherwise?"

I swallowed. "I guess not. What's Lizzie's gift?"

"Her what?"

"Lizzie's talent. Her magical gift. You know. What kind of witch is she?"

"Oh!" Rosalie laughed, gave her hair one last pat to make sure every straight, silken strand was in place, and headed for the door. "To be honest, we're not really sure yet. She's very good at glamours. Heavens, I better get back out there. The professor's speech was only supposed to last twenty minutes! I've let him drone on *way* too long about West Harbor history."

I nearly choked on my mouthful of chocolate, peanuts, nougat, and caramel. "*Glamours?*"

"Uh-huh." Rosalie flung me a sunny smile on her way out of

the restroom. "Lucky little thing. Haven't you noticed how great she always looks? Her selfies are just perfection, no need for filters. She was outside on the dock with her friends taking some last night when she saw me with Derrick. That's how I got that photo. She was worried he was being mean to me, can you believe it? So she took that snap. More proof she's the Bringer of Light—so protective! Well, got to run. See you later."

Derrick

As Witches, we recognize that our intelligence is vastly superior to that of the non-magical, and that is why we have a moral duty to nurture and guide them.

Rule Number Nine of the Nine Rules
World Council of Witches

Derrick was seething, more at himself than at anyone else. He ought to have known that Bart would insinuate himself into the situation somehow.

But he lived all the way in London. What was he doing, concerning himself with a small-town hell rift, when he had the corporate offices of the World Council of Witches to run?

Not that it mattered, Derrick supposed. Bart had always done exactly as he liked.

Annoying prick.

As he stood in the chilly parking lot, listening to his call go to his mother's voice mail, Derrick reflected that most grown men got along with their brothers—even with their half brothers. Most of them didn't have to call their mothers when one of their brothers was doing something underhanded. They dealt with the situation themselves.

But then again, most brothers didn't have a mother like his and Bart's.

"Hello, darling," purred his mother's voice in his ear. "I can't answer the phone right now because I'm busy doing . . . other things. But if you leave a message, I promise to get back to you . . . someday."

His mother's voice mail message never failed to irritate him, which was too bad since he had to listen to it more often than not. She "didn't have time to text."

"Mother," he said. "It's me. You'll never guess who's here in West Harbor. I'll give you a hint. It's one of your many other sons. And not one I like. Call me back and tell me what you want me to do about it. And if fratricide is on the table, I'm all for it."

He made sure his phone was on vibrate so that when she called back, the ring wouldn't disturb the proceedings inside, then went back into the dining room—only to find an empty chair beside his.

"Where's Jessica?" he leaned over to ask Esther.

"She went to look for you," the kid whispered back. "Didn't you see her?"

Derrick shook his head. He didn't like the sound—or look—of any of this. The Hopkins woman was gone, too, he noted. It was only his jackass brother on the stage, still droning on about pre–Revolutionary War West Harbor. The gasbag had never been able to resist an opportunity to listen to his own voice over a microphone.

"I'll be right back," Derrick whispered to Esther, whose only response was a long, bored suck through the straw of her cranberry juice.

Exiting the dining room, he nearly collided with Rosalie Hopkins, who was coming back in.

"Pardon me," she said, giving him a hefty dose of side eye.

He held the door open for her. "No, pardon me, ma'am."

She sailed past him with a self-satisfied little smirk. Derrick couldn't help thinking what a good pair she and Bart would make. Too bad she was already married.

Back out in the bar, the jazz trio were nearly packed up.

"Hey," Derrick said. "Did you see a woman in a blue dress with dark curly hair—"

"And the face of an angel?" the drummer said. "Yeah, she was looking for you. She was in there with the blonde who just came through." He pointed toward the door to the ladies' room. "Blonde came out, brunette is still in there."

Derrick grinned, then reached into his pocket for his wallet. "Thanks, guys. Have a good night," he said as he slipped a hundred-dollar bill into the tip jar the drummer was holding. They wouldn't be able to tell it was a hundred until one of them unfolded it. Derrick was always careful to crease his tip bills nine times, so the recipient would receive good fortune.

But even without knowing this, the musicians beamed in appreciation.

"Thanks, man," they said, and left with all of their equipment.

"Drink?" the bartender asked Derrick when he settled onto a barstool, his gaze locked on the door to the ladies' room.

"Club soda would be great, thanks," Derrick replied. He needed to keep his head clear for what he knew was about to occur . . .

And then it did.

The door to the women's restroom swung open, and Jessica slowly emerged, looking shell-shocked—though whether it was from what she'd heard in the dining room moments before, or just now, from Rosalie, he had no way of knowing.

"Jessica." He rose from the stool, the drink that had only just been placed on a coaster near him completely forgotten. "I—I can explain."

Her gaze rose from the floor to center on his face, and his gut immediately twisted from the pain and betrayal he saw in those twin dark pools.

"You can *explain*?" Her voice was rough with sarcasm—and possibly even some unshed tears. "Oh, really? Just how can you *explain* the fact that you've been lying to me this whole time, Derrick?"

The bartender, who'd been standing behind him polishing glasses, took that as his cue to beat a hasty retreat for the kitchen, and then the two of them were alone . . . except for the hundred or so people Derrick could hear laughing in the dining room next door.

"Look," he said, taking a step toward her, his hand outstretched.

But to his utter heartbreak and horror, she retreated from him, shrinking against the wall as if she were afraid of him—of his touch.

He knew she had a right to be.

"Jessica, I never lied," he said. "I just couldn't tell you the truth."

"What truth?" Her dark eyes flashed. "The truth that your own brother founded the most exclusionary and screwed-up organization for witches that's ever existed? You mean *that* truth?"

He dropped his hand. This was going to be much more difficult than he'd thought.

And that was the problem, really. He hadn't thought. Not with his head.

"Okay. Yes, you're right. But I didn't tell you that because I knew how you felt about the WCW. And also because the truth is so outrageous, I never thought you'd believe me."

"Uh, the fact that I'm the *Chosen One* is more believable than whatever else you're hiding?"

"No. I mean yes." He couldn't stand the pain in her voice. He wanted to walk over and put his arms around her and sweep her back in time, back to this morning and the warm coziness of her cottage, of her bed, where the rain pattered against the roof and the outside world couldn't intrude and it was just them and Pye and her endless supply of leftovers and miniature chocolate bars and coffee.

But he hadn't been blessed with the gift of time travel.

He'd been given a different gift, instead.

"Bartholomew Brewster *is* my brother—half brother." His voice sounded as rough and as raw as hers. "And he *did* found the World Council of Witches. All of that is true. But it's also true I've never been a member. I hate clubs. I also hate my brother, for whatever that's worth."

That didn't earn him the laugh he was hoping for, only a reproachful look.

"But I *was* sent here to help save your town," he went on, desperate now. There was nothing else he could do. He was going to have to tell her the truth, even though doing so might be worse than letting her think he'd lied. "Just not by the World Council of Witches."

She let out a tired sigh. "Who sent you, then? Go ahead, lay it on me, Derrick, I've heard it all. I'm a witch, remember? Conspiracy theories have been getting people like me killed since the beginning of time. So who was it? The CIA? Homeland Security? MI6?"

"No," he said. "My mother, Gaia."

Jessica

To rid thyself of sadness, peel the whole of an onion.

Goody Fletcher,
Book of Useful Household Tips

Of all the excuses I'd expected Derrick to give for his behavior, claiming to be the son of the goddess of all creation was not one I was expecting.

I had to admit, it was pretty creative. It made me laugh.

Not *ha ha ha* laugh. But metaphorically.

Rosalie was right: I really did have the worst luck where men were concerned.

"Good one," I said to him. Then I straightened. I didn't need the wall to support me anymore. I could manage the way I'd been managing for all these years: on my own. And with Dina's shoulder to cry on. "Look, I'm going to go in there and be with Esther. Even if it turns out she's not the Bringer of Light, she's still my mentee, so—"

He looked genuinely confused. "What are you talking about?"

I smiled at him—very sweetly in my opinion, given the circumstances. The circumstances being that what I wanted to do was knee him in the balls.

"Gosh, Derrick, didn't you know? That prophecy you showed me last week was written by Rosalie Hopkins's witchy old ancestress Elizabeth back in the sixteen hundreds. Which makes *Rosalie* the Chosen One, and her daughter *Lizzie* the Bringer of Light—a fact I would have thought that you'd be aware of, considering that you claim to be *the son of the Mother Goddess*, who is all knowing. Oh, well." I'd started back toward the dining room doors, stopping only to pat him on the shoulder along the way. "Better luck in the next town, champ. I don't care how magic your mother is. I think you should find different accommodations than my house tonight—"

He reached up and, with lightning-fast reflexes, seized my wrist, anchoring me to his side.

"Hey," I said, looking up at him in surprise. Not because his grip hurt—it didn't. The contact of his skin against mine was sending waves of painless gold fire all up and down me. He was playing with an unfair advantage, and he had to know it.

He didn't let go, however.

"Who told you that?" He breathed down at me. "About the prophecy? Was it Rosalie?"

"Yes, of course it was Rosalie. Your *best friend*, who you snuck out onto the dock with last night at Trivia. Who else?"

"It's not true." He kept his hold on my wrist. The tingles continued, in parts other than my wrist, unfortunately. Honestly, I should have known all along that he was otherworldly. What mortal man could touch you on the wrist and make you wet between the legs? Dammit. "Yes, I talked to Rosalie last night on the dock, but to warn her about the muffins, nothing else. Can't you see they're trying to play us, Jess?"

"Who is? And I swear to God, Derrick, if you say demons, I'll—"

"I don't mean demons."

"Who then? Your brother?"

"Yes. And Rosalie."

"To what *purpose?*"

Derrick's silver-eyed gaze had gone hard as flint. A drunk man in a tux came barreling through the dining room doors, evidently set on ordering something a little harder than wine from the bar, but got one look at Derrick's steely-eyed gaze and muttered, "'scuse me," and trundled right back into the dining room.

"You *know*," he said. "Rosalie is a narcissist, so desperate for power and attention that she'll do anything, anything at all to make sure she gets it, even put the lives of everyone around her at risk. Look what she did to you when she found out the boy she liked loved you instead. This is no different."

I rolled my eyes. "We're talking about an entire town, not a high school crush. It's a *little* different, Derrick."

"Is it? My brother has always had exactly the same issues as Rosalie, always needing to be the center of attention. He calls himself a *Grand Sorcerer*, for God's sake. I've always had a relationship with our mother that he envied. I'm the one she asks for help when there's a problem with a town like yours, not him, and it's always driven him crazy."

"Wow, that's so funny, because Rosalie says that he says the *exact same thing* about you. Unfortunately for you there's *proof* Rosalie's great-great-granny wrote the prophecy. And Rosalie says Lizzie's a witch. She can cast glamours."

"Rosalie's great-granny may very well have written the prophecy," Derrick said, releasing his hold on me, and leaving me feeling warm and tingly . . . and regretful he hadn't touched me in more places. But he dragged a hand through his hair instead.

"And Lizzie very well may be able to cast glamours. But glamours won't save us tomorrow night. You and Esther will."

"Oh, I see. And that information came from your mother, the ancient pagan deity Gaia, I suppose."

"*Yes*. I know how hard it must seem to believe, but *yes*." He spat the words through gritted teeth. "It's not information I generally share, because of exactly the reaction you're having right now. I don't relish people knowing that my mother makes a regular habit of roaming the earth looking for lonely, virile men by whom to impregnate herself, and then abandoning the baby with them nine months later because she has no interest in child-rearing, then going off on her merry way to find some other poor sap to screw. But she is literally *the mother of creation*. It's what she does for fun. She's been doing it since the dawn of time and will probably keep doing it until Armageddon."

I stared at him. "Wait. Your mom got pregnant by your dad and then just . . . *left* you with him?"

"Yes." When he noticed my expression, he jabbed a finger in my direction. "Don't. Do *not* look at me like that. I do *not* have abandonment issues or whatever else Rosalie told you that my brother said. Dad and I were—*are*—fine."

"I'm sure you are." Still, my heart wept a little for the motherless little boy raised all alone on that desolate farm in Montana—if, in fact, what he was saying was true. "How many siblings do you have?"

"Far, far too many to fit into any normal venue for a family reunion, with the possible exception of the Grand Canyon."

I shook my head. "I really . . . I really don't know if you're telling the truth. Or how to process this information if you are. Because if your mother is Gaia, that means she's immortal. Which must mean that you are, too."

He was shaking his head, as well. "No. No, it does not. Why do you think she keeps having children? She can't bear watching us grow old and die. Every one of us leaves her, in the end."

"Oh." Now my heart swelled with pity for his mother. "*Derrick.*"

It all made sense now. . . .

Wait. No, it didn't. *None* of this made sense. Nothing I'd heard this evening—this whole week—made sense. Why was I even standing here having this conversation? This guy was a stark, raving—

Except.

Except that if I believed magic was real—and I had incontrovertible proof that it was—why shouldn't I believe that this was real, too?

Because *none* of it made any sense.

"But if you and Bartholomew Brewster have the same mother," I asked, "why would she tell *you* that I'm the Chosen One and *him* that Rosalie is?"

"She didn't," he said. "Brewster and my mother don't speak."

I raised my eyebrows. "They don't?"

"No. Does everyone in your family get along?"

"Yes."

His eyebrows practically hit his hairline. "But your parents don't even know you're a witch."

"Well, yes. But aside from—"

"Aside from you *actively lying* to them about the most important thing in your life, you mean."

"Not *actively*. I told you . . . I consider it more omitting a truth they wouldn't understand, and would only hurt them. I'm *protecting* them."

"Oh, so it's fine for you to omit truths to your parents to

protect them, but wrong for me to omit truths to you for *your* protection?"

I glared at him. "Yes! Because I'm not a senior citizen. And stop trying to change the subject. Why don't your mother and brother get along?"

"Have you *seen* him?"

"Stop it, Derrick. Is it because he founded the World Council of Witches?"

"For starters."

"Because she believes it's better to keep the existence of magic secret?"

"Not at all. Because she, like me, agrees that it's too exclusionary. Magic is everywhere and in everyone. It isn't an inheritable trait. But Brewster is so proud of having magic on both sides of his family—Mom chose a little bit *too* big of a loner when she picked out Bart's dad—he made inheriting it the first of the nine rules of his organization."

I thoughtfully fingered the amulet I still wore at my throat. "And the symbol of Gaia as its insignia."

"Yes." Derrick's eyes narrowed with regret as he looked down at my throat. "She wasn't too happy about that decision of Bart's, either. But it *is* a protective symbol. I didn't lie about that. I know I should have told you the absolute truth from the beginning. But she—I—we both didn't know how you'd react. And you have to admit, it sounds—"

Completely insane? That's what I'd been about to say when a huge burst of applause came from behind the dining room doors.

Then they broke open, and a flood of people came streaming out, most of whom went straight toward the bar. Like clockwork, Randy the bartender reappeared from the kitchen, along with several of his colleagues, and began taking cocktail orders.

I bit my lip, looking around. I saw Billy headed straight for me. "This isn't the best—maybe we should continue this conversation another time. Like . . . tomorrow."

"*Tomorrow?* Jessica. You can't be serious." Derrick's fingers were on my skin again, but this time taking my hand, the look in his eyes pleading. "I—"

But he never got to finish whatever it was he'd been about to say, because a rainbow-haired meteor hit us out of the blue, crying my name.

"Jessica, Jessica!" Gabby threw her arms around me, burying her face in my chest. "Thank you so much! Because of you, I won! I'm a Harvest Princess!"

She was, indeed, wearing a crown of dried roses, spray-painted gold, with gold ribbons trailing down the back. Although the thorns had been removed, the leaves were still a bit stiff, and pointy enough to jab me all the way through my bra as she clung on to me.

Still, I hugged her back, wincing against the pain. "Congratulations!"

"It never would have happened if it weren't for you," Gabby said, releasing me finally to dash tears of joy from her professionally made-up eyes.

"It would, actually." Esther, who'd followed along behind Gabby, wore her seemingly permanent expression of wry amusement. "Only nine girls showed up in the end. There were nine crowns. So you all won."

"Stop it, Essie!" Gabby's mother had followed her daughter into the bar area as well, and now she smiled gratefully up at me. "Gabriella would have won anyway, no matter how many other girls she was up against."

"She would," I said. "And just to be clear, contests that judge women on their looks are sexist and limit—"

"Dad!" Gabby's shriek of joy was so piercing it nearly broke my eardrum. She darted through the throng toward a balding older man in a business suit. He threw his arms around first her, and then his wife when Mrs. Aquino joined them.

"Sorry I was late, *mija*," Mr. Aquino murmured affectionately into his daughter's hair.

I was startled from my enjoyment of this family reunion by Billy saying my name. He seemed to have got his facial coloring under control. "Jess, how are you? So glad you could come. Are you thinking about joining the club? I'm on the selection committee and I'd be happy to put in a good word for you—"

"Uh, no, thank you," I said. "Just here supporting a friend. I don't exactly own a yacht. I only own a car thanks to you."

"Do you like it?" His smile was wide. "I know it's not the same as your old car, but it has some impressive features. The amount you'll save on fuel alone—"

"I *love* it." I couldn't help being aware of Derrick's burning gaze.

"And you know you don't have to own a yacht to join the Yacht Club," Billy assured me. "There are all sorts of membership privileges besides reduced dockage fees—"

"You know what? I left my phone at my table with my coat." I gave him a smile that wasn't nearly as wide as his, but at least I tried. "I'm just gonna go grab them. But we'll talk later, okay?"

"Oh." His face fell. "Okay."

I spun around and headed quickly back into the dining room to snatch up my things. I just wanted to put on my coat, make sure Esther had a ride home with the Aquinos, then head out— alone. I needed some time by myself to clear my head.

Derrick and Bartholomew Brewster were the sons of Gaia?

Gaia was real, and walking the earth, and making baby daddies out of lonely farmers in Montana (and apparently Oxford deans in England)?

I could believe that my hometown was located on a hell rift. But the Mother Goddess, not being a particularly good mother?

That was a hard one to swallow.

All of this was just too much, too fast. If Rosalie wanted to be the Chosen One, that was fine with me. All I wanted was to be left—

And then it happened. I walked out of the Yacht Club dining room, my coat on, bag in hand, and spied Bartholomew Brewster talking to Esther near the grand piano in the bar.

No. Just no.

That was *not* happening.

Sure, Rosalie and her daughter, Lizzie, were both standing right there as well, looking dazzling in their matching ice-blue sheaths.

And I spied Derrick a few feet away, looking tall and fairly menacing in his all-black ensemble, his gaze still burning, but in a different way, and this time directed at his brother.

But this just wasn't okay.

I walked up to the little circle and said, "Esther, I'm leaving. Can I give you a lift home?"

Esther looked surprised. She'd evidently been enjoying whatever Brewster had been saying.

"Oh," she said, glancing around the crowded room. "I thought I'd get a lift home with Gabby."

"No."

Everyone glanced in surprise at Derrick. His gaze met mine, and stayed there. "Change of plans. You're going with Jessica."

Esther looked from one to the other of us, bit back whatever sarcastic remark she'd been about to make, then said quickly instead, "Let me go get my coat," and ducked back into the dining room.

"Derrick!" Brewster held his arms open wide for a hug that his brother didn't step into, and eventually, he dropped them. But he didn't drop his jovial tone. "What a pleasure to see you. I'd heard, of course, that you were here in town." He shook a finger at his younger sibling as if at a naughty child. "You see? I always know. I have spies everywhere. How have you been, my boy?"

Derrick looked as if he wished Esther had blown his brother's head off with her hands. But he only said, "Fine. And you?"

"Well. Very well. Sad that the only time I get to see you is at functions like this. What do you say to coming back to my hotel after this, and joining me for a nightcap so we can talk—*really* talk? This lovely young woman here arranged for me to have the most spacious suite—" He gestured at Rosalie, who ducked her head, managing to look modest for what was probably the first time in her life.

It was loud in the bar, and I was standing a few feet away from him, but I could have sworn I heard Derrick grinding his teeth.

Still, his reply was the height of politeness. "That'd be great."

Then Brewster turned his eyes—the same silver as Derrick's, only somehow lacking their brightness—on me. "And feel free to bring your young friend here, Miss, uh—"

"Sorry," I said, since I'd seen, with a burst of relief, that Esther was coming toward me with her coat and backpack. "I have to go. Maybe some other time. But this was a lovely evening." I plastered a wide fake smile across my face. "Thank you so much."

"I guess we'll see you both tomorrow, then," Rosalie said, looking from my face to Derrick's, "at the ball?"

"Maybe," I called back over my shoulder as I took Esther by the arm and began to steer her through the crowd and toward the exit. "Bye for now." I'd had to wrench my gaze away from Derrick's. His stare seemed to plead with me for my forgiveness.

But I needed the one thing I knew we didn't have: time.

"*Maybe?*" Esther echoed as I dragged her to the door. "What do you mean, *maybe?* You aren't going tomorrow?"

"Of course I'm going tomorrow," I said. "I just don't know if I'll see them."

"Who? Mrs. Hopkins? Or—" She gasped, her eyes widening. "Oh my God. Are you and—"

Gabby came rushing over, her gold rose crown askew on her rainbow-colored hair. "Wait! You're not leaving yet, are you?"

"We are," Esther informed her, soberly. "Mommy and Daddy are fighting."

Gabby sucked in her breath, looking anxious. "No! *Why?* Is it demons?"

"No, it's not demons." I paused in the vestibule to open my bag for my key fob. "Derrick and I are not fighting. We had a little disagreement, that's all."

"How do you know it's not demons?" Gabby asked. "It's nearly Halloween. Maybe demons have possessed Derrick's body and are making him fight with you."

"Yeah." Esther nodded. "As a Sagittarian, he'd be especially susceptible. Sagittarians are always up for adventure."

I glared at both girls. "It's not demons. Esther, say good night to Gabby. We have to go."

"Hold on," Gabby said. "I'll come with you. My parents never get a night out alone. It will be fun for them to hang out at the Yacht Club. You can drop me off at Esther's, if you don't mind, Jess."

Which is what I ended up doing, chauffeuring the two girls in the back seat of my new car like I was a rideshare driver. The moon was only a day away from being full, so bright in the cloudless night sky that I could easily see the road before me despite my headlights, shining like a river. . . .

As well as the sleek body of the gray wolf running alongside my car.

Yes. That's right.

Though I was certain I had to be imagining it, there it was, the mythical wolf everyone else had been reporting.

Or at least an extremely large, light gray dog, loping fast as lightning, leaping over hedges and under guardrails in order to keep up with me.

Since I was fairly certain that no canine could keep up with a car going forty miles per hour, I wondered if this was some sort of hex Rosalie had put on the rearview mirror, so that every time I glanced into it on a moonlit night, I'd think I was being followed by a wolf. And not only one. As my speed increased, so did the number of wolves. First one, then two, then four, until finally we were being followed—or escorted—by an entire pack of wolves, their silver coats and eyes gleaming in the moonlight, their paws silent on the frozen grass.

The girls in the back seat didn't notice. They were giggling away with one another, flipping through images from the night on their phones. I wasn't about to ask them, *Hey, do you see those wolves out there?* and freak them out. Well, freak Gabby out, anyway.

I was relieved when I pulled up in front of Esther's house and saw not only every light in her house blazing (as usual), but also that the wolves had vanished.

They'd probably never been there in the first place, I told myself. I'd probably imagined the whole thing. Maybe the entire village of West Harbor was suffering from mass hallucinations. Something in the drinking water?

"Good night," I said to the girls as they got out of the car. "Try to get some sleep. Big day tomorrow."

Esther paused before closing the door. "Thanks. And hey, Jessica? I don't know what Derrick did, but I personally don't think you should be too hard on him."

I blinked. "Oh?"

"No. He's not really that bad—for a guy." She shut the door, then ran up the steps to her front porch, where she waved good night.

I waved back, then drove away. I didn't see a single wolf during my ride home.

Jessica

Insert a needle into the wick of a candle, then light it. Concentrate on thy love. His thoughts will be pierced, and thou wilst hear from him within four and twenty hours.

Goody Fletcher,
Book of Useful Household Tips

"Technically Derrick didn't lie to you," Dina said.

"Dina." I was in my bed, alone—unless you counted Pye, curled at my feet on top of my comforter. "You aren't saying you actually believe this craziness that he's the son of Gaia?"

"Why shouldn't I believe it?" I could tell by the way she was huffing that Dina was on her phone outside, being dragged by the three beagles she co-owned with Mark. "There's no way to disprove it, especially since you didn't stick around long enough to ask Old Bart if it was true."

"Dina." I had the television on in my bedroom—a luxury I hadn't had much of a chance to enjoy since Derrick had moved in, as I'd been preoccupied by . . . other things. Now I flipped through the channels with the sound on mute, vainly looking for something to distract me from the feeling that I'd been wrong to ask Derrick to find alternative lodgings for the night. Not only because I knew hotel rooms were so limited in the area, but also because my best friend wasn't on my side. Even worse: I missed him. "Are you out walking the dogs? In the dead of night? With a pack of wolves on the loose?"

"It's ten thirty," Dina said. "And there are no wolves. Certainly none that can run as fast as a car."

"I know what I saw. Text me when you get home so I know you're safe."

"Text me when Derrick gets there with a dozen roses and you two are done having hot makeup sex."

But although I received Dina's text a few minutes later, letting me know she and the dogs were home safe, I wasn't able to send her one in return saying that Derrick had come over and he and I had had hot makeup sex. Because none of those things happened.

When I woke up Thursday morning after evidently having fallen asleep watching a marathon of *Halloween Cake-Off*, not only was all of Derrick's stuff still in my house, his hail-battered rental car was still in my driveway, as well. His running clothes from the day before were still in my dryer. His book about Plutarch was still cracked open on the table by his side of the bed. There was evidence all over inside and outside my house that Derrick Winters had lived there for days . . . but there was no Derrick Winters. It was as if he'd vanished entirely—like magic.

Only not the good kind.

"It's what you asked him to do," Dina said when I swung by her office that morning to complain about it.

"I know," I said, handing her a cheese Danish—Derrick's favorite. There'd been no sign of him at Wake Up West Harbor when I'd gone in there, though—not to look for him. Not at all. I simply enjoyed their breakfast special. And when I asked her,

Stacy said she hadn't seen him since the day before, either. "But I didn't think he'd really do it."

"That's because you're used to stalkers like Billy," Yasmin said.

Dina ignored her sister-in-law. "Look, Jess, why don't you do yourself a favor and just *call* him? Talk it out. Both of you made mistakes."

"*I* didn't make a mistake," I said. "He lied to me." How could I explain to Dina how much this stung? It was true I hadn't known Derrick for very long, but I'd thought that what we'd had was the start of something promising. Not necessarily long-term, of course, since he had demon fighting to do. But definitely extremely close friends with *major* benefits. "You can't build a relationship on lies—"

"First of all, he didn't lie," Dina interrupted. "He just didn't tell you the whole story. And second of all, we only have Rosalie's word that she's the real Chosen One. And since when have we ever believed anything she said? I personally refuse to."

I didn't want to believe it, either, but not for the reason Dina didn't. I didn't believe it because I couldn't imagine Derrick doing something as cruel as going around the country, convincing impressionable young witches that they were the saviors of their town, only to turn out to be making it all up. The thought of it turned me right off my breakfast.

"Um, I don't care who is the real Chosen One," Yasmin said, brushing pastry crumbs off her skirt, "so long as one of you fixes the Internet. I've hit my data cap on my hot spot. And between the cafeteria and the football field flooding, Sal's losing his mind. This morning he found out there's black mold growing beneath the Emo Dome."

"Gross!" Dina cried, at the same time that the ground beneath us rumbled.

And though at first I was tempted to think it might be the rift, opening a yawning chasm to hell beneath our feet, a quick glance out the Sisters In Law office windows showed me that it was only a massive truck from Connecticut's Best Catering driving toward the village square.

"Oh, yeah," Yasmin said, noticing my questioning look. "Those have been going by all morning. They're setting up for tonight. You should see it. Only Rosalie would choose to have a ball *outside* in Connecticut at the end of October. They've already got the tents up, in case it rains. Or snows. But it looks like it's going to be a beautiful day."

"Rosalie will make sure of that," Dina agreed with a snort.

I nodded and checked my phone for the hundredth time that morning.

No message from Derrick. Not that I was surprised. Why would he call when I'd told him to stay away?

"Just *text* him," Dina said, noticing what I was doing.

"No," I said, and put my phone away. "It's fine. I have to go to the bank to get cash, then open the shop anyway. It's going to be a busy day."

Predicting the future isn't one of my gifts, but I wasn't wrong. Enchantments was flooded with shoppers, many looking for last-minute finery to wear to the ball, and others simply browsing. I'd had to call all hands on deck to manage the crowds, so both Becca and Zahrah were working, as well as one of my extra holiday helpers, Naomi, who normally only did gift wrapping.

I'd even pulled in Gabby—not so much because I needed her, as because I knew she'd drag Esther along with her, and I wanted to be able to keep an eye on her. I had no way of knowing what kind of tricks the WCW might pull to get their candidate for Bringer of Light in place instead of mine. I didn't have any reason to think Lizzie Walker-Hopkins was in league with the forces of evil. But I wasn't so sure about her mother.

I put Gabby and Esther in my office in the back, sorting and pricing new merchandise.

"You have to be kidding me," Esther said when she saw the boxes of formal sequined jumpsuits for New Year's Eve. "It's *Halloween*."

"Gotta keep up with demand, kid," I said, and handed her a box of price tags. "Get to work."

"Capitalism is wild," she said with a sigh.

But both she and Gabby happily began tying tags to the merchandise, leaving me free to roam the store, offering help to customers in search of that special something to wear to the ball. Like the dark-haired older woman with the enormous—and expensive—designer tote bag I saw combing the evening wear rack. Judging from the bag—and her matching shoes—she had style and taste. She was going to be a delight to dress.

"Excuse me, ma'am," I said, making a beeline to her side. "Are you looking for something in particular?"

"I am," the woman said, turning to me. She had dark eyes—expertly made-up à la Cleopatra to accentuate their already immense size—and a sleek helmet of shoulder-length, jet-black hair. Her smile was wide and bright, her taste in jewelry—thick gold chains around her neck and bangles at her wrists—exquisite. Her voice was hoarse, as if from overuse, her accent crisply, untraceably European. "Can you help me, darling?"

She pronounced it *dahling*.

"I hope so," I said, instantly charmed. Purple, I thought. This woman should be awash in amethyst and turquoise. Some white, too, around her face, to bring out her lovely brown skin tone. "But I think you're in the wrong section. You see, you want petites. Everything over here will be swimming on you."

The woman looked surprised, then tossed back her head and laughed. It was a delightful sound, so happy and infectious that I couldn't help smiling, too.

"No, darling," she said, reaching out to lay a hand on my arm. "I'm not here to shop. I'm looking for this lovely little shop's owner, Jessica Gold. That's you, isn't it?"

I nodded, slightly dazed by the warm touch and even warmer manner. "Yes. But I'm afraid I don't know—"

"Oh, yes, you do." Still smiling, the woman reached out and took me by the hand. "You know me very well. I'm Gaia, Jessica. Derrick's mother."

Derrick

Character is simply habit long continued.

Plutarch

Derrick couldn't remember being so hungover.

Falling asleep on the couch in his brother's hotel suite hadn't contributed much to his night's rest, either. Now not only was his head pounding, but his neck was stiff.

He knew he shouldn't have drunk as much as he had. But his brother had kept pouring, and Derrick had felt so miserable, remembering the wounded look in Jessica's eyes as she'd asked him to stay away, it had seemed only right to keep drinking.

He regretted it now. Especially since his brother had ordered nearly everything on the room service menu for breakfast, and was still in the room, eating it.

"What I find most appalling about Americans," Bart was saying, "is their portion sizes. Look at this. Just look at these fried potatoes. A family of four in any other country could make an entire meal of these alone."

Derrick staggered into the bathroom, stripped off his clothes, and stepped under the shower. He ran it as hot as he could stand it for two minutes, then as cold. Then he toweled off and got dressed again.

He used one of the spare toothbrushes provided by the hotel to clean his teeth, then came out of the bathroom to find his brother complaining about the ketchup.

"Is it true they count this as a vegetable in American school lunches?" Bart asked, holding up one of the mini bottles from the room service cart. "I don't understand how you can stand living in this country. What was Mother thinking when she begat you with that uncultured yeoman?"

Derrick knocked the ketchup bottle from his brother's hand and seized him by the collar of the hotel robe he was wearing.

"Wh-what are you doing?" Bart demanded, shocked. "Have you lost your mind?"

"What are *you* doing?" Derrick shot back. "You know Rosalie Hopkins isn't the Chosen One."

"Oh, that's right." Bart's voice dripped with sarcasm. "Because I'd go to all this trouble for someone I *didn't* think was going to be able to save this village."

"You would," Derrick said. "You would if you thought it might result in a spectacular enough bloodbath. That would get Mom's attention, wouldn't it? Because that's all you've ever wanted."

"Don't try playing amateur psychologist on me, little brother. It won't work, any more than your healing hands or that ridiculous theory of yours that demons are the spirits of those who died unjust deaths. Bloody New Age nonsense. Demons are demons, and deserve to be sent right back where they came from—hell. And that's what Rosalie and I intend to do here tonight."

Derrick blanched. "An *exorcism*? That's what you're planning to do with the restless spirits that are causing this rift?"

"Please call them what they are, brother: demons."

"They've only become demonic because they've gone so long without—"

"So we should waste time coddling them? Allow them to *heal* and all of your other New Age piddle when we could simply banish them? I know it might be hard for you to understand—a man who thinks the best way to honor his mother is to get a *tattoo* of her favorite symbol on his body—but when you're in possession of a hammer, the best way to deal with a nail is to flatten it."

"That's *not* how that saying goes," Derrick growled, tightening his grip. "And I think there's a simpler explanation for why you're doing this: not only do you want Mother's attention, you want to get into Rosalie Hopkins's pants."

"No, that would be you, little brother. At least *I've* never been foolish enough to fall for my Chosen One. I always thought you were smarter than that."

Derrick released Brewster in disgust and went to the window. Of course Rosalie had arranged for the Grand Sorcerer of the WCW to have the penthouse suite, so the view looked out across all of downtown West Harbor, including the village square—now tented in preparation for tonight's ball—and stretching all the way to the sea.

"So did I," Derrick murmured, as he gazed down at the front entrance to Enchantments, which he could just make out through the red-and-gold treetops that lined the main road. "So did I."

Jessica

For long life, vitality, and attractiveness, drink wine.

Goody Fletcher,
Book of Useful Household Tips

"Of course I wanted to meet you," Gaia said, tearing at the bread in the basket Mark had reverently delivered to our lunch table. Not that Mark knew Gaia was the mother of all creation. I highly doubted Dina had shared that piece of information with him.

But I'd introduced her to him as Derrick's mother when we'd shown up at Mama Giovanni's without a reservation after Gaia asked me to have a late lunch with her.

"Oh, *Mrs. Winters!*" Mark cried, his dark eyebrows nearly hitting the roof. "Yes, of *course* we have a table. You know, we're big fans of Derrick's."

"Isn't that a delight?" Gaia looked from me to Mark with eyes that shined. "One *does* so want one's children to be liked. It's a pity when they aren't. I do have some children who aren't very much admired, you know. It's the risk of having children. There's no guarantee that all of the seeds we plant will flourish. Some can turn out to be damaged at the root. But everyone does seem to like Derrick."

Mark's eyebrows hit his hairline at the "damaged at the root" line, but he gamely escorted us personally to the best table in the house, the white-tableclothed table for two in the front picture window looking out over the Post Road.

"Here you are," Mark said, pulling out a chair for Gaia, then handing us both menus. "Don't hesitate to ask for anything we can get in order to make you more comfortable. And *buon appetito*."

Then he was gone, leaving me alone with the Mother Goddess.

Or at least as alone as we could be, considering that right outside the window streamed hundreds of tourists and locals alike, coming to take in the official start of the Tricentennial festivities. The construction of the tents and dance floor for the ball had been completed, and the Post Road was now closed to vehicular traffic along the courthouse square, so pedestrians had taken over the thoroughfare to stroll in the late afternoon sunlight with Tricentennial Tricorns (cookies shaped as tricorn hats) and Connecticut Confections (bags of kettle corn). Soon, Gabby would change into her Harvest Princess gown and go out to offer unsolicited facts about West Harbor history to the tourists.

And I'd have to keep Esther from being attacked by either demons or wolves or both.

"Oh, Jessica," Gaia explained with a sigh, "all of this is my fault. I'm the one who sent Derrick to find you."

I stared. "You did?"

"Yes. I normally don't interfere in my children's affairs. It's better if parents don't, for the most part. Otherwise, how will they ever learn to stand on their own two feet? But I do so want Derrick to be happy. And Bart. Oh, *Bart*. He's my damaged root. I've had several, of course, but he's the latest."

She waved to the server, who came hurrying over to refill our glasses from the bottle of pinot gris she'd ordered. She waited until he'd gone away before continuing. "He was so thoroughly spoiled by his father, he grew up to be convinced of his own superiority over others. Now the only voice he'll listen to is his own. It pains a mother to have to admit that about one of her own offspring. But in Bart's case, it's true."

I was still trying to digest the fact that I was sitting at Mama Giovanni's with Derrick's mother, Gaia, and so had barely touched my wine, let alone any of the bread she was genuinely attacking. For such a tiny woman, Gaia had a pretty voracious appetite.

"So let me get this straight," I said. "You sent Derrick to find me."

"I did, yes."

"Because you believe there's a rift in West Harbor—"

"I don't *believe* it, Jessica, darling. I *know* it. I think that should be obvious to anyone."

"And you want him to be happy."

"I do. Of course it's wrong for a mother to have favorites, and I'm not saying that I do, but Derrick—he's *sensitive*, don't you think, Jessica?" Her dark eyes glittered intelligently at me over the top of her wineglass. "Perhaps every mother says her son is sensitive, but I've had many sons, and I know some of them have—how shall I put this? Lacked empathy. Derrick's positively brimming with it. And I want him to be happy."

"And you think . . . *I* could make him happy?"

It was a guess. A wild swing at a ball I wasn't even sure she was throwing in my direction.

She smiled and wagged a finger at me.

"Ah-ah-ah," she said. "I told you. I don't like to interfere— except when I have to, of course. I'm not saying whether or not you make Derrick happy. That's for the two of you to decide."

"Right," I said. "But you *do* think I'm the Chosen One."

She laid a hand over mine, smiling warmly. "I do, darling. You saw for yourself what Esther was able to do in your presence. She really is a most remarkable girl."

"She is," I agreed. "And you're really *Gaia*? As in . . . the *Mother Goddess*?"

She nodded, her shining black curtain of hair—curled under just where it skimmed her shoulders—swinging. "Yes, darling. I swear it. I know it's been a difficult past few days for you. *Years*, even. And I know that Hopkins woman has been an absolute shit to you. I'm sorry for swearing—but sometimes it's called for. But you've handled all of it so admirably—really, very admirably. And you've only the next few hours to get through, and then everything will be all right. I'm almost sure of it."

"*Almost* sure?"

"Well, no one can be absolutely sure of anything, Jessica."

"Not even a goddess? That's what you are, aren't you?" When she smiled and nodded at me, I plunged on. "Then why can't you just get rid of the rift? Why can't you prevent evil in the first place?"

"I *could*, of course, but I already told you: I don't like to inter-fere. Children never learn from their mistakes if their elders are always swooping in to rescue them—and, from my experience, that applies to adults, as well. You've all been given free will. You must make your own choices. All I can do," she went on with a sigh, "is hope those choices will be good ones, and try to guide you as best I can when they look as if they aren't. But I will say that, in most cases, your choices have not disappointed me."

"By 'your choices,'" I said, "do you mean humans in general, or my choices specifically?"

"Humans in general," she said, and let out a surprisingly hearty laugh. "Why, Jessica? Do you think I've been spying on you?"

"No!" I reached for my wine, hoping she was telling the truth.

Because I wasn't sure she'd have such a good opinion of me if she'd seen what her son and I had been choosing to do to one another all over my house the past few days. "Not at all."

"Well, I have," she admitted, causing me to almost choke. "That's why I knew you were West Harbor's Chosen One—and my son's. But I only looked a little. And it was because you've performed so many spells over the years, invoking my name. Even a goddess can't help looking when she hears her name over and over again. Oh, how heavenly!" She glanced past my shoulder, then rubbed her fingers together, looking excited. "Our stuffed artichokes are here. I haven't had one of these in *ages*."

"Special of the day," Mark said, proudly setting a plate down in front of each of us. "Would either of you care for pepper?"

"Now how would I know before I've tasted it?" Gaia asked, showing a bit of her flirtatious side.

Mark played along. "Good point. You taste it and let me know."

"I will," Gaia said, and gave him a smile that looked the way Derrick's fingers felt—like the sun coming out after a long winter's day. Mark went away grinning, while I continued to sit there in complete disbelief.

What was happening? What was happening to my life? My hometown was sitting on the precipice of apocalyptic disaster, and I was eating stuffed artichokes with the mother of my not-so-fake witch boyfriend? A mother who also happened to be a primordial deity, who freely admitted to having been spying on me—but "only a little"?

How was any of this even possible?

"What's wrong, darling?" Gaia asked. "Why aren't you eating? Do you want pepper? How rude of me, I didn't think to ask. Don't worry, I'll get him. Mark? It's Mark, isn't it? Oh, Mark!"

"No," I said, gripping the tabletop. "I don't want pepper. I just . . . I know it probably sounds rude, but I just . . . I'd love some kind of proof that this—*any* of this—is true. That you're really . . . Gaia."

"Oh, is that all?" She laughed. "Well, why didn't you say so sooner, darling?"

A second later, I looked out the window beside our table and saw Derrick, dressed in a full tuxedo, riding down the street on a motorcycle.

Derrick

The mind is not a vessel to be filled, but a fire to be kindled.

Plutarch

Derrick didn't think he could remember a time when he'd been quite so simultaneously annoyed and elated. One minute he'd been packing up his things at Jessica's house, taking care not to let Pye escape outside despite the cat's persistent efforts to do so.

And the next, he was riding a motorcycle down a closed road, narrowly avoiding striking pedestrians.

It was only when he slammed on the brakes and skidded to a halt in front of Mama Giovanni's Italian Trattoria, then looked through the wide picture window there that he had any clue as to what was going on.

That's when he saw Jessica staring at him, slack-jawed in astonishment . . . and his mother sitting across the table from her, lifting a glass of wine in a saucy salute to him.

Of course. Gaia. He should have known.

"Hey!" yelled an angry father of three, yanking his children from in front of the cycle's path. "Can't you read? The sign says *Road Closed!*"

"Sorry," Derrick muttered as he switched off the bike. He glanced down at himself, noticing an unfamiliar flash of white. What had Gaia dressed him in? A *tuxedo*?

He looked at his mother through the window and shook his head. She shrugged, smiled, and took a sip of her wine.

Jessica, meanwhile, had thrown down her napkin and headed outside. Her cheeks were bright pink—whether from the wine or seeing him drive down a closed road like an idiot, he had no idea—and her hair its usual chaotic mess of curls. She looked beautiful and warm and sexy in an oversized Fair Isle sweater and jeans, and Derrick wanted to kick himself for ever having left her side in the first place. He should have stayed last night and begged on his knees for her forgiveness.

Maybe he'd do it here, on the street, instead.

"Jess," he began, swinging his leg from the bike.

But she didn't let him say another word.

"Where. Have. You. Been?" she demanded, her fists on her hips.

Now he knew her cheeks weren't pink from the wine or secondhand embarrassment. She was angry.

"I—You told me—You said to stay away," he stammered.

"Yes," she said. The blush was deepening. "But I didn't think you'd do it."

"I'd do whatever you asked me to do." He was aware that people were gathering around them—some from the street, some from inside the restaurant, including his mother and Mark—but Derrick had eyes only for her. "Anything. You should know that by now."

"Except wear a suit," his mother said. She was standing on the sidewalk holding her glass of wine in her hand, thoroughly enjoying herself. "I put him in the suit, Jessica, because he'd never wear one otherwise, and I knew you'd like it. Doesn't he look handsome?"

Derrick sent his mother a withering look. "Mom. Please."

"Well, you *do* look handsome!" she cried, defensively. "Tell him, Jessica."

Jessica grinned. Her blush was abating. "Your mother's right. You do look handsome."

He found himself grinning back at her.

"And the bike is for you, you silly boy," his mother cried. "You've been complaining about that rental car for days, so I thought, why not give him one of those terrible motorbikes he likes so much? That way they'll both be happy."

Mark nodded at the Ducati. "Sweet ride there, man."

Derrick's grin widened. "Thanks, man."

"Ma," Mark said to his mother, who was standing on the sidewalk beside him, watching their little drama unfold. "Why don't you get me a bike like that?"

"Why don't you get married?" Mrs. Giovanni demanded, smacking him on the back of the head.

A crack of thunder sounded overhead, startling everyone. It was so long and so loud, it seemed to be coming from everywhere all at once. Derrick glanced toward the square, thinking it had come from that direction, but he saw no clouds in that part of the sky. Then Jessica nudged his shoulder.

"No," she said. "Look there."

He looked where she was pointing. To the east, storm clouds were growing, piling up above the Sound like wrecked cars on an expressway.

He and Jessica weren't the only people who'd noticed. Many of the tourists had seen the clouds, too, and were checking their phones, confused since the forecast for the evening had called for clear skies just seconds before.

Locals, however, used to the intemperate northeastern weather, merely shrugged and headed for the square.

"Is this Rosalie?" Derrick asked his mother, urgently. "Or you?"

"*Me?*" Gaia's eyes widened. "When have *I* ever tampered with the weather, especially to spoil a party? I love parties."

But Jessica was the one who knew the answer.

"It's not Rosalie," she said firmly. "She worked hard on this event. She'd never ruin it with a storm—especially with Lizzie there."

"Then this is the rift," Derrick said. "It's starting. And it's worse than I'd thought. Brewster intends to try to exorcise the demons."

Jessica shook her head. "And that's bad because—?"

"It will only make them angrier, and put the people of this town in more danger. Demons feed off negativity. What drives them away is positive energy, understanding, and justice, not attempts to cast them into eternal damnation."

"Come on." She seized Derrick's hand, and before he realized what was happening, he found himself being tugged toward his new bike. "We've got to find Esther."

"You two go on," his mother called to them as they strapped on the matching black helmets he found in the bike's storage compartment. "I've already involved myself more than I should. I'm staying here with my new friends."

"Yeah," Mark said, putting one arm around Derrick's mother, and the other around his own mother's. "I'll take good care of our moms."

"Good luck with that," Derrick muttered, as he heeled back the bike's kickstand.

Then Jessica wrapped her arms around his waist, and he felt her soft breasts against his back. His heart staggered as if he were a boy again.

"Is your mother *really* not going to help?" she asked.

"She's already helped," he said. "She brought you and me together. The rest is up to us. Are you ready?"

He felt her grip on his waist tighten. "I'm ready," she said.

He flipped on the ignition. "Let's go."

Jessica

During a waning moon, perform spells to banish. During a waxing moon, perform spells for growth. During a full moon, perform spells for power.

Goody Fletcher,
Book of Useful Household Tips

Of course I had a lot of feelings about my boyfriend's mother forcing her son to show up in a tuxedo at the restaurant where she and I were having lunch.

Even though Derrick seemed to get over his indignation with her pretty quickly, this didn't feel to me like the healthiest relationship, especially since she wouldn't help save my town from possible demonic annihilation.

But unfortunately I didn't have time to sort through my emotions about that.

When Derrick pulled his bike up in front of Enchantments, I hopped from the back and whipped off my helmet, hoping my curls would come streaming out and then bounce right back into place like the hair of models always does on shampoo commercials.

But I'm not a model. And there was so much dampness and

static electricity in the air from the storm brewing out east off the ocean, most of my curls seemed to stick wetly to my face instead.

Even so, Dina and Yasmin, who'd heard the rumble of Derrick's bike engine, came out of their office across the street and hooted appreciatively.

"Yeah, lady!" Dina catcalled me. "Looking good!"

I turned around. Dina and Yasmin had already changed into their evening wear for the ball—gowns I'd selected for them at Enchantments, in which they seemed to glow, despite the growing darkness.

I waved to them—I didn't have time for more—and hurried into the shop. Becca, Zahrah, and Naomi had changed into their gowns as well and were closing up. They glanced up at me in surprise as I burst in.

"What are you doing here?" Zahrah asked.

"Is that a *motorcycle helmet* in your hand?" Becca teased. "Bold fashion choice for a formal event."

"Where are the girls?" I asked, my gaze tearing frantically around the shop. I didn't see them anywhere in it. "Gabby and Esther?"

"They went on up to the square," Zahrah said, looking confused. "Esther said she got a message to meet you there. Did you not—?"

"*No.*"

I swallowed back the sudden fear I felt welling inside me, then spun away from their confused expressions and pelted back out onto the street, where Derrick was waiting with the bike still running.

"She's already at the square," I told him, tugging my helmet once again over my damp curls. "Someone sent her a message telling her to meet me there."

"One guess as to who it was," he said as I swung up onto the seat behind him.

"I don't need to guess," I said, wrapping my arms around his waist. "I know."

"Hey!" I heard Dina yell behind us as the Ducati's engine roared. "Where are you going? The road is closed! You two are gonna get yourselves killed—or arrested!"

Good thing I know a couple of lawyers, is what I would have yelled back—if I hadn't been too busy clutching Derrick in anxiety as he thundered down the narrow, cobblestoned road, now clogged with West Harbor citizens in formal wear, all attempting to jam themselves beneath the multiple tents that covered the town square.

They had to line up to show their tickets first, however, in order to be admitted, and it was past this line Derrick rumbled. And though his bike's engine was loud, I could still hear the occasional shout and comment leveled at us: "The road is closed!" "Get to the back of the line!" "People think they're so *entitled* these days."

I'm sure Derrick heard them, too, but he didn't stop until we'd reached the red velvet ropes at the entrance to the closest tent at the very front of the line—just as the first drops of rain began to fall from the heavy blanket of clouds that had closed over West Harbor.

"Hey," I said, flinging myself off the back of Derrick's bike and rushing to the ticket taker, who was wearing full Colonial garb—a serving wench costume, complete with corset, scullery cap, and a surly expression. "I'm not here for the ball. I just need to run inside and talk to someone." And save West Harbor from becoming a hellmouth. "I swear I'll only be a second."

"No ticket, no entrance," she said without skipping a beat as she scanned the tickets of the guests in front of her. It had grown dark enough that she needed to use a mini flashlight to see them. Either that, or Rosalie was so worried about forgeries, she'd told the staff to use flashlights to check the tickets for authenticity. "And you'll have to get back in line and wait your turn like everyone else."

"I have a ticket," I said, opening my bag and rooting through it. Where had I put those tickets Rosalie had given me the other day? "I just don't know where they are right now. Is there a list? I'm sure I'm on it."

"There's no list." The barmaid spoke in a bored voice. She'd evidently been asked this question a lot. "Ticket holders only will be admitted."

"You know, you can't park that bike there," a man in full British redcoat uniform said to Derrick, pointing at a sign that had been calligraphed in Old English script. "The street is closed to vehicular traffic today."

"I was hoping you could make an exception," Derrick said, removing his black helmet and blinking at the barmaid with his silver eyes. "It's an emergency."

Something in Derrick's voice caused her to actually look up from her ticket inspection—but not magic, which is what I'd thought at first. She lifted the frilly rim of her scullery cap.

"Oh, hey," Stacy the waitress from Wake Up West Harbor said with a smile of recognition. "It's you guys."

I'd pulled off my helmet, as well. "Oh, hi!"

"You found him, I see." Stacy grinned at me knowingly.

"I did, yeah." I laced my fingers through Derrick's. "Finally. So, um, would it be okay if we—"

"Oh, yeah, sure." She casually waved us through the velvet roped entrance using the beam of her flashlight. "Take all the time you need. I'll watch the bike."

"What?" objected the haughty British redcoat. "You made me

go back to my car for my tickets, and I'm parked all the way by the train station!"

"*Next*," Stacy said, in a bored voice, ignoring him.

"*Thank you*," I said to her, and Derrick and I ducked through the entrance just as the cold, stinging rain began to fall with more earnestness.

Inside the tent, however, it was a completely different world. Warm and dry, strands of white party lights hung from the branches of trees to give a festive, even otherworldly glow. Tables strewn with white cloths and decorated with dancing votive candles were placed in front of a stage that backed up onto the courthouse steps, on which sat a podium and small orchestra, playing a piece that certainly sounded as if it had come from the seventeenth century. Servers dressed similarly to Stacy milled around, offering champagne and small dishes to the many party-goers who'd already managed to make it inside the tents.

Looking out over such a picture-perfect scene, listening to the lovely music and seeing all the happy, beautifully dressed people, it was hard to believe anything could be amiss.

Until I heard another crack of thunder—this time sounding as if it was right overhead. People all around us ducked, looking up, then giggled as if at their own foolishness for forgetting how safe they were, beneath this series of tents.

Except of course they weren't safe. They weren't safe at all.

Derrick and I scanned the square.

"I don't see Esther," he said. "Do you?"

"No." I'd already fished my phone from my bag and called her. No response. "I doubt she can hear her phone, with all this racket."

"That 'racket,' as you call it," Derrick said, "is the Allegro from Bach's Brandenburg Concerto Number Four."

"Wow," I said, pretending to be impressed. "You know a lot,

for a farm boy from Montana. Oh, wait, I almost forgot. Your mom is *the creator of all life*."

He gave me a pleading look. "I'm sorry. I wanted to tell you."

I squeezed his hand in mine. "I know," I said. "It's all right. Truthfully, even if you had told me, I wouldn't have believed you."

"And now?"

"Now I believe you. But I also think your family needs a lot of therapy."

He lifted my hand to his lips, his eyes seeming to burn into my soul.

"You know I love you, don't you? You're the only thing my heart beats for," he murmured, and despite the music, despite the chatter of all the people around us, despite the rain pattering even harder against the tent, I heard every word, as if he'd burned it across my skin with the golden fire of his touch.

I wanted to tell him that I felt the same. I wanted to tell him a lot of things. But I didn't get the chance, because suddenly his grip on my hand tightened.

"There she is," he said, his gaze sharpening on something behind me.

"Esther?" My head whipped around, but all I saw was Rosalie, standing at the edge of the stage with her tablet and headset again. The only difference between tonight and last night was that tonight, her sheath dress was red. My shoulders sagged with disappointment. "That's Rosalie."

"I know," he said. "But she'll have an idea where Esther is. Come on."

He kept his grip on my hand as he steered me toward the stage. I was glad he did, since we could easily have become separated—not simply by the ever-growing crowd, but by leaks which had begun to appear in the seams between the tents. Rainwater was sluicing down in steady rivulets, some between tables, some even onto them, dousing the candles, and causing partygoers to leap from their chairs unexpectedly, directly into our path.

Derrick didn't care. He veered past them, until we reached the stage—and Rosalie.

"This is inexcusable," I could hear her barking into her headset as we approached, even though the orchestra was playing as energetically as ever only a few feet away. "The city paid over a hundred and fifty thousand dollars to rent these tents. I was told they'd stand up to driving rain and gale force winds. I want somebody here to fix this *right now!*"

"Rosalie," I said. I'd noticed that Billy, dressed in his tux, was slouched at a nearby table, nursing what looked like a whisky on the rocks. He lifted his glass upon meeting my gaze, then went back to drinking. Beside him, Billy Junior slumped in a tux of his own, playing video games on his phone, and Lizzie—Rosalie's contender for Bringer of Light—was hunched a few chairs away, wearing a red gown that matched her mother's, only with a crown of gold roses instead of a headset.

Rosalie held a single index finger out to me, to indicate that I should wait a minute until she was done on her call.

"What do you mean, the roads have become impassable?" she asked, in a voice that was as cold as the rain that suddenly began streaming down in the middle of the string section of the orchestra. "What—"

She tapped the headset several times, then looked at me, her eyes wide with astonished outrage. "They hung up. *They hung up!* Can you believe—?" She looked around, noticing that the orchestra had ceased playing and the musicians were rising from their seats. "What's wrong? Why has the music stopped?"

"We can't continue playing until the rain is over, Mrs. Hopkins," the conductor informed her. "It's a liability issue. Some of these instruments are worth an enormous amount of money, and if they get wet, they'll be ruined. That's not to mention the risk of electrocution from the sound system."

"Great." Rosalie's gaze fell on me, and when it did, I took a staggering step back, and Derrick's hands went protectively around me. Rosalie didn't look like her normally cool, collected self. She didn't even look like a storm witch. She looked like hell. "There wasn't even rain in the forecast. Where did this storm come from, huh? Are you the one causing this, Jess? *Are you?*"

But before I could reply, a man's deep voice rang out. It had a British accent.

"Of course it's not Jessica, Rosalie," Brewster said, sounding amused. I spun around to see him standing behind me.

And he had one hand on Esther's slim shoulder.

"We all know exactly what's happening right now, don't we?" Brewster went on, amiably. "So why don't we sit down and discuss it, like civilized witches?"

Jessica

When the Bringer of Light is joined by the Chosen One, her power will increase tenfold.

"I'm sorry," Billy said, putting down his drink with a thump. "But did he say *witches?*"

"I did, my boy."

Brewster, his hand still resting on Esther's shoulder, propelled her forward. She'd changed from the clothes she'd been wearing earlier into one of the New Year's Eve jumpsuits. She'd chosen my cross-neck sequin jumpsuit in silver, with flared wide-leg bottoms. She was walking a little stiffly, but otherwise seemed all right.

Except for her eyes. Her eyes, behind the lenses of her glasses, were huge. And terrified.

"Your wife is a witch," Brewster informed Billy. "A very powerful witch who is going to help me send the demons who've been plaguing your village for centuries back to their graves, where they belong."

Witch? The word rippled through the crowd. Not horrified. Amused, mostly. There was a smattering of giggles, and even some snickers. It seemed to me that many people thought this was some kind of pre-ball theatrical skit for their entertainment.

But not Billy. Billy shot Rosalie a look so hurt, you would have thought she'd stabbed him. She, in turn, cried, "It's not true!" She was sticking to Rule Number Eight: A True Witch keeps the existence of magic and witchcraft a secret from the non-magical, knowing that their minds are too fragile to handle the truth.

Looking at Billy's stricken face, it wasn't difficult to see why this rule had been created.

Rosalie whirled upon Brewster. "Excuse me, but what do you think you're doing? None of these people here"—on the word *people*, she gestured toward those of us who were still in the audience, and included no less dignitaries than the mayor and her wife, multiple city commissioners, and the fire chief—"are interested in hearing about—"

"Well, they should be, Rosalie," Brewster interrupted as a crack of thunder so loud it felt as if it might tear the sky in two shook the tent. "Because this concerns all of them."

"That's enough, Bart," Derrick said in a hard voice, stepping into his brother's path.

"Oh, it's not *nearly* enough," Brewster said. "But get ready. It will be—"

Pop!

One of the bulbs in the strand of party lights above our heads exploded. I wasn't the only one who let out a shriek and ducked as tiny shards of glass rained down on us—especially as another, and then another popped. Lizzie and her brother screamed, too, and dove for safety beneath the table at which they'd been sitting. All around us, guests went running for the exits— then stumbled, since the rest of the tent was quickly plunged into near total darkness. Most of the votive candles had been extinguished by the rain, and the other fairy lights appeared to have shorted out.

The only light to see by was that of the full moon, low in the night sky, and barely visible through the slowly dissipating clouds, shining through the rips in the tents.

But that light was seeming to glow brighter with every passing second.

"The demons!" Professor Brewster cried, covering his eyes as a bulb burst above his head. "I warned you!"

"Demons are the least of your problems," Derrick snarled.

And then his right fist landed on Brewster's face with a sickening thud—the sound they never get right on-screen, not a *smack* so much as a *squelch* of flesh striking flesh, and bones breaking.

Brewster went staggering back. Rosalie, stunned by such a violent display, let out a scream, and Esther came running down the stairs from the stage—and into my waiting arms.

"Are you all right?" I asked her.

"Yeah," she managed to choke. She was clutching me as tightly as I was her. "Fine. I'm sorry. He sent me a text message saying to meet up, that he was with you—it wasn't until I got here that I saw that he was lying. I would have blown his head off, but Gabby was there the whole time. I didn't want to upset her—"

I knew then that she'd never actually been terrified. Nor was she hurt, or even slightly annoyed: she was angry. Esther was simmering with rage, and had only managed to keep that rage in check because she hadn't wanted to frighten her girlfriend. Brewster didn't know how lucky he was.

"Where's Gabby now?"

"Somewhere around here, harvest princessing."

"Was that you?" I asked. "Who blew up all the lights?"

"No." She was holding me so close, I could feel her heart

drumming against mine. "I would never. Glass is dangerous, and there are kids here. Was it . . . was it the *demons?*"

Crap.

Rosalie came rushing over to us. "Why are you just standing there?" she shrieked. "Aren't you going to do something?"

I released Esther and turned toward her. "I thought you were the Chosen One, Rosalie. Why don't *you* do something?"

"What am I supposed to do about *this?*" She waved her hands in the air, indicating the wrecked tent, sodden tables, the sound booth that was now on fire, and the two men on the steps to the stage who were still slugging it out. Derrick definitely seemed to have the upper hand, however. Brewster had collapsed against the muddy ground, with Derrick standing above him. "Can't you put a stop to *that*, at least?"

To be honest, I was kind of enjoying the view. Derrick's bow tie had come undone, and so had his ponytail. He looked like an avenging Viking in evening wear.

Still, I realized that this wasn't exactly the positive energy that Derrick had said we'd need in order to combat the demons. Even in the semidarkness, I could see that Rosalie was crying.

"Please." She sounded more desperate and unhappy than I'd ever heard her. "I have no idea how this became such a disaster—" She pointed toward the table where she'd been sitting with her kids, and where Billy, now slumped with a bottle of whisky he'd stolen from somewhere, was drinking. "But if you have any idea how to fix it, *please* help me."

My high school nemesis, asking for my help? Was *this* the work of demons?

But before I had time to figure it out, Esther stepped forward. "I think I know what might help," she said.

Then she reached into the pocket of her jumpsuit, withdrew

what appeared to be a letter, and climbed the stairs to the stage. Miraculously, when she reached the microphone and gave it a tap, it let out a sound. It might have been the only object left in the tent that was still electrified.

"Testing," Esther said, leaning into the mic. "Can you hear me?"

"We hear you!" someone called from the back of the tent. I was fairly certain it was Gabby.

"Good," Esther said, and unfolded the letter she'd drawn from her pocket. "My name is Esther Dodge, and I just wanted to say a few words."

My mentee—the Bringer of Light—was about to give a speech.

I tensed, half expecting the demons I'd heard so much about to come swooping out from the darkness and attack her. At the very least, I thought Brewster would yell at Esther to get off the stage.

But he didn't. Instead, I saw him lying there at the bottom of the steps, staring up at her with a look of horror on his face. At first I didn't understand why.

Then Derrick staggered through the mud and broken glass to come stand by my side, and I saw him staring in the same direction. He wore a look of wonder, not horror.

When I looked back at Esther, I saw why.

The silver sequins on her jumpsuit had caught the reflection of the moonlight, and were casting a sparkling light show all around the tent. Like sunbeams dancing on the surface of water, the reflection of the sequins swayed across the walls of the tents, as dazzling as diamonds. Dozens of them, hundreds, they tilted dizzyingly around us, as disorienting as the glitter from a disco ball, but just as pleasing.

"I wrote to the mayor the other day," Esther said. "And she was kind enough to write back. I'm holding the letter I received from her. Some of you may know that back in the sixteen hundreds, right here in America, a number of men and women were wrongfully accused of witchcraft. The very first witch trials in this country occurred here in Connecticut. Most of the records from those days have been lost, but we know for sure that nearly forty people were indicted, and eleven actually executed in a spot very close to where we're standing now. I know that's not as many as were accused and executed in other places, but none of those people deserved to die. And to me, that's the real crime—the crime of persecuting someone for their supernatural beliefs, a crime for which people around the world even today continue to be accused, and to suffer and die. I believe the court systems should be held accountable for this."

That's when the reflections on the sides of the tent changed. Before they'd merely been round, like the sequins on Esther's jumpsuit. The more she spoke, however, the brighter they grew—and the more distinctly identifiable in shape.

And that shape was . . . wolf. Dozens, hundreds, maybe thousands of shining gray wolves, all the wolves that had ever existed in West Harbor, back before they, like the witches, had been hunted to extinction—glowed all around us.

I caught my breath. I'd never seen anything more beautiful. I could tell Derrick felt the same way as he fumbled for my hand. I could see it in his eyes—the same silver as the wolves, and the light from the moon.

"I asked the mayor if there was some way she could clear the names of all of the poor people who were accused of witchcraft back in the early days of West Harbor," Esther went on, seemingly unconscious of what was occurring all above and around her. "And she said that unfortunately, she didn't have the authority. But she said that she would do all she could to help get my request to the right people. People who could help."

The wolf-shaped lights began to shift and sway, like sunlight on the Sound, as if the pack was on the move—in celebration, or in thanks. It was hard to tell. All I knew was that I was in tears—but they were tears of joy.

"The wolves were never here to hurt us, were they?" I leaned close to whisper to Derrick. "They were here to protect us."

He nodded. I saw that his eyes were looking damp, as well.

"Are demons always this beautiful?" I asked.

He shook his head. "No. That's because of Esther—and you."

I smiled through my tears.

"All I want," Esther continued, "is for the souls of all those wrongfully accused to be able to rest in peace. They did nothing criminal. And I intend to fight for them . . . and I hope some of you, at least, will join me in my fight."

"I'll join you," I heard Gabby's voice cry, clear and strong, from the back of the tent.

"Me, too," cried someone else.

"M-me, too," Rosalie choked. Tears were streaming down her face as she gazed around the tent, and at Esther. "I—I'm sorry."

Rosalie had so many things to apologize for, it was impossible to say what, specifically, she was sorry for.

But the Bringer of Light, unlike me, wasn't petty enough to question it. Esther merely smiled at her kindly, as in the distance—the far distance—thunder rumbled. The storm was moving on. Around us, the wolf lights were beginning to fade. Justice hadn't yet been restored for those in West Harbor who'd been wrongly killed so many centuries ago. But something like it was pouring in to repair the rift, like a touch from Derrick's fingers, filling the hurt with golden warmth.

"It's all right," Esther said to Rosalie. "You didn't know better."

Brewster—who'd sunk to his knees in the mud—lifted his own tearstained face. "I'm sorry, too," he murmured. "*Please . . .*"

Esther looked down at him, and her expression hardened. "You *did* know better," she said, and she raised her hand, exactly as she had with the pumpkins—

"No!" I cried.

Esther looked at me and lifted an eyebrow. "Why did you two bother teaching me how to control my powers if you don't want me using them?"

"You *did* use your powers," Derrick said. "Your powers of compassion and empathy."

She rolled her eyes. "Boring."

"Isn't it better not to be like him, though?" I asked, nodding at the sniveling Brewster.

She thought about it for a moment. I could see her considering her options—then she shrugged.

"Yeah," she said. "I guess you're right. Besides, I can always blow stuff up when I get to college."

Then, just like that, the last shaft of wolf light disappeared, the party lights in the rest of the tent turned back on, and Esther was herself again.

And Professor Bartholomew Brewster slumped down into the mud in a dead faint.

Jessica

To show gratitude to the Mother Goddess for all her bounty, place sacrifices of wine upon her altar. Or simply drink it in her name.

Goody Fletcher,
Book of Useful Household Tips

It took the EMTs a while to get into the tent, because of the crowd and the road closures.

But when they finally got a chance to examine Derrick's brother, they found his pulse and blood pressure completely normal. He begged them to take him to the hospital anyway, and hold him overnight for "observation."

I guess I can't really blame him. I wouldn't want to hang around, defenseless, against a whole bunch of powerful witches who hated me, either.

It was as they were trundling him away on the gurney that we turned around and saw the mayor walking up to our table, her wife in tow.

"Good evening," the mayor said. "That was certainly an interesting performance piece."

"It wasn't a perf——" Esther started to say, but Rosalie jumped in before she could finish.

"Oh, Madam Mayor, I can't apologize enough," she gushed. "I was assured the tents would be wind- and waterproof."

"That's quite all right." The mayor shrugged sympathetically. "These things happen, especially in New England in the fall. We can't control the weather."

None of us said anything—especially those of us who knew better.

"I don't think it's too late to try to salvage the evening, though." She looked up at the dripping tent ceiling. "Well, what's left of it, anyway. The sky is clear now, and there are still quite a few people left, including the caterers."

It was true. The servers had begun putting out the first course—a somewhat soggy lobster bisque. Cold, hungry party-goers were drying off their chairs with their napkins with good-hearted cheer, and sitting down.

"And look," said the mayor, pointing to the stage.

The orchestra was back, apparently no longer fearing either damage to their instruments or electrocution, and had resumed Bach's Brandenburg Concerto Number Four.

"Aw, see, honey," Billy said, beaming down at his wife. "Things haven't turned out so badly, after all."

I have no idea what Billy had seen—or did not see, or told himself not to see—in the hour before. But whatever it was, the whisky seemed to have caused him to decide it was all right. He was back to being the happy-go-lucky Billy he'd been ever since he'd married Rosalie.

Was that because of the spell Dina and I had cast upon the couple, so many years earlier? Or simply because he loved her, witch or not?

Whatever the reason, Rosalie seemed relieved. She swayed against him, and he put an arm around her to support her.

"Yes," she said. "Yes, you're right. I guess things are turning out all right, after all."

"I've often found," the mayor said, "that nothing bonds people more closely together than a little adversity."

Was that smile that she gave as she said it a secret one, meant for Derrick and me? Or had it been meant generally, for all of us?

Because we hadn't stopped holding hands since Esther had narrowly saved West Harbor and all its residents from the apocalyptic deluge.

Not that she seemed to be aware of it. She'd turned back to the serving of bisque she was sharing with Gabby, who'd finally managed to find her, and was astonishing Esther and Lizzie with tales of the adventures she'd had while volunteering as a Harvest Princess.

"And then," she told them, "these people from Ohio asked me if we catch our own lobsters. Just go out to the pier and catch our own lobsters. With fishing poles. I almost died."

Esther laughed gently. She seemed as unfazed as Billy by her brush with the supernatural. That was probably, I was sure she'd say, because she was a Scorpio.

"Oh, Esther." The mayor reached into the inside pocket of the red velvet tuxedo I'd designed for her, then pulled out an envelope. "I almost forgot, this is for you. I wish I'd gotten it to you earlier, but . . . well, you have it now."

Esther looked surprised as she took it. "*Another* letter? Should I open it? Here?"

"I think so," Mrs. Dunleavy said encouragingly, looking radiant in the gown I'd sold her. "I know what it says. I think you're going to like it."

Curious, Esther opened the envelope, then pulled out and un-folded a stiff piece of paper.

"What's it say?" Billy Junior asked.

"It's a proclamation," Esther said. She had a funny look on her face, one I didn't recognize. That's when I realized it was emo-tion. Esther didn't "do" emotions, except the teen basics: sar-casm, amusement, and an occasional combination of both.

But she looked genuinely touched by whatever the mayor had written.

"A proclamation of what, Ess?" Gabby asked.

"Declaring my witch ancestor pardoned of all charges against her." Esther smiled up at the mayor, her eyes shining. "Thank you. This means a lot."

"It's not official, of course," the mayor said apologetically. "Mayors can't officially pardon people—especially people who lived over four hundred years ago, and records of whose trial no longer exist. But like I said, I'm happy to help you through that process."

"*You* have an ancestor who was accused of witchcraft?" Rosa-lie asked, sounding stunned.

"Yes." Esther folded the proclamation and put it in her backpack—which of course she'd kept close to her all evening. "On my mother's side. Elizabeth Fletcher. She wasn't executed, though, just banished."

I felt a delicious shiver down my spine. Maybe it was because Derrick was touching me. Or maybe it was something else.

"Us, too!" Lizzie cried, delighted. "Hey, Mom, isn't Elizabeth Fletcher the name of our great-great-whatever-grandmother who was banished for witchcraft?"

Rosalie's lips went very small as she looked at Esther. "Yes. Yes, that's her."

"Hey!" Lizzie laughed. "I wonder if we're related!"

Esther grinned. "That'd be cool."

It was clear from the way Rosalie was struggling to smile that she did not yet consider this cool—but she was trying to get there.

"Did you know about this?" I asked Derrick, under my voice.

"That the witch who wrote your book left it behind after moving to New York, then wrote Rosalie's? I'll admit, I suspected. The handwriting is similar."

"Didn't everyone back then write the same way? Besides, the ink is so faded, it's almost impossible to read the thing."

"Almost," he said with a knowing smile, "but not quite. You certainly managed."

I shook my head, amazed that a witch who had lived so long ago could have had such an impact on not only my own life, but the lives of so many others—and had even managed to create a happy ending for herself, as well.

"Look!" Billy cried, pointing. "People are starting to dance. Isn't that nice, Rosalie?"

I looked. I saw dozens of people—including people I knew, like Dina and Mark, and Yasmin and Sal, and even Becca and Zahrah and Naomi and their partners—had finally made it to the village square. All of them were dancing. Dina noticed that I'd caught sight of her, and smiled and lifted a hand to wave. I smiled and waved back, my heart filled with a sudden gladness. So many people I loved were here, right here, under these sodden tents. This had truly turned into a celebration—thanks to Goody Fletcher, Esther, and the other witches.

Rosalie, however, barely glanced up, she was so devastated at discovering her daughter wasn't only not the Bringer of Light, but not the only witch descendant of her great-great-grandmother. "Yeah. That's great."

I had something else that was going to make Rosalie mad—if she ever found out about it, that is. I would have to do everything I could not to let that happen, of course.

"Hey, Esther," I said to her as she and Gabby got up to dance.

"Yeah?"

"I think I have something of yours," I said. "Something that belonged to Elizabeth Fletcher. Or Goody Fletcher, as she was called back then."

Esther's gaze sharpened with interest. "Oh, yeah? What?"

"You'll see," I said. "I'll bring it by for you tomorrow."

"Yeah, but what is it?"

"A book."

Esther rolled her eyes. "A *book*? After everything I just did, you think I still have things to learn?"

"Oh, you do," Derrick said, severely. "And you'd better listen to her."

Her gaze sharpened even more as she looked at him. "What about you? Are you sticking around?"

I couldn't help stealing a questioning look at him as well, my heart, which had felt so full before, suddenly seeming to stand still.

"Oh," he said. "West Harbor won't be getting rid of me as easily as it got rid of my brother."

And with that, he tightened his grip on my hand and dragged me toward my friends.

Relief flooded through me. Relief that he was staying. Relief that I wouldn't have to beg him not to go. Relief that I wouldn't have to put up a brave front when he did go, and pretend I didn't care, and that I'd be fine without him.

I *would* be fine without him.

But my days wouldn't be as sweet. Like dinner without dessert. Like candy without chocolate. Like life without magic.

Only when I saw that we were headed toward the dance floor did I dig in my heels.

"*No*," I cried, putting on the brakes. "I do *not* dance."

"You do now," he said, and pulled me playfully forward.

And then—I don't know how—something in me loosened, and I was in his arms, dancing, my long dark hair swaying around my shoulders, which were suddenly bare, because I was in a slim-strapped, satin-topped, tulle-skirted evening gown of midnight black in a style I don't even sell in my shop. Someone had magically transposed it upon me. It couldn't have been Lizzie casting a glamour, though I saw her bright face laughing joyously as Derrick spun me around the room.

Could it have been Gaia?

I didn't care. I didn't care because I was the Chosen One.

Chosen by him.

Jessica

For lasting love, laugh much, quarrel little, and keep thy heart and mind open.

Goody Fletcher,
Book of Useful Household Tips

I threw open the front door. My little brother stood on the front porch, looking rumpled and tired and surrounded by duffel bags. Only he wasn't so little anymore.

"Ethan!" I threw my arms around him.

He seemed surprised. I guess I couldn't blame him. We'd never really been huggers.

But when you're happy, you want to hug everyone.

"You look good," Ethan said, coming in the door and dragging his bags with him. "God, the ride from the airport was a bitch. Since when did they shut down the coast road?"

"Oh, that." I laughed and closed the door behind him to keep out the heat. "Yeah, I should have warned you. They're redoing the high school cafeteria while school is out for summer break. Did you know they found out it was built over the exact place where they used to hang witches, back in the sixteen hundreds? That's why the Emo Dome was always leaking and growing mold and stuff. Sal's going bananas, but at least he's relieved to know it's not any kind of structural fault."

Ethan looked shocked—although maybe not so much by my words. His gaze was roving around the house.

"I like what you've done to the place." He let his backpack slide off his shoulder and fall to the ground with a thump. "Are those new windows? They've really brightened it up."

"Thanks," I said. "So let me show you where I keep Pye's food. Want a beer or some coffee or something? You must be thirsty after your flight. How many hours was it? Twenty-two?"

"Twenty-four." Ethan followed me into the kitchen. "Sure, I'll take a beer. But you don't have to show me Pye's food now. There's plenty of time for that, isn't there?"

"I'm afraid not."

Both Ethan and I turned at the sound of a man's deep voice. It was Derrick, coming downstairs with our bags.

And as always, my heart did a little dance inside my chest when I saw him, even after all these months of living together. He was freshly showered from his morning run, dressed in his ubiquitous black T-shirt, jeans, and motorcycle boots.

He looked absolutely delicious. And he was mine, all mine. And I was his.

And we both had every intention of keeping it that way.

"Hi," he said, setting down our bags. I'd finally learned to pack light, so it's not like they weighed much. "I'm Derrick, Jessica's friend."

"Hi," Ethan said, sticking out his right hand. "I'm Ethan, Jessica's brother."

"Great to meet you." Derrick pumped Ethan's hand. "I've heard so much about you. In fact, can I—"

And then Derrick pulled a startled Ethan in to his chest. Because Derrick had turned into a hugger, too.

"Uh—I mean, I guess," I heard Ethan say, sounding a little strangled from Derrick's embrace. He was awkwardly holding the beer I'd given him, trying to keep from spilling it. "I've heard a lot about you, too, man."

Then Derrick let Ethan go, but only to hold him by both shoulders and stare deeply into his eyes. "I want you to know that I love your sister," he said. "And I intend to marry her."

"Uh," Ethan said, his gaze darting toward me as he tried to hide a smirk at this overshare. "That's great. I'm glad to hear it."

"Okay." Derrick gave Ethan a friendly slap on the shoulder and then released him. "Got that out of the way. Now your only job is to keep Pye alive while we're gone. Think you can handle that?"

Ethan looked down at the cat, who was sitting where he could usually be found . . . at Derrick's feet. "Seems simple enough."

"It is," I said. "I've left a list of instructions about his care in the kitchen, but since he spends most of his time outside, you probably won't even see him much. We used to have to keep him locked in because of wolves, but that problem got solved."

"Wait . . . *wolves*?" Ethan trailed after me because I'd headed to the front door after Derrick and the bags.

"Yeah," I said. "No need to worry about those anymore, though. I'm leaving you the key to my car. Just make sure you plug it in every once in a while. Dina and Mark know you're here, so call them if you need anything and can't reach me. Dina can't wait to hear from you, as a matter of fact. Didn't you used to go to school with Mark's little sister, Cat? She's back in town, too. I think Dina wants to have you both over for dinner, or something."

"Uh, great. Wait," Ethan said, as I lifted my motorcycle helmet from the hall bench. "You're not even going to stick around for a few days to hang out? I haven't seen you in ages. Do you have to leave *now*? Right *now*?"

"We do," Derrick said, soberly. "I'm sorry. But there's a town that's in very grave danger, and we have to go help save it."

Ethan looked at us—at me—like we were crazy. "Danger? What kind of danger? Jessica, you own a *clothing* shop. What is there, a fashion emergency? What the hell is going on?"

I glanced at Derrick and saw his eyes—eyes that I'd once thought so hard and flinty, like silver, but which I now knew were soft and warm, like goose down—and knew what he was urging me to do. It was so hard, though, after so many years of not telling.

Still, for Derrick—and for Esther, who was growing not only into a powerful witch, but a mature, responsible young woman under my continued mentorship, and for all the other witches who'd hidden their powers for so long because of fear of persecution—I did it.

"Ethan," I said gravely. "I'm a witch. Derrick and I are both witches. Derrick's mom, in fact, is the ancestral goddess of all life, Gaia. And when there's a town that's in trouble of a super-natural nature, she lets us know, and we go there and see if we can help out. That's what's happening now. So I can't thank you enough for cat sitting while we're gone. Becca and Zahrah can't do it because they're already taking care of the shop, and Esther and Gabby really aren't old enough to house-sit on their own."

"Though they'd love to," Derrick added.

Ethan stared at us without expression. "Witches," he said, finally. "You two are a couple of witches."

"Yes," I said, biting my lower lip. "Does that freak you out?"

This time Ethan didn't bother to hide his smirk. "No, not at all, actually. It explains a lot of what went on around here while you were in high school." Then the smirk faded. "You haven't told Mom, have you?"

"Oh, God no." I shook my head. "We're going to drop by and

see her and Dad this trip—and Derrick's parents, too. But I don't think—I mean, we're going to tell them we're getting married. But the witch thing just doesn't feel like something Mom and Dad would be quite ready to—"

"Yeah." Ethan shook his head. "I wouldn't tell Mom if I was a witch, either."

I smiled at him. Then I reached up and kissed him on the cheek. "Thanks again for helping."

He grinned down at me. "Anytime, sis. I'm just glad to see you so happy—*finally*."

"Thanks." I beamed at him and tugged my helmet over my head, while Derrick grabbed our bags.

"See you, Ethan," he said.

"Yeah, see you, man." My brother came to the front door with Pye at his heels to see us off. "Take care of my sister."

Derrick threw Ethan one last, glorious smile. "I will. But she doesn't need me to. Your sister is magic."

Acknowledgments

I owe an enormous debt of gratitude to many individuals—most of all you, my amazing readers, without whom this book would never have been possible. But first a word about the subject matter:

West Harbor is a fictional town. This fact doesn't excuse any mistakes I may have made in writing about Connecticut, a place I've visited many times, and which is filled with wonderful people, a few of whom I'm lucky enough to call friends.

Unlike West Harbor, the Connecticut Witch Trials are not fictional. But at the time this book was being edited, Connecticut state lawmakers were considering posthumous exonerations for all residents there who were accused of witchcraft. Such exonerations were unheard of up until a few years ago, when amateur historians, descendants of those accused of witchcraft, researchers, and even schoolchildren began demanding them.

So additional thanks are owed to all of those who have been fighting so hard and for so long for the "witches." Like so many members of marginalized communities, these people—the vast majority of whom were women—had no one to fight for them while they were alive. I'm so grateful that this is changing, and I hope the change continues.

Specific thanks are owed to the following people: my agent, Laura Langlie; editor, Carrie Feron; and assistant editor, Asanté Simons, for their kindness and patience while I was writing this book, as well as to Beth Ader, Gail Ader-Fecci, Jennifer Brown,

Gwen Esbensen, Mark and Dina Gambuzza, Trish Thomas, Rachel Vail, and especially Michele Jaffe, all of whom helped so much in so many different ways while I was writing this book.

And finally, my biggest thanks of all to my husband, Benjamin Egnatz: there'd be no magic in my life without you.

About the Author

MEG CABOT's many books for both adults and teens have included numerous #1 *New York Times* bestsellers, with more than twenty-five million copies sold worldwide. Her Princess Diaries series was made into two hit films by Disney, with a third on the way. Meg currently lives in Key West, Florida, with her husband and various cats.

EXPLORE MEG CABOT'S OTHER NOVELS

──── LITTLE BRIDGE ISLAND SERIES ────

──── THE PRINCESS DIARIES ────

──── HEATHER WELLS MYSTERIES ────

──── THE BOY SERIES ────

──── OTHER TITLES ────